RITA BRADSHAW

The Storm Child

PAN BOOKS

First published 2020 by Macmillan

This paperback edition first published 2020 by Pan Books
an imprint of Pan Macmillan
The Smithson, 6 Briset Street, London EC1M 5NR
Associated companies throughout the world
www.panmacmillan.com

ISBN 978-1-5098-9812-1

Copyright © Rita Bradshaw 2020

The right of Rita Bradshaw to be identified as the
author of this work has been asserted by her in accordance
with the Copyright, Designs and Patents Act 1988.

1 3 5 7 9 8 6 4 2

A CIP catalogue record for this book is available from the British Library.

Typeset by Palimpsest Book Production Ltd, Falkirk, Stirlingshire
Printed and bound by CPI Group (UK) Ltd, Croydon, CR0 4YY

Visit www.panmacmillan.com to read more about all our books
and to buy them. You will also find features, author interviews and
news of any author events, and you can sign up for e-newsletters
so that you're always first to hear about our new releases.

For dear Jayne, so brave, steadfast and faithful, with a heart that embraced the world. Your passing has left such a hole in so many lives, but we're the richer for having known you.

And remembering my little Alfie, loved and treasured beyond words and so special to his mum.

Acknowledgements

The following books were invaluable with research for *The Storm Child*:

Chronology of World War Two by Edward Davidson and Dale Manning
Our Wartime Days: The WAAF in World War II by Squadron Leader Beryl E. Escott
The Nazi Officer's Wife by Edith Hahn Beer with Susan Dworkin
Hitler's Girls: Doves Amongst Eagles by Tim Heath
Yesterday's Farm by Valerie Porter

Contents

The Storm Child

The storm child came at the break of dawn
and eased my aching heart,
speaking words of love and hope
she soothed my troubled soul.
Arms outstretched, she beckoned me
to the promise yet to come,
a time when joy and strength would flow
and peace and faith be mine.
I believed the storm child that winter's morn,
I believed the day would come
when tears and grief would be no more
and light would flood my world.
She left me then, her purpose done,
although I begged her stay,
that ethereal child from another time
beyond life's mortal plain.
But still I think of her sweet smile,
of her beauty and her grace,
and long to see her once again,
my child, my love, my life.

Anon.

PART ONE

The Arrival

1921

Chapter One

Sophia Maliana lifted her head to look up into the whirling snowflakes and knew she couldn't go on. She had long since lost all feeling in her frozen feet and now she was falling as much as she was walking. The blizzard had taken the last ounce of her strength and she couldn't fight it any longer.

She'd just toppled headlong into a drift at the side of the lonely country lane she had been following since daybreak and it was now twilight, the snowstorm that had gathered pace since mid-morning showing no sign of easing. Drawing her knees as far towards her chest as her swollen stomach permitted, she put her arms round them and closed her eyes. She had to rest.

The sides of the five-foot drift had fallen in on her to some extent, and with visibility practically non-existent, the keenest pair of eyes wouldn't have noticed the snow-covered mound. Too weak and spent to resist the deep blanket of exhaustion she felt into semi-consciousness, vaguely aware of the wind howling and the snow falling but too numb in mind and body to move. She was comfortable and for the first time in days she didn't feel chilled to the bone – strange that . . .

Released from the necessity of willing her body to take the next step and the next, her mind floated back to the night of the party at the big house. They had all been so excited, the rest of the staff and her, for it wasn't every day the son and heir got engaged. The preparations for the celebrations had begun weeks before, the huge, fifteen-bedroomed country residence of the Right Honourable Charles Richmond and his lady wife and their two sons having been cleaned from top to bottom, with new curtains and carpets throughout downstairs, although, as the sixteen-strong indoor staff had agreed amongst themselves, it hadn't been necessary.

The enormous hall at the back of the house which overlooked the manicured gardens had been cleared of its furniture so the dancing could take place in there, and in the drawing room and dining room everything had been rearranged to allow the guests to eat and drink from the tables lining the walls. Hothouse flowers from Mr Weatherburn's glasshouses in the grounds had been displayed in magnificent arrangements, perfuming the air, and although Mr Weatherburn, the chief gardener, had mourned the stripping of his precious blooms en masse, the result had been breathtaking.

She had been happy that night. Tired, because she and the other upstairs housemaid had been commandeered to join the three downstairs ones who, along with the footmen, had been kept busy scurrying here and there seeing to the guests under the watchful eyes of the butler and housekeeper. But it had been worth it to see the beautiful dresses and glittering jewellery of the female guests, and the men in all their finery. The house had been filled with music and light and gaiety and had taken on a fairy-tale magic.

It had been well after two o'clock in the morning when the party finished and the guests dispersed, those who were staying overnight disappearing upstairs to their suites and the rest taking their leave in the multitude of motor cars and carriages outside. Almost immediately the long row of bells in the kitchen had started tinkling as the guests demanded attention. Hot water for the hip baths in each suite; refills for the stone hot-water bottles which had been placed in beds earlier that evening; hot chocolate for the ladies and brandy for the men, and so on.

The Richmonds were unusually considerate employers and rarely called on their staff after dinner in the evenings apart from Lord Richmond's valet and his wife's lady's maid, but that night the footmen and the maids were sent hurrying hither and thither. She had been sent to a suite at the end of a long corridor in the west wing with a tray holding a cup of hot chocolate, dainty iced biscuits and a glass of brandy for the occupants. She had knocked at the door, and when a voice had bidden her come in, she had nearly dropped the tray as a middle-aged man in a state of undress casually told her to put it on a side table, slurring his words as he spoke.

She had placed the tray where he said, bobbing a curtsy as she had straightened and turned to face him.

'Pretty little thing, aren't you.' He had moved to stand between her and the door, and as she'd smiled nervously, he'd added, 'Doesn't look as though my wife will want her chocolate, she's dead to the world,' waving his hand across the room to the big double bed where the sound of genteel snores could be heard. When he had reached out a hand and pushed her into the dressing room behind her, shutting the door as he had followed, she had been too surprised to react for a moment, and then as she realized what he was about, she'd opened her mouth to scream only for him to grab her and put his hand over it. He'd been a big man and broad with it, and at five foot and slender as a reed she'd had no chance to prevent what had followed. The rape had been short and brutal, her muffled protestations against the iron hand clamped over her mouth and her struggling both futile.

When he'd expended himself, he'd dragged her back into the bedroom, obscenely unbuttoned and still with his hand smothering her sobs, reaching for some coins scattered on the dressing table. 'Here.' He had fumbled for the pocket of her uniform and thrust the money inside. 'Our little secret, eh? That's a good girl.' And with that he had pulled her across the room and shoved her outside into the dark corridor, shutting the door. She had stood shaking and crying quietly, unable to take in the enormity of what had just occurred, the pain and smarting between her legs proof it was real.

She'd reached the end of the corridor and was on her way downstairs to tell Mrs Finnigan, the housekeeper, what he had done to her when Beattie, the other upstairs maid, met her. 'What's up? You bin crying?'

Still in shock she had mumbled what had happened and that she had to see Mrs Finnigan, but Beattie, two years older and wiser to the ways of the gentry, had shook her head.

'You do that an' you'll be out on your ear afore you can say "Jack be nimble",' she'd whispered darkly. 'It'll be your word against his and guess who they'll believe? He'll either say you're making it up an' you pinched the money when he wasn't looking, or that you offered yourself to him on a plate and bein' in his cups he was tempted. Either way, your reputation will be ruined. That's Colonel Hewitt and his wife in that room and they're great friends of the family.' She had put her hand on Sophia's arm, her voice matter-of-fact but not unkind as she'd added, 'It's done now, lass, and if nowt else it'll teach you to be more careful in the future. I've met the odd beggar like him and bringing your knee up where it hurts always works for me. Come on, Mrs Finnigan said we could go to bed once we'd taken the trays and everything'll seem better in the morning.'

She had taken Beattie's advice but for the rest of that night had lain awake in the women servants' quarters beyond the kitchen and scullery and dairy, crying softly and in pain from his handling of her. And the next morning nothing had seemed better.

Deep in the drift, she was sheltered from the bitter north-east wind that gusted above and sent the snowflakes whirling in a frenzied dance, her breathing slowing as she fell more deeply asleep. Now she was transported back to the life she'd endured before the big house, to the miserable existence in the workhouse.

She had been six years old when she had entered its austere surroundings after the death of her Italian parents. They had died from cholera in a record heatwave that had swept the country shortly after the three of them had arrived in Newcastle from Italy, making her a homeless orphan. Only vague memories of her place of birth remained, but they were ones of warmth and sweet scents and dazzlingly bright colours, of her mother's laughing face and her papa throwing her up into the air and catching her in his strong arms. The workhouse couldn't have been more different. The dingy, drab, soulless confines of the grim Victorian building had terrified her from the moment she had walked through its doors, and when she had been undressed and bathed and her long hair examined for fleas and lice, she had sobbed the whole time, her cries increasing when one of the officers had shaved off her thick brown ringlets and dressed her in workhouse clothes.

Sophia moved restlessly in her sleep, terrified by the path her subconscious was leading her down. The master and mistress had been harsh and tyrannical, and their officers had followed suit. Beatings had been commonplace, and the discipline room, a small square windowless structure, had been feared by every child, even if they had never had cause to enter it. At seven years old the girls and boys attended the nearby council school, sticking out like sore thumbs in their paupers' uniforms and being segregated from the other children where possible, for the local mothers didn't want their offspring associating with 'workhouse vermin'.

A memory surfaced in Sophia's sleep-drugged mind, and now she moaned softly. Eleanor Todd had been a bully, a big fair-haired girl with rosy red cheeks and small beady eyes, and she had always been accompanied by her small band of devoted followers. Sophia had been frightened of her and she had let it show which had been a big mistake. The persecution had been relentless but she'd endured it silently until one day, when Eleanor had deliberately tripped her up and she'd landed in a sticky patch of mud in the school playground, her fighting spirit had been aroused. The group of girls had been laughing as she had struggled to her feet, and when Eleanor had further compounded the victimization by calling her filthy workhouse scum and spitting in her face, she had seen red. She'd had no chance of winning – Eleanor had been twice her size and strong and well fed into the bargain – but her first punch had taken the other girl by surprise and made her nose bleed. After that it had been a blur but she did remember the pain as Eleanor had knocked her to the ground and started kicking her in the stomach again and again.

For a moment, as the terrible pain caused her to cry

out, Sophia thought she was still in the playground with Eleanor and her cronies, her mouth stretching as she became aware this was no dream. She was lying in the snow and the pain in her stomach meant the baby was coming. Groaning, she heaved herself to her knees, fully awake now from the stupor that would have taken her life within a very short while, and that of her unborn child.

As the contraction began to ease she was tempted to lie down again but no, she had to find shelter, she told herself, whimpering as she stood up and brushed the snow from her clothes. But where? She had no idea where she was. It had been over a week since Mrs Finnigan had become aware of her condition. Up until then, lacing herself tightly into the closely fitting, corset-like under-garment Beattie had helped her make had concealed her changing shape. But once rumbled, it had been as Beattie had forecast. The butler and Mrs Finnigan had called her wicked for daring to accuse one of the Richmonds' guests of forcing her, suggesting instead she had dallied with a lad and got herself in the family way. Despite her protest-ations, and even Beattie standing up for her and stating what she had seen on the night of the party, she'd been turned out of the house within the hour even though she had nowhere to go. Mrs Finnigan had told her to get herself to the workhouse where she belonged and that was that. They'd washed their hands of her.

The night was icy and the cold had seeped through her damp clothes and chilled her to the bone, but she slowly pulled herself up on to the lane and began walking again, only to double over as the next pain hit. It was too early at seven months for the child to be born, she knew that, but these pains could only mean one thing. She drew in a long breath and straightened up a little, testing her body, and once again began to walk, still bent slightly to the side.

How long it was before she saw the farmhouse and the barns and other buildings clustered in a small valley she didn't know, but now the contractions were coming more frequently. Turning off the road into the farm track which was knee deep in snow and bordered by drystone walls she stumbled on, but it was a while before she reached the first barn. With no thought in her head but that of being able to lie down out of the wind and snow, she pulled at the door, managing to open it enough to squeeze in. She saw immediately the building was used to store hay. Walking fully into the fragrant surroundings and past stacked bales she made for an area where a heap of loose hay was lying and sank down into it.

Beattie, who seemed to know everything about anything, had told her that labour started with griping type pains which gradually got more frequent and stronger, but this wasn't like that. The pains had started suddenly and fiercely and seemed to be tearing her insides apart. Now she didn't care if she lived or died as long as the agony eased because she couldn't bear it.

She must have fallen asleep for a minute or two until the pain shot through her again, forcing her into wakefulness. In spite of the cold she was sweating and as the contraction peaked she cried out, writhing in the hay. Was she going to die? Here, alone? The baby too? But perhaps that would be for the best, better than the workhouse at least. When she'd made the decision not to make her way there in the last few days, she'd faced the fact that she might be imposing a death sentence on the two of them.

Now the pains were tumbling one on top of the other, causing her to scream and moan without ceasing, and she was quite unaware of the sound of hobnailed boots or the be-whiskered face staring down at her muttering, 'What the dickens?'

Kenneth Redfern had been born at Cowslip Farm, as had generations of Redferns before him, and when his father had died some years previously he had inherited the lot, having no siblings and his mother having passed away when he was a young boy. He was a dour, tough individual and would have stated on oath that nothing surprised him, but the sight in front of him this night had caused his mouth to fall into a gape and sent his bushy eyebrows up into his hair. A young lass, little more than a child by the look of her, having a bairn of her own in his barn? Where the hell had she come from and in the middle of the worst storm of the winter thus far? And then, as the girl let out a piercing cry, her body arching and heaving as her legs bent and fell wide apart, he turned on his heel and practically ran out of the barn back to the farmhouse for his wife.

Elsie Redfern was sitting in her rocking chair in the

huge farmhouse kitchen with her feet resting on the fender of the range when her husband burst in. He startled her so much she gave a little scream, causing the baby at her breast to lose his hold on her engorged nipple and let out an indignant squawk of protest. He was Elsie's fourth child and a disappointment to her in as much as he was another boy; his brothers, Robin who was two years of age and twins Edwin and Larry who were five, being stocky, somewhat unaffectionate replicas of their father. She had been praying and hoping for a girl for the nine months of her pregnancy, a little lassie who she could teach to cook and sew and who would be company for her when the boys were older and working with their father on the farm. But just days ago her time had come and out had popped another little lad. Her husband, who seemed to look on his ability to produce male heirs as proof of his virility, had been unable to hide his satisfaction, but she had cried bitter tears, even while chastising herself for being ungrateful that another healthy little boy had been given to them. He'd patted her on the shoulder, declaring that males populated the Redfern line and there hadn't been a girl child for generations, which had been of no comfort whatsoever. When she had stated this in no uncertain terms he'd retired in a huff, and the last few days had been a little frosty on both sides.

'Ken, for goodness' sake—'

Her words of admonishment were cut short as he gabbled, 'There's a lass in the hay barn an' she's on her time.'

'On her time?'

'Aye, a little lass an' she's having a bairn.'

'I know what on her time means but there can't be a woman in there, where's she come from?' Nevertheless, she put the baby in his crib by the side of her chair where he immediately began to make his feelings known about having his meal curtailed. Standing up, she said, 'Are you sure?'

'Am I sure? Damn it, woman, what do you take me for? I know a lass when I see one and this one's having a bairn as we speak.'

Because of the weather Elsie hadn't put her nose out of the door since having the new baby. They had been snowed in for a couple of weeks and she had delivered the child herself with Kenneth following her instructions about hot water and boiling the scissors and a clothes peg for little James's umbilical cord after she'd cut it. The other three had been delivered by the local midwife but as she lived in a village some miles hence, and James had got himself born with some urgency in under two hours from start to finish, there had been no point in Kenneth trying to fetch her. Elsie had little time for the woman anyway, considering her something of an old soak as she always arrived at the farm smelling of gin no matter what time of the day or night.

Pulling on her coat and stout boots and still only half-believing what her husband had told her, Elsie followed him to the barn, hearing the girl before she saw her.

In the last little while Sophia had had the urge to push,

and now, as she gave a long piercing scream, her knees up and wide apart, it was clear to Elsie the baby was about to be born. Turning to Kenneth, she said, 'Get some towels and boil a kettle quick, go on,' pushing him as she spoke, although he needed no encouragement to escape the scene in front of him.

'Dear oh dear, dear oh dear . . .' Elsie was muttering to herself as she knelt down in the hay, and as the child beside her – for she was little more than that, Elsie thought – opened her eyes and looked at her, she said softly, 'It's all right, it's all right, hinny, you're safe now.'

The girl groaned horribly, heaving as her body arched again, her skirt and coat tumbled back about her thighs, and Elsie just had time to pull her bloodstained knickers down before the head of the baby was born in a gush of blood and fluid. Feeling that something was terribly wrong, because her own births hadn't been like this, Elsie kept up a steady soothing, 'Come on, come on, that's it, it's nearly born now and then the pain will stop,' as the girl rested for a moment, her legs shaking, before pushing again and expelling the baby straight into Elsie's waiting hands.

The tiny body was limp and still, and through instinct rather than knowledge, Elsie manoeuvred it over her knees and began rubbing the little back with the head hanging down and its arms flopped either side of her leg. Suddenly there was a choking sound between a cry and a gasp, and then a stronger cry as the baby took breath. Thanking God, and wondering where Kenneth was with the towels,

Elsie placed the baby on the chest of its young mother and then took off her own coat and lay it on top of them both.

The girl seemed to have collapsed now the child was born, but as the baby gave another cry, she opened her eyes and her arms feebly came up to cradle it as her gaze met Elsie's.

'You've got a little lassie, hinny,' Elsie said softly, but even as she spoke, she wondered if the little mite's next breath would be its last. It was so tiny and fragile, nothing like her hefty lads when they'd been born. Even the twins had been more solid and chunkier.

'A –' the whisper was so faint Elsie had to bend closer to hear – 'a girl?'

'Aye, lass. You've got a daughter.'

'Her – her name's G–' A long shuddering breath followed before Sophia could say, 'Gina. After my mama.'

'Right you are, hinny.'

Kenneth came clomping back in the next moment, cursing as a scalding drop of water from the big black kettle in his hand dropped on to his skin. He was carrying clean towels in which he'd wrapped the scissors and a clothes peg, and when Elsie said, 'You've scalded these?' he nodded, his eyes wide as he took in the baby lying on its mother's chest.

Sophia lay perfectly still as Elsie separated mother and child before wrapping the infant in a towel and handing her up to her husband. 'I'll clean you up a bit, lass, and then we'll get you indoors in the warm.'

There was no answer. Sophia was as white as bleached linen and her eyes were closed. Kenneth said uncertainly, 'Elsie?' as he nodded to the pool of blood that was seeping out from beneath the thick pile of hay and inching over the barn's dusty dirty floor.

'Hinny?' Alarmed, Elsie shook the girl's shoulder and when there was no response, said loudly, 'Lass, lass, open your eyes. Come on now.'

'Is she breathing?'

Elsie didn't answer him but she undid some buttons on Sophia's blouse and pressed her ear against her skin. After some thirty seconds or so, she raised her head, looking at her husband with horrified eyes. 'I don't think she is, Ken. Here, give me the babby and you listen.'

'I'm not doing that.' He actually took a step backwards. 'All this blood, she's haemorrhaged, like that cow a few years back. You can't do nowt when that happens.'

'She's not a cow, Ken.' Elsie's voice was sharp. 'We've got to do something. She's only a bairn herself. I doubt she's more than fourteen or fifteen. Give me the babby.'

Swearing under his breath, Kenneth passed her the child and then knelt down, taking care to avoid the pool of red. After a few moments he said quietly, 'She's not breathing, lass. She's gone.' Standing up, he shook his head. 'Did she say her name or where she's come from?'

'Just – just that she wanted the babby named Gina after her own mam.' Elsie stared at him. 'The poor lass.'

She might be a poor lass but ten to one she was no better than she should be, Kenneth thought. Nice lassies didn't tramp the roads in this weather with their belly full unless their kith and kin had turned them out as a result of their shenanigans. Grimly, he said, 'You can't do owt here, lass, and you shouldn't be standing in the cold not long having had our James. Come on, come back to the house.' So saying, he picked up Elsie's coat and put it round his wife's shoulders, peering at the baby in her cocoon of towelling as he added, 'That'll be joining its mam afore the night's out by the look of it.'

It was at moments like this that she wondered why she had ever married him. Her voice a growl, Elsie said, 'That's a horrible thing to say.'

'Why? Best thing that could happen to it. It'll have no life as a bastard with no mam or da, will it.'

'She's a little lass, not an it, and I'll thank you to keep your opinions to yourself.'

'All right, all right, keep your hair on. I was only saying.'

'Well, don't say.' Elsie paused. 'I'll take the littl'un into the house but what are you going to do with her poor mam? You can't leave her like that, Ken. Not with the rats.' The hay barn and grain store and other outbuildings had their fair number of rats and mice, and although the farm cats kept them down to some extent, the smell of blood would bring them skulking about.

'I'll sort it out. Go in the warm.'

Elsie plodded back to the farmhouse, James's cries greeting her as she opened the kitchen door. The baby was red in the face and clearly furious at having his feed interrupted, but she ignored him for the moment. Putting the bundle in her arms down on Kenneth's big armchair which was close to the range, she quickly heated some water in a pan, her kettle still being in the barn, and tipped it into the enamelled bowl she used as a baby bath. Praying the tiny infant was still alive, she picked up the cocoon of towelling and was rewarded with a pair of milky grey eyes looking at her.

'That's it, that's a good lass,' she crooned softly, unwrapping the baby from the towels whereupon she immediately began to grizzle. 'You're just going to have a clean-up and then we'll find somewhere nice and warm for you, all right, my pet?'

Tiny arms flailed as Elsie placed the baby in the warm water and she began to cry in earnest, but within moments Elsie had her clean of the blood and pasty-looking matter that had clung to her skin and downy black hair, wrapping her in one of James's blankets once she had finished and rocking her as the cries began to subside.

Looking down into the small face, Elsie wondered if the child was too premature to be able to feed in the normal way, but as there was only one way to find out she sat down in her rocking chair opposite Kenneth's armchair and put the baby to the breast. There was a great deal of frantic snuffling and squirming, the small mouth blindly searching, but then Elsie felt the baby latch on to her and begin to suck. 'Thank God, thank God.' It meant the child had a chance if she could take some nourishment. Feeling quite weepy, Elsie made sure her flesh didn't cover the minute nose and continued to thank God that the baby seemed to know what she was doing. She only suckled for a few moments but she was definitely swallowing, and once Elsie couldn't persuade her to take any more, she walked across to the bread oven at the side of the range. This was always warm as the range was on day and night, and as Elsie felt inside she nodded to herself. This would keep the bairn warmer than she could.

Reaching for the largest of her earthenware jugs, she tilted it on its side and thrust it into the oven to warm up, before lifting the still-screaming James out of the crib Kenneth had made when she was expecting the twins, and placing the tiny girl in his place. Once James had been fed, the enormous jug in the oven was warm enough for her to slide the little girl, still wrapped in the blanket, into what had become a heated cocoon.

It was the best she could do, she told herself, standing and staring into the oven's depths. It was up to the bairn now, but if the child's persevering and taking some milk was anything to go by, she was a fighter in spite of her outward shell of tiny helpless limbs and underdeveloped body. Gina. Elsie's face softened into something resembling a smile in spite of her anxiety. It was a bonny name. Gina Redfern . . .

And it was at that moment the idea took form.

Chapter Two

'I want to keep her.'

'What do you mean, you want to keep her?'

It was Christmas Day and Gina was two weeks old. Since her arrival at the farm, Elsie had fed her every hour day and night, catching naps in her rocking chair when possible if she wasn't seeing to James and her other sons or attending to her household chores as well as working in the dairy.

The snow hadn't let up for more than a few hours now and again, and they had been cut off from the outside world for some weeks, but they were used to times like this in the harsh northern winters. The farm was self-sufficient and they had everything they needed.

They had just finished Christmas dinner and the older three boys were playing with the wooden fort and little lead soldiers that had been their Christmas present in the farm's sitting room across the hall from the kitchen, while Elsie and Kenneth sat drinking a glass of home-made blackberry wine at the kitchen table. It was Kenneth's third glass, and Elsie had waited until her husband was mellow before she had broached what was in her heart.

'Just that, I want to keep her. We're all she's got.'

Kenneth had straightened in his chair, his eyes narrowing. 'Don't be daft, woman. You can't keep someone else's bairn. Once I'm able, I'm taking her into Hexham and the authorities can try and trace her kith and kin.'

'How?' Elsie too had sat upright. 'You tell me how. We don't know her mam's name or where she came from, nothing about her at all except she was on the road in the midst of winter. If she had family they'd clearly thrown her out, you know that. So they wouldn't take the babby in, her being born on the wrong side of the blanket, even if they could be traced which would be impossible. The bairn'll end up in the workhouse nursery, that's what'll happen.'

'You don't know that.'

'Aye, I do, and so do you an' all.'

Kenneth stared at his wife. This was exactly what he had been afraid of from the moment he had walked into the kitchen that first night to see Elsie in her rocking chair with the baby at her breast. He'd had a gruelling couple of hours moving the body of the girl to the farm's cold store, a concrete structure his father had made which was partly underground and used to store cuts of meat and other produce in the summer, and then hauling out every scrap of hay that had blood on it and burning the lot in the yard. He'd then washed the floor of the barn where the girl had lain, scrubbing it with bleach once it was clean. Until he could get into the town and report what had happened and get someone to come and collect the body, the girl would have to remain in the cold store, there was nothing else for it, but at least it was freezing in there this weather and no rodents could get in.

Trying to keep his patience, because he could see Elsie was het up, he said, 'You're not thinking clearly, lass, now then. I know you've taken to the little mite –' feeding the baby had been a big mistake in his book because what woman wouldn't have maternal feelings in such circumstances? – 'but she's not ours and there's the end of it. How would you explain her suddenly making an appearance for one thing, and what about her mam lying in my cold store?'

'I've thought of that.'

'Elsie—'

'No, listen.' There was a light in her eyes now and her voice was quick and eager. 'I've just had James and we could say Gina's his twin. It'd explain her being so small. You often get one twin bigger than the other – our Larry was a sight heavier than Edwin, now wasn't he?'

'Not that much.'

'Well, a boy and a girl is different to two boys or two girls. As for that poor lass, the way I see it we've got two options. We can either bury her somewhere in the fields once the winter's over and the ground's soft, or . . .'

As Elsie paused, Kenneth, who was staring at his wife as though she had taken leave of her senses, said, 'Or?'

'We can let the river take her now. They do burials at sea, don't they, so to my mind that'd be no different.

When the body turns up somewhere they'd think the lass just fell into the river and drowned. It happens, especially when the weather's so bad. Look at that farmhand who worked at Stone Farm. He fell into the river, didn't he? They found him miles downstream.'

'He was in his cups after a drinking bout at the Swan and Duck,' Kenneth began, and then shook his head. 'Why am I even discussing this? The lass needs a decent Christian burial and the child passing over to the authorities.'

'She won't get a decent burial, not in the circumstances. The best they'd do is a pauper's grave.' Elsie's voice was low but grim when she continued, 'And this is all about the bairn for me. I'm not letting her go to the workhouse nursery, Ken. I tell you straight, I'm not. It'd break my heart. She's as much mine as our four.'

If Elsie had spoken the truth here, she would have said that the baby girl felt more hers than her lads ever had. She had prayed for a daughter even before the twins were born and with each son the longing had grown. Kenneth was an unemotional, taciturn man. What she had seen as quiet strength in their courting days, she'd soon come to realize was more an ingrained coldness once they were wed. And their sons, bless them, seemed to be cut from the same cloth. Of course, it was too soon to know with James, but certainly the other three were undemonstrative, sober little lads. The farm was relatively isolated and she hadn't understood how much that would affect her until it was too late. Having been brought up in a village with umpteen brothers and sisters and a close community where everyone knew the ins and outs of their neighbours, she had begun to crave female company. Kenneth's two farmhands came from the nearest small hamlet and in her seven years of marriage she had never met their wives and families or visited the place, although she had been hoping that when the twins started school at the nearest village with a schoolhouse a few miles away, things would change.

Kenneth drained his glass and poured himself another, feeling he needed it. He had been up since half-past five that morning, milking his cows in the whitewashed cowshed by the light of his old faithful storm lantern while the farm cats waited patiently for their ration before he went indoors for his breakfast. With the snow so thick and unrelenting and with ten-foot drifts in parts, his farmhands hadn't been able to make it through to the farm for a while, and so seeing to the cows, the pigs in their sty, the hens in their coops and the hundred and one other jobs about the farm was all down to him and he was dog tired. Tired and irritable. He'd come in for his Christmas dinner an hour ago, looking forward to a good meal, a nice drink to toast the Christ child and putting his feet up for a bit before he went out again, and now Elsie had started on about the bairn.

Holding on to his temper by the skin of his teeth, he said flatly, 'Whether you like it or not, she's not ours though, is she, and that's the bottom line. See sense, woman. Where would the world be if folk went round snatching any bairn they took a fancy to? You've got four healthy lads, be content with that.'

Elsie said nothing for a moment. Bending slightly forward, she glared at him and when she did speak Kenneth thought the voice that came through her tight lips was hardly recognizable. Slowly and steadily, she said, 'She's mine and she's staying and if you don't back me in this I'll never forgive you. I prayed to God for a daughter and He gave me what you can't. I've given her life just as much as her mam did – she'd have died within the first few hours without me feeding her – and this was meant to be. I've given you your lads and I'm glad for you, but she is mine.'

Kenneth's mouth fell open slightly. Since his marriage he had congratulated himself many times on his choice of wife. Elsie was a hard worker and a good breeder – four sons in seven years of marriage was a feather in his cap and one he was proud of. Moreover, she was a grand cook, kept the farmhouse and dairy as clean as a new pin and wasn't one for idle chatter or fancies. But this . . . Stuttering slightly, he made one last effort: 'It – it's not right, lass, you must see that? And wh-what if someone finds out? Us keeping the bairn as our own would make folk think something dodgy went on. They might even say we did away with the mother. We could go down the line for it.'

'No one will find out. The lads have accepted her being here with no questions, same as they did James, and we tell them the same as we do everyone else, that she's ours and James's twin sister.'

'And what happens when Frank and Walt get through and come back to work? The ground's frozen solid. I can't bury her, for crying out loud. What if they find a body in the cold store?'

'So let the river take her like I said.'

He could hardly believe that his wife, his respectable God-fearing wife, was suggesting such a thing. 'You're condemning her to an unconsecrated grave if the body's found or decaying slowly on the bottom somewhere if she gets caught in weeds.'

'The body is just an outward shell, Ken. Wherever her soul is, it's not with her body and she'd want me to do my best for her child. My conscience is at peace.'

Their eyes held for a moment or two before his gaze dropped away. He was in no doubt she meant every word she said, including the fact that she would never forgive him if he defied her in this. Her whole being had been geared to the tiny infant over the last two weeks and despite the odds stacked against her she had pulled the little lass away from the very brink of death. His mistake had been in not taking the infant and her dead mother to the authorities that first night, but how could he have done? The roads had been blocked and his horse and cart wouldn't have got more than a few yards.

He lifted his glass and threw the last of the wine down his throat. 'This is wrong, lass.' He'd work his fingers to the bone for Elsie and his lads, but taking in the flyblow of a lass who had clearly been caught out in sin stuck in his craw. 'But if your mind's made up, so be it.'

And then she surprised him by doing something she had never done throughout their courting days or seven years of marriage. Springing up, she came to him where he was sitting, settling herself on his lap and putting her arms round his neck as she kissed him full on the lips.

'Thank you,' she said softly. 'It's meant to be, I know it is, and you won't regret it, Ken.'

He was too taken aback to do more than nod. She gave him another swift kiss and then, as James began to grizzle in his crib, got up and deftly changed the baby's nappy before settling herself in her rocking chair and putting him to the breast. Kenneth watched her feed his son who made the odd loud slurping noise, and after a few moments his gaze wandered to the open door of the bread oven and the cocoon in the massive jug.

How Elsie had got through the last couple of weeks with virtually no sleep he didn't know, but although she must be exhausted he hadn't heard a word of complaint, neither had she been short with the lads or him. She was a good woman. He nodded mentally to the thought. Which made what she was proposing even more astonishing, because whatever way you looked at it, it wasn't right.

His big Christmas dinner, the warmth of the kitchen, and not least the wine he'd consumed which was strong with a kick like a mule, caused his heavy lids to close. It was quiet in the kitchen, just the ticking clock on the mantelpiece and James's snuffles and snorts breaking the silence. Faint chatter and laughing filtered through from the sitting room where the older lads were playing, and Kenneth's head began to droop. Within moments he was snoring.

James having guzzled his fill, Elsie placed the now-sleeping baby in his crib and then eased Gina out of her nest. Until now, the infant had done little more than feed and sleep, and every time Elsie changed her nappy or held her she marvelled how tiny but perfect she was, as light as a feather compared to James. This time as she held her, a pair of round bright eyes peered over the top of the blanket the baby was wrapped in, causing Elsie to smile as she whispered, 'Oh, so we're awake, are we? That's good, me bairn.'

The baby still had her moments of struggling to latch on to the breast, but today tiny lips closed firmly round the nipple and began softly pulling. Every time this happened, Elsie sent up a quick prayer of thanks. God had given her a daughter. Not in the way she had expected but that didn't matter; didn't the good Book say that His thoughts were not our thoughts, and His ways not ours? she told herself. Gina was hers. She would keep the name the poor lass had wanted, that was only proper, but in every other respect the little girl was her daughter, and now Ken was in agreement, the future would pan out.

She glanced across at her husband, and in that moment she loved him more than she ever had or would ever do again.

Chapter Three

It was a beautiful soft evening in early August. The day had been one of intense heat with deep-blue skies and no breeze, but had mellowed in the last hours into a perfect summer twilight.

Gina was five years old, and the day had begun badly and continued in the same vein. It being the summer holidays there had been no school, and she and the lads had spent most of the day helping their parents about the farm, she with her mam in the farmhouse and dairy, and the four lads accompanying their father and the farmhands in their numerous jobs.

Even before breakfast, she'd fallen foul of her da. She and James had been having one of their arguments, and her father had clipped her round the ear but not James, causing her to protest indignantly whereupon he'd cuffed her again. The slaps hadn't been hard – it had been the unfairness which had made her cheek him. Or at least he'd said she'd cheeked him, Gina thought now as she hung out of the window of her little bedroom and gazed across the farmyard to the faint shimmer of fields of corn in the distance. As she'd said to her mam later, she had only been saying that James should have got the same treatment her da had meted out to her.

Gina sighed heavily. And then later that morning her da had *had* to be watching when she'd dropped the basketful of eggs she'd collected from the hen coops. She'd been watching the skylarks whirling and diving in the thermals high above and had tripped as she'd entered the farmyard, sprawling headlong on the cobbles. He'd hollered at her, ignoring the state of her bruised bleeding knees. And yes, she *had* cheeked him that time, Gina admitted to herself, but she didn't care. He was always going on at her for the slightest thing.

A bat shot silently past the window, flying so fast her eyes couldn't follow it, and then more joined it as they hawked for insects in the dying light. She watched, entranced, and suddenly the world was an amazing place again, full of wonder and beauty and a joy that made her hug herself in awe. Lots of things could cause her to feel this way: a glorious sunset when the sky ran red and gold and purple; the dew hanging on the delicate tapestry of spiderwebs in the hedgerow; a field of poppies dancing in the sunlight; the list was endless. She had learned not to express these feelings to the rest of the family, though. Her da called her doolally and said she was a penny short of a sixpence, and her brothers teased her, but it was because of her mam that she kept quiet. Her mam always looked worried and kind of sad if she spoke her thoughts out loud at these times, and because she loved her mam more than anyone in the world she didn't want to upset her.

This last thought caused Gina to bite down on her bottom lip. She'd upset her mam tonight, even though it hadn't really been her fault – it had been her da again. After tea the lads had said they were going to paddle and splash about in the brook that ran through Bluebell Wood, and she had automatically made to join them, thrilled with the idea of cooling her legs and feet after the endless hot day. And then her da had forbidden her to go, citing her smashing of the eggs and then cheeking him as his reason.

Gina now shut her eyes as she relived the scene that had followed, which had ended with her da dragging her upstairs to her room and throwing her in, whereupon he had locked the door as he had left her screaming and sobbing, red marks on her arms where he'd manhandled her. She hated her da, she did, she hated him, she told herself vehemently. She'd said this once to Edwin and Larry after some to-do or other, and Larry had ponderously replied that she was sinning and breaking one of the Ten Commandments that said you had to honour your father and mother, and when in answer to this she had turned her back on the twins and lifted her short skirt and thrust her bottom out at them, Edwin had said she was wicked and would go to hell.

Gina gave another deep sigh. She would have loved to go to the brook with James and the others. Although it was nearly dark it was still really warm outside, and her room was hot and sticky. She would never be able to sleep. When she and James had started school in January, after their fifth birthday, and she had told the new friends she'd made about her life at the farm, they'd said she was lucky to have a bedroom all to herself. They had to share with at least two or three siblings, and her best friend, Daisy May, had to top-and-tail with four sisters. She hadn't said any more but deep inside she'd felt they were the lucky ones. She would have liked to have a sister to talk to and play with and would gladly have shared her bedroom, small though it was, being the box room. And because it was only just big enough to fit her bed and a chest of drawers in, on nights like this it got unbearably stuffy.

The lads had long since returned from their little jaunt and the rest of the household were asleep, but in her mind's eye she could see the brook and hear the water tumbling over the smooth pebbles and rocks and smell the earthy scent of the wood.

As the last of the daylight faded the moon came out in all its splendour, casting its silvery light over the land-scape below and surrounded by a myriad of twinkling stars. Gina stretched like a small kitten and suddenly the idea of staying indoors one more minute wasn't to be borne. She was in her nightie and she didn't bother to get dressed, pulling on her sandals before opening the window as wide as it would go and climbing on to the sill. Thick, sweetly scented wisteria covered the walls at the back of the farmhouse where her room was situated, its ancient trunk as sturdy as a small tree in parts. She had considered this means of escape before when her father had locked her in for some misdemeanour or other but had never quite drummed up enough courage to try.

Her heart pounding fit to burst, she edged out of the window backwards, her feet probing for footholds as she held on to the windowsill. It was much easier than she had imagined. With the heady scent of the flowers in her nostrils she descended to the ground like a small monkey, delighted with herself. Once on the ground, she stood for a minute as her heart slowed and resumed its normal pattern. Her da would go mad if he caught her. The thought had the power to turn her stomach over and then she brushed it away. He wouldn't catch her. She'd have a splash about in the stream and get nice and cool and then she'd be able to sleep.

There was an occasional hoot from an owl as she made her way to Bluebell Wood about a half-mile from the farm. The moonlit night was bright in places and black and shadowed in others but this didn't worry her. She had never been frightened of the dark, unlike James who wouldn't go to sleep unless he had a candle burning in the bedroom he shared with Robin. She shook her head at the thought of her brother, making her dark curls bounce. He was such a baby sometimes, she told herself without a thread of malice but rather a maternal kind of affection. Although they were the same age, she had played the protective role of an older big sister for as long as she could remember, both of them accepting that she was the leader in any games they played and that at school in the playground she would fight James's battles as well as her own, in spite of him being a head taller than her.

On reaching the wood she spent a blissful hour paddling in the crystal-clear brook before retiring to the grassy bank covered in wild flowers and letting the warm air dry her. The contrast to her hot little box of a room made her in no hurry to retrace her steps, and after a while she lay back in the scented grass, her eyelids heavy and her small limbs relaxing. She'd have to start back in a few minutes but oh, this was so nice.

It was her name being called in the distance that brought her wide awake. For a moment she couldn't recall where she was and then as the events of the previous night came to her she gave an 'Oh!' of dismay and jumped to her feet. Early-morning sunlight was streaming through the trees, and as she heard her name again she realized the cat was well and truly amongst the pigeons. Pulling on her sandals she fairly flew back the way she had come the night before, exiting the wood as fast as she could and following the lane beyond to the stile which led into the first of the farm's cornfields, the pastureland where the cattle grazed being on the north side of the farm. The corn was high and ready for harvest, reaching to the top of her head, but as she stood on the stile she could see her mother and one of the twins in the distance and heard her name again.

She yelled back as loudly as she could, waving her arms for good measure before losing her balance and falling in a heap on the ground, whereupon she picked herself up and ran along the narrow track between the hedgerow and the beginning of the crop. Her heart hammering, she covered the distance between them in moments, and as she came in sight it was her brother who yelled, 'What have you been up to this time?'

Her normal response to this might have been, 'That's for me to know and you to find out,' because she considered the twins unbearably bossy and pompous, but the look on her mother's face checked any retort.

As she reached them, she said quickly, 'I'm sorry, Mam, I'm really sorry.'

Elsie was panting – her round little body didn't take kindly to dashing about but since she'd gone into Gina's room first thing and found it empty and the bed not slept in, she'd been running around like a chicken with its head cut off. The last twenty minutes or so had been the worst of her life as she'd imagined all sorts of things. Her hand pressed to her heaving bosom, she said, 'Where have you been? And the truth, mind.'

Hurt that her mother could suggest she'd tell anything but the truth, Gina said again, 'I'm sorry, Mam, but I was so hot last night and I couldn't get to sleep so I thought I'd have a paddle in the stream, that's all.'

'That's all?' Edwin's voice verged on a shriek but Elsie waved her son to silence.

'I must have fallen asleep on the bank, I didn't mean

to. I was going to climb back inside last night . . .' Her voice trailed away. She had never seen her mam so angry.

'You climbed out of the window.' It was a statement, not a question, but Gina nodded anyway. 'How often have you done that before?'

'Never.' It was immediate and carried the ring of truth.

Elsie nodded slowly and again raised her hand to stop Edwin who had made an exclamation of disbelief, and now she spoke the thought that had been at the front of her mind ever since she had unlocked Gina's bedroom door that morning and seen the open window. 'You could have brained yourself if you'd fallen. You know that, don't you?'

'I never fall.'

That was true enough, the child had the agility of a small monkey, Elsie told herself wryly. It was James who had fallen out of the apple tree following her lead last summer and broken his arm. 'Be that as it may, there's always a first time, and how do you think I'd have felt if I'd have found you hurt or worse this morning? It was bad enough finding you gone and being worried to death.'

'Oh, Mam, I'm sorry.' Gina flung herself at her mother, clutching her round the waist as she buried her head in the folds of her apron. 'I am, I'm sorry.'

There had been the catch of tears in the child's voice and now Elsie gathered her close, lifting her up and into her embrace. When a pair of thin little arms went round her neck and she was kissed over and over again, she hugged Gina to her as she said, 'Promise me you'll never do that again, hinny. Promise me,' but even as she said it she was thinking this whole episode was Kenneth's fault. Locking the bairn in like that last night and forbidding her to go to the stream with the others; that was cruel. Where Gina was concerned he was cruel. He had never taken to the child, that was the thing. Gina's elusive endearingness had never touched him. And she was such a pretty little girl with her dark brown curls and bright cornflower-blue eyes, in spite of being a proper tomboy. But it was the lass's spirit that caught him on the raw. He had no idea how to handle her, and because he couldn't control what he saw as her defiance against his authority it brought out the dark side of him.

Her thoughts caused her to turn to Edwin and say, 'Run back and tell your da and brothers we've found her, and I'm dealing with it. Your da can get on seeing to the cows before breakfast.'

Edwin stared at his mother. He was fully aware of the hidden message in her words to his father, but if she imagined she could turn his da's wrath away from Gina by saying she'd deal with his imp of a sister herself, she had another think coming. And he could understand his da in part, to be fair. The things that Gina got up to were enough to make your hair curl, like this latest escapade.

His gaze dropped to the small figure in his mother's arms and there was an element of grudging admiration in his eyes. He and his brothers would no more have thought of climbing out of a top-floor window and shinning down to the ground than flying. But that was Gina all over. He remembered one evening a few weeks ago when he'd had the toothache and crept downstairs to find his mam. It had been late and his parents had thought they were alone. They'd been talking softly but intensely and he knew they were arguing, but something his da had said then had stuck in his mind since, not so much because of the words but because of his mother's reaction.

'She's a damn cuckoo in the nest, that's what she is,' his da had growled, and his mam had gone for him so vehemently he wouldn't have been surprised if she'd belted him one. It had been then he had noticed Gina sitting on the landing, her hand to her mouth, and he'd known she'd heard every word by her white face and the tears running down her cheeks. He'd gestured for her to go back to her room before he'd made his presence known to the two in the kitchen – he didn't want her getting in more trouble for eavesdropping – and his mam had made him a warm drink and put oil of cloves on the offending tooth. He'd thought since about what his da had said and the fact that although James was Gina's twin, the two of them were nothing alike, not in looks or nature or anything. Gina didn't resemble any of them. His mam always maintained that Gina looked like her own mam, but as his maternal grandmother had died before any of them were born he had no way of knowing if that was true or just wishful thinking on his mother's part. He knew his mam had thought the world of her mother – she often said their grandmother had been the finest woman to draw breath – and his mam thought the world of Gina too, that was for sure.

There was no rancour in this observation, it was just how things were. He knew his mother loved him and his brothers but Gina was her favourite, with her being a little lassie and all, and perhaps the way his da was always going on at his sister had contributed to his mother's feelings?

'Go on then, go and tell your da. I don't want him rampaging over here.'

His mother's voice brought him out of his reflections and he nodded before reaching out and tweaking his sister's curls as he muttered, 'Behave yourself at breakfast and don't cheek him, it'll only make things worse. Just say you're sorry and then keep quiet.'

Gina turned and reached out an arm, pulling him close for a moment as she pressed her cheek to his before burying her face in her mother's neck again. It took Edwin aback, not an uncommon occurrence where his sister was concerned. She could aggravate him and Larry like no one else could with all her antics and her air of superiority and refusal to accept their seniority, and then she'd go and do something like this show of affection and – as Larry had put it once – cut the ground from under your feet.

He shook his head at his mother, bringing a smile to her face as she said for the third time, 'Go and tell him she's found.' She understood her son's bafflement. Gina was like a bright exotic bird in the midst of a flock of ordinary pigeons. Even she, who adored her bairn beyond words, didn't know what the child was going to do next. But she and the lads loved their little bird.

Edwin was some distance away before she set Gina on her feet. Bending, she cupped the small chin in her hand and brought the little girl's eyes to hers. 'Your da's going to be very angry, you know that, don't you? Like Edwin said, I want you to say you're sorry and nothing else. No answering back, hinny. I mean it.'

Gina nodded, her bottom lip trembling. 'I didn't mean to fall asleep, Mam.'

She never did mean to do the things she did that had Kenneth ranting and raving. But no, that wasn't fair, Elsie told herself as she straightened. He'd never given the bairn a chance, that was the truth of it. From day one he'd been determined to be proved right that taking the child in was a mistake. Even if Gina had been a model daughter in his eyes, it would have been the same. For the first twelve months or so she'd thanked God every day that the bairn's mam's body had never been found, certainly not to their knowledge, anyway. She'd imagined that everything in the future would be hunky-dory. She hadn't realized then that Kenneth had an obsessional dislike of the infant. Any disagreement they had always had Gina at the core of it.

As she took the child's hand in hers, they began to walk back to the farmhouse. Everything about Gina was different to the lads; she was as bright as a button and even at five and a half could read better than Edwin and Larry. And she loved that her bairn was the way she was, she did, but it constantly served to remind Kenneth that she wasn't his flesh and blood. Unconsciously her free hand touched the swell of her belly under her linen apron. And now there was another babby on the way, something she could have done without although she wouldn't say that to Kenneth. She'd gone so long without falling for another bairn that she'd assumed, foolishly it appeared, that her childbearing days were over and she had been glad.

Once in the farmhouse, Gina went quietly about her morning task of setting the kitchen table for breakfast. Elsie placed the big pan of porridge that had been soaking overnight on the range, and then put more than a dozen thick rashers of bacon in her black frying pan. The lads were helping their father with the morning milking, and once that was finished they would carry two big pails of foaming milk through to the dairy between them, ready for Elsie to make her cream and cheese and butter. This routine never varied winter or summer, but both Elsie and Gina knew today was different. They were waiting for the sword of Damocles to fall, and although this sword might not be hanging by a hair it was just as stomach-curdling.

Elsie glanced across at the child who was the light of her life. For once there was none of Gina's chatter or humming as she went about her duties, and although Elsie knew the bairn had been naughty, she couldn't bring herself to upbraid her further, mainly because she felt the whole incident could have been avoided if her husband hadn't dealt so harshly with the child the night before. When Gina asked in a small voice, 'Shall I slice the loaves,

Mam?' she smiled at her as she said, 'Aye, pet, an' go careful with that breadknife,' as she brought two crusty loaves from the batch she'd baked the day before to the table.

By the time Kenneth and his sons came into the house the breakfast was ready and waiting as it was every morning. On hearing their approach, Gina had moved close to her mother. She always brought the bowls of porridge to the table once the menfolk had washed their hands in the scullery, but today she didn't look up as her father walked through from the small room. He sat down in the big chair with carved arms at the head of the table, but it wasn't until the four lads had taken their seats that he said, 'What's she doing down here?' to his wife although his gaze was fixed on the small figure at her side.

Warning herself to go careful as her temper rose at his tone, Elsie began ladling the porridge into bowls with her back to the room as she said, 'If you mean Gina, she's helping me with the breakfast same as always.'

'*I want her upstairs now.*'

Elsie turned and looked at him. He was even angrier than he'd been earlier that morning when they'd discovered Gina had gone. His whiskered face was a turkey red and his eyes were like bullets. Quietly she said, 'Gina's no use to me upstairs, I need her down here,' before handing Gina a bowl and saying, 'Take that to your da, hinny, and be careful not to spill it.'

Gina kept her eyes on the bowl in her hands as she

walked to the table, and as she placed it in front of Kenneth, she whispered, 'I'm sorry, Da.'

'Sorry? I doubt that but you will be, m'girl. You can bank on that. And look at me when I'm speaking to you.'

She raised her eyes to the big hairy face. This man's treatment of her over the five years of her life had engendered a whole host of feelings, ranging from hurt and resentment to fear and humiliation, but it had only been in the last few months that she had come to hate him. Before this, if anyone had asked, she would have said that she loved him because he was her da and that's what you did. She had accepted that he treated her differently to the lads in the unquestioning way small children have, but since starting school after Christmas and seeing the way some of her school friends' fathers were with their daughters, it had dawned on her that her da didn't like her. She had never been swung up on to his shoulders or given a hug or kissed, but as he didn't do that with her brothers either the physical manifestations of his attitude weren't what hurt her. But her friends' fathers never looked at them in the cold nasty way her da looked at her, as though he wished she was somewhere far away, neither did they snap and snarl at the slightest thing or recoil from their bairn's touch. She'd realized it wasn't because she was a girl that her father treated her the way he did. It was because she was *her*.

She had fought against the realization at first, crying herself to sleep at nights and praying to God every morning that that day would be different, but after a little while her natural fighting spirit had reared its head. Her da might not like her and only love the lads, but she didn't like *him* either, she'd told herself painfully. And her mam loved her, that was all that mattered. And it had been from that point that she had stopped trying to win his affection, something that she'd done without being aware of it from when she could toddle. The inevitable consequences of this had been confrontation after confrontation in the last months, because even when she knew she should keep quiet she'd found herself unable to.

Gina was small for her age and Kenneth was a big man in height and width, but as they stared at each other what he read in the child's face transfigured her in his mind's eye. The lads had always respected his authority as head of the family and with that respect there was an element of fear which didn't displease him, but this creature was something else entirely. When he looked back at the years before she'd arrived at the farm they had taken on a utopian quality but now everything was wrong.

He glared at her, and it made his blood boil when she stared back unblinkingly, a reflection of the deep loathing he felt for her showing on her own face. 'How often have you been off gallivanting who knows where when the rest of us are asleep in our beds, eh?'

'I haven't. Done it before, I mean.'

'Don't lie to me.'

'She's not lying.' Elsie had come to the table with two bowls of porridge which she placed in front of the twins. 'Gina, fetch your and James's porridge and let's all get on with our breakfast.' She turned Gina and pushed her in front of her as she spoke, and once she had given the child the bowls she picked up her own and Robin's.

Kenneth stared at his wife and then growled, 'The hell she's not lying. She pulls the wool over your eyes, woman, and always has done, but not me. I told her to stay in her room and she defied me. Are you condoning that?'

'Of course not.' Elsie had to nudge Gina forward to take her place at the table beside James. 'She went too far. She understands that and she is sorry.'

'Sorry, my backside. Well, you can make the usual excuses for her but it won't wash this time, I'm telling you.'

'Eat your breakfast, Ken.' Elsie raised her head and husband and wife exchanged glances, his full of frustrated fury and hers holding a different kind of anger, the quality of which checked his next words. He glared at her, his rage mixed with bitterness and indignation that yet again he was being put in the wrong. That little madam had wilfully disobeyed him and caused a right panic and hullabaloo, and yet it was as clear as the nose on his wife's face that she was blaming him for this.

Standing up so suddenly that his chair skidded on the stone flags and tipped over, he grabbed his bowl of porridge and threw it against the wall where it shattered into several pieces. 'To hell with you,' he ground out through clenched teeth, grabbing his cloth cap and stomping out into the yard.

The children sat in a frozen silence staring at their

mother, but Elsie made no response other than to say calmly, 'Eat your porridge before it gets cold. The eggs and bacon are nearly ready.'

White-faced, each of them obediently picked up their spoons and began their breakfast.

Chapter Four

The hot days of summer were a distant memory. It was the middle of November, and for two weeks hard frosts and zero temperatures had made the ground as hard as iron. It made certain jobs on the farm easier because the autumn had been a wet one before the cold spell, and wading through acres of mud had been filthy and time-consuming. But every coin has two sides and other jobs were nigh on impossible. The old-timers were predicting a difficult winter and Kenneth had already brought the cows into the byres, which had their own separate yard so the animals had a chance to stretch their legs and see daylight. One or two farms in the district had enclosed cow houses with no natural light at all, and when the time came for the spring turnout into the fields, the cows' legs could hardly support them and their eyes were almost blind. Nevertheless, the animals still tried to do what all cows do at turnout: dance and scamper and kick and buck with joy, their udders swinging with gay abandon. But on Cowslip Farm Kenneth did what his father and grandfather had done before him, and that was to treat his animals with consideration.

This thought came to Elsie as the family sat at their evening meal, and it was followed by a realization that if her husband showed an ounce of the kindness to Gina that he did to his animals, their home would be a happier place. Since the incident of Gina climbing out of her bedroom window in the summer, Kenneth had taken the tack of ignoring the child's very existence. He didn't look at her or speak to her if he could help it, and days could go by in this fashion. When it had first begun she had challenged him about it, and his reply had been short and blunt.

'You've made it clear I'm to have no say in her upbringing so I'm giving you what you wanted. I wash my hands of her.'

In one way it made for a quieter life, but the atmosphere in the house when Ken was around was tense and they all felt it. Looking back, she didn't regret the stance she had taken that day, not really, but if she'd known that Ken would keep this new attitude up for so long she might have behaved differently. It had certainly driven a wedge between them. He hadn't touched her since the summer, and him a man who liked his oats. Not that she minded that, if she was being honest, not with her as big as a house with this bairn, but nevertheless him turning his back on her in bed every night had hurt.

Elsie sighed as she finished the last of the cow-heel pie she'd made for their evening meal. She just wished this babby would hurry up and get a move on; she'd feel better once it was out and her body was her own again. She was as big as she'd been with the twins but the midwife reckoned she could only feel one in there.

As though the thought had prompted it, the next moment she felt the familiar cramping pain and instinctively her hand went to her stomach. She hadn't been aware her husband was watching her, but now as he said, 'What is it, the babby?' she looked at him and nodded.

He got up, coming round the table to pat her on the shoulder before he said, 'I'll go for the midwife. Edwin and Larry, you get some hot water and towels ready for when we come back and keep an eye on your mam.'

The pat on her shoulder had brought a rush of emotion that surprised her. Not trusting herself to speak, she nodded again. Once Kenneth had departed, everyone sprang into action. James and Robin cleared the table and brought the dirty dishes to Gina who was washing up at the kitchen sink, and Edwin and Larry filled the kettle and several milk churns with cold water from the well situated just inside the far wall of the farmyard. Putting the kettle on the hob to boil, the twins, along with Robin and James, went out into the bitterly cold night again and fetched armfuls of logs from the wood store, piling some against the side of the range and taking a good amount upstairs to their parents' bedroom. The fire in the small blackleaded fireplace had been kept going day and night for the last couple of weeks in view of Elsie's impending confinement, and the temperature was markedly different to that of the other three bedrooms, all of which were freezing cold with a layer of ice coating the inside of the windows.

Elsie remained sitting at the kitchen table while all this was going on. The pains were increasing in intensity and pace and she was wishing she had told Kenneth to stay rather than going for the midwife. They had managed perfectly well by themselves when James was born.

After a while, when the twins had got the fire blazing in the bedroom, she went upstairs and Gina helped her change into her nightie and get into bed while the lads filled the stone hot-water bottle and brought it up to place at her feet. Elsie looked fondly at the small figure perched by her side on the bed. Gina had sent the lads downstairs again to wait for the midwife, saying she would call them if they were needed, and it had amused Elsie how the four of them, even the twins big as they were, had done what they were told. She reached out a hand and immediately small fingers slid into hers. As soon as she had begun to show she had told the children about the baby. Her sons had been politely uninterested on the whole, but Gina had been excited, and when the old baby clothes had been fetched out and washed and the crib got down from the loft, Gina had spent hours folding and refolding the tiny garments and pretending the cloth doll Elsie had made her years ago was the new arrival in the crib.

Now Elsie said softly, 'You'll have to help me look after your baby brother, hinny. I'm relying on you.'

Gina's blue eyes with their long thick lashes smiled at her. 'I will, Mam,' she promised. Boys were no good with babies, everyone knew that, so the lads would be no use.

'There's me bonny lass.' Unable to say any more as a particularly strong contraction took over, and feeling she wanted to push already, Elsie willed herself not to moan out loud. She hoped Ken made good time, because the signs were that this babby was going to be born shortly with or without the midwife.

It was another half an hour before Maggie, the midwife, came running up the stairs, and in spite of Elsie's prediction the baby hadn't made an appearance despite her pushing for the last thirty minutes. Eight o'clock came and went, and then nine. Kenneth sent the children to bed but no one could sleep, the sounds coming from their parents' room were too harrowing. Gina lay curled up in a ball praying with all her might that her mam would be all right. A girl's mother in her class at school had died in the spring having a baby, and ever since she'd known her own mam was pregnant the thought had haunted her.

It was gone ten o'clock when a baby's cry sounded, and both mother and child were exhausted. The reason for the delayed birth had become apparent when the little girl suddenly shot out of her mother like a cork out of a bottle after being wedged inside the birth canal. The child was enormous.

'She's at least twelve pounds or more,' Maggie said in awe as she laid the baby on Elsie's chest. 'She's a whopper, lass, but perfect, praise be to God.'

'It's a little lassie?' Elsie murmured in disbelief. Never for one moment had she expected the child would be a girl.

'Aye, an' a bonny one. I'll get you cleaned up, lass, an' then once I've washed and dressed her you can put her to the breast.' Maggie went deftly about her business and once the child was clothed in a little nightie, bonnet and nappy, brought her to her mother. The little girl took to the breast like a duck to water, and the midwife stood surveying mother and child fondly for a moment or two before she said, 'I'll go and tell himself he can up and see his daughter, shall I?'

Elsie nodded. 'Thanks, Maggie.' She had never really liked the little Irishwoman but she had been glad of her tonight, she thought as Maggie disappeared. *Her daughter.* She looked down into the chubby little face, amazement uppermost. The child's eyes were closed but the rosebud lips were pulling at her nipple with a strength that belied her only being a few minutes old, and already Elsie could see the baby was a Redfern. She had the look of the lads about her.

Kenneth walked into the room with Maggie just behind him, and Elsie saw he was smiling widely. It surprised her because she knew he had expected, like her, that they would have another boy, but he clearly wasn't disappointed. The feeling that filled her was the same as when he had patted her on the shoulder earlier, and it made her voice soft as she murmured, 'A little lassie, Ken.'

'Aye, an' like Maggie here said, she's bonny.'

Maggie walked round the other side of the bed as she said, 'By, she knows where her grub is to be found, all right. I reckon she'll let you sleep till morning after this, lass, 'cause I dare bet she's as tired as you. I'll say me goodbyes then and get home.'

'Aye, all right, Maggie, an' thanks. Thanks a lot, lass.'

Kenneth didn't immediately follow the midwife downstairs. Instead he came closer and bent over, kissing the top of his wife's head as he muttered, 'Happy, lass?'

'Oh, Ken, I never expected her to be a girl. Not in a million years.' She smiled mistily up at him. 'And she's such a big baby, Maggie couldn't get over her.'

'Aye, she's a Redfern all right.' He touched the downy head with one finger. 'What do you want to call her?'

She could afford to be magnanimous. He'd been more like the old Ken tonight and she knew he was genuinely pleased for her. 'I thought Betty, after your mam?' she said quietly.

'Aw, lass.'

For the first time in her life she saw tears in his eyes and it melted her. Reaching up her hand, she stroked his cheek. 'Betty it is then,' she said softly, and as they smiled at each other she thought, this is a new beginning. Everything would be all right now. Having his own daughter would mellow him towards Gina, she knew it would, and they could be a proper family again. She felt a fierce surge of love for the baby in her arms, as much because of what her coming would mean for Gina as anything else.

A movement in the doorway brought Kenneth turning and they saw the lads and Gina clustered on the landing. It was Robin who said, 'The babby's here?'

'Aye, she's here,' said Kenneth, his voice hearty. 'Come and see her, all of you, but quietly mind, and then back to your rooms so your mam can get some rest.'

There were a lot of oohs and aahs and smiles, but as the children were shooed back to their rooms by Kenneth, it dawned on Elsie that Gina had been more subdued than she would have expected. But then it was the middle of the night and the bairn was tired, she reassured herself. Gina would be full of it in the morning, no doubt.

Once they were alone again, Kenneth said, 'Right, lass, I'll take Maggie back. I shouldn't be long. She was finishing at another birth in the village when I got there earlier so that's why we were a while. I was beside meself thinking the littl'un would arrive, and you on your own with the bairns.' He picked up the crib and placed it at the side of the bed as he spoke, positioning it so Elsie merely had to lean over and deposit the infant inside. 'You need anything afore I go, lass?'

'I've got all I need.' Elsie looked down at their daughter and then smiled at him.

'She's as bonny as her mam, that's for sure.'

Elsie listened to Kenneth and Maggie leave the house and once all was quiet, sighed contentedly. The child had stopped suckling and was sound asleep, and so she placed the baby in the crib, tucking the blankets round her. Leaning back against the pillows propped behind her, she gazed across at the flickering flames in the fireplace. She couldn't remember feeling so tired in all her life, but it was a happy tiredness, filled with joy and peace. Her and

Ken were all right again, and now she had not one but two daughters. Who would have thought it?

She fell asleep still smiling.

Kenneth Redfern wasted no time getting Maggie home and returning to the farm. Once there, he released the horse from the cart but didn't walk it to the stables, instead fetching a saddle and reins. Once it was saddled up he tied the reins to a post and then entered the house holding a sack. Making no sound, he tiptoed upstairs.

From the moment Maggie had come into the kitchen and informed him they had a daughter, a plan had been formulating in his mind. The basic idea wasn't new to him – he'd considered variations on the same theme more times than he could remember – but it had never been viable before, not without him coming under suspicion anyway. But tonight the circumstances were such that he could see he could get rid of the thorn in his flesh for good, although what he was about to do was risky.

There was no sound from the bedroom he shared with his wife when he reached the landing. He crept inside and stood looking down at her sleeping figure before his gaze moved to the crib. Elsie had her daughter now, and it was a child of her own flesh, and his. Aye, and his. They could be a proper family again once Gina was out of the way.

He left the room as quietly as he'd entered, checking on the lads' rooms before pushing Gina's door open. No one was awake. The previous hours had been traumatic for everyone and now that they could sleep, they were. Walking across to the small chest of drawers, he gathered the clothes Gina had worn during the day from the top of it and stuffed them in the sack, along with her buttoned boots. Moonlight was streaming in through the uncurtained window and by its silvery brightness he could see the small shape in a ball under the covers. Carefully he opened the window wide and then stood for a moment, his heart beating fit to burst. Once he had done what he was about to do there was no going back, for better or worse. What if someone awoke before he got back, or Marigold threw a shoe like the horse had done the week before – or what if he couldn't get the child out of the house without attracting attention? His goose would be well and truly cooked.

The brief second or two of hesitation gone, he gently peeled back the covers from the little form. In one swift movement he put his hand across Gina's mouth and lifted her into his arms, her back against his chest. As she began to struggle, he muttered fiercely, 'Quiet now, quiet. We've an errand to do for your mam, all right?'

She took no heed, fighting him for all she was worth, but her cries were muffled by his hand and he quickly carried her out on to the landing and down the stairs to the kitchen and then into the farmyard. It was bitterly cold and the child was wearing nothing but her flannelette nightdress, her small limbs flailing frantically. As he tried to undo the reins from the post she managed to free her mouth enough to cry out, and immediately he dropped the sack and slapped her across one side of her face and then the other, her head jerking like a rag doll's. The blows were hard enough to shock her into a stunned silence, whereupon, taking advantage of her dazed state, he bent and picked up the sack before undoing the reins and climbing into the saddle, his hand once again firmly over her mouth. As the horse began to move it brought her fully to her senses and she began to struggle wildly again, but it was as ineffectual as the efforts of a tiny sparrow in the talons of a bird of prey.

Once out on the track leading from the farm, Kenneth put the horse into first a canter and then a gallop, and Gina became frozen in terror. It was some miles before Kenneth brought Marigold to a halt, and by then Gina was numb with cold, her teeth chattering uncontrollably. Sliding to the ground with one arm still round her waist, he said roughly, 'There's clothes in the sack for you to put on,' but as he released her she fell to the ground, unable to stand. Yanking her up, he growled, 'Put these on, do you hear me?' but then found he had to virtually dress her himself as the cold and shock prevented her from obeying. She wasn't crying; she was paralysed in body and mind by what had happened to her. Pulling the clothes on over her nightie he then forced her freezing feet into her boots, almost snapping her ankle bones in the process, but still she made no sound. After being terror-stricken for hours that her mam was going to die, so much so that she had been quite unable to express her overwhelming relief when she had seen her mam and the new baby, the night had taken on a further nightmarish quality her mind was unable to comprehend.

She submitted to Kenneth roughly hauling her up on to the horse again, and when Marigold was urged into a trot with her seated in front of him and his arm round her waist, she wasn't even aware of the tears streaming down her face until the freezing air chilled her skin. Instinct told her not to anger him, but when they passed through a small hamlet and she took the opportunity to shout for help in spite of her fear, he said fiercely, 'You do that again and I'll find a river to throw you in, you hear me? I mean it, mind. No one can hear you anyway, it's the middle of the night. Keep quiet and you'll be all right. I don't want to hurt you but I will if I have to.'

Gina believed him. She didn't know where they were going or what was happening, but she believed he would do what he had threatened.

Kenneth knew exactly where he was bound. Keeping to country lanes and byways and dirt tracks as much as possible, he made his way eastwards towards the coast. The thick frost which coated the ground and trees and hedgerows with a glittering layer of white, along with the bright moonlight, made visibility easy. He knew he was limited by both the speed and length of journey the horse could accomplish without doing herself harm, and the time he could afford to be away from the farmhouse. With regard to the latter he was hoping Maggie was right and that Elsie and the baby would sleep for most of the night. The farm was situated in a valley to the south-east of Hexham and some sixteen or so miles from Gateshead where he was headed.

He had only been to Gateshead a few times. Any business he needed to do such as the buying and selling of produce or animals was conducted in Hexham, the town being much closer to the farm and having a fine market day every month. Most of the folk he knew had never travelled more than a mile or two from their own front doors; it was the country way.

Gina was quiet now and Marigold had found a comfortable pace, trotting through the silent night quite happily. It was a couple of hours before they reached the south-west ward of Gateshead and Kenneth made straight for his intended destination. On reaching Workhouse Lane, he pulled Marigold to a halt. As Gina twisted round to look up at him, her eyes huge in her white face, he said, 'I've brought you to your new home and this is where you are going to live from now on. Do you understand what I'm saying?' The child's silence had him wondering if she'd lost her senses.

'I want to go home.' It was a tiny whisper.

'This is going to be your home.'

'I want Mam.' She was shivering with cold and her bottom lip was quivering, but there was no pity in the be-whiskered face staring down at her.

'She's not your mam, she was never your mam. You were given to us to look after for a while by your real mother, all right? But now your mam –' he stopped abruptly – 'now my wife and I have decided it's time for you to leave and we don't want you back. There's no room for you any more, not with the new baby an' all.'

She had started to cry, and he said roughly, 'Stop that, it'll do no good. I'm going to leave you in a minute and you tell them that you have no mam an' da, no family, you hear me? You're an orphan. Remember that. An orphan.'

'I'm not.' She was struggling wildly now and as he shook her hard so her head wobbled, she cried, 'I want my mam. She is my mam, she is.'

'She's not.' His voice a growl, he measured his words as he said, 'She – is – not – your – mam. She never was. We took you in when your mother died, that's all. Now be still or so help me I'll throw you in that river we passed a while back.'

'I don't care, I want Mam.'

Rage uppermost, he shook her again and again so savagely that she suddenly went limp in his grasp and for a moment he thought he had killed her. Panicking now, he turned her fully to face him and when he saw that she was merely unconscious he breathed a sigh of relief. He didn't want her death on his conscience, just to have her out of their lives for good.

He clicked his tongue and urged the horse to begin moving again towards the sprawling collection of buildings in front of them. Gateshead workhouse had four main areas and he was making for the entrance block with the porter's lodge and the receiving wards. Gina was stirring again but as he bent and looked at her he saw her eyes were dazed and unfocused.

'You'll be all right here,' he said gruffly as he reached the lodge which was in darkness, but she made no response. 'I'm goin' to ring the bell and then be off but someone'll come out to you in a minute or two.'

So saying, he slid off the horse with her in his arms and walked across to the gates of the lodge whereupon he put her on her feet. But she fell to the floor in a small heap. He looked at her for a moment. Her eyes were closed and she looked bad. Telling himself it was not his concern any more, he pressed the bell set in the gates and hurried back to Marigold. Mounting swiftly, he dug his heels in the horse's flanks and they cantered off at some speed, Marigold neighing in protest at the rush. He didn't look back. He had done what he had set out to do and it was for the good of the family as a whole, he told himself. Things couldn't have gone on as they were. Elsie had her daughter now and in time she'd forget about Gina. Life would go on, it always did.

He got back to the farm just after five o'clock in the morning and after settling Marigold in her stable he entered the house with his heart in his mouth. If Elsie had been aware of his absence she would smell a rat when it was discovered Gina was gone, but he'd just have to brazen it out somehow. Divesting himself of his coat and boots downstairs, he crept up the stairs to the bedroom. The house was hushed and silent, and as he pushed the door open Elsie and the bairn were fast asleep, but now the baby was lying in the crook of his wife's arm. Stripping off his clothes he pulled on his nightshirt, sliding carefully between the covers. As he did so, Elsie stirred and opened her eyes, saying sleepily, 'What time is it?'

'Milking time.' He sat up. 'I'm just going to get dressed and go down. I won't wake the lads – they had a late night and they can sleep in for a bit for once.'

'Aw, Ken.' She smiled at him and then as the child in her arms gave a little whimper, she said, 'Isn't she good, letting us sleep all night. She woke up once, I don't know what time it was but it was before you got back after taking Maggie 'cause you weren't here. So it was early on. If she sleeps like this every night we'll be in clover.'

'Aye, well, she's a big babby so she might, but don't count your chickens yet.' He smiled at her, sending up a silent prayer of thanks that things had gone so well. 'She made a few noises once or twice,' he added for good measure, 'you know how they do, but then she went off again and you were dead to the world, bless you, and no wonder. That was a birth an' a half, wasn't it. Nothing like any of the lads.'

'She's worth it, though.' Elsie watched him as he began to get dressed, the glow from the embers of the fire in the grate sending shadows on to the ceiling, and then as the baby began to grizzle she unbuttoned her nightdress and put her to the breast.

Kenneth stoked up the fire in the grate once he was dressed and put a log on to burn, saying as he did so, 'I'll see to the milking and then bring you a cuppa, lass, before I get the lads and Gina up. You stay in bed, you hear? We can all manage atween us for a day or two while you have a bit of a rest. The bairns can stay off school for once and help in the house, it won't hurt. Now

I'd better get meself downstairs. Frank an' Walt'll be here any minute and it'll take us a bit longer with the milking, the lads not being about. I won't open the curtains yet, you doze if you can.'

Once he'd gone, Elsie lay back against the pillows with a blissful sigh, feeling like the luckiest woman in the world. The thick stone walls of the farmhouse deadened any sound from outside, but in her mind's eye she saw him telling the farmhands about little Betty and her smile deepened. He was genuinely pleased about her being a girl and that was nice, and Betty was going to be a good babby, she could tell. Her arrival had healed something between herself and Ken, and they were a united family again, the tensions and difficulties of the last year or two forgotten. And Gina would be tickled pink about having a sister once she got used to the idea; the lassie had just been a bit taken aback last night about her being a girl, that was all. She nodded at the thought. She had come to this conclusion in the night when she was feeding Betty, and once the reason for Gina's quietness had dawned on her it had seemed so obvious. From the moment she'd become pregnant she had referred to the baby in her belly as a he, and so had everyone else. Of course, her little lassie was surprised, but she'd love the babby, boy or girl, Gina was like that.

Betty having nodded off again at the breast, Elsie placed her back in the crib and settled down for a nap, happier than she had been for a long time.

PART TWO

The Cottage Homes

1927

Chapter Five

'And you say she has said nothing at all since the porter found her?'

'Not a word, Matron. Dr Taylor thinks she might be in shock or has banged her head, although there is no obvious sign of injury. Of course, she could merely be simple and unable to communicate, although she looks normal enough. Dr Taylor feels the fact that she keeps slipping in and out of consciousness indicates a physical accident of some kind. She is not malnourished and appears to have been well looked after.'

'Hmm.' Matron Heath gazed down at the small figure fast asleep in a narrow iron bed in one of the receiving wards. It was eight o'clock in the morning, and she had just come to the entrance block at the request of the senior doctor, Adam Taylor, after leaving the main building of the workhouse where she had finished making her usual rounds of the male and female wards. She had expected the doctor to be on hand to greet her, but the nurse he had left in charge had informed her Dr Taylor had had to rush off to attend an emergency in the infectious diseases ward of the hospital on the south-east of the site. The matron was not impressed. Any emergency involving an inmate should rank well below giving her the courtesy she expected from her staff.

Turning her steel-blue eyes on the nurse, she said, 'Who left her at the gates?'

'The porter saw no one, Matron, but he thought he heard a horse galloping away in the distance. He couldn't be sure though.'

'Most unsatisfactory.'

'Yes, Matron.' The nurse had been at the workhouse long enough to know that you agreed with everything Matron Heath said.

'Tell Dr Taylor to keep me informed of the child's progress. She will either have to be moved to the hospital or to the cottage homes in due course.'

'Yes, Matron.'

Once the matron had swept out in a crackle of black starched linen, the nurse continued looking down at her tiny patient. She had been at the workhouse for less than a year and was not yet hardened to the misery and heartache. Someone had left this beautiful child here, she thought sadly. Abandoned her. And yes, it might be because of extreme poverty or ill health or a whole host of other reasons, but could anything really justify committing a young innocent to the grim confines of the workhouse without any explanation or any means of contact? Dr Taylor had told her he'd feared he was going to lose the child for the first hour; she had been virtually unconscious and as cold as ice and getting her body temperature up to normal had been a struggle. He had hoped that as she'd warmed up she would revive enough to speak, but her dazed state had continued, which had led him to suspect she'd been ill-treated in some way despite no apparent wounds.

As she watched there was a slight movement of the small body and then the child's eyes flickered open. This had happened a few times before and like then the nurse said quickly, 'Hello, my dear. Are you feeling better?' On the other occasions the vacant stare had not registered her and the child's eyes had closed again within seconds, but this time they stayed open.

'My head hurts.'

It was a faint whisper but, relieved beyond measure that the little girl was able to speak, the nurse said softly, 'That will soon pass. Would you like a drink?'

'I feel sick.'

As the nurse whisked her up into a sitting position and held an enamel bowl under her chin, Gina brought up the contents of her stomach in a bout of nausea that continued for a few minutes. Once she had finished and was lying down again, she whispered, 'Where am I?'

The nurse hesitated. She was well aware the poor had a paralysing fear of the workhouse from birth to death and she didn't want to frighten the child.

She was saved from having to reply by the appearance of Dr Taylor who, on seeing that his patient was awake, said cheerfully, 'Well now, that's good, back in the land of the living, I see. You had us worried there for a while, missy.'

Gina looked at the man in the white coat. He had a kind voice, like the lady. Again she murmured weakly, 'Where am I?'

'Somewhere where you'll be well looked after, m'dear, don't you fret.'

It wasn't really an answer and Gina was aware of this but she couldn't find the words she wanted to say. Her head was muzzy and ached so much that all she wanted to do was to close her eyes. 'My – my mam . . .' Even as she spoke the words she spiralled downwards into the darkness again.

'Matron was here,' the nurse said quietly. 'She said the child will have to be moved to the hospital or to the cottage homes.'

Dr Taylor straightened his shoulders. He had just spent a traumatic twenty minutes attempting to save a young woman with typhoid. Beth had had the face of an angel but had been working the streets as a prostitute from childhood, living in the appallingly overcrowded housing close to the docks where disease was rife. One of her pals had brought her to the workhouse hospital the day before, after Beth's pimp had thrown her out of the house he owned, saying she was of no use to him any more. Dr Taylor had suspected it was too late to save the young woman the moment he had examined her but he'd done his best. He sighed deeply. That seemed to be the soul-destroying pattern of his life these days – doing his best and failing miserably. But then most of his patients were destitute and poverty-stricken before he even laid eyes on them, meaning that years of starvation and disease had already taken their toll.

But not this child. His gaze returned to Gina. The girl appeared fit and healthy, and he would think she had been well looked after before she had been abandoned at the workhouse gates.

'I'm not transferring her to the hospital,' he said quietly. 'By all means inform Matron of my decision if she pays another visit. We'll see how the child progresses and I'll look in later. For the moment she remains here under your sole care, is that clear?'

The nurse looked at him in surprise. Apart from the fact that no one contradicted Matron's orders with her being the wife of the master of the workhouse, there were never enough staff per ratio to patients as it was and the guardians wouldn't stump up any more money for extra nurses. Instead they'd decreed that the inmates of the workhouse cleaned the wards, emptied the bedpans and urine bottles, made the beds and did any other menial tasks. Many of these women were brutal and ignorant and often mentally deficient, and the nurse wondered if that was the reason Dr Taylor seemed set on keeping the child here in relative isolation until she was well enough to be sent to the Union's cottage homes at Medomsley, near Shotley Bridge. The homes had been constructed nearly thirty years before, when it had been decided to remove pauper children who had formerly resided within the workhouse to separate premises some miles away.

The site was a large one, and as well as the boys' cottages and girls' cottages – each home housing a 'family' group of fifteen to twenty children looked after by a house mother – there was the master and mistress's premises and an administrative house, the porter's lodge, a hospital situated upon the highest part of the grounds, a group of buildings consisting of workshops, general stores for grocery, haberdashery and so on, the superintendent's quarters and office, a committee room and surgery.

She had visited the hospital there several times with Dr Taylor, and there was no doubt both the hospital and the place as a whole made a far better environment for children than the original workhouse. Nevertheless, the taint of the workhouse still clung to the little ones. She'd heard reports of bullying by the local children when the cottage home occupants attended the Benfieldside council schools which were a short distance from the site.

As the doctor left the small side room on the receiving ward, the nurse glanced at her patient. However this poor child had fared before this, she was going to have to adapt to a whole different life now, unless, of course, the person or persons who had left her here came back for her.

She sighed, in much the same way Dr Taylor had done a few minutes before, because she doubted very much that would be the case.

*

It was another two days before Dr Taylor agreed for Gina to be transferred to the cottage homes. She had been able to tell him it was her father who had brought her to the workhouse but not where she lived, simply because she had no idea except that, 'It's a long way away.' He had listened to her story with immense pity and, when she'd related how her father had struck and shaken her, immense anger.

It had become apparent to him that the man's treatment of the child had been the cause of her incoherent and dazed state in the first hours of being admitted. The brain wasn't meant to endure such violent vibration; it was a wonder that she had recovered as quickly as she had.

He had spent some time patiently drawing out the events of that night amid her tears. She had told him her father's assertion that she was an orphan and had been taken in by them after her natural mother had died, but it was clear she had no real idea of what it meant and that she had been abandoned for good. She asked for her mother constantly, begging to be taken home umpteen times a day. Of course, it was anyone's guess where 'home' was, and the workhouse had neither the resources nor the inclination to dig deeper.

Children were brought to the workhouse for all sorts of reasons. Death of the parents; a family being turned out on the streets; a father abandoning his wife and children and the mother being unable to provide; dis-ablement of little ones, either physically or mentally – the sad list was endless. Gina wasn't the first child to be deposited at the gates under cover of darkness and no doubt she wouldn't be the last, Dr Taylor thought grimly as his nurse dressed the small patient for the journey to the cottage homes. She had been able to tell them that her name was Gina Redfern but that was all, and more than once over the last forty-eight hours he had told himself that it was a mercy, with the child being such a pretty little girl, that this man she had called her father hadn't dumped her on the streets. The pimps and brothel keepers in certain parts of the town were always on the lookout to procure boys and girls for certain of their clients who had a predilection for young flesh. It was a brutal and uncaring world.

The same nurse who had been caring for the child was accompanying her to the cottage homes, much to the annoyance of Matron Heath who hadn't been able to understand what she called the 'fuss' being made over one small patient. Dr Taylor didn't fully understand why he had made a stand against the matron either, but there was something about this particular little girl that had got to him. She seemed to embody the hopeless plight of so many he dealt with on a daily basis, and he had wanted to make her painful circumstances as easy for her as he could. But now he had to do something he had been putting off for the last hour or so. He had to explain the truth of the situation to her, because once she got to the cottage homes it would be better if she was prepared.

Once she was dressed for the outside in the hat and coat they had acquired for her, the nurse brought her to stand in front of him. He squatted down so his head was on a level with the child's, as he said gently, 'Do you understand where Nurse is taking you, Gina?'

Gina stared at him for a moment, her gaze moving momentarily to the nurse and then back to the doctor. She liked him, he was nice, the doctor, not like the lady the nurse called Matron who had come to look at her once or twice and glared at her with a nasty face like she was smelling something bad. After a second or two, she said, 'The cottage homes?'

'Yes, that's right, and you are going to stay there from now on. There will be lots of other children for you to play with and—'

'When will my mam come for me to take me home?' She stared at him, unblinking.

The nurse moved from one foot to the other but the doctor ignored her. Keeping his eyes on the small face in front of him, he said even more gently, 'I'm afraid your mother won't be able to do that.'

'She will.' Her chin jerked as though to emphasize her words, and when he continued to stare at her, she said more loudly, 'My mam will come, you'll see. She will. I'm going to help her look after the new babby.'

'I don't think—'

'*She will.*' Her body had stiffened and then, as though realizing she had shouted, Gina said more quietly, 'My mam will come and take me home, I know she will,' as tears began to trickle down her cheeks.

Wishing he had never started this, Dr Taylor fished in

his pocket for his handkerchief, handing it to the child as he stood up and said, 'Now come, come, no tears, not from such a brave girl.' He looked helplessly at the nurse for a moment before saying, 'Let me put it this way, Gina. Until your mother comes for you, you will be staying at the cottage homes and you have to do what they tell you. Do you understand? The people there have lots of children to look after and they won't tolerate anyone being naughty or answering back or . . .' His voice trailed away.

Gina continued to stare at him and she didn't speak for a moment, but when she did it was to say again, 'My mam will come.'

Dr Taylor was out of his depth. The child imagined she only had to stick to her guns and her beloved 'mam' would materialize, but he had had experience of the house mothers at the homes. Some were more tolerant than others but they all expected their charges to be seen and not heard, and a child having their own opinion about anything was out of the question. She was a bright little thing and he had to make her understand for her own sake. She had to fit in or her life would be untenable. He searched for the right words and then said hesitantly, 'Some people won't understand about your mother coming for you so it will be better if you say nothing about it. It can be your secret, all right? It's nice to have a secret, isn't it? And until she comes I want you to promise me that you will be a good girl and do everything you're told. Will you do that?'

Gina paused as her mind raced, blinking at him the while. *He didn't believe her about her mam.* The terrible feeling took over again, the one that had her wanting to scream and cry and shout at the thought of not seeing her mam again. But she would, she would see her soon, she had to. Her mam would tell her da what was what and she would come for her whatever her da said. Her mam loved her.

'Gina? Do you promise?'

She bit down hard on her bottom lip to stop herself crying again, then she brought out, 'Aye, yes, I do.'

Dr Taylor nodded and smiled. He had done all he could and he was late for his morning rounds. Nevertheless, he delayed a further moment. Squatting down again, he said quietly, 'Everything will seem much better in a little while, Gina. I know you're sad now but things have a habit of working out in the end, take it from me.'

She nodded because she knew that was what he wanted her to do, but she didn't believe him. Nothing would be better until she was home again with her mam.

Chapter Six

Elsie knew she was losing her mind. It had been over a week since Gina had gone and she had barely eaten or slept; how she was producing enough milk for the babby she didn't know but her breasts seemed to be working independently from the rest of her. She had enough milk to feed umpteen babies.

She looked down at her daughter guzzling her feed and already dressed in clothes that Gina had worn at six months old. Little Betty had a voracious appetite during the day, but after her last feed at ten o'clock at night she slept through until five in the morning. Elsie knew she ought to be grateful for this and in the normal run of things she would have been, but in the present circumstances it just meant she lay awake with nothing to do but imagine horror after horror concerning her bairn. Gina floating in the same river that was her mother's last resting place or caught in weeds and debris under the surface; Gina frozen in a little ball somewhere in the countryside beyond the farm where animals would savage the body; Gina in the hands of one of the tramps or vagabonds that walked the lanes and byways, or snatched by someone in a carriage or horse and cart and taken away to do goodness knows what to her.

Rising quickly from her rocking chair by the range she deposited Betty in her crib and ran to the deep stone sink and retched. Her child was gone, lost, and she was going stark, staring, raving mad. She retched again but her stomach was as empty and painful as her heart. Kenneth kept trying to persuade her to eat but she knew his patience was running out. Only that morning he had stated grimly that she had to look after herself for Betty's sake, that her refusal to eat would start to affect the baby's well-being if she wasn't careful. It was all Betty with him, Elsie thought bitterly. From not being bothered about having a daughter, he was now besotted with the infant. If he had shown a smidgen of the affection to Gina that he showered on Betty everything would be different now.

But no, that wasn't altogether fair, Elsie told herself amid Betty's cries at having her feed interrupted so arbitrarily. She should have realized the night Betty was born, when Gina came in with the lads to see the baby, why her bairn was so quiet and subdued. All along she had told Gina she was going to have a brother and then when Betty had arrived of course the child would wonder if she was going to have her nose pushed out. She should have reassured her bairn that the baby's arrival would make no difference to the bond they shared, that her love for Gina was something nothing could change. But now it was too late. Raising her head, she looked wildly about the kitchen. Where was Gina at this moment? Was she dead or alive? Would nothing ever be heard of her again? Kenneth and the farmhands and the lads had scoured the countryside calling for her, and after that first day Kenneth had ridden into Hexham to inform the police of Gina's disappearance. She had expected someone to come to the farm but Kenneth had told her the police had taken Gina's details and would conduct their own search and let them know if anything came of it.

Betty's wails were making her head pound, and after picking the baby out of the crib she recommenced the feeding, gazing down at the plump little face against her breast. Over the last days she had realized a feeling of resentment for the baby had crept into her heart. If Betty had been a boy Gina would still be here. However much she tried to rid herself of the thought it kept intruding. And it was wicked, she knew it was wicked because the baby was innocent in all of this, but nevertheless, that was how she felt. Or maybe it was more that it felt terribly disloyal to love this daughter when her Gina was gone? Oh, she didn't know. She didn't know anything any more except that life wouldn't be worth living if her bairn didn't come back. For the child to climb out of her window in the dead of night she must have been feeling wretched, but she didn't believe Kenneth's assertion that Gina had run away. She might have gone for a walk that night – the child had a habit of doing that if anything troubled her – but she wouldn't have intended to stay away. She hadn't taken her hat and coat, for one thing, and Gina was a sensible bairn. No, she'd planned to take a little walk and come to terms with the fact that the new babby was a girl, that was all. Elsie nodded mentally. But something had happened.

There had been continuous flurries of snow in the last few days but now a blizzard was blowing, the wind howling like a banshee. Elsie's weary gaze strayed to the window as Betty fell asleep at the breast and tears trickled down her cheeks. Gina had come to her in a winter's storm like this one, her precious, beautiful bubbly storm child. So tiny and yet so perfect, with a strength and will to live that had been all at odds with her minute frame. Pray God that will had kept her bairn alive the last few days.

She was still sitting in a kind of stupor when Kenneth walked into the kitchen some time later saying, 'We're in for a load, the sky's full of it.'

She looked at him. Did he really think she cared one way or the other? Her bairn was gone.

He stared at her for a moment. 'Where's me grub?'

Of course, he'd come in for his lunch, she hadn't realized the time. It was on the tip of her tongue to tell him to get his own meal but she bit the words back. Standing to her feet, she placed the sleeping baby in her crib and walked over to the range where a meat roll had been steaming for three hours. In the winter Kenneth expected three hot meals a day although he was agreeable to a supper of bread and cheese and ham. She took the roll out of the pan and peeled off the cloth it had been wrapped in, bringing it to the table and then fetching a crusty loaf and pat of butter along with their plates and knives and forks. Putting the kettle on for a cup of tea, she joined him at the table where he'd already helped himself to a good portion of the steak-and-ham roll. After cutting several slices off the loaf and spreading them liberally with butter, she placed them at the edge of his plate, receiving a grunt of thanks as he continued to eat.

She sat watching him for a moment. How could he eat with every appearance of enjoyment when their lives were in turmoil? Some fragments of the meat roll had caught in his whiskers and she looked away in distaste, her stomach heaving. Getting up quickly, she walked across to the hob and poured hot water into the teapot, spending a couple of minutes mashing the tea with her back to him before bringing two mugs to the table and setting his in front of him.

'It's getting cold.' He gestured at the meat roll.

'I don't want any.'

'Don't be stupid, woman. You've got to eat.'

'I said I don't want any.'

Her voice had risen but instead of backing off as he had done in the last few days, he said flatly, 'You'll damn well eat something, now then. What will happen to the rest of us if you're taken bad? That little baby needs you – we all do.'

'That's all that bothers you, isn't it? Her and the lads and you being looked after? You don't care how I feel.'

She had expected him to answer in the same angry tone she had used, so when he paused and then said gently, 'That's not true, lass. You must know that. Of course I care,' it was her undoing. As she began to sob he got up and came to her, drawing her into his arms where he held her, both of them rocking backwards and forwards as he murmured, 'Aw, lass, lass, don't take on. Things will get better. I know you don't believe that now, but they will. And if it's any comfort I don't believe the bairn is dead. She's out there somewhere and being looked after, I feel it in me bones. In fact, I'd stake me life on it.'

It was the first time he had said this and now she drew away to look into his face, her eyes streaming as she said, 'Do you mean that? Really mean it?'

'Aye, I do. I wouldn't say it otherwise. I've felt it all along.'

He wasn't a man given to fancies and in spite of her grief and despair, she felt a ray of comfort.

'Now come and sit down and have something to eat. Gina wouldn't want you bad because of her, now would she?'

The name had stuck in his craw but when she sat down and then reached for a slice of bread and butter, he said, 'That's right, that's right. We don't want you faded away to nothing by the time she's found.'

Elsie had worried him the last few days. He hadn't expected her to take it so badly about the bairn, not with Betty having been born, but then women could be weepy after childbirth. It would pass. He had told himself this every day when his conscience had pricked him. And it wasn't as if the bairn was flesh of her flesh, not like Betty and the lads. No, once Elsie got over having the baby she'd get back to her old self. It might take a while but he could be patient. Everything would settle down. People would forget about the bairn in time; folk had their own lives and problems to deal with, after all. He might have to pretend to go into Hexham again and say he'd check with the police there, but he'd do the same as he'd done before and go for a jar or two in one of the public houses. Elsie would never know the police hadn't been informed.

He took a gulp of his tea, watching Elsie nibble at the slice of bread, and when he cut her a small portion of the meat roll and placed it on her plate, saying, 'Try and eat it, lass. For me,' he was rewarded with a wan smile.

Aye, he'd done the right thing in taking the girl to the workhouse, which was where she'd been destined for all along. It had only been Elsie insisting they take her in that had prevented him giving her to the authorities when she was born, and look at what a mistake that had turned out to be. She'd never fitted in. Making out his lads were dim-witted because they weren't much cop at school, and flaunting the way she could read and write and what have you, and the tongue on her! Cheeky as the day was long. If she'd have carried on living here she would have split the family in two, because Elsie had thought the sun shone out of the lass's backside. In a way Elsie had brought her present unhappiness on herself. All this upset could have been avoided if she'd listened to him in the first place. Now it would be just them and their own bairns, which was as it should be.

He watched as Elsie forced the meat roll down, and when she had finished he picked up her plate and his and took them to the stone sink, saying, 'You sit a while and finish your cuppa, lass. I'll see to the dishes.'

This was a great concession. To her knowledge Kenneth

had never lifted a finger in the house since they had been wed. Indoors and the dairy were her domain, outside was his. Elsie sipped at her tea as she watched him wash and dry up, and again his kindness brought tears pricking at the backs of her eyes. He was doing his best, she told herself, and although it was true he and Gina had never got on, he was probably feeling in his own way the loss her going had left in their family. And certainly the distress and pain of the lads was obvious. Poor little James had been inconsolable.

The rhythmic beat of the headache that had been with her for days caused her to close her eyes for a moment or two. She was tired, so tired but she couldn't sleep apart from the odd catnap and doze now and again. She had made the mistake once or twice of looking into a future that didn't contain her bairn and it had terrified her, the absence of joy and hope and peace, of anything that made life worthwhile. All the beauty had been sucked out of the world and it wouldn't return until Gina was back with her.

'I'll ride into Hexham the morrer, weather permitting, and see if they've heard owt, if you want?'

She opened her eyes to see Kenneth peering down at her. She nodded wearily. 'Thanks, Ken.'

Please God there would be some news, a sighting, anything. Please, *please* God.

Chapter Seven

'You're barmy, you are, liking school. No one likes school.'

Gina was standing in the dormitory by her bed facing her accuser, a tall, thin-faced girl with sharp eyes who had a little band of followers behind her. She had got the measure of this girl, Peggy Turner, from her first day at the cottage homes. Peggy had been assigned to take her up to the dormitory after she had been introduced to everyone by the house mother, and once there Peggy had pointed to one of the eight beds the room held. 'That's yours, by the window. No one likes that bed, the window's draughty.'

Gina had been too heartsore to care, saying woodenly, 'I don't mind.'

'Doesn't matter if you mind or not, a little squirt like you. You'll do as you're told and I'm in charge of the dormitory when Mother isn't here.'

The girl's tone had jerked Gina out of the lethargy that had taken her over since the nurse deposited her at the receiving station situated near the porter's lodge. This was so placed that children, when admitted to the cottage homes, were taken directly to the receiving building without passing any other establishment. She had been collected from there by her house mother, a Mrs Bainsby, and walked to what had appeared to Gina's fevered gaze as an unending maze of houses set in landscaped grounds with lawns and trees and bushes. Each cottage consisted of a living and dining room, mother's room, kitchen, lavatory and bathroom on the ground floor, and on the first floor two dormitories for the children, a mother's bedroom, and a linen room. She had arrived shortly before lunch and it being a Saturday none of the children were at school. Once taken to the dining room, she'd sat in numb misery following the introductions by Mrs Bainsby, quite unable to eat anything, and then Peggy had taken her upstairs.

Remembering that day over a week ago, Gina suddenly realized that she had been waiting for Peggy to show her hand ever since. The girl didn't like her, she knew that, but then Peggy didn't seem to like anyone except Ethel, Vera, Gladys and Martha, her four friends who always did exactly what Peggy told them. Gladys and Martha were twins, thin, scrawny little things with bow legs due to rickets, and Gina felt they were frightened of Peggy, but then most of the children seemed to be. But she wasn't. Gina looked at Peggy, sizing her up. The other girl was a head taller than her and always wore her hair in a high ponytail which made her appear even taller, and Gina knew she herself looked young for her age, being small and slim. She had always hated being small but no one would have guessed this as she straightened her narrow shoulders. 'Barmy yourself,' she said clearly, 'and it's up to me what I like and don't like so mind your own business.' There was a collective gasp from the rest of the girls in the dormitory. It was a few minutes before lights-out and everyone had been scrambling into their nighties, but now as one they watched the scene unfolding in front of them.

Peggy glared her outrage. For someone in her dormitory to answer her back was unheard of. Everyone knew she was Mother's favourite, and if they didn't she soon acquainted them with the fact. Born to a young single mother in the workhouse, she had been brought to the cottage homes as an infant and the life here was all she'd known. Naturally cunning and manipulative, she had adapted to her surroundings like a chameleon, inveigling favour with the staff and using her limited power to control the other girls in the dormitory, which she saw as her own little kingdom. For this new girl, this upstart with her curly hair and big blue eyes, to challenge her was insupportable. 'Don't you dare talk to me like that,' she hissed furiously. 'I'll tell Mother on you.'

'Tell her,' Gina hissed back with equal venom. 'See if I care.'

The other girls, even Peggy's four minions, stared in rapt fascination. Peggy might be taller and older than her adversary but it was clear to everyone that in repartee and temper the two were equally matched.

'I'll smack your face for you,' said Peggy, taking a step forward and seeming to tower over Gina.

'You raise your hand to me and I'll take a lump out of it.' Gina bared her small white teeth. 'You see if I don't.'

Peggy hesitated, more than a little taken aback. It was plain Gina meant what she said; her blue eyes were blazing with an anger that had turned her cheeks scarlet and her small hands were clenched into fists. Knowing she couldn't afford to lose face but utterly at a loss as to what to do, Peggy turned and appealed to her little band. 'Look at her,' she said with as much derision as she could muster up. 'She's like a little animal. Wherever she's come from it's obvious she's been dragged up, not brought up respectably. Scum, her folk must be.'

The slur on her mother was too much. Gina launched herself on her enemy with all the ferocity of a tiny wild cat, and as Peggy screamed and tried to fight her off, Mrs Bainsby's voice cut through the resulting hullabaloo like a thunderclap. The next minute or two was sheer pandemonium but eventually Mrs Bainsby carted Gina off in a kind of headlock with Peggy trailing behind and sobbing for all she was worth. The show over, the rest of the girls slunk into their beds and tried to make themselves invisible, each one knowing that the new girl wouldn't fare well in this but full of admiration for her fearlessness.

Once in the mother's room downstairs, Mrs Bainsby pushed Gina roughly in front of her with the command of, 'Stand there and don't move.' Glancing at Peggy, who was still trying to force some tears out, she said crisply, 'What happened?'

'She went for me, Mother, just because I said I'd tell you she'd been disrespectful to me.'

'That's not true.' Gina's voice was quivering, not with tears but with rage. 'She said my family were scum and that I'd not been brought up properly.'

Mrs Bainsby was fifty years old and an embittered woman. After only three years of marriage her husband had run off with another woman twenty-five years ago, an event which had shaped her life ever since. The girl in question had been a pretty flibbertigibbet according to those who had known her, and at first the wronged wife had expected her husband to come crawling back with his tail between his legs when he realized what he had landed himself with. This girl wouldn't keep a house spick and span and have his meal waiting when he got home at night, his slippers warming by the fire; even his own parents had said as much when Mrs Bainsby had gone to see them. But the husband hadn't come back and the years had passed and Mrs Bainsby had had to accept that some men preferred a pretty face and an enthusiastic partner in bed – one of the necessities of marriage Mrs Bainsby had found repugnant from day one – to a good respectable woman.

She surveyed the child in front of her, one of the prettiest little girls she had ever seen, her thin nostrils flaring as she said, 'I see nothing in your behaviour to convince me that Peggy has said anything other than the truth.'

Far from being intimidated, the injustice made Gina even angrier. 'She doesn't know my family, none of you do.'

'Is this the same family who left you at the workhouse gates with no explanation or means of contact?'

'That was my da, not my mam and brothers.'

'But according to what Dr Taylor wrote in his report, this man is not your father, neither are you related to his family. That is what you told him your father said, is it not?'

Gina stared into the thin face. She had known she disliked the woman she was supposed to address as Mother from the moment Mrs Bainsby had collected her from the receiving station and marched her back to the cottage without a word, just not how much. The hard lump in her chest that had been with her since she had woken up in the workhouse and realized the horrible dreams she had been having weren't a nightmare but true rose up into her throat, but telling herself she couldn't cry, not here in front of Mrs Bainsby and Peggy, she narrowed her eyes. 'Just because he said it, it doesn't make it so.'

'Oh, so he's a liar, is he?'

'Aye, he is.'

The child could have been sixteen in her speech and attitude rather than five or six. Mrs Bainsby had received the initial report from the schoolmistress at Benfieldside school in charge of the infants, which had stated that Gina was a lot more intelligent than most of the other children, and were they sure she was only coming up for six in December as the child claimed? It was annoying. Intelligent children were always a problem, girls in particular. But she had broken the rebellious spirits of other girls before Gina and brought them into line, and this child would be no different. Raising her hand, she hit Gina on the head with such force that she fell backwards, landing on her bottom on the polished floorboards with a resounding thump.

'That's for your sauce, madam. I won't be talked back to and I won't tolerate insubordination from my girls. Do you understand?'

Gina's ears were ringing and lights were darting before her eyes, the pain in her coccyx where she'd hit the hard floor making her want to be sick. Peggy, too, was stunned at the sudden violence. She had seen Mrs Bainsby smack the inmates in her charge before and if a girl was taken to the punishment room, a small cupboard type affair with no windows and no furniture, everyone knew the unfortunate child would be severely beaten on their bare bottom by Mother so they couldn't sit down for a day or two. But this was different. If Peggy had been able to verbalize what she was feeling she would have said that it was the uncontrolled ferocity that had shocked her, but as it was she felt repulsed and fearful and, to her surprise, sorry for the new girl, an emotion that was unfamiliar to her. Knowing Mother wouldn't like it if she made a move to help Gina to her feet, however, she did nothing as the other girl struggled up.

'I don't know what liberties you have been used to taking before this, but from now on you do exactly as you are told, m'girl. And make no mistake, the master and mistress will hear of this when they make their next inspection.' Mrs Bainsby stepped back a pace as she regarded the child, who was swaying slightly and clearly in a great deal of pain. Turning to Peggy, she said, 'Take her back to the dormitory and I don't want any of the other girls talking to her until she shows me that they won't be contaminated by her wayward tongue.'

'Yes, Mother.' Now Peggy did take Gina's arm to turn her around and lead her out of the room, but as she did so, Gina vomited over the floor.

'Filthy little thing!' Mrs Bainsby practically screamed at Peggy as she said, 'Get her out, get her out of my sight.'

Once outside the room and with the door closed behind them, Peggy muttered, 'You all right? Do you want to be sick again?'

Gina shook her head. The pain in the base of her back was fractionally better and now her stomach was empty the awful feeling of nausea was passing.

'Look, I didn't know she'd go for you like that. I mean –' Peggy paused. She didn't know what she meant, truth be told, but through the confusion and guilt she was feeling about her part in the proceedings, she murmured, 'I didn't mean it, about your family, that's what I'm trying to say.'

Gina wasn't in a position to know that this was the first olive branch Peggy had proffered to anyone in her whole life, but nevertheless, she nodded. 'It's all right.'

'I shall have to tell the others what Mother said about not speaking to you, but I'll say we're only going to do it when she's around.' They were mounting the stairs to the first floor now, and as they reached their dormitory, Peggy said, 'Just keep your head down for the next little while and don't upset her. She can be horrible when she's got it in for someone.'

'I thought you liked her?'

Peggy shrugged. 'She's the mother,' she said, as though that answered the question.

'She's not my mam and I'm not going to call her that.'

'You'll have to or else she'll go mad. Anyway, your mam can still be your mam, can't she, and mother isn't the same as mam.'

The two girls looked at each other and in that moment their unlikely friendship was born.

The next weeks were hard and painful for Gina as she was forced to adapt to the alien world in which she found herself. Rules, both written and unwritten, governed every aspect of her new life. The site was a massive complex and run as strictly as any military camp, and the children were expected to do what was required of them with no argument or opinions of their own.

Very quickly Gina learned that the boys' cottages were given the names of trees – Ash, Oak, Beech and so on – and the girls' cottages those of flowers. Mrs Bainsby was the mother of Lilac House, and it was unfortunate that she was one of the harshest disciplinarians among the staff with little patience or understanding of a child's needs. All the cottage home children were expected to work for their keep, and work hard. Beds had to be made in a certain way and their dormitories kept spotless along with the rest of the cottage. Washing, scrubbing, polishing and dusting were part of every day. Everything was kept immaculately clean and the long wooden tables where they ate their food were scrubbed and polished four times a day after each meal. The rotas pinned to the living-room wall allotted each child their tasks for the week, including cleaning the toilets and bathrooms and bringing in wood and coal for the fires.

Before bedtime at eight o'clock each night, everyone had to clean their shoes or boots ready for morning, have a good wash, and then present themselves to their house mother to show how clean they were before they were given permission to retire. They were woken at six o'clock in the morning and had to carry out any chores before breakfast at seven-thirty prompt. If any work didn't meet the satisfaction of Mrs Bainsby, there was no breakfast.

At eight o'clock the younger children were escorted out of the site in long crocodiles to the Benfieldside council schools, and the older boys and girls would make their way to the various workshops and training buildings in the grounds where they learned a trade of some kind. The boys were taught shoemaking, tailoring, gardening, painting and woodwork, and the girls made frocks and petticoats and nightdresses, did knitting, cooking and ironing, and were versed in the various aspects of house-keeping. At the age of fifteen each youngster who was mentally able would be found a job in the outside world, the girls often ending up in service.

Within a couple of days after the incident when Gina had fallen foul of Mrs Bainsby, the master and mistress of the cottage homes made their weekly visit of inspection.

They had a master key to all the cottages and every building on site, and always started the inspection by examining the cottage bedrooms before going downstairs. Any criticisms or complaints by the master and mistress were noted in the foster mother's book and expected to be rectified immediately, and likewise it was the chance of each mother to voice any concerns or grievances.

When Gina had got back from school that evening, Mrs Bainsby was waiting for her. 'Don't take off your hat and coat, the master wants to see you.'

Without further ado she had been whipped out of the cottage and marched briskly through the site of light, honey-coloured stone buildings, their green-slated roofs black in the thick November twilight. The master had been at his desk in the administrative house when they had arrived, and when they had been shown into his office he had looked up unsmiling.

'Please be seated, Mrs Bainsby.' He gestured towards a hard-backed chair to one side of his desk and then fixed his gaze on Gina, who had been left standing in front of him. 'This is the disruptive influence you spoke of today, Mrs Bainsby?'

'It is, sir.'

The master's eyes narrowed. On the wall behind the desk was a selection of thin wooden canes. He leaned back in his big leather chair, turning to glance at them as he said coldly, 'The punishment for insolence and disobedience is without favour here. Do you understand?'

Peggy had already warned her about the master. A

harsh, grim man, he saw the docility and obedience of the children as a direct reflection on his authority. Every child had heard the tale of a boy the master had whipped so severely he had later died in the hospital. Whether it was true or not didn't matter; it had had the effect of terrifying the children under his charge. Normally each house mother dealt with any problems and it was considered the worst possible fate to be sent to the master.

Remembering all Peggy had told her, especially what to say and do if she came before this dreaded individual, Gina said tremblingly, 'Yes, sir.'

'You are a fortunate girl to have been brought here where you are clothed and fed and will be educated. Ingratitude is one of the worst sins, along with insubordination.'

Gina wasn't sure what this last word meant but she said, 'Yes, sir,' anyway.

Julian Preston continued to stare at the girl Mrs Bainsby had complained about so strongly. He hadn't expected her to be such a tiny little thing but he had read the copy of her school report and knew she was above average intelligence. He didn't like intelligent children; they were always the ones who caused trouble.

'Due to the fact that you have only been at the homes for just over a week, Mrs Bainsby showed you great kindness and forbearance in the severity of your punishment, especially in the face of your rudeness to her, but such behaviour will not be tolerated in the future.' He turned again and glanced at the canes for a moment. 'If I see you here again, you will bitterly regret it, believe me. While you are under our care here, you will work hard, do as you are told without question and respect those in authority.'

Gina's bruised back was still preventing her sleeping at night and making it difficult to walk or bend over, and she didn't see how this could be considered 'great kindness', but, nevertheless, she said, 'Yes, sir.'

'You may now return to the cottage with Mother and I suggest, when you say your prayers at night, that you thank the Almighty for such a good and worthy woman to look after you.'

For the life of her Gina couldn't force a 'Yes, sir' in answer to this, but Mrs Bainsby had already risen to her feet, saying, 'Thank you, Master,' in a simpering sort of way, and so the moment passed.

That night in her bed Gina had cried herself into a kind of stupor, but the interview with the master had shown her one thing. She had to manage here until her mam came and took her home, because if she did anything out of turn and the master killed her like he'd killed the boy Peggy had told her about, she would never see her mam again. And once she was home she'd be a good girl, she'd never be naughty and upset her da again. She nodded to herself in the darkness, the narrow iron bed hard and uncomfortable compared to the one at home and the draught from the window making her shiver. Her mam would come, she knew she would come, perhaps even tomorrow.

Chapter Eight

It was the afternoon of Christmas Eve. After breakfast, the children in Lilac House had been absorbed in making coloured paper chains for the living and dining room, and these now hung in gay splendour criss-crossed over the ceiling, adding a touch of festive colour to the normally clinically clean and austere surroundings.

An air of subdued excitement hung in the air. On Christmas morning, once the children got back from church, the guardians would make their customary visit to the cottage homes bringing stockings for the children, each containing an orange, an apple, a silver thruppenny bit, a candy cane and a few sweets. Once they had taken their leave, it would be time for Christmas dinner followed by charades in the afternoon.

It was the best day ever, Peggy had told Gina earlier in the week. Even Mrs Bainsby had been known to crack a smile or two. And at night, before they went to bed, there were hot teacakes and warm milk, rather than the usual bread and jam for supper.

Gina had listened and made the appropriate noises but she had known she wouldn't be there on Christmas morning. Her mam wouldn't let her spend Christmas at the cottage homes; she would come for her before then. Anything else was unthinkable. And so while the other girls had made their paper chains and then gone out to build a snowman in the snow that had fallen the previous night, she had sat at the window of the dormitory watching and waiting for a figure to appear on the path outside. When Mrs Bainsby had asked her what was wrong and why she wasn't downstairs with the others she'd replied she had the stomach ache, because she knew she mustn't mention her mam after what Dr Taylor had told her about it being a secret.

'In that case you won't want any lunch,' Mrs Bainsby said with her usual asperity, and when this received nothing but a 'No thank you, Mother,' Mrs Bainsby felt her forehead. 'You haven't got a temperature so there's no point in getting the doctor to look at you. Sit here then if you must, but if you haven't been sick I shall expect you downstairs later.'

At four o'clock Peggy was sent with a message to say that Mother said Gina must come down for tea right now. She went, but due to the feeling of dread that was choking her was unable to eat more than a bite or two. She and Peggy and Vera were on the rota to clear away the dishes and do the washing- and drying-up, and once in the tiny scullery attached to the kitchen, Peggy said grumpily, 'Me an' Vera had to do the lunch things by ourselves 'cause you weren't here. It took ages.'

'Sorry,' said Gina woodenly.

'You still feeling bad then?'

Gina nodded. She couldn't share her secret with anyone, not now, because in the last hour or so when it had got dark, hope was dying that her mam would come. And if she didn't, if her mam wouldn't come to collect her at Christmas which was so special, then . . . She couldn't follow this thought through to its natural conclusion, not with Peggy and Vera staring at her, and so she forced herself to say, 'It's just the tummy ache, like Martha had the other day.'

Peggy clucked her tongue. She had limited patience with the twins, who were always ailing. 'Trust her to pass something on for Christmas,' she said uncharitably. 'Look, let's get the dishes done and then we can play a game till bedtime. Hangman or noughts and crosses or something.'

Gina concurred, but once in the living room with the others she lost every game, one ear cocked for the knock on the door that would announce her mam's arrival. At supper she managed one teacake, mainly due to Mrs Bainsby's eagle eyes being fixed on her along with the command of, 'You *will* eat something, girl,' and then, shoes cleaned and toilet completed to Mrs Bainsby's satisfaction, she followed Peggy upstairs to the dormitory. Everyone was giggling and whispering about the following day and the stockings they'd receive, but she quietly slid into bed and lay in silent misery. Her mam hadn't come. She was never going to come. Her mam didn't love her or want her and that was why she had been put in this place. Her da had spoken the truth about her not being their real child, but what had she done to make her mam suddenly decide her da could take her away? She lay racking her brains as one by one the others settled down for sleep and only heavy breathing and little snores filled the room.

It was some time later when she finally worked out the reason for her banishment. Her mam had the new baby, a little girl, to take her place and she didn't want her any more. And her da had never wanted her. Because he wasn't her da and her mam wasn't her mam and James and the others weren't her real brothers.

Tears trickling down her face she lay in utter desolation, all hope gone. She would have to stay here until she was old, as old as Sally McHaffie who had left the cottage homes the week before to take up her place in service at a big house somewhere. Never again would she sleep in her own bed in the little room that had become infinitely precious over the last weeks, or hear her mam humming to herself as she went about her baking, or walk in the cornfields in the summer where the poppies raised their scarlet heads and waved in the breeze. She wouldn't hear the owl, her owl, as he hunted at twilight, or climb trees with James, or paddle in the brook or— She gave a great gulp, her heart breaking. She couldn't even run away from here and try and find her way back home because if she did find her mam she would just be returned to the cottage homes.

The bitter pain of rejection, a pain she was too young

to even begin to process, engulfed her. The certainty that her mam would come for her was gone, never to return, and with its going something died in her.

She lay awake all of the long winter's night, and when morning came and she knew the baby Jesus had been born and was lying in His crib with the animals around Him, she felt none of the rapturous wonder this normally inspired.

Peggy and the others woke early, whispering and quietly giggling to each other because it was forbidden to talk until Mrs Bainsby rang the bell for them to get up in the morning. Gina pretended to be asleep, her head buried under the covers and her body curled into a tight ball. She knew Mrs Bainsby wouldn't let her stay in the dormitory two days running, especially with the visit of the guardians later. Peggy had told her there was a great deal of pomp and ceremony involved in this. First the girls, one cottage at a time, would be marched over by the mothers to the master and mistress's house where the guardians would be, and once there would be lined up in the hall ready for when the eminent visitors came out of the master's sitting room. They had to curtsy and say thank you, sir or madam, when they were given the stockings, Peggy had emphasized, and once the last girl had received her present they all curtsied together before leaving the hall. Once all the girls had finished, it was the boys' turn. Then, unless it was raining hard or something, all the children from the cottages formed a big semicircle on the grass outside the master's house and sang the carol everyone had been practising for weeks to the guardians.

Peggy had been beside herself with excitement when she had related all this, and Gina hadn't liked to say that she couldn't share her friend's anticipation. She wasn't quite sure why she felt as she did, but it went hand in hand with the way the workhouse children were kept apart from the other boys and girls at school wherever possible. They had to use a different playground to the local children and even the worst dressed and poorest of these looked down their noses at her and the others. Words like 'workhouse scum' and 'dirty mongrels' had been bandied about by some of the local children when they were sure the teacher, Miss Middleton, wasn't in earshot, and more than once since she had been at the cottage homes Gladys and Martha had walked home in tears. Knowing she wouldn't be at the cottage homes for long because her mam was going to come for her, Gina had been able to shrug any comments off and whisper back as good as she got like 'dirty pig face' or something equally insulting, but now it was different.

Mrs Bainsby's arrival in the dormitory cut short further introspection and Gina was forced to come out of her burrow and face the world. The snow of the last days was not thick, not by northern standards, just an inch or two, but as the children formed crocodiles outside their respective cottages after breakfast it was beginning to snow in the wind again. They were marched off to the Christmas Day service at the parish church in the town of Consett four miles away, it being larger and better able to accommodate the cottage homes children en masse than the smaller one in Medomsley, and many little legs were tired by the time they reached the stone building. Inside the church was barely warmer than the freezing conditions outside, but with their arrival the building was full to bursting and huddled together like sardines in a can on the pews, the children began to thaw out.

Gina sat between Peggy and Ethel, and when they excitedly pointed out the manger to one side of the altar containing the baby Jesus with Mary and Joseph standing looking down at their new son, their carved hands clasped in prayer, she nodded but couldn't speak for the lump in her throat. Last year Edwin and Larry had proudly come home with a little crib they had made at school, and she and her brothers had filled it with straw and her da had fashioned a baby Jesus from a lump of wood. Her mam had drawn a little face on the figure which had instantly brought it to life.

Once the service was over the mothers marshalled the boys and girls out of the church and they began the long trek back through lanes turned into a winter wonderland. The frozen landscape intensified the slightest trace of colour, highlighting the few brightly toned leaves still clinging to the occasional beech tree or the gleam of bright scarlet berries in the seemingly barren hedgerows.

For once, Gina's eyes were blind to the cold beauty of nature as she trudged along at Peggy's side, Ethel and Vera chattering nineteen to the dozen behind them and

Gladys and Martha making up the rear. It was Christmas Day, and somewhere her mam and da and the lads would be having a lovely time without her.

It was Peggy, who'd glanced at Gina a few times, who broke the wretched misery of her thoughts when she suddenly said, 'What's the matter? It's not your tummy, is it. What's wrong?'

Gina looked up into the thin face and found she was too desolate to try and lie or put on a brave front. 'I thought my mam would come for me but she hasn't – she's never going to.'

'You don't know that.'

'Yes, I do, because she's not my real mam and she's got the new baby now, a girl. She doesn't want me any more.' She hadn't talked about her family before other than to say that her da had brought her to the workhouse but she didn't know why, but now as they walked it all came pouring out in a dull whisper. 'My da, well, he's not my da, said my real mam died and that's why they took me in. He said I was an orphan.'

Peggy didn't know why she liked Gina so much but she did, and it moderated her usual acerbity when she whispered back, 'So am I. My mam had me in the workhouse and died a little while later. Mother told me. So we're the same, you and I. We'll have to look after each other, all right? I'm older than you so I can be your big sister.'

In spite of her grief, a spark of the old Gina raised its head. 'That doesn't mean you can boss me about,' she said warily.

Peggy grinned. 'Only sometimes,' she compromised, 'like when Mother tells me what you've all got to do. I *am* head of the dormitory, remember.'

She could hardly forget. Peggy mentioned this fact to one or another of the girls every day.

'We can be our own family, you an' me, and Ethel and Vera an' all,' Peggy said conspiratorially. 'We'll stick together no matter what.'

'And Martha and Gladys.'

Peggy glanced back down the crocodile at the twins who as usual were struggling to keep up with everyone else. 'Aye, them an' all,' she said grudgingly.

At this point Mrs Bainsby at the head of the procession turned to call, 'No more talking for now, girls. Keep your breath for the walk home, we don't want to be late for the master, do we.'

Gina didn't care a fig about being late for the master, but as everyone fell silent, well aware that Mother was quite capable of giving someone a whack round the head for disobedience, Christmas Day or no, she followed suit. But now as she walked, she didn't feel quite so desolate as she had a few moments ago. Her mam and da and the lads might not want her but Peggy and the others did. She wasn't completely alone.

The visit to the master and mistress was every bit as bad as Gina had feared it would be. After they had filed into the hall of the house, which smelled pleasantly of beeswax and lavender, and had a fine rug on the polished floorboards, the guardians were escorted out of the sitting room. The men were wearing frock coats and top hats, and their wives elegant dresses, but it was the two children one of the married couples had brought with them who took all of Gina's attention. The two young boys couldn't have been older than seven or eight and were dressed beautifully, but it was the expression on their faces that kept her gaze. They held their heads high, staring down their superior little noses for all the world as though they were surveying animals in a zoo, and somewhat smelly, undesirable animals at that.

Someone had thought it a good idea for these children to present the Christmas stockings to the needy, and as they did so each girl was expected to curtsy her thanks. Gina didn't know if it was the way the two boys held the stockings with the tips of their gloved fingers as though the contact was repellent, or the highfalutin voices saying flatly, 'Merry Christmas,' as they stood swathed in matching fur coats and caps, but when it was her turn to move forward, she kept her head up and stared the boy who held her stocking straight in the face without smiling.

'Thank you,' she said coolly, unconsciously mimicking the refined tones of her teacher at the Benfieldside school, Miss Chapman, before turning on her heel and walking back to her place in the line.

She thought she heard a little gasp of surprise from the boy's mother, and she saw the mistress quickly move to her side and murmur something in the woman's ear which caused her to nod. Gina kept her eyes straight ahead but even though she didn't look at Mrs Bainsby she could feel her wrath.

Once they had trooped out of the house and begun to walk to where the other classes who had collected their stockings were gathering, Gina suddenly found herself caught by the scruff of her neck and shaken like a rat by a furious Mrs Bainsby.

'How dare you behave with such a lack of modesty and respect towards your betters? How dare you?' she hissed, spraying spittle as she spoke. 'You knew exactly what was expected of you, m'girl. I've never been so mortified in my life.'

Propelled along at such a speed that her feet hardly touched the ground, she was deposited at the back of the assembled throng and shaken once again for good measure before Mrs Bainsby let go of her. 'You stay here and don't move an inch. Do you hear me? Not an inch,' Mrs Bainsby ground out before flinging her aside and returning to the rest of the group who had filed into place at the front of the assembly.

Parked where she was behind everyone Gina couldn't see a thing, not that that bothered her. She rubbed her neck and took a swallow, feeling as though she had been strangled. A girl in front of her turned round to say, 'What have you been up to then? Old Ma Bumblebee looked as though she had smoke coming out of her backside.'

'I didn't curtsy when I got my stocking.'

'Oh, my word, you've broken one of the ten commandments.' The girl was much older than Gina but her voice was kindly. 'Why didn't you curtsy then? Did you forget?'

Gina shook her head. 'I didn't want to, not to those boys.'

'Well, whatever you do, don't say that to Ma Bumblebee. Say you forgot and you're sorry and you might just get away with it, it being Christmas Day an' all.'

The girl didn't sound very hopeful though and Gina wasn't either, but she nodded. She was already regretting what she had done although she knew if she was placed in the same situation again, she wouldn't do any different. The way those two boys had stared at everyone, as though they were less than muck under their highly polished boots, had been horrible. Why should she curtsy to them? They weren't any better than her even if they did have a rich mam and da.

The boys were entering the house now, a cottage at a time, and then coming out to form two wings either side of the girls where they would all sing to the master and mistress and the guardians. It was bitterly cold with a cutting north-east wind, and most of the children were shaking and shivering long before the dignitaries made their appearance. Hidden as she was at the very back of the crowd Gina made no effort to join in the carol they'd been practising for weeks; it was the only Christmas song she had never liked. 'Good King Wenceslas' always seemed such a bleak song to her, all about walking through a winter storm and being cold and miserable, not like 'O

Little Town of Bethlehem' or 'O Come, All Ye Faithful', they were lovely. She'd had a slap round the head from Mrs Bainsby for asking if they could sing something more cheerful and had been sent to bed with no supper that night.

Wrapping her arms round her waist and hugging herself in an effort to keep warm, she listened to the others bellowing out the carol with more enthusiasm than tunefulness. Everyone knew that once it was over they could get back to the cottages and Christmas dinner, but first the master would give a little talk thanking the guardians for their kind gifts and saying that their presence would have been gift enough for the children. Apparently he said the same every year, Peggy had told her, and they all had to smile and nod and then cheer the guardians off to their grand carriages and motor cars.

Her mam and da and brothers would probably be sitting down for *their* Christmas dinner about now, and everyone would be happy and jolly. Would they think about her at all? The answer came hard and fast, like a punch in the solar plexus, and in reply to it she muttered, 'I don't care, I don't,' even as tears pricked at the backs of her eyes and drained away the last of her bravado.

As the cheers rang out for the guardians she surreptitiously wiped her eyes with the back of her hand, the stocking that had caused her present fall from grace hanging limply in one hand. It had a drawstring at the top of the sacking and each child had been warned that they were not to open the stocking until they were back in their respective cottage. She doubted Mrs Bainsby would let her keep it now, but she didn't care one way or the other. The stocking didn't matter, nothing did. She wanted her mam. She didn't mind if her mam couldn't love her any more now she had the new baby; she wanted her anyway, and she would do anything, *anything*, to go home. Please God, she prayed fervently, closing her eyes, please let her come this very minute, let her appear in front of me now and I'll never be naughty again in the rest of my life, I promise. Please, *please*.

When her name was called in the next moment and she opened her eyes it was to see a ferocious Mrs Bainsby bearing down on her, the other children parting before the furious woman like the waves of the Red Sea. But Mrs Bainsby was no Moses and neither did she have a trace of the festive spirit about her. Once again Gina found herself gripped tightly and borne along at a rate of knots that had the other girls running to keep up. No one said a word although everyone was thinking the same thing; they wouldn't want to be in Gina's place for all the stockings in the world.

She was going to have to get used to the way things were and get through each day the best she could. Elsie glanced round the table where Kenneth and the lads were tucking into their Christmas dinner with every appearance of enjoyment. Even James, who'd cried on and off for Gina constantly the last few weeks, seemed to be calming down. And she supposed that was a good thing – it hadn't helped the atmosphere in the farmhouse to have James moping and bursting into tears at the slightest thing and Ken telling the child to pull himself together. When she had objected to this, saying it was natural James would be upset, Ken had maintained it was her he was concerned for and he didn't want James's behaviour putting more strain on her. But she didn't believe it was her feelings he was worried about. Ken just wanted everything to get back on an even keel. He had gone through the motions of looking for her bairn and appearing to be concerned, but he wasn't grieving like her and the lads were. And Betty, well, she was the apple of his eye. You'd have thought she'd had no hand in their daughter's conception or birth, it was all Betty this and Betty that. Was that why she couldn't take to the bairn?

Immediately, with the thought came the surge of guilt which caused her to protest silently. It wasn't that she hadn't taken to the baby, it was just that Gina was all she could think about, she told herself. In the dead of night when the rest of the household was asleep and there was nothing to distract her, she tortured herself with one grim scenario after another. It was all very well for Ken to insist he felt it in his bones that Gina was alive and well, but he didn't *know* that, did he, and she felt he would say anything to have her back to normal. But that would never, *could* never happen unless they found Gina. He'd never understood the bond between the bairn and herself, he'd merely resented it, feeling it took something away from himself and his lads. And maybe it had at that, she didn't know any more, but one thing she did know was that her life would for ever be split into two distinct parts; the time before Gina had gone and the aftermath.

She became aware Ken was looking at her as her eyes refocused from her thoughts. He held her gaze for a moment or two but didn't smile and neither did she. When his eyes fell away and he began to eat again, she forced herself to pick up her knife and fork and begin her own meal for which she had no appetite whatsoever. Her precious bairn was lost, and most days she felt she was hanging on to her sanity by a thread. Left to herself she would roam the countryside, shouting and screaming for her bairn like a demented soul, she knew that, but as Ken reminded her every day, her family needed her. And so the urge to run, to fly hither and thither searching every hamlet, every village, every farm, every barn and outhouse, had to be curtailed. But, and help me God, she prayed, because I know it's a sin, she bitterly resented it. Her home had become a prison and her family's needs felt like a millstone round her neck. The future stretched ahead of her without the faintest glimmer of light to make it bearable.

PART THREE

Where There's a Will . . .

1937

Chapter Nine

'So, the day has arrived' – the words 'at last' were implied but not voiced – 'when you will be leaving us. I trust you are aware that you will carry the unblemished reputation of the master and the cottage homes with you into your place of employment, and conduct yourself with decorum and modesty at all times?'

Gina stared into the hard, tight face of Mrs Bainsby, making no effort to conceal her loathing of the woman who had gone out of her way to make her life a misery over the last endless years. 'Of course,' she said coolly, waiting just a fraction of a second before she added, 'Mother,' knowing how much this would infuriate her.

'Are you being insolent, girl?'

'No, I am agreeing with you.'

Mrs Bainsby gritted her teeth, her hand itching to slap Gina across the face. She had meted out punishment after punishment on this vile girl in the past but nothing had quenched her spirit. 'You'll come to a bad end, m'girl.

I've seen others like you who thought too much of themselves, and they all ended up the same.'

Gina's chin rose a notch and her blue eyes darkened to violet. 'That will be up to me now, won't it, and I can assure you I shall make a success of my life. My years under your care have taught me the value of resilience and determination, and I shall put that to good use in the outside world. I suppose I ought to thank you for that.'

They eyed each other a moment more, the strikingly lovely young girl and the bitter older woman, and their mutual hate vibrated the air. Mrs Bainsby's hands were clenched into fists to stop herself striking the girl who was viewing her coldly and with such open disdain, a girl who had the whole of the rest of her life stretching out in front of her. If her wish could have been granted Gina would have dropped down dead on the spot.

As it was, she contented herself with growling, 'Get out of my sight, you ungrateful chit. At least I'll never have to look at you again.'

'Certainly – Mother.'

As Gina closed the door behind her, something crashed against it on the inside of the room, making her jump before she grinned to herself. Hateful old crone.

Her smile faded, however, as she walked back to the dormitory to collect her meagre belongings. She could hardly believe the long-awaited day had finally arrived and she was leaving this place for good. If it hadn't been for Peggy and her other friends and their constant support, she wouldn't have got through the beatings and stints in the little windowless cell called the punishment room. And the fact that she could escape the cottage homes and Mrs Bainsby for school most days had been a lifesaver.

She had enjoyed her time with Miss Middleton in the infants and Mrs Appleby in the juniors, but it wasn't until she had moved into the seniors and Miss Shawe had become her teacher that the passion for learning had really blossomed to the full. Miss Shawe was young, well educated and dedicated, and she had told Gina she had an intelligence and aptitude far beyond that of her peers. Miss Shawe had believed in her. Gina nodded at the thought. And liked her, really liked her. Not only that, Miss Shawe had seemed to understand that if she informed the master or Mrs Bainsby about this, it would be looked on with extreme disfavour. A workhouse pauper needs to know his or her place in the world, that was the master's motto. And so Miss Shawe had quietly given up her lunch breaks to introduce her to history and geography and poetry, and even the background of the emancipation of women. These extra lessons had had to be surreptitious, of course, because Miss Shawe was employed to teach English and arithmetic and other subjects up to a certain level and Gina knew her private lessons went far beyond this. They had been wonderful. She had learned so much. And on her last day at school before Christmas when she had told Miss Shawe the master was finding a job for her, the teacher had taken her aside and told her that she had to continue her education by going to night school and training to become a teacher.

'You have the ability to do it easily, Gina,' Miss Shawe

had said warmly, her owlish eyes in their thick glasses blinking at her earnestly. 'You can't waste your life in service or something similar, you know that, don't you? You must have a vocation.'

She had thanked the teacher and told her she had no intention of remaining for long in whatever job the master arranged, but because of Miss Shawe's kindness she hadn't voiced that she had no wish to become a teacher either. The thought of being ensconced in a classroom and doing the same thing over and over again for years on end had no appeal whatsoever. The trouble was, though, she had no clear idea of what she *did* want to do. But whatever it was, she wanted to travel and see all the marvellous places Miss Shawe had introduced her to in the geography lessons. But that would have to wait. She knew that.

The dormitory was empty when she walked in. Peggy had left the cottage homes some time before and was in service in a big house in Newcastle, and Ethel and Vera had recently been placed in respective positions elsewhere. Gladys and Martha were a year younger and still at school, and it being the beginning of January they and the other girls were presently at their lessons at Benfieldside. The twins had shed a few tears when they'd said goodbye that morning after breakfast and she'd had a lump in her throat, but the knowledge that this was her last morning at Lilac House had buoyed her up.

Gina sat down on her bed with a little plump. The master had arranged for her to begin work as a live-in kitchen maid at a large hotel in Newcastle, and the porter of the cottage homes was taking her there in his little van that was used for collections and deliveries and workhouse business. She had wanted to get there under her own devices but Mrs Bainsby wouldn't hear of it, suspecting, no doubt, that Gina might abscond if she got half a chance. She just might have done so too, Gina thought, getting up and peering out of the window above her bed for the last time. She wanted nothing more than to throw off the taint of the workhouse and begin a new life – it was all she had dreamed of for years – but at the same time she knew it was sensible to establish herself somewhere first and get a little money behind her. At the moment she was a girl of fifteen with nothing to commend her, no power to forge her own path, no prestige, but it wouldn't always be that way. She would rise above her beginnings, like Coco Chanel had done.

The thought prompted her to reach under her mattress and draw out the dog-eared copy of a travel magazine that Miss Shawe had given her when she was teaching her about France. The spread about the country, its ways and customs, had been interesting and informative, but it had been the article about the woman who had built up the celebrated Paris fashion house of Chanel that had gripped Gina. She knew the words off by heart – she'd read them so many times – but she read them again anyway, needing the boost they always provided. The writer of the piece gushed:

Coco Chanel is known as the woman who dominates the world's fashion circles and has made Paris the fashion centre of the world, and after conquering that world she then added several subtle and exotic perfumes to the mix which have been just as well received by her adoring admirers. The incomparable Chanel No. 5, which, Coco maintains, consists of natural essences found in the South of France, is marketed as a perfume for the slim and beautiful women of Paris and has been adopted as the world's most exclusive perfume. Her encouragement to women to wear trousers and bob their hair goes hand in hand with her assertion that independence is the greatest achievement a woman can aspire to, and in her own words, 'We must cast off the chains of husbands and babies.' This self-made millionairess has been friends with many famous men, including the painter Pablo Picasso, the Russian composer Igor Stravinsky, the eccentric French novelist/playwright Jean Cocteau, and Cecil Beaton, the English fashion photographer, as well as the English aristocrat the Duke of Westminster. But what is known of the real Coco Chanel, or Gabrielle Chanel as she was christened?

Gina sat forward on the bed, pausing for a moment to relish the next part of the article, which was what had fascinated and bewitched her from the moment she had read it.

Gabrielle was born in the year 1883 and her father was disappointed she was a girl. He refused to call her by her real name but always called her 'Coco' after the circus clown. It was not said in an endearing way and their relationship was not a happy one, and when the young Gabrielle was six years old her mother died of TB and her father deserted her. She was put in an orphanage and then later a convent where she hated the discipline and harsh rules.

'Like me,' Gina breathed as she did every time she got to this part of the story. She had been the same age when she had been abandoned by her father at the workhouse gates, and she had hated her life ever since. Coco had had nothing and no one of her own when she was a child and a young girl.

Coco ran away from the convent and earned her living as best she could, and by her early twenties she had saved enough capital to open a millinery shop in the town of Compiègne. When that was well established, her next move was to open a salon in Paris and from then on it was success all the way.

Gina sat back with a little sigh of satisfaction. She had no interest in entering the world of fashion or anything like that, but if Coco could start off with nothing and rise to fulfil her dreams, so could she. She read on:

Now in her fifties, Coco is the symbol of the new Parisienne woman, beautiful and elegant but always in control. Some say her use of her father's old nickname 'Coco' is a mark of her contempt and defiance against the man who deserted her so cruelly, and certainly she is known for advising her three thousand female employees to save their salaries to ensure their independence from men. In spite of many proposals from rich and influential men Coco has never married, valuing her autonomy and freedom as a 'pearl of great price'. One thing is for sure, the abandoned child who grew to be the queen of a business empire has no one to thank for her rise to fame but herself and that will perhaps be her greatest legacy of all. All hail the queen.

Gina sat for a moment more and then began to pack the few clothes and personal items she owned into the cloth bag Mrs Bainsby had dropped on her bed that morning, putting the magazine at the very top before she zipped it shut. It was clear Coco trusted no one but herself and neither did she. Just as Coco's father had deserted her, so had her own family washed their hands of her and that was all right. She didn't need them, not any of them, including her mam. Friends were nice to have but even they could let you down. Peggy had promised to write every week when she left the cottage homes but she rarely received a letter from her, especially now her friend was apparently courting a stable hand at the big house where she worked. For years she had cried herself to sleep, longing to see her mam just one more time and wondering if there was something in her, some fault, that had made the family she'd thought of as hers abandon her – but even if that were so she didn't care any more.

A pang in her chest challenged the thought and now out loud she said defiantly, 'I don't care, I don't.' Walking to the door of the dormitory, she turned and looked at the clinical room with its two rows of single iron beds. She had been desperately unhappy here but there had been some good times too with Peggy and the others, she had to remember that. It was natural Peggy was making her own life now and the bond they'd had was gone; she would be the same once she left here. In fact, she'd already made up her mind that when she could she would create a new past for herself if anyone asked, along with a different persona. She didn't want to be poor little Gina from the workhouse, it was up to her after all.

Once downstairs she left Lilac House quietly and walked to the porter's lodge. The January day was bright and cold and there had been a heavy frost the night before that still remained in places where the sun hadn't penetrated. She knocked on the front door of the lodge and the porter's wife answered after a moment or two. Eyeing Gina up and down she said shortly, 'He'll be a few minutes,' and shut the door again. This didn't surprise Gina. Mr Irvin, the porter, was nice enough but all the girls knew his wife was a shrew and he was hen-pecked.

She put the cloth bag on the step and stood gazing up into the high blue sky above her that was devoid of even the merest wisp of a cloud. It was a beautiful day, she thought with a sudden surge of excitement. It was silly, and she had only just realized it, but right up to this moment she had feared something would happen to prevent her leaving the cottage homes. But it was happening, she was going. A feeling similar to the ones she had experienced as a little girl before she had come to the workhouse assailed her, a kind of bubbling joy that transported her right up into the blue sky with the flock of birds that were whirling about high in the thermals. She closed her eyes for a moment, letting the cold January sun wash over her face as she breathed in the crisp frosty air.

This was the beginning of her life, she told herself, and what had gone before was just shadows now. She would make something of herself and live as she wanted to, like Coco Chanel, not being tied to society's view of what a woman should be as a wife and mother. That was fine for girls who wanted it but not for her. What had Miss Shawe said to her as they had said goodbye before the Christmas holidays? Oh, yes: 'The world is your oyster, Gina, and you can do anything you want, become anything you want if you just set your heart and will to it.' Miss Shawe had been speaking about her becoming a teacher, she knew that, but the principle was the same.

The door opening brought her out of her reverie, and as she turned a bright face to Mr Irvin he said kindly, 'Well, you look chirpy if you don't mind me saying, lass. Glad to be off, I dare bet?'

'Oh, *yes*, Mr Irvin.'

He grinned at her. 'Best we're on our way then, don't you think?'

And the answer came even more fervently. '*Yes, please.*'

Chapter Ten

Gina stood looking about her. The small room had a distinctly musty odour with an undertone of smelly feet. Three narrow iron beds were squeezed into the limited space and they looked as uncomfortable as the ones at Lilac House. The room held no other furniture whatsoever but on the wall above each bed a few hooks provided somewhere to hang clothes, and she could see bags and bits and pieces under two of the beds where presumably the girls she was sharing with stored personal possessions. The walls were distempered a sickly green and the floorboards were bare. One high rectangular window positioned just below ceiling height let in a shaft of natural light, but this was merely a pane of glass with no handle to open it. Altogether, this room made the utilitarian dormitory at the cottage homes seem positively luxurious.

'Awful, isn't it,' the girl who had shown her up to the attic room at the back of the hotel said cheerily. 'We all hate being up here – it's too cold in winter and we fry in the summer. I'm Milly, by the way. I'm in the room next to this with the other two housemaids, Tessa and Becky. You share with Hilda – she's the other kitchen maid – and Ada. She's the scullery maid and not quite right in the head. She's all right,' Milly added hastily at Gina's look of alarm. 'She's friendly and all that but a bit simple, poor lass.'

She gestured to one of the beds. 'That's yours. Chef has his own room downstairs off the kitchen and so does the under-chef. Mr Skelton, the manager, doesn't sleep in, he's got his own house in town and it's very nice by all accounts. The waiters and the bell boy live over what was the stables in time gone by – they're separate from us in case of any shenanigans.' Milly giggled. 'Mind, if anyone was going to try it on it'd be Mr Skelton, although to be fair he's bin all right since Tessa took up with him. Hands like an octopus he used to have. Always trying to cop a feel, you know? According to Tessa he's never married, fancied himself as a ladies' man, I think, but he's a bit long in the tooth now if you ask me. Tessa plays him like a violin though, but then she's no better than she should be if you know what I mean. She'll come to grief one day and end up with a bellyful, that's what I tell her, but she just laughs and says she's too careful to catch her toe. There's always a first time though, isn't there.'

Gina felt a little dazed. Milly talked so fast the words tumbled out in a never-ending stream.

'Mind, the old goat let her have a whole week off at Christmas so she's canny with it, I'll say that for her. The thought of him doing *that* to me revolts me though. I said that to her and she said she just lies back and thinks of England.' Milly giggled again. 'She's one on her own, Tessa is.' She glanced at the little watch pinned to the front of her pretty frilly apron. 'Oh, flip, I'd better go. I talk too much – in case you haven't noticed. Your uniform's there –' she pointed to a grey dress, thick linen apron and little cap lying on the bed – 'and Chef will want you downstairs as soon as you've changed. He's been in a right fit since the last kitchen maid left with no notice. You just go back down the stairs and along the corridor and the kitchens are in front of you, all right? Whatever you do, don't turn right and go through the green baize door into the hotel proper or else you'll be in hot water. Kitchen maids aren't allowed out front.'

Gina nodded. She was overwhelmed. 'Thanks,' she said feebly.

'I know it's a lot to take in straight away but you'll be just fine,' Milly said kindly. 'Just do exactly what Chef tells you and don't worry if he shouts and goes on a bit – he yells at everyone except Mr Skelton. He's foreign,' she added, as though that explained everything. 'Ada drives him round the bend but then she'd try the patience of a saint.' She pulled a face. 'See you later.'

Left alone, Gina sat down on the edge of the bed that was hers and then jumped up again as she realized she'd creased the carefully folded clothes. Shaking them out, she stared at the dress and apron. It was a horrible uniform. The dress was a dirty muddy grey colour and the bleached calico apron looked enormous. Realizing time was ticking by, she quickly divested herself of her frock and cardigan and once standing in her petticoat pulled on the grey dress. It hung on her like a sack and the apron was no better. Tucking her long wavy brown hair into the stiff cap that tied at the back of her head, she wondered what she looked like. A fright. The answer came immediately and her mouth turned down ruefully. Milly's uniform had been quite pretty, a black dress with a lacy apron over it and the little cap perched on the back of her head had been lacy too, but then Milly was a housemaid and apparently that was a big step up from a lowly kitchen maid.

If anyone had told her that she would have fond feelings for Lilac House she would have laughed at them, but for a split second she found herself longing for the dormitory and the companionship of Gladys and Martha and the other girls with all her heart. From the moment Mr Irvin had escorted her into the grand lobby of the Star Hotel in Fernwood Road in the centre of Newcastle, she had felt terribly out of her depth. The hotel was set in its own gardens and Mr Irvin had told her it had once been a private house before being used for its present purpose. Sweeping steps had led up to the wide wooden doors of the hotel, and Mr Irvin had taken her arm and led her past the doorman dressed in black and red and over to a very pretty receptionist sitting behind a huge low desk. They'd been treated to a sweet attentive smile before Mr Irvin had stated their business, but then the smile had cooled to freezing and the girl had eyed them up and down as she'd informed them that they should have used the back door to the hotel situated in the yard by the dustbins. The staff entrance. The main entrance was reserved for guests only.

The girl had brought her hand down on a bell at the side of her and after it had pinged, a young lad dressed in the same coloured uniform as the doorman had appeared. 'Could you take Miss—?'

Cold green eyes had stared at Gina.

'Redfern,' Gina supplied falteringly, crimson with hot embarrassment.

'Miss Redfern through to the kitchens, please, Terence, and tell Chef his new kitchen maid has arrived.'

Mr Irvin had just had time to hand over her bag and wish her well before Terence whisked her away. Once in the back of the hotel they had met Milly before they'd reached the kitchens. It seemed a housemaid was more important than a bell boy in the hierarchy of the hotel because once Milly had enquired who she was, she had told Terence she would take Gina straight up to her room to change into her uniform.

'Chef's tearing his hair out in there,' Milly had said to the bell boy, 'and he wants her working as soon as possible. Go and tell him she's arrived and is changing into her uniform and will be down shortly.'

And now she had to go 'down'. Gina smoothed the voluminous apron over her practically non-existent hips. Although she had suddenly shot up in height over the last year her figure had yet to develop into womanhood. She thought for a moment of the receptionist's styled blonde bob, full figure and immaculate clothes, but then her chin came up as it always did when her fighting spirit was aroused. That girl might think she was the cat's whiskers and could talk to folk as though they were muck under her shoes, but she'd show her, she told herself grimly. Quite what she would show the other girl she didn't know, but she would do it anyway.

Taking a long deep breath, she prepared to leave the room, but as she did so she noticed a pair of horribly ugly black-laced shoes sitting under her bed which clearly were meant to be part of her uniform. Drawing them out, she stared at them in dismay. They had obviously been the property of the kitchen maid she was replacing and were the size of boats. She had small feet and when she tried the shoes on found them to be several sizes too big, besides which they stank to high heaven. She pulled on her own boots again. She wasn't going to break her neck trying to walk in those things and if anything was said she would say exactly that. Her own boots weren't exactly fashionable or attractive, but at least they fitted and didn't smell like mouldy meat.

Feeling as though she was going to war, her stomach turning over, she left the musty little room and stepped out on to the equally musty landing. This wasn't going to be for ever, she comforted herself as she walked down the perilously steep narrow stairs and made her way to the kitchens. Whatever it was like, she could stick being here for twelve months or so until she had managed to save a little money and could look for somewhere else. And at least she was in the centre of Newcastle and not stuck out in the middle of nowhere like Peggy in service in a big country house. She would have hated that. No, this was going to be far better.

Gina found she had to remind herself of those words frequently in the next few weeks, and she often wondered if Peggy could possibly be working as hard as she was at the hotel. It apparently had twenty bedrooms, three of which were superior suites, although as a lowly kitchen maid she never got to see further than the kitchens.

The hotel employed a staff of fifteen consisting of Mr Skelton, the chef and under-chef, Miss Wynford the receptionist, two young waiters and an elderly doorman, a bell boy, three housemaids, two kitchen maids and the scullery maid, Ada, plus an old gnarled gardener called George. Like Mr Skelton, the receptionist, doorman and George didn't live on the premises. Gina suspected this was as much because the rest of the staff were squeezed in the rooms at the back of the hotel and over the stable like sardines in a can as anything else. There simply wasn't room for more people. According to Tessa, who cleaned the staff rooms, the chef and under-chef's accommodation was basic to say the least, and the long room over the stables was barely fit for human habitation. The rooms of the hotel guests were apparently in stark contrast, being carpeted throughout and furnished to the highest standard.

'They don't have chamber pots under their beds and a privy in the yard by the dustbins,' Hilda, the other kitchen maid, grumbled to Gina in her first few days at the hotel. 'There's a lovely bathroom on each floor and Milly says the suites each have their own. Here's us expected to make do with washing in the wash house in the yard and all having to share a privy. I wouldn't mind so much if the lads had a separate one to us – they're dirty beggars at the best of times. Still, my mam says it's typical to treat the workers like scum.'

Gina nodded. She didn't like using the privy in the yard, especially if one of the menfolk had just been in.

'Mr Skelton's told Tessa that the owner, Mr Jefferson, has umpteen hotels here an' there so he must be rolling in it, him an' his lady wife. They live in one of them great big country estates with an army of servants inside and out, and them just a family of four. Me da says it's criminal how the gentry live. Aye, it's one law for them and one for us, lass. For two pins I'd tell Mr Skelton where to stick his job.'

Gina was to learn in the days ahead that this was a daily saying of Hilda's, but apparently the required two pins never materialized. Mind, Gina often told herself, Hilda did have a point. They were expected to be up with the lark and then would be rushed off their feet until bedtime with an endless list of tasks for which they never received a word of thanks. Chopping vegetables, herbs and meat; boiling and roasting potatoes and other vegetables; preparing trays of coffee and easy items like toast and sandwiches for the housemaids to take through to the dining room or the guests' rooms; preparing soups for the evening meals, and snacks for elevenses in the morning and mid-afternoon or a late supper at night, and this as well as seeing to the staff meals wherever possible and being at the beck and call of the chef and under-chef on all occasions. Ada, the scullery maid, was charged with keeping the kitchen clean and doing all the washing and drying-up in her grim little room off the kitchen and numerous other menial tasks, but as she was as slow as a snail and liable to burst into tears and fling her apron over her head if she couldn't cope, Gina and Hilda did half her work as well as their own.

Lawrence, the under-chef, was a young man of twenty-five who did most of the routine cooking and who apparently was in training under the chef, Monsieur Fontaine, who was an expert at creating the fine dining experience in the evenings most of the guests demanded. Gina found out very soon that the chef was the absolute ruler in his territory and as tyrannical as any monarch. His rages would cause poor Ada to run and hide in the privy in the yard and even Lawrence had been known to turn as white as a sheet and have trembling lips. Hilda was frankly terrified of him, and when the housemaids and waiters came into the kitchen they tiptoed about as though treading on eggshells.

It was on her first full day in the kitchen – the afternoon and evening before had been too rushed for the chef to do anything but bark orders at everyone – that

Monsieur Fontaine noticed her footwear. She had already learned from Hilda that the previous kitchen maid had disappeared without giving notice thereby causing the chef to become apoplectic, a mood in which he had remained ever since, so when his black gimlet eyes fastened on her and he snarled, 'These things on your feet, what are they?' she smiled sweetly and said, 'They are boots, Chef.' She had been warned to address him in this way and never by his name, something she thought very strange.

He had drawn himself up to his full height, which at five foot wasn't exactly towering although his temper often made it appear so, and the rest of the kitchen had suddenly become hushed. 'I know this. I am not, as you say, the imbecile,' he bit out in his heavy accent. 'Why are not the shoes on your feet?'

'You mean the ones the girl before me used?' she said calmly, although now she was under the full force of his rage she felt a trembling inside. 'They are far too big, Chef. They won't stay on my feet and I didn't want to trip and spill something.'

Poor Ada regularly dropped and spilled most of the stuff she handled to the accompaniment of his screams of anger.

He glared at her. 'Fetch them.'

She forced herself to walk steadily out of the kitchen and once in the attic room picked up the offending shoes. She had been conscious of their smell the evening before and had contemplated leaving them on the landing every night. Once back downstairs, she entered the kitchen with her head held high, a pose Mrs Bainsby would have recognized if she had been present.

'Show me.' Everyone appeared frozen in a tableau and as though noticing this for the first time, the chef growled ominously, 'Have I told you to stop the busy-busy?' and like the release of a paused film everyone sprang into action again.

Hating the fact that she had to put the wretched things on her feet again, Gina slipped off her boots and pulled the shoes on. A blind man could have seen they swamped her small feet. Quickly removing them, she said, 'I can't walk in them.'

'I see this.' He considered her for a moment. 'You have the small hands and feet, like the aristocracy I think, yes?'

She didn't know what to say to this and so she said nothing.

'Lawrence, dispose of these.' He gestured at the shoes. 'And until we get the shoes that fit the feet you may wear your own in my kitchen.' This was said in a manner that made it clear it was a great concession. To her 'Thank you, Chef,' he gave an imperious nod, and then as Ada dropped a massive bag of Brussels sprouts sending them rolling like marbles into the four corners of the kitchen, his roar announced that normal service had been resumed.

It was a small incident, and Monsieur Fontaine continued to bark at her like he did everyone else, but in a strange way Gina found the episode made life at the hotel bearable. New shoes were obtained in her size, and when she put them on she found them comfortable if ugly. She quickly realized that the chef was a perfectionist who suffered fools badly. He didn't miss a thing in his kitchen and on the occasions when she anticipated a job that needed doing and got on with it without being told, his sharp eyes would assess her silently. He never gave praise to anyone but as time went on it was noticeable that she got the more intricate jobs like icing the little cakes and fancies for afternoon tea or preparing dainty sandwiches when Lawrence was tied up with something else. She apologized to Hilda about this – the other girl had been working at the hotel far longer than her after all – but Hilda was quite philosophical about the situation.

'I don't mind, lass,' she said good-naturedly. 'I hate doing them fiddly things, I'm all fingers and thumbs and he always picks fault. You do 'em far better than I ever could an' twice as quick an' all.'

She liked Hilda and Ada, and the three housemaids were easy to get on with too, but she couldn't understand Tessa's association with the manager for the life of her. Tessa was plump and pretty with curly blonde hair and big blue eyes. Gina would have thought she could have any lad she wanted, and yet she let Mr Skelton – as Milly put it – paw her about. Mr Skelton, of all people, Gina thought for the umpteenth time one day when she watched the manager whispering something in Tessa's ear that made her giggle. He wasn't exactly an unpleasant man, quite affable on the whole and in his youth had clearly been good-looking, but at well over fifty he was balding with a distended stomach and bad breath.

The girls had every other Monday afternoon off in a staggered rota which meant there was always at least one housemaid and one kitchen maid working, and at the end of February, when Gina had been at the hotel nearly two months, it happened that she and Tessa were free together. Becky was off too but as she had a streaming cold she announced that she was going to stay in bed for the afternoon, whereupon Tessa suggested she and Gina go for a walk.

Before now on her free afternoons, Gina had explored the surrounding area when the weather permitted, but the last couple of times winter storms had prevented her leaving the hotel and so she had sat on her bed in the attic room and read the pile of magazines the other girls were always buying. Tessa in particular was fixated on the latest fashions and had even had her ears pierced in the summer as this new craze had swept the smart set in London. Normally this was unusual before middle age or later, but the season's debutantes and young married hostesses had decided it was the in thing to do and suddenly hundreds of women a week in the capital were following suit. Milly was less interested in fashion but being a romantic soul had been gripped by the love story between Edward VIII and Wallis Simpson, which had caused the King to renounce the crown in December after the cabinet and the Archbishop of Canterbury had refused to agree to him marrying the twice-divorced American woman while he was monarch. The fact that the King chose abdication as the price of freedom to wed the woman he loved had thrilled Milly, but the down-to-earth Tessa had been scathing.

'Silly beggar,' she'd said scornfully as Milly was poring over the latest magazine snippets at the beginning of February where it was reported the ex-King and Wallis Simpson were residing in France. 'All that fuss and palaver when she could have just carried on being his mistress on the quiet. They'd been at it for years apparently and all the nobs have mistresses, everyone knows that. At it like rabbits they are.'

'Not the King,' Milly had protested hotly, shocked to the core. 'He wasn't like that. He's a decent man.'

Tessa had snorted. 'Oh, take the rose-coloured glasses off, lass, for goodness' sake. He had lots of women before he met the American, you can bank on that. Young beauties offering themselves on a plate because of who he was, you can't blame him, now then. Any man would. He was knocking about with Lady Furness, according to the papers, when he met Wallis Simpson at a party Lady Furness gave, so he wasn't exactly the shy, retiring type.'

'I don't believe it.' Milly had been close to tears. 'All that's just vicious rumours. And what he said about finding it impossible to carry on as King without the help and support of the woman he loves was just beautiful.'

'Daft more like.' Tessa shook her head. 'And to give everything up for some old biddy who's been round the block a few times like her—'

'*Tessa!*' Milly couldn't have been more affronted.

'Well, she has. She's been married twice before.'

Milly didn't comment on this. As a stout Catholic it was the only thing that spoiled the romance a little but she didn't let herself dwell on it. For a King to give up his throne for love was the stuff of fairy tales in her opinion. Tossing her head, she glared at Tessa. 'He's lost his heart to her and her to him, and I think it's awful he couldn't marry her and still be king.'

'And have a twice-divorced woman from a different country with a face like a smacked backside as queen? I don't think so.'

Mortally offended, Milly had thrown down the magazine and stalked off out of the bedroom where she, Tessa and Gina had been sitting, banging the door behind her.

Tessa had grinned at Gina. 'Silly mare,' she'd said fondly.

Gina had shaken her head. 'You shouldn't tease her. You know how starry-eyed she can be.'

'Gullible, more like.' Tessa had suddenly become serious. 'And that'll get her nowhere in this world, especially with men. They want one thing and one thing only – they're all the same, and you have to play 'em at their own game, lass. I know, believe me. You can have a bit of fun but always look after number one, that's what I say. My mam married my da for love and ended up with four bairns before she was twenty. She's due with her fifteenth any day now and still goes out to work cleaning to make ends meet. An' me da lets her. If he didn't drink half his wage away afore me mam got hold of it they'd be a sight better off. She's coming up for forty, me mam, and she looks seventy if a day. I'm not going to end up like her, dropping a bairn every year and working me hands to the bone for a selfish so-an'-so who couldn't give a monkey's jig. Not on your life.'

This conversation had troubled Gina for a while, less because of what Tessa had said than the look on the other girl's face when she'd spoken about her parents. She had seemed so bitter and angry, not like her usual bubbly, funny self at all. The two of them hadn't been alone since then before today, and as they left the hotel muffled up to the eyeballs against the cutting wind, Gina said tentatively, 'I thought you normally went to see your mam on your afternoon off?'

Tessa's family lived in the grid of streets to the east of the north-eastern railway. It was only a mile or so from the hotel but it could have been in another country, so different were the dwellings to the big grand houses in the street the hotel was in.

Tessa shrugged. 'I popped in last night with me wages.' Tessa had been out with Mr Skelton the night before and hadn't returned to the hotel until the early hours. No one else would have dared to act in such a way but Tessa was Tessa and no one took much notice, especially with Mr Skelton being her beau.

Snowflakes were beginning to blow haphazardly in the wind and the sky looked heavy and low. Tessa shivered and pulled her smart hat that matched her coat further down over her forehead. Milly had told Gina the outfit was yet another gift from Mr Skelton, one of many. 'I know a little café that'll be open.' Tessa glanced at Gina. 'Fancy a cup of tea and a sticky bun?'

It was over half a mile to the café situated at the back of Ginnett's Amphitheatre, which was no distance in the summer, but with the wind picking up and the snow coming down more thickly every minute Gina was glad to enter the warm confines of the little building that smelled of toast and fried bacon. It was as clean as a new pin, and once they'd sat down at a table by the window, a middle-aged woman came bustling over.

'What can I get you?' she said, before looking more closely at Tessa and adding, 'Oh, hello, lass. I didn't recognize you straight off.'

Once they'd given their order for a cup of tea and a bacon sandwich – the tantalizing fragrance had proved irresistible – and the woman had disappeared, Tessa said softly, 'Me an' Howard come in here sometimes. She thought he was my da the first time and put her foot in it, poor thing. She felt awful, went as red as a beetroot.'

Gina didn't know what to say. Tessa was just eighteen years old and Mr Skelton could have been her granda let alone her da. He must be getting on for sixty.

As though she'd read Gina's mind, Tessa said, 'He's fifty-four by the way.'

Gina nodded. 'Oh.'

'You don't approve, do you.' It was a statement, not a question.

'Me?' Gina stared at her in surprise. 'It's not up to me to approve or otherwise, is it. You can do what you like.'

'Aye, that's what I told Milly the last time she got on her high horse. She seems to think that Howard's taking advantage of me.' Tessa rolled her eyes. 'If anyone is taking advantage, it's me, not him. I knew what I was doing when I started going out with him and he's all right, he really is. I know he's old but he's got a wicked sense of humour and he's not brash and cocky like younger lads. I like him.'

The last three words were said with an air of defiance and again Gina said, 'You're a free agent, Tessa. You can do what you like. It's no one's business but yours and Mr Skelton's.'

'He's not mean. He buys me nice things, anything I want. I only have to mention it and he's got it straight away. And his house is lovely. It's got a little garden at the back with fruit trees an' that. He's never wanted to settle down in the past – he said he wanted to live somewhere nice and buy his own place and go on holidays abroad, but he's done all that now.'

There seemed to be more to what Tessa was saying than the surface content, and this was proved when she suddenly leaned forward over the table. 'Can I tell you something? It's going to be common knowledge in the next day or two anyway. Howard's asked me to marry him an' I've said yes.' Tessa sat back in her seat, her eyes intent on Gina's face.

The defiance was still in evidence but then when Gina smiled and said with genuine warmth, 'Congratulations, Tessa,' the other girl seemed to deflate.

'You see, that's what I like about you.' Tessa's voice

was merely a whisper. 'You don't immediately jump to the conclusion the rest of them will, you're not like them. Mind you, they'll be right. I *am* expecting a bairn.'

Gina swallowed. She was completely out of her depth and it showed.

'Milly will be cock-a-hoop thinking she's been proved right and I caught my toe, but it's not like that.'

The arrival of their tea and bacon sandwiches caused Tessa to pause, but as soon as they were alone at the table again, she said, 'No, it wasn't like that. You won't repeat what I'm going to say, will you?'

Gina shook her head. 'But you don't have to tell me anything if you'd rather not.'

'No, I need to share it with someone and although we've not known each other long I trust you, lass. I wanted to get pregnant. I wanted it because I knew it'd give him the push he needed to marry me. He'd got it all his own way before then, having his cake and eating it as Milly would say. And so I—' She hesitated. 'I made sure we slipped up.'

Gina didn't have a clue what this would entail but she nodded as though she did.

'I felt bad about it at first but then when I told him I was expecting he was so pleased it made me feel all right. He said he'd reached a stage in his life where a wife and family would be nice, and if anyone's sown their wild oats, Howard has.' She smiled ruefully.

'But I thought—' Gina paused. She didn't want to offend Tessa.

'What? Tell me?'

'I thought you'd said you didn't want to be like your mam and marry someone and have bairns.'

'I don't want to be like her.' Tessa shuddered. 'That's why Howard is exactly right for me. I'll let him have this one bairn, that's only fair, but then I'll make sure I don't have no more. I'll be a good wife, look after him and the bairn and keep house and that'll be a pleasure. It's so lovely, his house, and there's the garden to sit in and it's a semi-detached in a nice tree-lined avenue. I couldn't believe it the first time he took me there.'

She sounded as though she was more in love with the house than Mr Skelton, Gina thought with disquiet.

'He wouldn't expect me to work after we're wed, not with him earning what he does and being well set up with money in the bank and the house bought and paid for and everything. And let's face it, when he goes eventually I'll still be young enough to enjoy what he leaves me. Even before that I'll be my own mistress, so to speak. And we'll go on nice holidays an' that. I've never been further than Newcastle in my life.'

Gina stared at the other girl. Tessa was young and pretty and far from being stupid – in fact she was the most intelligent of all the other girls – but as she saw it the only way she could escape ending up like her mother was to marry an older man, a much older man who was, as Tessa herself had put it, well set up. She had said she liked him. Not loved him. She'd talked about being her own mistress when in fact she would be tied to a man she didn't love in a marriage that was little more than a convenience, on her side at least. Gina rubbed her forehead.

'What?' said Tessa again, reading her body language.

'Nothing.'

'You're shocked, aren't you. That I tricked him.'

'No, it's not that.'

'What then?'

'I just wondered—' Gina didn't know how to put it. 'I just wondered, what with the way you feel about your mam, if you'd ever thought about getting a good job eventually and being independent of any man until you met the right one and fell in love.'

'I don't want to fall in love. That's a weakness. I'd never give a bloke that power over me.'

'Well, if not that, then just the job bit. Maybe going to night school or something and bettering yourself so you could buy your own home in the future, travel, do the things you want to do.'

Tessa's eyes narrowed intuitively. 'Is that what you want?' she asked softly.

Gina's gaze had been on the oilcloth on the small table. Now she raised her head and met Tessa's eyes. 'Aye, yes, it is.'

Tessa nodded. 'You could do it an' all, lass, I see that. But I'm not made like you. It's the easy way for me.'

Gina didn't think marrying an older man you didn't love with a bairn on the way *was* the easy way, but she smiled and said, 'If it's what you want then I'm happy for you, Tessa. I mean that.'

'Aye, I know you do. You're a nice lass. What my grandma, God rest her soul, would have called an old head on young shoulders. I dare say you've known it hard.' Tessa, like the other girls at the hotel, knew she had come from the cottage homes.

Gina shrugged. She didn't like to discuss her past.

'So you don't want to marry a lad and have a family like Milly and the rest of them?'

In answer to that, Gina said, 'My old teacher said the world's my oyster and I could do anything I want, become anything I want if I set my heart on it.'

'That wasn't what I asked.'

She had understood exactly what Tessa had meant when she'd said she didn't want to fall in love and give anyone power over her. She wasn't even sure if she believed in the concept of love any more. She had thought her mam and brothers loved her but they hadn't, and if your family didn't care about you why would anyone else? People weren't to be trusted. She smiled. 'No, it wasn't, and no, I don't want to marry anyone, Tessa.'

'Not ever?'

Gina shook her head. 'I'll make my own way in the world, sink or swim.'

'Oh, you'll swim, lass. Take it from me. You'll swim.'

They tucked into their bacon sandwiches then, the snow continuing to swirl outside the window and the afternoon as dark as twilight, but inside the café it was warm and cosy and Gina felt strangely contented. Talking to Tessa had reaffirmed her plans for the future and when in a few months she found herself a new job she wouldn't carry anything of the past with her. She didn't intend to remain the 'poor cottage-home lass' as she'd heard herself referred to once or twice when people hadn't realized she was listening. She would be someone else, creating her own past and a new persona. She could do it. Tessa had faith that she could, and Tessa was as tough as they come. She *would* swim.

Chapter Eleven

In the last couple of years or so since Gina had left the cottage homes several changes had taken place in her life. The most important to Gina herself was that with the onset of puberty, her figure had filled out and she had grown a few inches. She was on the willowy side, but could easily have passed as a young woman of twenty rather than her actual age. When, in the spring of 1939, she'd applied for a job as an usherette at the Olympia cinema in Northumberland Road in the centre of Newcastle and stated her age as eighteen, it hadn't been challenged.

She had been offered the position and had found herself a room in a lodging house, and within two weeks had begun to take driving lessons. It was another new start, and one where for the first time in her life she felt she was in control. It was a heady feeling.

When she had left the hotel she had let contact with the girls there drift away after a month or two. In addition to which, Peggy's letters had become few and far between and then stopped altogether, and although she had felt hurt at first she'd told herself it was all for the best. Peggy had a different life now and so did she, and this way she could enter the future with nothing of the past hanging on her coat-tails. To anyone who enquired, she said she was an only child and her parents were both dead but that was all.

Although it had been a little daunting at first, the fact that she had to rely on herself and herself only proved exhilarating. When she had saved enough money, she intended to move down south and then her new life would really begin. She had no ties in the north-east, no real relationships, and that was the way she wanted it. She was free and unencumbered. The technicalities of what the new start in the south would entail she hadn't worked out but that didn't matter. She was young and she had plenty of time to plan the finer points. Travelling would be part of it, she was sure about that, and she would definitely attend some evening classes to further her education as Miss Shawe had suggested. Not with a view to becoming a teacher, but she would like to learn a couple of languages and maybe do a course in short-hand and typing. This could only help to widen her scope for a good job.

The only thing that troubled her when she considered the months and years ahead, were the rumours of war with Germany which had gathered pace with alarming speed recently. She hadn't been aware of what was going on in the outside world when she'd lived at the cottage homes; it had been very much a little world of its own, and they hadn't been taught anything about the political situation at school. She'd only realized how ignorant she was about current affairs when she had begun work and listened to the discussions about Hitler and the Nazis during mealtimes in the kitchen of the hotel. Shortly before she had left there the Germans had marched into Czechoslovakia, and it had been then that she had fully understood the threat to peace. Since then the newspapers had been full of the Nazis' atrocities against the Jews in Germany, the death camps for those German citizens who dared to disagree with Nazi ideology, the cosying up of Mussolini and Hitler, and the plans to introduce conscription in Britain in readiness for a possible conflict.

Gina looked up from the newspaper she'd been reading while she ate her breakfast of fried kippers in the lodging house. Mrs Hogarth always cooked kippers on a Tuesday even though Gina and her other two lodgers didn't care for them. The newspaper had reported that Italy and Germany had signed a 'Pact of Steel', a military and political alliance, committing the countries to support each other in time of war with 'all military forces'.

Her stomach turned over and she couldn't continue eating. This was the most serious development yet.

Lorna, a middle-aged woman who occupied the room next to hers, nodded at her from across the table. 'Doesn't look good, does it,' she said, waving at the paper. 'Chamberlain's the one I blame for all this. Hitler's a bully and Chamberlain should have stood up to him last year in Munich. I reckon Britain was doomed from the minute Chamberlain announced he was a man of peace to the depths of his soul, and armed conflict between nations was a nightmare to him. I mean, even if you think that, you don't say it if you're the Prime Minister, do you. Weak as dishwater, that man is.'

'Oh, be fair, Lorna,' Enid, the other lodger, piped up. She was a tiny woman of indeterminable age who worked at the local laundry and had apparently lived at Mrs Hogarth's for decades. She and Lorna were great friends and spent most of their evenings sitting in the front room with Mrs Hogarth, the three of them knitting and gossiping and generally putting the world to rights. 'You can't blame Chamberlain for how Hitler is. He was always going to be the same, the man's evil in my opinion. What he's doing to them poor Jews is wicked and all the governments round the world are turning a blind eye 'cause they don't want to upset him and have him turn on them. He's banned them from being dentists, vets, pharmacists and the rest, driving, going to the theatre or the pictures or concerts, closed their businesses down and taken their money – it's terrible. And his Nazi thugs beat them up and worse. Why doesn't someone *do* something?'

'That's what I'm saying, isn't it? If Chamberlain had stood up to him over Czechoslovakia, it might have brought him up short.'

'Nothing will stop him.' Enid gave a big sigh. 'The world's in a terrible mess. There's Franco and his lot in Spain, and Mussolini in Italy – all that trouble in Palestine and the Japs killing the Chinese. Where's it all going to end? Makes me glad I never had any bairns. I wouldn't want to bring a child into this world, I tell you straight.'

Gina stood up. She agreed with everything Enid and Lorna had said but it was a depressing way to start the day, besides which she had her driving lesson in a little while. She had taken to driving like a duck to water and was due to take her test the following week, but Enid and Lorna had told her they thought she was wasting her money.

'Throwing good money after bad,' Enid had stated. 'What's the point? You're never going to own your own car, are you, not unless you catch a wealthy husband, besides which it's not quite seemly, a woman driving.'

The two of them were full of such opinions, as was Mrs Hogarth. 'Nice' girls didn't smoke or drink or wear make-up or a hundred and one other things the three women considered beyond the pale. Gina always listened politely, smiled sweetly and then did exactly what she saw fit, as in the matter of the driving lessons. Once she had moved down south and left the provincial north and followed through on her plans for evening classes, she intended to get the sort of job where renting a flat and buying her own car wouldn't be out of the question. She knew it wouldn't happen immediately – she had a goal to work towards – but it would be of no use to explain this to Mrs Hogarth and the others. They wouldn't understand. One day when Lorna had been lamenting the fact that due to the Great War and the lack of eligible men afterwards she had never married, Gina had proffered the view that independence and autonomy had their own benefits. Enid had also been present and the two women had looked at her as though she was mad.

'Another driving lesson, is it?' Enid now said with raised eyebrows, and it was with considerable effort that Gina kept her face smiling as she nodded and left the room.

Once upstairs, Gina sat down on her bed. It was a nice enough bedroom, spotlessly clean like the rest of the house, but with just one small window providing natural light and the wardrobe and chest of drawers in a deep mahogany, a colour reflected in the curtains and bedspread, it was always dark and somewhat dreary even on the brightest day. But then that seemed to be the story of lots of women's actual lives here in the north from what she could make out, those who were married in particular. With work outside the home vehemently disapproved of by all decent respectable family men once a woman was wed, a wife's lot was destined to be that of housewife and mother.

Gina's brow wrinkled. She never intended to get married anyway, but if she'd harboured such a notion that would be enough to put her off. The world was big, huge; why would anyone be content to remain within a few miles of where they were born, for goodness' sake? And even more so, why would they agree to being told what to do and what to think just because they had a gold band on the third finger of their left hand? She'd made the mistake of saying exactly that at the breakfast table one day – breakfast was the only meal she shared with Lorna and Enid, as she started work at midday at the cinema and didn't leave till well after ten at night – and the two women couldn't have been more shocked if she'd come down to breakfast stark naked. She'd realized then that it was going to be wiser to say little in the future. They were nice ladies, Mrs Hogarth too, but as different to her in the way they thought as chalk to cheese.

She stood up, opening the wardrobe and reaching for her hat and coat. It was the last few days of May but the weather had remained cold and rainy for the last two months in spite of the winter officially being over. Still, at least she had had plenty of practice in driving in all kinds of conditions, she thought ruefully, from thick snow and ice to endless pouring rain. She felt ready now to take her test and Mr Briggs, her instructor, said she had every hope of passing.

She paused before leaving the room, glancing round the dismal surroundings again. This wouldn't be for ever. She nodded at the thought. Everything she was doing now was a means to an end. The small nest egg under her mattress was steadily growing too, and she enjoyed her job at the cinema. It was a piece of cake compared to the hard grind as a kitchen maid and it paid more too, and she got to see all the films and newsreels free, which was a bonus.

The cinema had been packed for day after day in the last week or so since *Goodbye Mr. Chips* had come to town, although personally she preferred something with a bit more action, like a western. Mr McCabe, the manager, had told the staff that *Stagecoach* would be coming shortly, and she was looking forward to that. There was talk that *Gone with the Wind* would be released next year and would be a big spectacle. She'd taken the book out of the local library some time ago, and she'd admired Scarlett's strong spirit even if the ending of the story had left her somewhat torn between feeling the headstrong and heartless Scarlett had got what she deserved, and wishing she and Rhett could have lived happily ever after.

She shook her head at her thoughts and walked out of the room. Who did live happily ever after? she asked herself grimly as she went downstairs. Only the rare few. Life wasn't like that. She of all people knew that and it would be foolish to forget it.

In the next weeks, as Europe walked in the shadow of impending war, the only bright spot that occurred as far as Gina was concerned was that she passed her driving test with flying colours as Mr Briggs had predicted.

Britain's farmers were encouraged to 'dig for victory' and plough up grazing pastures in a government drive to increase the proportion of food produced at home in case of the outbreak of war; the first military conscripts were enrolled and the newspapers reported that seven hundred and fifty planes a month were under construction for the RAF; the King approved the formation of the Women's

Auxiliary Air Force, and the Registrar General announced that everyone would have a personal identity card and number in the event of hostilities. And all the time, every day it seemed to worried British citizens, Adolf Hitler flexed his muscles and did exactly as he pleased.

The newsreels at the cinema had become more popular than the films in the last months, and Gina watched them with a kind of horrified fascination. It seemed incredible to her that the small nondescript figure of Hitler with his little moustache and somewhat wizened face could inspire such fanaticism in his followers, but there was no doubt Germany's Führer was adored with a fervour that amounted to worship by millions.

July was a beautiful month as the long-awaited summer arrived at last and the weather turned hot and sunny, but like everyone she talked to Gina couldn't enjoy it with the threat of war forever in the forefront of her mind. It was alleged that the Germans were smuggling arms and military instructors into the Baltic port of Danzig, a Free City under the League of Nations mandate, and that local Nazis in the predominantly German city were acting as though it had been returned to Germany. They were treating the Poles in the city of Danzig, which sat at the mouth of the Vistula river and occupied a vital strategic position that enabled Poland to have access to the Baltic, as enemies and usurpers, a newsreel at the cinema declared one evening. Poles employed in the shipyards and docks were being arrested and deported to concentration camps in Germany, whilst other workers were being attacked and viciously beaten. '*Poland, however, has no intention of allowing Hitler to get his own way,*' a reporter on the newsreel announced to cheers from everyone in the cinema. '*Britain has promised that if Poland should feel obliged to use force to maintain the status quo in Danzig, then she'll go to her aid.*'

Gina glanced round the shadowed cinema. She was standing at the back of one aisle with the other usherette positioned on the opposite side of the auditorium. In a moment or two the lights would go up and then customers would queue for ice creams once she walked down to the front. She wondered if everyone was thinking the same as her, that Hitler would never back down over the Danzig issue or anything else, come to that. It was as plain as the nose on your face he was set on war, so would Chamberlain renege on his pledge to go to Poland's aid if Germany invaded? Chamberlain had thrown poor Czechoslovakia to the wolves, after all. All this was horrible, Gina thought as the newsreel ended, and ordinary folk were powerless to do anything about it except wait and see what transpired.

She didn't want a war – no one in their right mind would – but Hitler had to be stopped, didn't he? Gina's eyes narrowed. Or at least people had to try. The whole of Germany's Jewish community was being subjected to an unbelievable reign of terror without precedent in modern times, and everyone except Chamberlain seemed to know it. Already an unknown number of men and women and even little bairns had died. If Hitler could do that in his own country he'd do it anywhere. If war came, and it looked inevitable to her, she knew she couldn't sit at home twiddling her thumbs. The thought had been at the back of her mind for a long time, but as the newsreel went on to describe how loutish Storm Troopers had beaten a young couple senseless with lead piping while respectable-seeming middle-class Germans looked on laughing, one woman even holding up her baby to watch the sickening scene, it became a cast-iron decision. Sheer evil had been let loose in the world, and if good people did nothing and stood by hoping it wouldn't touch them, it was tantamount to condoning it. She was young and fancy free, she had no family and no one to miss her, she couldn't *not* volunteer.

The lights in the cinema flickered and then came on as the news ended, and as Gina walked down the steps to stand and turn to face her customers, she knew the course of her life had just changed yet again. Moving down south, going to night classes, getting a job that could become a career would have to wait. She was going to join the WAAF.

PART FOUR

*Corsets with Bone and
Vests Tied with Tape*

1939

Chapter Twelve

Gina sat on the train clutching her newly bought suitcase to her, her rail warrant safe in her handbag. She couldn't have explained how she felt to anyone because she didn't know herself, except that a mixture of excitement, trepidation and moments of sheer terror warred with pangs of homesickness and the feeling that she had well and truly burned her boats. Although the last wasn't quite true if she analysed it, she corrected herself. The recruiting officer had told her that as volunteers were enrolled and not enlisted they were basically civilians in uniform and free to leave and return home, for the time being at least.

Not that she would do that, she told herself firmly as the train steamed its way across country on the last leg of her journey to the training camp in Morecambe she had been assigned to. After she'd passed to join the WAAF she'd made up her mind there was no looking back. Whatever she had to put up with, it wouldn't be as bad as what the poor Polish people had suffered when the Germans invaded their country at the beginning of

September a month ago, forcing Britain and France to declare war on Hitler and his Nazis.

She had applied to join the WAAF within a few days, in spite of Mrs Hogarth and Lorna and Enid pleading with her to wait a while and reconsider. 'Work in a munitions factory or something like that if you want to do your bit,' Lorna had said. 'I'm going to do that, we could do it together. Our soldiers are always going to need weapons now, aren't they?'

She had pointed out as gently as she could that her situation and Lorna's were quite different, and that furthermore the WAAF was where she wanted to be. They had tut-tutted and fussed about the danger she was putting herself in, not from Hitler's bombs or anything of that nature but from the lecherous advances of the airmen she would come into contact with who all – according to the three older women – had one thing and one thing only on their minds, and it wasn't the war.

'You're so bonny, lass,' Enid had lamented. 'It'll be like a lamb to the slaughter in one of those camps, and you'll be mixing with all types of girls too, some of whom will be no better than they should be.'

Gina thought of Enid's words now as the train stopped at a station and a young woman in a bright red coat and hat with far too much make-up on her pretty face got into the carriage, looking straight at her as she said, 'Mind if I sit next to you, ducks?' She plonked herself down in a wave of cheap scent, placing a suitcase at her feet shod in high-heeled fashion shoes. Before Gina could reply, the girl went on, 'I'm on my way to the WAAF training camp for my sins. How about you?'

'The same.'

'Thought you might be.'

The only other occupants in the carriage were an elderly couple and a young vicar complete with dog collar, and as the girl's gaze took him in she crossed and then re-crossed her shapely legs clad in silk stockings, putting her hand over her mouth as she said in a stage whisper to Gina, 'Wonder if they know how attractive wearing that garb makes them? Sort of a challenge, know what I mean?'

As the young man blushed to the roots of his hair, Gina fought back a giggle. The girl was outrageous but there was something about her she liked, probably because she reminded her of Tessa in a way, being blonde and plump. However, Tessa had been a natural blonde whereas she rather thought this girl's colour came out of a bottle.

'I'm Kitty by the way, Kitty Routledge.' She held out a red-taloned hand, and Gina shook it as she said, 'Gina Redfern.'

'Bit of a lark this, isn't it,' Kitty said, settling back in her seat. 'Never would have guessed this time last year I'd be in the forces. What did you do, before you volunteered, I mean?'

'I was an usherette at my local cinema.'

Kitty nodded. 'My sister did that before she had her first bairn, it was how she met her husband. Bought an ice cream off her and they never looked back.' She chuckled. 'I'm a hairdresser, or was.' She fluffed her immaculate hair under the fashionable hat. 'I'd got a bit fed up with it anyway to be honest. Same old biddies coming in every week for their wash and sets. I was thinking of applying to be a dancer at a club in town.'

The young vicar cleared his throat but the elderly couple appeared fascinated.

'It was a bit near the mark, tassels here an' there, you know?'

Gina didn't but she nodded anyway.

'But one of my pals works there and she earns shed-loads, and I thought, what the heck. You only live once. But then old Hitler did his thing and I thought I'd give the WAAF a try. Can't hurt, can it?' She grinned wickedly. 'And of course, there'll be plenty of nice young pilots around with any luck.'

'Wouldn't your parents have minded? If you'd gone to work at the club, I mean?'

A hard look came over Kitty's pretty face. 'You don't know my mam an' da.' She shrugged. 'We all, my sisters and brothers and me, left home as soon as we could so I suppose that speaks for itself.' She delved into her black patent handbag and brought out a box of chocolates, opening it and offering it to Gina. 'Here, have one. I treated meself 'cause no one else was going to and who knows what the grub'll be like where we're going.' She grinned again and Gina smiled back. She had no doubt that Mrs Hogarth and Enid and Lorna would thoroughly disapprove of Miss Kitty Routledge but she liked her. There was something very disarming about such honesty.

The rest of the journey went by far quicker with Kitty chattering at the side of her. They had finished the box of chocolates by the time they reached Morecambe station where a station bus was waiting for them and the other volunteers who got off the train.

It was the beginning of October and a bitter wind gusted round the girls as they huddled together before a male warrant officer counted them on to the bus. He was gruff and impatient and clearly irritated at having to deal with a bus full of chattering, giggling women, barking at them to sit down as though he was the headmaster and they were all schoolgirls.

Kitty wrinkled her small nose as they took a seat together at the back of the bus. 'Hope all the men aren't like him else I'd have been better off at the Starlight Club,' she whispered. 'Still, this is an adventure, isn't it. I've never travelled out of Yorkshire before. I'm glad we're both northerners,' she added, slipping her arm through Gina's. 'We'll stick together, eh, lass?'

The bus was old and rickety, and as it bumped along the level of noise rose as the girls recovered from the warrant officer's less than welcoming manner. He was sitting at the front beside the driver, stiff and still, and he didn't turn round once, not even when one of the girl's suitcases slid off the rack above her head, hitting her on the shoulder before depositing its contents all over the floor.

The bus stopped at the guardroom at the entrance to the camp and the warrant officer wound down his window to talk to the service policeman at the gate.

'You got the short straw this time then?' the SP said with a sympathetic grin, nodding at the women in the bus who had all become silent as they'd approached the camp.

'McKenzie's sick,' the warrant officer said briefly.

They spoke a little more and then the bus drove through the now open gates and drew up outside a reception area, where the warrant officer bellowed at them to disembark. There was a great deal of huffing and puffing as the girls dragged their suitcases off the racks and staggered down the steps of the bus. The girl whose suitcase had fallen off the rack on the journey tripped over her own feet on the last step, causing it to fly open again dispelling clothes and undies and other items at the warrant officer's feet. Gina saw him shut his eyes for a split second and swear under his breath, but he said nothing as a couple of other girls helped the unfortunate rookie to stuff everything back inside.

Once in the building, they were told to dump their suitcases in one corner and were then taken through to another room where they had a very long lecture about rules and regulations, correct procedures and so forth from a WAAF corporal. The room was freezing cold and they all sat huddled in their hats and coats, their teeth chattering and their ears getting bombarded with so much information it was brain-numbing. Gina wondered if she was the only one who was no wiser at the end of the lecture than at the beginning. She glanced at Kitty, who was glassy-eyed, and decided she wasn't.

They were told they had their first medical inspection to look forward to the next day by the corporal as they left the lecture, with instructions to visit the washroom before they had to form a queue at the clothes store. The washroom was a shock. It was housed in a big corrugated-iron shack with a foot gap between the walls and the roof. Down one side were a number of wooden cubicles with a toilet in each and a washbasin at either end of the row, and on the opposite side of the shack was a row of baths divided only by a flimsy partition; under each bath ran a water gulley.

Gina and Kitty stared at each other. 'Flippin' heck.' Kitty shook her head. 'They don't believe in modesty here, do they. Talk about one for all and all for one. And to think I chose this rather than a nice warm club and dressing room, and the punters buying me cocktails. I must be mad.'

She didn't seem particularly upset though but Gina was dismayed at the lack of privacy. Still, it was what it was and she'd just have to get used to washing and changing in front of complete strangers; although they wouldn't remain strangers very long under these conditions, she thought wryly.

Once everyone had abluted, they filed out and made their way to the clothes store where two WAAFs who were easily in their fifties were waiting for them. 'Right, girls,' one of them said. 'I hope you all realize how lucky you are that we have some kit here? Lots of other stations haven't. This is not due to any lack of foresight on the behalf of the RAF, I might add, but rather that WAAF was not expected until a good few months after war broke out. However, those in authority changed their minds at the last moment and here we are.' She sniffed audibly, leaving no one in doubt as to what she thought about the matter. 'So be grateful for what you get, that's what I'm saying.'

'That sounds ominous,' Gina whispered in an aside to Kitty.

Within a short while she found out she had been right to be apprehensive. The collection procedure resembled a huge conveyor-belt system for one thing and took a very long time, but when the clothes came the girls stared aghast at the underwear. It appeared so ancient that their grandmothers might have worn the same. Corsets with bone and vests tied with tape, and the regulation knickers were massive things.

'Talk about passion killers,' Kitty said in disgust. 'I bet they've done it on purpose to put the men off. And look at the pyjamas – they've got to be men's, haven't they? They're awful. When I think of my frilly nighties . . .'

There were similar murmurs from other girls, and the dispensing WAAF eyed them with a steely gaze. 'Before any of you ask, yes, you *do* have to wear the underwear and no, you *cannot* wear any you've brought with you. Rules are rules and have to be obeyed.'

Other items were added to the pile including a camou-flaged ground sheet, a rain cape, shoes and what Kitty insisted were men's greatcoats. They probably were. It was clear much of the clothing had been obtained hastily and from who knew where. Lastly they were issued with what the WAAF called their 'irons' – a knife, fork and spoon – which apparently they were to take to the cook-house for each meal.

Once each girl was staggering under her pile of things, a male sergeant appeared and told them to line up outside the clothes store. 'I'm going to read your names against the number of each hut,' he said in a voice that made it clear he had better things to do. 'You will take your kit there before collecting your suitcases. You will not be expected to change into your uniforms tonight but from tomorrow morning kit must be worn at all times. You will have twenty minutes to accomplish this before forming an orderly queue outside your huts after which you will be escorted to the cookhouse for your evening meal. Anyone who is not ready will not eat. Have I made myself clear?'

A few nods and murmurs and a couple of 'Yes's answered him, and then he suddenly frightened the life out of everyone, causing a couple of girls to drop their bundles, when he shouted at the top of his voice, 'Yes, *sergeant*!'

'Flippin' heck,' Kitty whispered again. 'Old Hitler's not a patch on him.'

The huts were allocated by order of the girls' surnames in alphabetical order, so to their delight Gina and Kitty found themselves together. That brief pleasure soon faded when they were marched to a line of Nissen huts in the far distance, their corrugated-metal covering almost invisible in the blackness that had fallen while they had been in the clothes store. Two other girls had also been allocated to their hut, one of whom was the unfortunate creature who'd spilled the contents of her suitcase on the bus. It seemed to be something of a pattern with her as twice on the way to the huts they all had to stop while she picked up items she'd dropped, much to the fury of the sergeant.

Various girls filed off as their names were called outside the huts, and then it was their turn. The sergeant opened the door of the hut and stood aside for them to enter, after which he closed it behind them. The four of them stared about them. A row of beds on either side of the hut each had a small cupboard beside them and in the middle of the hut stood a black, pot-bellied, floor-fixed stove made of cast iron. It had a large pipe as flue and had probably been alight earlier in the day but now was cold and dead. The inside of the hut felt as cold as the outside air. Most of the beds had suitcases beneath them and items on the cupboards, but there were four at the far end of the hut, furthest away from the stove, that appeared to be vacant.

'Home from home.' Kitty's voice dripped sarcasm. 'Oh, well, let's dump our things and then get our suitcases. I'm starving, I don't know about anyone else?' So saying she walked down the middle aisle and dumped her things on one of the beds, gesturing for Gina to put her pile on the next bed, while the other two girls followed suit on the opposite side of the hut.

'Let's introduce ourselves,' Gina said once they were all relinquished of their burdens. 'I'm Gina and this is Kitty.'

'Stella,' said a rosy-cheeked, dark-eyed girl, and the other one who seemed so accident prone said apologetically, 'Wilhelmina. I know it's a mouthful – I don't know what Mother was thinking of – but everyone calls me Minnie.'

They had no time to say any more before Kitty hurried them out of the hut to get the suitcases, but on the way to reception and then back to the hut, Gina learned that Stella was from Durham and Minnie from the Yorkshire Dales, and for both it was their first time away from home. The girls seemed warm and friendly and down to earth, and after having deposited their suitcases under their beds, the four of them stood chatting outside their hut while they waited for their escort.

The cookhouse was packed full with WAAFs when they filed in armed with their irons. They queued up to be served by two harassed cooks and the nearer she got to them the more Gina wondered what it was that was on the menu. Something with onions for sure. Kitty was in front of her and Minnie and Stella behind, and when Kitty groaned and said, 'Liver. I *hate* liver,' Gina's heart sank. She didn't like it either. But that wasn't the worst of it. The liver had a greenish tinge and was served out of galvanized buckets along with the onions, overcooked cabbage that resembled seaweed, and greyish potatoes. On the other side of the same plate the cook dumped a heap of prunes and custard that gradually swam to meet the liver and onions.

Gina swallowed hard as she looked at her food. Hungry as she was, she didn't think she was going to be able to eat this.

The four of them had to split up to find seats as the long rectangular tables were mostly full. On Gina's table everyone was in uniform which meant she was the only newcomer, and she sat down nervously, feeling very small. She tentatively tried a spoonful of custard. It was disgusting, having already taken the flavour of the onions. As she winced, the girl next to her smiled. 'Dreadful, isn't it,' she said, pushing her empty plate to one side, clearly having devoured the lot. 'But you wait until you've been on a route march for hours and you'll be so hungry you'll want seconds.'

Gina made a face. 'Is every meal as bad as this?'

'It varies, to be fair. Breakfast isn't too bad – porridge and toast with jam or treacle – and you can fill up on that. Dinners are –' she shook her head – 'pretty foul on the whole, like today, but then everyone hates liver.' She eyed Gina's plate hopefully. 'Are you going to eat that?'

'Be my guest.'

'Thanks.'

Another WAAF was walking round pushing a trolley with two great urns on it, and as she stopped by Gina, she said, 'Tea or cocoa?'

'Er, tea, please.'

'Where's your mug?'

'What?'

'You're supposed to pick up a tin mug when you get your food. Didn't you see them stacked at the side?' the woman said irritably.

'No, sorry.' She'd been so horrified by what had been put on her plate she'd been blind and deaf to anything else.

'Here, have my mug. I've finished my tea and I don't want another one.' The girl who'd taken her plate had been wolfing down the food so fast it was nearly gone; she pushed her empty mug forward. 'And give her a break, Maud,' she added to the other WAAF. 'It's her first day, for goodness' sake.'

The said Maud glared at them both, filled the mug and flounced off. 'Don't mind her, we all hate urn duty. I'm Joyce, by the way – and you are?'

'Gina, Gina Redfern.'

'Don't worry, Gina. It gets better. In a week or so you'll know the routine and you won't be missing home so much.'

Gina smiled and took a sip of the tea, which was actually quite palatable. She supposed that was one advantage of having no family – she wouldn't be feeling as wretched as some of her companions.

'The sugar's all gone,' Joyce added apologetically. 'They put out a bowl per table and it's never enough. It pays to get here as soon as you can for each meal.'

Her new friend chattered on between mouthfuls and by the time everyone was standing up and leaving the cookhouse, Gina felt better. Joyce had introduced her to the other WAAFs in their immediate vicinity, all of whom were just as sociable. As they'd spoken, the hangar which was the cookhouse and which had appeared so huge when she had first walked in, seemed to have shrunk in size and become less overwhelming.

Kitty, Stella and Minnie were waiting for her by the door, and the four of them walked back to hut number fourteen together, all complaining about the food. 'I've been trying to lose my spare tyre for months,' Kitty said ruefully. 'I needn't have worried. A couple of weeks here and I'll be like Greta Garbo, all sunken cheeks and allure.'

'Or Merle Oberon,' Minnie put in. 'Did you see her and Laurence Olivier in *Wuthering Heights*? Her waist's so tiny I couldn't believe it.' Like Kitty, Minnie was nicely rounded. 'Trouble is, I love my nosh and Norman's no help.' She had already told them that Norman was her 'intended' although they weren't officially engaged. 'He says he likes a good handful.' She giggled and then dropped her irons in the foot-high grass they were ploughing through. After a few moments, when they'd retrieved the utensils which had seemed intent on disappearing for ever, they continued on. The huts were a good few hundred yards from the cookhouse and as they had been among the last to leave, all the other girls were already inside when they got to number fourteen – as the noise when Gina opened the door testified to.

The four of them stared around, standing awkwardly together just inside the doorway. Someone had lit the stove so the room was several degrees warmer, and on one of the beds nearest the warmth a girl was sitting, yoga fashion, on her bed in a big thick jumper and bare legs, brushing her long blonde hair that resembled a silken curtain. Several others were reading or writing, but a group in the middle of the room were swaying to the music coming from a portable wind-up gramophone. Gina recognized 'In the Mood' by Glenn Miller in the moment before one of the girls came forward saying, 'Hi there, you must be the new intake. Welcome to hut number fourteen. I'm Bridget, by the way, but everyone calls me Biddy.'

Then it was introductions all round, and while Tommy Dorsey sang about 'Cocktails for Two', Gina and the others were offered biscuits and cocoa from one of the girls which they accepted eagerly. The cocoa had come from a big flask and on her first sip Gina realized it had a kick to it. The girl grinned at her. 'What's a bedtime snack without a spot of whisky?' she said. 'You need something to warm you up in this ice box.'

'That's Vicky's excuse and she sticks to it,' another girl said good-naturedly. 'She can take on the most hardened drinker in the RAF, can't you, Vicky.'

Vicky laughed. 'According to my mother she used to put whisky in our bottles when we were babies to make us sleep, so I blame her. I acquired the taste early.'

Gina didn't care what was in the cocoa – she was famished, and biscuits had never tasted so good. The four of them ate the whole packet between them, encouraged by Vicky, who looked on sympathetically. 'I know the food's a shock on your first day,' she said commiseratively, 'but I promise you by the end of a week you won't care what you're eating you'll be so hungry.'

'And half the time you won't be able to guess what it is anyway,' put in Biddy, laughing.

A couple of hours later, when lights-out sent the hut into darkness and all the girls were snuggled under their scratchy blankets in bed, Gina lay awake contemplating the events of what had been the most exhausting day of her life. From across the hut she could hear muffled sobs from either Minnie or Stella. She suspected it was Minnie, who had already confessed to homesickness. From other beds came snoring and heavy breathing interlaced with grunts and the odd girl talking in her sleep. It was clear the girls who had been in the training camp for a day or two had no problem in falling asleep as soon as their heads touched the pillow. They had seemed like a nice bunch on the whole and the spirit of camaraderie was strong in spite of the girls coming from all kinds of different backgrounds.

She had paid a visit to the wash house just before lights-out – a miserable walk there and back in the freezing cold with the wind blowing – and Biddy had accompanied her and filled her in on some of the girls in the hut as they'd chatted. Apparently two of them – one of whom was the girl with the sheet of blonde hair – were from the aristocracy with a pedigree as long as your arm. At the other end of the scale there was Nancy, a former prostitute who'd made no secret of her past and was 'a card', as Biddy described her, and Primrose, a girl from the slums of Manchester who'd been lousy with lice and fleas when she'd arrived. At least three of her new house-mates, one being Primrose, were underage; the youngest in the hut, a tough Welsh lass only being fifteen years old. Of course, they'd all declared they were eighteen to the recruitment officer and as birth certificates weren't required, they hadn't been challenged.

Gina turned over in bed, bringing her knees up to her chest as she curled into a little ball, trying to get warm. In spite of the stove it was absolutely freezing cold and it was only October, she thought. She'd noticed quite a few of the girls had gone to bed wearing a full set of clothes under their regulation pyjamas and she decided she'd do the same tomorrow. There were eight beds on each side of the hut and only the ones close to the stove would feel any benefit from it.

But she didn't regret joining up, she told herself firmly, and however many rules and regulations there were in the WAAF it had got the same in the outside world in the last month or so since war had been declared. Decrees, exhortations and petty officialdom had been bombarding everyone. Britain's citizens had been told to carry luggage labels stating their name and address; the blacked-out streets rang to the cries of the air-raid wardens telling folk to 'Put that light out', and giant posters had appeared, urging the populace to save, dig, work, buy war bonds, not to travel, not to waste or to spread rumours – all for victory. The government leaflets that had showered Britain covered everything from ordering householders to obtain a hand-operated stirrup pump and long-handled shovel to deal with incendiary bombs, to painting the edges of their windows black so that not even the slightest chink of light could be seen at the side of their blackout curtains. Heavy fines were given out seemingly at the drop of an air-raid warden's tin hat, and unlit buses and trams caused chaos to drivers and passengers alike.

But at least the country was pulling together, Gina thought as sleep began to overtake her at long last. And everyone had been excited when it was announced that 'Winnie was back' and Winston Churchill was First Lord of the Admiralty again, the post he'd held twenty-five years ago at the outbreak of the last war. She hadn't known anything much about him but the newspapers and newsreels had declared in no uncertain terms that such a man was needed to fight the strategies and wiles of their enemy. All she'd heard of him before the outbreak of war was that he was no friend of the working class, but perhaps he didn't need to be to help win the war against the Germans?

It was all somewhat confusing, and as her tired brain finally gave up the fight and she sank into sleep, her last thought was that she was glad to be where she was, in spite of the food, the accommodation and not least the RAF corporals and sergeants.

Chapter Thirteen

The next day Gina woke to the groans and moans of a hut full of girls who didn't want to leave their beds for another day of basic training. The service clothing felt strange and alien as she got dressed, but once in the uniform she began to feel that she really was in the WAAF at last. Kitty lamented her high-heeled fashion shoes as she tied the laces of the ugly black ones that were part of the kit, but once they were both ready she grinned at Gina. 'Look out, RAF, here we come,' she giggled, fluffing out her hair and winking.

Gina smiled back. It felt like they were firm friends already and it was heartening. They had to wait a few minutes before leaving the hut as Minnie had managed to lose her tie, eventually finding it as she pushed her feet into the 'black boats' as Kitty had christened the uniform shoes.

'Oh, yes, I remember,' Minnie said happily as she fastened it round her neck. 'I rolled it up in there for safekeeping before we left the clothes store.'

Kitty shook her head as she redid the tie which Minnie had managed to make into the most enormous knot. 'You're not safe to be let out on your own,' she said with a grin to soften the words. 'I can't believe you're nineteen years old, Minnie.'

Minnie wrinkled her nose. 'I know, that's what Norman says. I only volunteered once he was in France 'cause he wouldn't have liked me joining the WAAF. He worries.' Norman was part of the British Expeditionary Force that had been taken across the Channel to bolster the French defence.

'I can't understand why,' Kitty said wryly.

They had to run to the cookhouse through the sleet that was falling, arriving flustered and breathless. The meal was fractionally better than dinner the day before, although the porridge that was unceremoniously dumped onto each tin plate by one of the cooks was lumpy and made with water rather than milk. Gina ate it. She was too hungry this morning to turn up her nose at anything on offer.

The soup bowls in the middle of the table that had held jam and treacle for the toast were empty by the time they sat down with their porridge. 'Clearly it's a case of the early bird catches the jam,' Kitty said in a loud voice to no one in particular. Nevertheless, the four of them were able to gulp down several slices of toast washed down with two mugs of tea before they had to leave the cook-house for their first medical inspection, called the FFI or Free From Infection test. Biddy had told them the WAAFs had christened it the 'scabies, babies and rabies' test because it was to check on such conditions as pregnancies, head lice, fleas and venereal diseases. Kitty had taken this information in her stride but Gina, Minnie and Stella had been shocked to their core.

Now, as they entered the medical centre, Gina found herself wishing she hadn't eaten the porridge and toast as her stomach began to do cartwheels at what was in store. It was every bit as bad as she had feared. They were on parade for jabs and chest X-rays and a whole host of other procedures, and the whole morning was spent in various stages of undress waiting for doctors and nursing orderlies to do the necessary. No attempt to preserve the WAAFs' modesty was made, and at one point, as the four of them sat huddled on a hard wooden form with their better halves bare and Minnie looking close to tears, Kitty broke the tense embarrassment as she began to softly sing Fred Astaire's hit song 'Cheek to Cheek'. Their giggles verged on hysteria but after that everyone felt better. As Kitty said, they were all the same at heart even if they came in different shapes and sizes.

Gina couldn't help thinking of how Mrs Hogarth and Lorna and Edith would have viewed the FFI and the state of undress of all the girls. If anything would have been sure to confirm their suspicions that she'd entered a den of iniquity, this would, she told herself as a particularly large girl wobbled past them with not so much as a fig leaf to cover herself.

Once the ordeal was over and they'd escaped to the

cookhouse for lunch they were ordered to attend a parade in a large hangar for instruction on saluting and drill. Their flight sergeant was a big man with a steely glint in his eyes and a foghorn of a voice that sent Minnie into a dither straight away. The march round the hangar was a disaster, and the more the flight sergeant roared instructions, the more some of the girls went to pieces.

'What's the matter with you?' he bellowed at the top of his very powerful voice. 'You think you're going to play a part in this war and you can't even march properly? A three-year-old child could do this better than you lot! Now for the umpteenth time, just step off with your left foot and swing your right arm forward. No, your left foot, you morons.'

As the drill continued, the flight sergeant's language got more colourful and by the end of it the girls' vocabulary had increased enormously. There were several like Minnie who didn't seem to be able to get the hang of marching at all, and when she was singled out by the sergeant and he came over to where they stood, Gina thought she was going to faint on the spot. He must have thought so too because his voice was a few decibels lower as he ground out, 'I'm a patient man but you are trying me sorely. What don't you understand about left and right, for crying out loud?'

Minnie tried to speak and failed, but eventually she whispered, 'I'm left-handed.'

'I don't care if you're left-footed, left-handed or just plain stupid, you'll damn well march before this drill is over.'

By the time they left the hangar Minnie was shaking and everyone was exhausted. Biddy had told them that the WAAFs called the drills 'square bashing' but Gina thought 'ear bashing' would have been more appropriate. The sergeant had been impatient and sarcastic and at times just plain nasty, and already some of the newcomers from other huts were talking about going home. Surprisingly, Minnie, in spite of how she had been picked on by the flight sergeant, was determined to stay.

'Good for you,' Gina told her when Minnie voiced her resolve over dinner. 'Your Norman would be proud of you.'

Minnie beamed. 'I'll get the hang of marching if it kills me.'

'"Left, right, left, right and swing those blinking arms,"' Kitty said, in a perfect imitation of the sergeant's broad Scottish accent. '"Dig in them damn heels and move them damn arms, they won't drop off." Wish he'd drop off, over a high cliff preferably.'

They all burst out laughing. 'What *did* we look like,' Stella spluttered. 'All sailing off in different directions and falling over our feet. I wanted to laugh but I didn't dare.'

Vicky was sitting near them and now she leaned across and said, 'It's early morning PT for you tomorrow with the rest of us now your medical's over. And I warn you, whatever the weather we're marched off to the promenade in our shirts and knickers. All the old codgers from miles around come and sit on the benches to watch us do our exercises – all that bending and stretching, they just love it, randy old blighters.'

'Well, if they can get a thrill at the sight of us in our passion killers I'd say good on 'em,' said Kitty.

The others nodded. They were supposed to wear the regulation knickers every day but no one did – they were just so awful – and even the many inspections the WAAFs were subjected to didn't go so far as to ask the girls to lift their skirts and display their underwear.

'Hey, that bunch of airmen on the table near the door haven't taken their eyes off us since we came in,' Kitty said, after another minute or two of them eating what was supposed to be beef stew although it was almost entirely devoid of meat. They had been told during the lecture on their first day that there were two thousand airmen at the camp, but that on no occasion were they allowed to 'fraternize' with the trainee WAAFs. She fluttered her eyelashes in the men's direction and received some nods and grins in return.

'Oh, they're randier than the old codgers on the seafront,' said Vicky. She leaned even closer and whispered, 'See that one on the far left, the one with black curly hair? That's Perce. I met him last night at the back of the huts.'

'You *didn't*!' The four of them gazed at her in awe. Not even Kitty would dare to flout such specific orders.

Vicky smiled and nodded. 'He's a sweetie. It was his first time and he was like a dog with two tails after.'

Trying not to look shocked, Gina said, 'But what if you got caught by one of the corporals or sergeants?'

Vicky shrugged. 'Perce said it goes on all the time and they know it but don't bother unduly. We'll only be here for a little while to do our training and then we'll be shipped off to the real RAF camps anyway. Perce gave me a couple of bottles of whisky, by the way, so our cocoa will be all right for the next week or two. Oh, and he said that the reason our flight sergeant is such a so-and-so is because he shouldn't really be the one training us. The proper one broke both his legs in a motorbike accident the week before they started taking the WAAFs here, and so Ebenezer was ordered to do it. He's furious and says the other chap broke his legs on purpose.'

It was dispiriting to think the RAF sergeants considered training them such a terrible job that someone could be accused of breaking their legs on purpose to get out of it, but Gina and the others were more taken with their flight sergeant's name than anything else.

'That's never his name, Ebenezer?' said Gina as the others collapsed in laughter. It seemed ridiculously unsuitable for the big brute of a man.

'Cross my heart, hope to die.' Vicky was laughing too. 'It's like something out of Charles Dickens, isn't it.'

Kitty was still looking across the tables to the airmen. The WAAFs had to sit on the right side of the cookhouse and the airmen on the left so never the twain could meet. 'They all look gorgeous,' she said wistfully.

Later that night, after lights-out, Gina was aware of whispering and hushed giggles at the side of her and she sat up in bed. 'What's going on?'

'Shush.' Kitty bent over her with one finger to her lips. 'I'm just going to meet a couple of the airmen with Vicky and Nancy, that's all. Go back to sleep.'

'Or come with us if you like,' said Vicky's voice in the darkness.

'No, thanks.' Gina lay down again.

'Aw, come on, Gina,' said Kitty. 'It'd be fun.'

'I don't want that sort of fun and I need my sleep, thanks all the same.'

The other three left and once it was quiet again Gina lay trying to get to sleep but she couldn't drift off. The incident had bothered her, not because she minded what the others were doing – it was their business after all – but because it had brought to the fore the knowledge that she wasn't like them, she wasn't like any of the girls. They all seemed so young and carefree compared to her, flirting with the airmen and up for anything, eager for romance and whatever life had to offer.

She frowned to herself, trying to get comfortable on the lumpy mattress. Whereas she . . . She tried to pinpoint exactly what was bothering her. She didn't trust people in general and men in particular. She only trusted herself. Which didn't make her a properly rounded human being, she supposed.

She lay worrying about it for some time and then sighed deeply. This was ridiculous. She was what she was. She didn't want the sort of fun Kitty and the other two were having, and she didn't want to settle down with a Norman like Minnie either, but that was fair enough. It *was*. Caring for other people, whoever they were, only opened you up to be hurt and she'd had enough of that to last her a lifetime. She was happy and content with the way her life was and that was enough.

Having settled things in her mind, she turned over and was asleep within moments.

The next weeks were full of ups and downs, laughter and tears – especially Minnie's who with her two left feet and general clumsiness found many aspects of training particularly difficult – but then their training was over and examinations passed and it was the day of the passing-out parade.

The November day was freezing cold, bright and windy, and the parade took place on Morecambe Promenade, the scene of many a PT session. This time they were all fully clothed, the Air Force band was playing, and even the flight sergeant was smiling – whether because they were managing to march in good time or because he was getting rid of them at last no one was sure. The parade passed without a hitch and Minnie didn't miss a step, even when her hat blew off and sailed away in the distance much to the delight of some local children who had turned up to watch.

That night hut number fourteen had a party. Vicky's Perce had provided her with more whisky; someone else handed over a large fruit cake they'd received from home along with a box of biscuits; Amanda – the girl with the beautiful blonde hair who spoke with a plum in her mouth but who was incredibly risqué – donated a really huge box of chocolates her parents had sent her; and the airman Kitty had taken up with smuggled them in a few bottles of wine. The gramophone, which was hidden away in a big holdall under the owner's bed during the day, was brought out and they swayed and danced to Glenn Miller and Duke Ellington and some of the other big bands. Everyone drank too much and cried over Bing Crosby's 'Red Sails in the Sunset' and Billie Holiday's 'These Foolish Things', and on the way to the wash house at midnight Minnie fell over in the icy sleet that was falling and all but brained herself, forcing Gina and Kitty and Stella to carry her back to the hut, Gina and Stella taking an arm each and Kitty two legs. Having dumped Minnie – soaking wet and singing to herself despite a bump the size of an egg on her forehead – on her bed, the other three fell into their beds and within minutes the only sound was a hut full of snores.

Chapter Fourteen

It was very early in the morning and as Gina sat on her bed gazing round hut number fourteen the rest of the occupants were still fast asleep. When she had joined up she had stated to the recruitment officer that she wanted to be a driver, since she had passed her driving test and knew it was something she could do well. The woman had told her that this was always very popular and she could be disappointed and end up doing something different because the trade might be full, but when one of the training officers on camp had discussed the various occupations the girls would be doing – wireless operators, equipment assistants, radiographers, meteorologists, balloon repairers and umpteen other things – she had stuck to her guns and insisted she would be best used as a driver. At the time she had been told, sharply, that she would do what she was told to do, but the day before, this same training officer, a gruff Welshman, had informed her she had been successful in bagging a position as an MT driver. She had been thrilled but it had caused a little tension in the hut as Amanda, the blonde well-spoken beauty, had also wanted the same thing and had been turned down. She'd felt awful about it but Biddy had come alongside and whispered that the only reason Amanda had wanted the job was because she'd set her sights on driving the top brass around in a limousine!

She glanced at Kitty, who was snoring softly in the next bed. Later that morning they were all off to their first postings and for many of them it meant they were being torn from the arms of new-found friends and sent arbitrarily hither and thither, but as luck would have it she, Kitty, Minnie and Nancy were being sent to an RAF camp near Scunthorpe along with other WAAFs from neighbouring huts. It was on a need-of-supply basis, they'd been told, and presumably as Kitty and Nancy were both set for a wireless operator's course and Minnie had been designated as an equipment assistant they were the need that had to be supplied, along with herself as a driver and whatever any other girls were marked down for. They were all fully aware that the RAF wanted the WAAFs only in order to release its men for front-line duties, but Gina hadn't met anyone who minded that. They were doing their bit against the Germans and that was all that mattered in the long run. With Hitler and his Nazis determined to take over the world it was no time to be sensitive. Stella had been a bit upset that she wouldn't be with them, but had cheered up when she'd discovered that Biddy and another girl from their hut were going to her new camp. All the girls were looking on the move as an adventure, but it helped if they were being cast into the great unknown with a pal.

The Nissen hut was icy cold and even though she was fully clothed under her pyjamas with her greatcoat lying on top of the bedcovers, the chill began to seep through now she was awake. Gina lay worrying how she was going to fit all her things into the brand-new kitbag each WAAF had been given. The WAAF at the clothes store had told them to put shoes right at the bottom, followed by underclothes and then any other belongings with their RAF shirt and jacket right at the top with just their tin hat above them. Gas masks had to be carried over their shoulders at all times. Gina couldn't see why, as to date there had been no signs of Hitler and his fiends who were purportedly going to gas the whole of the country without mercy, but as she wouldn't be able to fit the mask into the kitbag anyway, the point was neither here nor there.

By the time the other girls were awake hunger pangs had taken care of the worry, and as they all trooped off to breakfast an air of excitement pervaded the atmosphere. Once back in the hut, they all got out their kitbags, tall, white, heavy tubes, and each girl laid out the mountain of stuff that somehow had to be fitted inside them on their beds. After a few minutes, despair was the prevailing emotion.

'This is ridiculous,' Gina panted. 'I can't believe they expect us to put a quart into a pint pot. This thing should be double the size.'

'It must be doable.' Kitty was looking positively wild-eyed, having emptied the kitbag twice and repacked it to no avail. 'My jacket already resembles a bit of rag it's so creased.'

Eventually all attempts to keep things neat and nicely folded went out of the window, and each girl crammed in their belongings by brute force. Once everyone was ready, the rope having been pulled to close the bag and made secure, and their gas masks slung over their left shoulders, they had a last group hug and then reached for their kitbags standing on the floor by each bed.

The WAAF at the clothes store had told them there was a knack to carrying the kitbags. 'Do as the men do,' she'd said. 'Hold the rope at the top, raise the bag and then swing it forward to land on one shoulder.'

It had sounded so easy.

Several of the girls managed to get their bag to swing forward a few inches before it thudded back on the floor, and others, like Gina and Kitty, couldn't move it at all. They looked at each other desperately, imagining what their flight sergeant would say if he came in.

'Come on,' Gina said. 'We've got to do this. That WAAF said there's a knack so let's find it.'

By now giggles had taken over, and everyone was helpless with laughter as Minnie managed to swing her bag to waist height and then lurched forward with the bag landing some distance away, where it knocked an unsuspecting Stella clean off her feet. The tin hat burst out of the top of the bag and clattered across the floor to land under Gina's bed, and as Minnie scrambled on all fours to retrieve it she managed to crack her head on the hard metal frame, whereupon she came out with a few very choice words.

'I see our flight sergeant's influence has already corrupted one poor soul,' said Kitty. 'I don't know *what* Norman's going to say.'

Once everyone managed to gain control, they gazed at each other helplessly. Only Bernice, a big strapping farm girl with arms on her like a fairground wrestler, had managed to swing the kitbag into the right position, and she'd gone as red as a beetroot with the effort.

'Right.' Gina took a deep breath. 'I'm sure we'll get used to it in time but for now the main thing is to get to the lorry before we have the flight sergeant in here breathing fire and damnation 'cause we're keeping everybody waiting. We'll have to do this together. Two of us can lift a kitbag on someone's shoulder at a time.' Everyone nodded. 'And Bernice, if you don't mind, you can lift the last one before you do your own?'

A few minutes later everyone was tilted over at an angle of forty-five degrees but at least the kitbags were in place between shoulder and neck. No one dared straighten up as they staggered out of the door, knees bent, bodies tilted and their gas masks threatening to strangle them. Their lorry was parked near the cookhouse in the distance and the walk seemed endless as they lurched along to meet the grinning RAF driver who watched their progress with obvious amusement. He threw the kitbags one by one into the lorry with practised ease, causing Kitty to mutter, 'Show-off,' and then helped each WAAF to clamber up, some more gracefully than others.

Flushed and breathless, Gina and the others sat huddled together in the back of the lorry as it trundled off with its human cargo for the train station, each one of them suddenly realizing that this was it. For good or ill, they were off to their first posting.

Hours later, when they arrived at the RAF station after a journey made more arduous by the thick snow that had begun to fall as they'd boarded the train, it was clear that the RAF were still struggling to make room for the influx of WAAFs that had descended on them. Their accommodation was yet again a row of hastily erected Nissen huts and these, along with the ablution facilities, were as spartan as at the training camp. The airwomen's accommodation, complete with its own guardroom this time, was separated from the rest of the camp and out of bounds to airmen, as a harassed RAF corporal informed them. If they went out for the evening they had to be in by 2300 hours, no exceptions.

'The airmen don't have to be in till midnight,' Kitty whispered at the side of Gina. 'Is that what we fought to get the vote for?'

Gina shrugged. It didn't bother her. She had no intention of dating or forming any liaisons, and with there being a camp cinema; a well-equipped NAAFI in a special building providing food, social and leisure facilities for the men and women on site; and among other things, a timber hut like a garden shed housing a library, she didn't think she'd be off camp much. She didn't want to touch her nest egg now nestling safely in a bank until after the war, and the fourteen shillings a week pay – a mere two-thirds of what an RAF airman received – might seem a lot considering she was housed, clothed and fed, but the girls had soon found it had to stretch a long way. By the time the WAAFs had bought their own shoe polish, button polish, soap, toothpaste, notepaper and stamps, face powder, lipstick and cream, cigarette and chocolate rations, extra collars and the occasional pair of thin lisle stockings for best, the pay was all but gone. Being young, Gina was always hungry too, and one of the girls they'd travelled up with had assured them they'd spend a lot on food from the NAAFI.

'They do nice cakes,' she'd grinned. 'Always a big plus after the camp food.' And even the camp cinema tickets were sixpence each, apparently.

'Mind you, there's no shortage of airmen willing to treat you,' the WAAF had said. 'They outnumber us four to one so you can pick and choose.'

Kitty and Nancy's eyes had lit up.

'And it's not like the training camp where relationships between airmen and airwomen are actively discouraged,' she'd gone on. 'My sister was posted here a few weeks ago and she says the NAAFI put on some right good dances, and if couples choose to leave early and make their own entertainment somewhere quiet and private, who cares. Old Hitler might be playing things slow at the moment but the word is it's going to hot up soon, so make hay while the sun shines, that's what I say.'

Kitty and Nancy nodded enthusiastically; the WAAF was preaching to the converted.

This camp was several times larger than the training camp and apart from their accommodation, the facilities were better. The fact that the four of them were kept together in their Nissen hut made it home from home immediately, though, in spite of it not only being shaped like an igloo but being as cold as one too. Yet again a black, pot-bellied stove was their only means of heat, but a big wooden coal store had been built in the middle of the Nissen huts with a good supply of coal inside for the stoves.

After the first few days Gina found the routine was not so very different to that of the training camp. The daily inspections of their hut and beds, the inevitable and exhausting route marches, the drills and exercises, parades and gas-mask practices, and a new phenomenon – once-weekly Domestic Nights.

The latter was bitterly resented by some because the airmen by virtue of their sex escaped them. The WAAFs were supposed to stay in and do 'housework' all evening, but apart from blackleading the stove, polishing the lino round their respective bed spaces, and taking articles such as sheets, towels and collars to be changed at the laundry, there was little else to do.

Secretly though, Gina found she enjoyed these evenings with the girls in her hut as they all got to know each other better. They'd have impromptu picnics sitting cross-legged on their beds and sharing whatever goodies they had to go with their toast and cocoa as they put the world to rights, telling stories, moaning about the senior NCOs and officers, and sometimes singing and dancing when the mood – aided on occasion by alcohol if someone had smuggled some in – took them.

The sight of a dozen and more WAAFs dressed only in their service bras and knickers – or 'harvest festivals' as Kitty called them, all being safely gathered in – doing the cancan would stay with Gina for ever. And she found, slowly but surely, that her fear of allowing herself to get too fond of her new comrades was fading as time went on. The sense of 'one for all and all for one' was impossible to resist, try as she might. It wore away at her resolution to remain autonomous and therefore less vulnerable, and Kitty and Minnie in particular became the sisters she had never had. She loved them and she knew they loved her.

She was finding she thoroughly enjoyed her job as an MT driver too, even if it was scary at times. To her astonishment she was expected to drive most kinds of transport, anything up to three tons, with no specific training, including the refuse lorries which were cumbersome and unwieldy and had minds of their own. The dump was some ten miles away from the camp along narrow country roads and each trip did her prayer life the world of good. Trucks, lorries, vans and staff cars, she mastered them all, and although one or two vehicles were delivered back to the camp with an extra dent or two, no one said anything. In fact, one officer told her, in a tone of great surprise, that she drove as well as any RAF driver and considerably better than some. She didn't know whether to take that as a compliment or an insult considering his air of amazement.

With Christmas approaching, Minnie and some other girls obtained seven days' leave over the holiday period, but Gina and Kitty were happy to stay on camp together. Kitty said that she had nothing to go home for as her parents wouldn't want her and she, like Gina, had given up her lodgings when she had joined up. Nevertheless, the two of them had a good time, throwing themselves into the concert that was put on for Christmas Day in which everyone did sketches, songs and quizzes, and the dance that was held on Boxing Day with food and drink provided by the commanding officer out of his own pocket. Gina had avoided getting involved with any one airman at the camp, although several had made it plain they would like to get to know her better. Kitty was already courting a rather dishy pilot officer called Rupert who had the inevitable 'friend' who, according to Kitty, was desperate to take Gina out. Gina had seen this particular airman with Rupert in the mess or NAAFI and had thought he seemed somewhat cocky and full of himself, but when she'd repeated this to Kitty, her friend had been adamant it was all show.

'Mark's all right,' Kitty said earnestly. 'He's just an ordinary working-class lad like Rupert and they have to hold their own with all the toffs from Eton and that. Just go out with him once and see how you feel. We could make up a foursome if you like, it'd be fun.'

Gina had declined and had kept on declining, but on Boxing Day she'd had a feeling what would happen. Sure enough, as soon as they set foot in the NAAFI where the dance was being held, Rupert and Mark were there in front of them, grinning like two Cheshire cats. Inwardly sighing, Gina smiled back. She didn't want to spoil Kitty's evening, besides which Mark was undoubtedly very good-looking, his black hair and deep brown eyes film-star material. It wouldn't do any harm to spend the evening with him and the other two, she told herself. It wasn't like an intimate date for two, far from it. The NAAFI was crowded and the RAF band playing on the stage were the only ones who weren't being jostled.

The men settled them at a table and then went to buy drinks, during which time several other hopefuls tried their luck. Kitty giggled. 'Look at Rupert and Mark's faces,' she murmured, glancing over at the bar. 'If looks could kill those other blokes would be six foot under. The shortage of women on camp does tend to bring out the caveman mentality in those who bag one.'

Gina smiled but with some effort. She didn't want Mark to think he had a claim on her, however tenuous.

'Relax,' Kitty whispered at the side of her. 'Just enjoy yourself for once, lass. Mark knows you don't want to get involved, for goodness' sake – you've made that plain enough over the last weeks. Personally, I think he deserves a medal for persistence. You don't exactly give off a welcoming aura for the lads, you know.'

'Good, I don't want to.'

'If you weren't so bonny you'd have frightened them all away by now.'

'That would suit me just fine.'

'You miss out on so much, Gina. There's a lovely little café in the village that Rupert takes me to and they serve a smashing tea of sausages, home-grown tomatoes, fried bread and chips and all for one and thruppence. They even have eggs sometimes. And the pub in the village is lovely an' all, really cosy. Everyone meets up there some nights and it's a real laugh.'

'You've told me this before.'

'Aye, and I shall keep on telling you until you put off your old-maid front and come out with us.'

Thankfully the men chose that moment to return with the drinks and Kitty dropped the subject, surreptitiously nudging Gina in the ribs as Mark casually rested his arm on the back of her chair in a manner that told any other alpha males to keep away.

As the evening wore on Gina had to admit to herself that she was enjoying Mark's company. He was funny and self-deprecating, which she hadn't expected, and something of a Don Juan, which she had. Even when he was flirting outrageously though, he managed to poke fun at himself and make her laugh at the same time, and he was a very good dancer. After a couple of hours the band took a break, and it was during this interval that Kitty and Rupert disappeared for a while, leaving them alone together at the table. Gina felt embarrassed. She knew exactly what Kitty and Rupert were up to – they hadn't been able to keep their hands off each other all evening – and that was fine except that it made her feel more awkward with Mark. He seemed quieter too in the others' absence and after a moment or two of uncomfortable silence, he suddenly said, 'Is it men in general, or me in particular, you don't like?'

Taken aback, she stared at him and saw for once his face was perfectly serious. 'I don't dislike you,' she said at last. 'I don't know you, do I.'

'But you didn't want to get to know me either.'

Gina shrugged. 'I don't date, that's all.'

'Why? Have you had your heart broken?' And then he added quickly, 'I'm sorry, I'm sorry, none of my business, I know.'

'No, it isn't, but if you have got the impression I'm some lovelorn female, you couldn't be further from the truth. I simply want to concentrate on doing my job, that's all. Romantic entanglements hold no attraction for me.'

'What about friendship?' He smiled slowly. 'Could we be friends at least?'

Gina shook her head, half-laughing in spite of herself. 'You don't give up, do you?'

'Never.' He settled back in his chair, his grin widening. 'So, as friends, tell me about yourself.'

She stiffened immediately. 'There's nothing to tell.'

He'd noticed her body language and it added to the consuming interest he felt in this woman. He didn't know why Gina Redfern attracted him the way she did – there were other beautiful WAAFs on the camp who were willing to give him what he wanted, after all – but she'd got under his skin somehow. He'd get nowhere by rushing things, though.

'I'll fill you in about me then, shall I?' he said with easy nonchalance. 'Just the best bits, of course.'

She smiled, knowing he was out to charm her but going along with it anyway. It was Christmas after all. 'Of course,' she said wryly.

'The name's Mark Hammond as you know already. I'm twenty-one years old and an only child adored by my mother and slightly less so by my father but only slightly, I might add.'

'Spoiled?' she put in with raised eyebrows.

'Absolutely,' he agreed. And then his expression became serious again. He leaned slightly forward in his seat. 'I know Rupert joined the Volunteer Reserve of the RAF for King and country to fight the Nazis, but actually for me it was just that I always wanted to fly, so you could say my motives are less noble. My dad's a farmer and I was always expected to follow in his footsteps but from a kid I could never imagine that happening. This war's a gift in a way.' He grimaced. 'Terrible thing to say, isn't it?'

Gina shrugged. 'Go on.' She hadn't expected him to be so honest.

'So I joined the Volunteers in January much against my dad's wishes, but it was my opportunity to fly and I knew I had to take it. We were all given the rank of sergeant and the RAF paid the fees for our flying lessons as long as we took the evening classes in navigation and signals and so on, which I loved anyway. I thought I was the bee's knees. I learned to fly at weekends in Tiger Moth biplanes and it was sheer heaven for me. I knew it was something I'd been born to do and we had such a good summer this year, didn't we, blue skies and endless days of sunshine. It was as if the weather knew what was to unfurl in September, but then I guess we all did. We knew there was going to be a war and that's why the VR were building up a supply of trained pilots, and to be honest I felt anything would be better than being stuck on the farm for the rest of my life. And then it happened.'

He looked at her. 'We'll never forget where we were when we heard Chamberlain speak, will we.'

She nodded. 'No, we never will.' She had been sitting in Mrs Hogarth's front room with the landlady and Lorna and Enid as the announcement had come through on the wireless, and even though it had been expected it had still been chilling. Outside there had been bright sunshine and birds singing, and inside the smell of Mrs Hogarth's Sunday roast in the oven – everything had been normal but so abnormal.

'I was called up to active service immediately and here I am being knocked into shape,' he said with another smile. 'But I can fly. I've flown Harts and Harvards and

Ansons, flying in formation, learning how to do rolls and loops and spins, all the stuff I'll need to know to get out of trouble. And I'm good at it. Like I said, it's something I've been born to do. In the spring we'll get to fly Hurricanes, now they are *real* planes.'

His eyes were glowing and in his enthusiasm he looked younger than his twenty-one years, boyish. It was endearing. Gina shook herself mentally, suddenly wary of the way her thoughts were going. Clearing her throat, she said, 'You're not nervous about taking on the German Air Force?'

'The Luftwaffe?' He paused for a moment. 'Not nervous, no, more . . .' He thought for a second or two. 'Impatient, I suppose. They're good, mind, no point denying it, but we're better. It's the Messerschmitts, the ME109s, we'll have to look out for, and the 110s. They have a gunner in the cockpit as well as the pilot, and the—'

He stopped suddenly, shaking his head. 'Sorry,' he said sheepishly. 'I must be boring you to death, which isn't at all the way I wanted this evening to go.'

'You're not boring me.' It was true, he wasn't.

'It's just that flying, planes, everything that goes with it makes me feel alive. I didn't do well at school and to compensate I made myself the class clown. The other kids loved me and the teachers loathed me.' He pulled a face. 'The number of times I was made to sit in a corner with the dunce's cap on my head were countless. I was told I was stupid by one master and only fit to work the land.'

I didn't tell my dad that, he'd have been up the school knocking the bloke's head off with him being a farmer. But the more you're told you're stupid and worthless the more you believe it.'

'But you're not,' she said softly, fascinated by this other side to the brash individual he presented to the world.

'No, I'm not,' he agreed just as softly. 'I realize now that the lessons at school seemed pointless and boring so I didn't try. I'm not saying that's right but it's how it was. Once I joined the VR the classes in navigation and signals and the rest of it were just the opposite and I was regularly getting one hundred per cent passes. I'd found my niche, I guess.'

She nodded. 'I've yet to find mine.'

'But it doesn't matter so much for a woman, does it. You'll get married, have babies—' He stopped abruptly, warned by her expression. 'That's if you want to,' he added hastily.

'Which I don't.'

'No?'

'No. I want to travel, see the world, and I definitely don't want to be tied to the kitchen sink.'

'Right.' He'd blundered. The gorgeous blue eyes that had been warm like cornflowers in the sun moments before were now icy. He took the bull by the horns. 'Sorry,' he said quietly. 'I like to think of myself as a modern man about town but breeding outs, I suppose, and before I joined up I'd never been further than the nearest town on market day. Of course, lots of young women today want a different life to the one their mothers and grandmothers had. I see that, I really do, and I'm all for it. This war is going to shake us all up and that's a good thing.'

As an apology it would do. She smiled at him – he looked so crestfallen.

'I suppose it works both ways,' she said. 'As a farmer's son no doubt your parents expected you to find a nice girl and settle down while you worked with your father.'

For a moment a strange look came over his face and then he nodded. 'Exactly that.' He paused. 'Gina—'

Kitty and Rupert's return interrupted what he'd been about to say, and the glow they had about them was telling. The men went off to get more drinks and Kitty immediately bent forward, murmuring, 'Well? What do you think?'

'He's all right.'

'Just all right?'

'Yes, Kitty, just all right. Take your matchmaker hat off.'

Kitty grinned. 'Sorry. It's just that you two are so *right* for each other and any fool could see he fancies you rotten.'

'Me and half the other WAAFs on the camp.'

'No, no.' And then at Gina's straight look, Kitty said, 'Well, OK, I suppose he's been a bit of a one in the past from what Rupert's told me but then they all are, aren't they? Especially now we're at war. But since he set eyes on you Rupert said Mark hasn't looked at another girl.

Honestly, Gina, he's mad about you. Rupert said he hasn't seen him like this before.'

'And that would have nothing to do with the fact that I haven't fallen into his arms like all the others? You know as well as I do that some men like a challenge and I think Mark's like that.'

'That's very hard,' said Kitty reprovingly.

'But probably very true. Anyway, we've agreed to be friends and that's all.'

'Well, it's a start and better than I thought he'd manage, if we're being honest.' Kitty settled back in her seat, seemingly satisfied. 'So if, as just friends, he wants you to come down the pub some nights with me and Rupert, you'll consider it?'

'I'll consider it, yes. But in these little chats you and Rupert have about us, you can mention that friendship is all I'm interested in so it gets back to Mark. I don't want him to waste time on me thinking it will lead to anything. He's a free agent and if he wants to play the field it's all right by me.'

'Oh, *Gina*,' Kitty sighed. 'You can be so annoying.'

'But you love me anyway,' Gina said lightly as the men approached with their drinks.

The rest of the evening passed in a whirl of dancing, drinks and conversation with plenty of laughter too. Mark had a wicked sense of humour and a way of seeing the funny side in everything. When the time came for the two men to walk them to the guardroom on the perimeter of the women's accommodation, he just gave her a quick peck on the cheek and walked off with Rupert without asking to see her again. Gina didn't know if she was relieved or disappointed but eventually decided it was a bit of both.

The next evening, she agreed to go to the pub in the village with Kitty, although neither of them mentioned Mark. The two men were already there with a bunch of their pals but left the others immediately when Gina and Kitty walked in. It was another nice evening. They walked back through a winter wonderland to the camp where they acted like children, the four of them pelting each other with snowballs and shrieking when the cold snow went down their necks. Again, all Mark asked for was a peck on the cheek, but this time Gina felt herself shiver inside and it had nothing to do with the snow. There was a faint lemony smell to his skin and he was a good foot taller than her, his broad shoulders and long limbs making her feel deliciously feminine.

That evening set the pattern for the next few weeks. If she and Kitty went to the pub the men were often there; they turned up on the same night at the camp cinema and more often than not appeared in the NAAFI too. Gina was fully aware that Kitty and Rupert were orchestrating these meetings but was content to go along with it as it avoided specific dates with Mark, something she wasn't ready for yet.

Her driving confidence improved in leaps and bounds and she had no qualms now about being in charge of the refuse lorry or driving the big Commer vans and the pig-swill vehicle, although she preferred the jeeps and officers' cars. Some of the lorries had a gatecrash gearbox and if, on changing down, you didn't get it just right when you brought it out of gear and double-declutched, the screeching and grinding was enough to wake the dead and resulted in the driver being scarlet with mortification.

She drove the CO's car once when his driver was taken ill. It was a filthy night with thickly falling snow, but nevertheless he had to get into town and so she gritted her teeth and drove him to his meeting, her heart in her mouth the whole way there and back. The only good point to the episode had been that the meeting was in a hotel with some of the town's dignitaries, and while they ate and talked in the dining room the CO had arranged for her to be served a three-course meal in the kitchen. The chef and kitchen staff made her very welcome and the food was wonderful, and as she left the chef pressed a bag containing pastries and iced cakes into her hand saying, 'For our fighting girls with my compliments.' That night the girls in the hut toasted him with cocoa while they munched their way through the bag of delicious goodies until not a crumb remained.

It was at the beginning of April when Germany invaded Denmark and Norway that the so-called 'Phoney War' started hotting up. Of course, it hadn't seemed like a Phoney War to the Polish people in the previous September, when after two weeks of nightmarish bombing Hitler's lightning invasion of the country meant sixty thousand Poles had been killed and seven hundred thousand taken prisoners of the Nazis. Neither had the war seemed phoney to the Czechs when less than six months after the Nazi dictator had declared that Germany had no more territorial claims in Europe, the jackbooted troops marched into Prague. Hitler himself entered the city as a conqueror, riding proudly in a powerful car decked with swastikas and surrounded by Nazi leaders, before raising his standard on the Hradzin Castle, the ancient palace of the Bohemian kings and residence of the president of the now vanquished republic.

Gina remembered reading sickening reports of how crowds of Jews and opponents of the Nazis sought to escape at railway stations knowing what was in store for them, and how civilians wept unashamedly as the victorious parade swept by. Others, the newspapers and newsreels declared, courageously sang the national anthem regardless of their own safety or hooted and hissed as the Führer and his Nazi guard passed. The crisis had followed the same pattern that had led to the occupation of the Sudetenland and forced the war seven months ago. Riots had been fomented and German newspapers had screamed headlines such as 'BLOODY TERROR OF THE CZECHS AGAINST GERMANS AND SLOVAKS CREATES AN INTOLERABLE SITUATION'. It seemed lies and manipulation on a grand scale were the order of the day and truth and sanity had gone out of the window.

But now it was May. The Nazis had invaded Holland and Belgium and were beginning to seem unstoppable. The British Expeditionary Force were in real trouble in

France and although Neville Chamberlain, totally dis-
credited, had resigned as Prime Minister and Winston
Churchill had taken his place forming an all-party coali-
tion government, many feared it might be too little too
late. The new Prime Minister had offered 'blood, toil,
tears and sweat' to the nation and promised to tell the
stark truth at all times to the people about its peril, but
also spoke of ultimate victory which was what every man,
woman and child needed to hear.

Gina, though, was fighting her own battle and it was
one that kept her awake for hours every night. Mark was
now flying Spitfires, the most beautiful plane in the world
according to him and one that even outshone his beloved
Hurricanes, and she felt she knew everything about the
planes – he'd rhapsodized about them so much. She knew
their wonderfully thin wings were 'a work of art', that
the Rolls-Royce engine was over a thousand horsepower
and could fly over three hundred and sixty miles per hour
and that there were four Browning machine guns on each
wing. 'She soars like an eagle above the clouds,' Mark
had told her, his face aglow. 'It's another world up there,
Gina, a world where nothing else matters but you and
the plane. You feel you could do anything, take on Hitler
and his damn Nazis single-handed.'

That last conversation had occurred a few days ago
and the resulting turmoil had forced her to admit a truth
she had been trying to deny to herself for weeks. She was
in love with Mark Hammond, much as she didn't want
to be. And the stark truth was he *couldn't* take on the

Luftwaffe single-handed, however invincible he felt. Hurricanes from the base had already been sent to France for the last little while, but Mark had told her it was common knowledge among the pilots that the top brass considered Spitfires too valuable to lose and were keeping them ready for when they were needed. With this escalation of events that would be any day soon and she felt sick to her stomach to think of him fighting against the Germans in something that seemed to her so fragile.

She hadn't gone out with Kitty the night after this conversation with Mark and had made excuses for the next few evenings too, but now as she walked towards the airwomen's accommodation and saw Mark waiting for her by the guardroom her stomach hosted a horde of butterflies suddenly. Over the last weeks their relationship had progressed from friendship to something more, although Mark had been careful to make no demands on her she was unwilling to give.

Their first kiss had been a sweet, non-threatening one but she had still trembled in his arms, terrified that she was allowing him to get closer to her and that she was finding she couldn't do without him. It wasn't what she wanted but she was powerless to resist his steady onslaught on her senses. He had told her he loved her many times when he'd held her in his arms, covering her face in kisses and whispering that she was the most beautiful woman in the world, and she knew he was waiting for her to say she loved him too. And she did, oh, she did.

He watched her as she approached him, his hands

thrust in his pockets and his face unsmiling. He had never appeared more handsome. He didn't speak until she reached him and then he hesitated after taking her hands in his. 'What's wrong, Gina?'

'Wrong? Nothing's wrong.' She tried to sound nonchalant and failed miserably.

He shook his head. 'You're a terrible liar, do you know that? They'd never recruit you as a spy. Is it me? Have I done something? Said something?'

'Of course not.' She tried to free her hands from his, but his grip tightened.

'Then why are you suddenly avoiding me?' he said softly, staring into the lovely face that haunted his dreams night after night. He had no idea what she was thinking but then he never did; she was a closed book. He'd imagined that they were getting on well in the last little while so this turnaround on her part had floored him. He'd played it straight down the line with Gina, no manoeuvring, no contriving to take advantage of her inexperience with men. She had told him she'd never had a boyfriend before and although it was hard to think why, with her being so beautiful, he knew it was the truth. She radiated innocence. Some nights after they had been kissing and cuddling and he'd come to bed, tossing and turning into the early hours with his body burning, he'd told himself he was crazy. The next time he saw her he would start making love to her until she couldn't resist him, he told himself through the long night hours, but he never had. When they had first met he'd thought she would be a notch on his belt like all the others. From the age of fifteen when he'd taken a giggling girl into one of the haystacks on his father's farm and had his way with her, he'd found that women couldn't say no to him, but none of them had meant anything, not even— He stopped his mind from continuing down that path. It was something he would have to sort very soon, he knew that, because he couldn't carry on like this now he'd met Gina and found out what love was. Gina was his nemesis, he told himself ruefully, staring down into her deep blue eyes. His beautiful, innocent, alluring nemesis.

Aware that she wasn't going to answer him, he said again, 'Why are you avoiding me, Gina? I want the truth. I think I have the right to know.' She still had told him very little about her past beyond that she had been orphaned in infancy and brought up in an institution, but he could see something had had a profound effect on her. He'd felt that until he got his own private life sorted out he couldn't push her but maybe that had been a mistake? One thing was for sure, he intended to have her in his life come hell or high water.

Gina stared at him. How could she explain what she didn't understand herself? She just knew that since she had admitted her feelings for him to herself, she'd been terrified. Terrified of the power it gave him, terrified something would happen to him, terrified she had got it wrong and he didn't love her despite his protestations, and more than anything, terrified to tell him how she felt because then everything would change. He would expect her to sleep with him and she wanted that too, but could she trust that he meant what he said about loving her? And so she had wanted to hide, to shut herself away, which was ridiculous. It didn't make sense to her so how could it to him if she tried to explain?

After a few moments she took a deep breath. 'It's the thought you'll be sent to France.'

He frowned, clearly puzzled. 'What's that got to do with anything?'

'I don't know.' She gazed at him, on the verge of tears. 'It just made me feel . . .'

'What?' His expression changed, his eyes narrowing.

'Frightened for you, I suppose.'

'And so because you were worried for me you didn't want to see me?' he asked softly, drawing her closer. 'I can't fathom you out, Gina Redfern.'

'I can't fathom myself out either.' She tried to smile but it was beyond her.

'So you'd care if I was sent into the thick of it?' he murmured softly. 'Is that at the bottom of this?'

She nodded. It was, partly.

'How much?' His dark eyes glittered. 'Tell me how much?' When she attempted to pull away, his arms tightened still more. 'I love you but you know that. I haven't exactly been able to hide it, have I. Are you saying you care for me a little?'

She swallowed hard. 'More than a little.'

'Say it. Say you love me.'

The moment was here and he would never know how

huge a thing it was for her but suddenly that didn't matter. 'I love you,' she whispered. 'I love you so much.'

Now he was kissing her as she had dreamed of being kissed until her head swam and she couldn't breathe.

When he finally raised his mouth, he said softly, 'I've got to get back for a briefing but I'll see you later, all right? You go to the pub with Kitty and we'll meet you there.'

She nodded, starry-eyed. It was going to be all right, she had to believe that. He loved her and whatever the future held that was the important thing.

He kissed her again and then as his name was called they turned to see Rupert beckoning him furiously in the distance.

'I have to go,' he said, drawing away before suddenly grabbing her again and kissing her frantically.

'Go, go.' She broke away, half-laughing and half-crying. 'I'll see you later.'

He grinned at her, kissing the tip of her nose, and then sprinted over to the waiting Rupert. She watched the pair of them gallop off. As he disappeared into the distance he turned and waved, but even as she raised her hand he had gone.

Chapter Fifteen

'I hope you got things sorted with her,' Rupert panted as the two men raced towards the briefing room. 'I've had more than enough of you mooning about the place like a lovesick cow the last few days.'

'Like a bull surely?' Mark said mildly.

'If you'd prefer. Just pray we're not late now else the CO will have our guts for garters.'

They weren't late, but only by the skin of their teeth. There was an undercurrent of excitement vibrating in the air as Mark and Rupert joined the rest of their squadron, and moments later the CO along with the squadron leaders marched into the room.

Since the Germans had invaded Holland and Belgium they had reached the Aisne River and Amiens on the Somme, just sixty miles from Paris, and then Vimy in France and Ghent in Belgium, followed by Boulogne, cutting off British and French troops. It was a dire situation and every man in the room knew it. The Nazis had the whip hand, and despite the Allies fighting every inch of territory, only giving up towns like Calais and Boulogne after terrible fighting, they had now been driven back to the coast by a ruthless German force that showed no mercy to either soldiers or refugees.

The CO, a fatherly middle-aged man, glanced round at the eager young faces before him. He was standing in front of a map showing the south-east of England, the Channel and the coast of France, and his face was grim. Part of the new legislation that had come into force a week ago, when Parliament had rushed in a law that was undoubtedly the most drastic constitutional measure known in British history, was that men in aircraft factories were to work ten hours a day seven days a week. The Emergency Powers Act gave the government other powers, of course, like practically unlimited authority over every person and all property in the land, and the banks, the munitions industry, wages, profits and conditions of work were now all under state control in an unprecedented mobilization of manpower and wealth. And while he considered the new Act necessary, he wondered how many young men would be sacrificed in the planes which the aircraft industry were being called upon to build in greater and greater quantities.

He pushed the thought aside. It did no good to dwell upon such things, or the fact that his three sons were all fighter pilots.

Clearing his throat, he said calmly, 'I'm sure you are all aware that the Belgian army surrendered at midnight on the twenty-seventh after a heroic resistance against the

Nazis. Our boys in the BEF have been ordered to make for the coast where they're fighting a desperate rearguard action around Dunkirk surrounded by German troops. An operation code-named Dynamo has been instigated to get as many of our boys home by sea as is possible. The Germans aren't going to let that happen if they can help it.'

A low murmur went round the room. Mark and Rupert looked at each other. This was it then, what they had been waiting for. They were finally going to do their bit. After the months of waiting the main feeling was one of relief and anticipation.

'The RAF have been ordered to supply air cover for the evacuation and if we're going to get the better of the Luftwaffe, we shall have to use everything we've got. That means you Spitfire pilots will now be helping to keep the Jerry bombers off the ships and boats sailing to the Allies' aid. Thousands of our boys are on the twelve-mile stretch of beach and the harbour has been bombed out of action. On top of that, the beach itself shelves away which means the big ships can't get close to the shore. This is going to be a blood-and-guts fight, gentlemen, with an enemy who are determined upon total annihilation of our boys. The BEF are being bombed and machine-gunned from the air as they wade out to the ships and boats in what observers have called nothing less than mass murder. Let's show the Jerries what we've got, eh?'

He smiled for the first time as a chorus of 'Yes, sir,' came ringing back at him.

'Your squadron leaders will give you more details

tonight but you leave at the crack of dawn. I suggest you all get a good night's sleep. Good luck, gentlemen.'

Far from getting a good night's sleep Mark found he couldn't sleep at all, less because of what he was going to face in the morning and more because he had been unable to say goodbye to Gina. After the talk with the squadron leader, which had seemed to stretch on for ever, they had been ordered straight to their barracks. He lay on his bed, his head buzzing. He knew she would guess what had happened when none of the usual crowd turned up and wasn't worried she'd think he'd let her down, but he just wanted to hold and kiss her one more time.

One thing he was determined about. As soon as he could, he would apply for a forty-eight-hour pass and go home and sort things out there. He should have done it before, he knew that. It had been sheer cowardice that had prevented him, that and not being sure of how Gina really felt about him. But now he did know – she loved him – and if he was certain of anything in this uncertain world he knew he loved her too.

The endless night was finally over and most of the camp were still asleep as they walked towards their Spitfires after a hasty breakfast of tea and toast. He was glad to see he wasn't the only one with no appetite. Nerves had kicked in and he felt as sick as a dog. This improved once he was in the cockpit going through the routine that was now second nature: putting on his flying helmet, plugging in the radio telephone and his oxygen, checking his instrument panel and then signalling to the airman below who yanked the chocks away from the Spitfire's wheels.

They taxied off in formation in the early-morning light, bumping across the grass before the plane took flight and soared up into the air. They were flying in tight formation which took all his concentration, leaving him no time to think of anything else but the job in hand. The Channel was a blue-grey expanse beneath him after a while and it was flecked with all kinds of vessels. As well as the Royal Navy ships, there were fishing boats and tugboats, yachts, pleasure steamers, barges and even rowing boats. It was an incredible sight. Britain united in one aim, to rescue their own from the jaws of death. Mark found he had a lump in his throat.

The blue sky changed to an ominous charcoal as they approached the beach of Dunkirk, a wall of black smoke in front of them. Mark stared down through shafts of sunlight at the grisly scene beneath him. He had known what to expect, had imagined it in his mind, but seeing it was so much worse than he had prepared himself for.

In the sea there were wrecks of ships and boats, some still on fire, and others hovering as close as they could to the shore for the men who were waiting to escape. Figures moved about on the sand below and others, many others, lay still on the beach, crumpled and broken. Bodies floated in the sea, gently bobbing in the waves. The twisted shapes of hundreds of battered vehicles covered the sand and already he could see lines of men wading out to the little boats which were waiting to transport them to the bigger ships, including naval warships, that were stationed in the deeper water. Even as he looked a Messerschmitt appeared out of nowhere and suddenly the radio was full of shouting and swearing as a swarm of ME109s dropped out of the clouds above them.

Their squadron leader was shouting orders through the R/T but it was a case of every man for himself as the Germans scattered and they scattered with them. Adrenaline surged through his body, his only thought to destroy the enemy before they destroyed him and the sitting targets on the beaches. He saw a Spitfire go down in flames and for a few seconds the sound of screaming came across the radio. A Messerschmitt shot across in front of him in his gun sight but although he fired off a quick round the German was too quick for him. Another plane followed the Messerschmitt and for a moment he almost shot at it before realizing it was one of theirs, a Hurricane.

He hadn't expected it to be like this, he thought wildly. This mayhem and chaos.

'Bandits dead ahead.' The squadron leader's voice came over the radio again and Mark wondered how he could sound so calm and untroubled. In all the training he'd had he'd always felt as though he was part of the Spitfire, as though he'd grown wings and swooped and dived as a bird would. This didn't feel like that.

The dull thud and bump told him what had happened before the pain hit and he saw daylight through the floor of the cockpit. He'd been hit and he hadn't even seen the plane that had got him. Shrapnel had made a mess of both of his legs but he was barely aware of it as he realized the Spitfire wasn't responding and he was losing altitude rapidly. The radio was dead and he could smell burning. Glycol fumes were leaking into the cockpit which meant the fuel tank could explode at any moment. He needed to bail out.

It had all happened so fast, in a few heartbeats, but as he became encased in a ball of fire he screamed Gina's name and the screaming continued as the wounded plane plummeted down, down, down into the sea. And then it stopped.

Gina, Kitty and Minnie and a couple of other WAAFs stood watching as aircraft descended out of the deep blue sky. It was a beautiful summer's day, white fluffy clouds heralding the squadron's return from France. Gina and Kitty were clutching hold of each other as in the distance the planes landed and came to a halt, the air crew running to help the pilots and one or two calling for assistance for those who were injured.

Minnie's Norman was part of the BEF stranded and under attack in France, but she had no idea if he had managed to reach the beaches of Dunkirk and whether he was alive or dead. Nevertheless, she was grateful the pilots on base had gone to do what they could. White-faced, the three girls stood together without speaking. In the last few days since France had been invaded the war had suddenly come very close and the threat of invasion to Britain seemed very real.

Gina saw Rupert before Kitty did. As he walked towards them she knew instantly something had happened to Mark from the look on his friend's face. Her grip on Kitty tightened for a moment and then she let go of her as Rupert reached them. He put one arm round Kitty's shoulders but his gaze was on Gina as he said quietly, 'I'm so very sorry.'

Gina nodded. An icy calm had taken hold and nothing was real. As Kitty began to sob, she said numbly, 'I have to drive the Commer into town. They're waiting for me, I must go.'

'Gina, wait.' As Minnie took her arm Gina gently shook herself free. She needed to get away because if they showed her any sympathy she would crumple and that couldn't happen.

When she reached the transport yard she found a couple of airmen waiting beside the lorry and was told they were to drive to several local farms and pick up sacks of potatoes and other supplies. She must have answered them normally because when they clambered into the back of the lorry they continued chatting, calling out to her and generally acting the fool. She was used to the narrow country lanes now, but they still demanded her full attention and for this she was grateful because she couldn't allow herself to think. She had a job to do and she had to do it.

She never remembered much of that afternoon and

couldn't have said which farms the airmen directed her to or what they loaded into the back of the lorry. Hours passed but it could have been minutes. Time had literally ceased to have meaning.

They arrived back at camp in time for the evening meal but Gina went straight to her hut. None of the other WAAFs were there and she sat on her bed staring blankly into the distance. Mark had gone. She would never see him again. Last night she had told him she loved him and now he was dead. She had dilly-dallied for weeks and as soon as she had confessed her love he had been killed. Was there something the matter with her, some sort of curse? Was she predestined never to know happiness which made her a threat to anyone who got close to her? Was this her fault? He had been so full of life, so young and handsome, and all he had wanted to do was to fly planes. He had been so happy last night.

When the tears came it was like a dam breaking, shock and grief causing a torrent of anguished sobbing, his name vibrating in her head. She cried herself dry, and when Kitty and Minnie and the others came back to the hut they found her lying on her bed, her eyes pink and swollen. She sat up as they came in, outwardly composed but exhausted.

'Lass, I'm so sorry.' Kitty and the others gathered round her. They had all been shocked and distressed when Mark and two other pilots, one flying a Spitfire and one a Hurricane, hadn't come home. Another of the girls had a sweetheart in the BEF like Minnie and was waiting for news of him too, and it was a very subdued atmosphere that evening with none of the usual banter and jokes. Kitty made Gina a cup of cocoa and fed her a few biscuits, standing over her until she had eaten them. No one suggested going to the pub or even the NAAFI and while Gina appreciated the moral support she would rather have been left alone, though she wouldn't have said so for the world.

It was getting on for ten o'clock and some of the girls had already turned in, when Kitty said, 'Come for a walk for a minute or two, Gina. I need to tell you something.'

It was the look on her friend's face rather than Kitty's words that made Gina blink and get to her feet, instead of getting ready for bed as she'd been about to do. They left the hut together and outside the air was warm and balmy and the twilight was soft. They had walked a few yards past one of the other huts before Gina said, 'Well, what is it?'

'I have been thinking about this all day and I don't know if I'm doing the right thing even now.' Kitty's voice was very small and as she glanced at Gina she shook her head. 'I feel awful, lass, just awful, but if it was me I think I'd want to know.'

'Know what?' Gina said dully. She really didn't care what Kitty was going to say. Nothing could be worse than Mark dying.

'The thing is, if you heard from someone else it'd be even more—' Kitty stopped abruptly. 'I'm so sorry.'

A chill of dark foreboding cut through Gina's misery.

Kitty was distraught. 'Kitty, whatever it is, tell me, all right?' And when Kitty just stared at her helplessly, she said quietly, 'Is it about Mark?'

Kitty nodded. 'I didn't know, I swear it, Rupert only told me today after—' She took a deep breath. 'And Rupert said he did love you, he knows that.'

'But?' said Gina flatly.

'He'd got a girl back home, he was engaged to her. She's the daughter of his parents' friends, they own a neighbouring farm, and it was sort of understood from when they were little that Mark and this girl would marry.'

For a moment Gina felt the same consuming pain and bewilderment that she had done as a child, on the day she had finally accepted that her mother wasn't going to come for her at the cottage homes. She was small again, a nothing, abandoned and unloved; no one cared about her and nothing was as she had thought it. The feeling eased a little as Kitty put her arms round her and hugged her close, saying again, 'He did love you, lass, he thought the world of you. Anyone could see that.'

It was no comfort. All the time he had been with her, from the very beginning, he'd had this secret and he had never even hinted about another girl. Not just a girl, his fiancée. Funnily enough after all the tears she had shed, she didn't want to cry now. A hard knot had settled in her chest where her heart should be. She hugged Kitty back before she gently disentangled herself. 'I'm glad you told me. It was the right thing to do.'

'Rupert was worried that if this girl accompanied

Mark's parents to get his things or something you might hear about her second-hand or find out about her from one of the crowd down at the pub. Mark had mentioned her to one or two of the men before you came to the camp, you know, in passing.'

Like someone mesmerized, Gina nodded. In passing. He had asked another girl to spend the rest of her life with him, and he had mentioned her in passing. She hadn't known him at all. He had appeared so open, so transparent, and she had felt horribly guilty that she wouldn't be drawn about her past the closer they had got or bare her soul like he had. Even last night, when she had told him she loved him, there had been no hint that he wasn't free to be with her. And she knew he had played the field a bit before she had arrived on the scene; there were still one or two of the WAAFs who tended to cold-shoulder her a bit because Mark had been out with them once or twice and then finished with them. And all the time . . .

'I've been such a fool,' she said softly, more to herself than Kitty. 'Such a stupid, gullible fool.'

'No, no, don't say that. Like I said, he'd fallen for you hook, line and sinker, lass, and I'm sure he would have broken his engagement in time.'

She stared at her friend. Kitty had tears in her eyes and was clearly distressed and she didn't want to upset her further, so she just said quietly, 'Maybe.' In spite of the warm night she shivered visibly. And maybe not. She would never know now. And would she have wanted him, if he had told her about his fiancée and that he had kept quiet about it for so long? She was sure he would have had a whole host of arguments for why he had done so, but could she have trusted him in the future? The answer when it came caused her to stand straighter, her eyes narrowing. Some girls could do that, she was sure, but it wasn't in her. Right or wrong, it just wasn't. And if that was a failing in her, a flaw, so be it.

The people she had thought of as her family had lied to her most cruelly, and it was the one thing she couldn't forgive. However hard and difficult the truth was, it was preferable to a lie. She'd loved Mark despite all her fears and misgivings about getting involved with someone, but it would never happen again. She didn't know how her life would pan out – who did, with this war making everything so uncertain? But one thing was for sure, whatever path she took from now on, she would never be so foolish again. Love, marriage, a family wasn't for her. She'd known that all along, hadn't she, so she had no one to blame but herself for thinking she could be like everyone else.

'Are you all right?' Kitty was staring at her anxiously.

'Not really, but I will be.'

'I'm sorry, lass,' Kitty said for the umpteenth time.

'You've nothing to be sorry about.' Gina took a deep breath. If the Nazis invaded, broken hearts would be the least of anyone's troubles; there were bigger things at stake than any one person's unhappiness. 'Come on, let's get back and go to bed. Tomorrow's another day.'

Chapter Sixteen

Over the next days Gina had to remind herself more than once of what she had said to Kitty. Grief that Mark had died, that his life had been snuffed out before it had barely begun, warred with anger and hurt and bitterness until sometimes she didn't know if she was coming or going. But other girls were suffering too. The other WAAF in their hut besides Minnie who'd had a sweetheart at the front learned that he had been killed, although Norman had made it back safely in the evacuation from Dunkirk. Two of their friends lost brothers, and a girl in the hut next to theirs discovered that her father, two uncles and a cousin had lost their lives in France. It was a grim time and it was only going to get worse.

In the middle of June German troops paraded up the Champs-Élysées, and Parisians had to decide whether to flee or face a life under occupation. The Nazi swastika was flying from the Eiffel Tower and the Arc de Triomphe and it was reported that two million Parisians had fled the city, roads to the south being blocked with women, old folk and children, pushing carts loaded with their possessions. From time to time German dive-bombers would come tearing out of the sky to rake the columns with gunfire, and civilians who remained in Paris had had to watch signs going up on cinemas, restaurants and even brothels, reserving them for German soldiers. A sign on the chamber of Deputies read, 'DEUTSCHLAND SIEGT AUF ALLEN FRONTEN' – Germany conquers on all fronts. And there were lots of people in Britain who feared that was true and they were next. Britain was fighting on alone and a bloody battle on British soil could well be the next phase of the war.

'Old Churchill's got a way with words, I'll give him that,' said Kitty one evening as she sat on her bed reading the newspaper. 'Listen to this. He went to see MPs in Parliament and this is what he said: "Let us brace ourselves to our duty and so bear ourselves that if the British Commonwealth and Empire lasts a thousand years men will still say, This was their finest hour."'

She glanced round the listening hut. 'And he said Britain will fight on for years if necessary.'

Everyone nodded.

'In the grounds of Buckingham Palace the King is practising revolver-shooting,' said Kitty, reading on, 'and he's said if needs be he'll die there fighting. The Queen's refusing to leave and fly to Canada with the princesses like some of the toffs have done. That takes some guts, doesn't it, when you could get your children away to safety.'

'The Nazis will never understand that,' said Gina quietly. 'They confuse power and force with courage, but our Royal Family is what being British is all about, standing for right against might.'

Now that France had fallen, everything changed rapidly. The new Local Defence Volunteers, originally armed with little more than armbands and hastily devised weapons, were renamed by Winston Churchill as the Home Guard. Most of them were veterans of the Great War keen to do their bit, and their aged rifles, shotguns, cutlasses borrowed from museums and broomsticks converted into pikes with carving knives, had been met with tolerant smiles from their friends and family at first. Now, with the introduction of uniforms and real weapons, military discipline kicked in.

Minnie received a letter from home and held up a photograph. 'Oh, bless him,' she said fondly, waving it about for the other girls to see. 'Look at my grandad in his kit.' The photo showed an ancient little man with a Father Christmas beard grinning like a Cheshire cat with a rifle slung over his shoulder. Everyone smiled and gushed about how sweet he looked, but with the German invasion of the Channel Islands at the beginning of July, Gina wondered how effective Minnie's grandad and his cronies would be at repelling invaders. Now that the enemy were just across the Channel the threat of invasion seemed inevitable. The obvious place for invasion was the east or south-east but Hitler seemed to have things so well worked out that he might not attack in the expected way.

There was always the fear of invasion from the air too, and the camp's CO decided that WAAF officers should be given instruction in the use of arms. They were taught how to use rifle, tommy gun, pistol and hand grenade. Gina and the others were filled with envy until one officer admitted that some of them were so clumsy at throwing they managed to drop the dummy grenades at everyone's feet in the sandbagged pit they practised in, and they dreaded the time when they would have to start using live grenades. After that Gina didn't mind so much.

The German air raids stepped up a pace the day after the Channel Islands were invaded when bombers carried out their first daylight raids, and shortly after this the Luftwaffe attacked British convoys in the Channel. It seemed as though every day the news got worse. Whether it was this that made the WAAFs bond together so strongly Gina didn't know, but as the weeks and months went on she found everyone shared their troubles and heartaches and did their best to help each other. Short off-duty recreation tended to end up with girls from their hut going out together dancing, going to the cinema, shopping or having tea in the local café, where the china crockery made a nice change from the tin mugs in the mess. Gina found it helped her come to terms with Mark's death and the revelation that had followed more than anything else could have done. When Kitty's Rupert died in the Battle of Britain in September Gina mourned with her friend, and when Minnie came back from a forty-eight-hour pass seeing her Norman in November sporting an engagement ring, the girls in the hut got together and arranged a surprise party, decorating the NAAFI and pooling their resources to buy food and drink. It was a lovely spread, followed by games and a sing-song, with Nancy, who had a surprisingly fine voice, singing Frank Sinatra's 'Our Love Affair' to a delighted Minnie.

As Christmas approached, Gina could hardly believe she had been at the camp for over a year, and that the war and the world in general had changed so dramatically in that time. The Luftwaffe had pounded London constantly since the Blitz in September and the King and Queen had been in residence at Buckingham Palace when six bombs fell on it, one of which had wrecked the chapel. So many cities up and down the country had had their landscapes changed for ever along with tragic loss of life, and now a bleak Christmas lay ahead for a besieged Britain. With vital shipping space needed for war supplies, food shortages had begun to bite hard. Carrots would have to take the place of dried fruit in many a Christmas pudding, and tight rationing meant housewives had their work cut out to provide even a whiff of meat in most dishes. Home-grown vegetables had become an important part of everyone's diet, and housewives were bombarded with recipes and food fact leaflets by the Ministry of Food for such dishes as 'mock goose', potato pancakes, semolina soufflés and carrot cookies. The word 'surprise' seemed to feature in many of these recipes, the surprise being – as many a disgruntled husband discovered – that be it rabbit surprise, duck surprise, lamb surprise or beef, the humble potato masqueraded as meat.

'Has *anyone* got any ham in their ham loaf?' Kitty asked plaintively a few days before Christmas as they sat eating their evening meal in the cookhouse. 'Mine's just potatoes and onions and turnips, I swear it is.'

'I've got a sliver.' Gina held up a tiny piece of ham on the end of her fork, smiling at her friend. Kitty had cried into her pillow over Rupert for a while but now she was dating another airman. This one was just for laughs though, she'd told Gina, and she didn't intend to get too fond of him. For airwomen who worked on airfields, death was never far away.

Gina knew her friend was right but she couldn't be as philosophical as the worldly-wise blonde, and even Kitty had been appalled and sickened when a little while ago two of their stricken bombers had crashed on landing at the airfield after a raid. Black smoke and fierce flames had leaped into the sky and the heat had been too intense for the rescue services to do anything. All the WAAFs had shed a few tears, but the next day things had carried on as normal. They had to if Hitler was going to get his comeuppance.

Gina gobbled the rest of her dinner including the eggless ginger pudding that was as heavy and solid as a lump of lead, and left the others still eating. She'd been ordered to drive the CO into the town, which was some miles away, for a meeting with the mayor, and had had to tell Kitty she couldn't accompany her to the village pub as they'd arranged that morning. She had driven the CO a few times now when his normal driver wasn't available, and although they hadn't exchanged more than half a dozen words, she liked the middle-aged man and found him less scary than some of the RAF corporals and sergeants.

The December evening was bitterly cold, and already the ground was coated in a fine layer of frost as she waited for the CO beside the staff car. A full moon sailed in a clear sky in which hundreds of stars twinkled and glowed, and as she gazed up at them she found herself remembering her mother. She never let herself think of the years before the cottage homes when she had been part of a family, when she had believed she had a mother and brothers who loved her, but like a bolt from the blue she heard her mam saying to her, 'You see them stars, hinny? Well, each one of them is a soul who's died an' gone to heaven and is looking down an' smiling on us, so there's nowt to be scared of, all right?' They had gone to a funeral in the village that day of one of her brother's school friends who had taken a fever and died, and seeing the coffin and knowing little Michael was inside it and unable to get out had terrified her, resulting in a screaming nightmare after she had gone to bed. Her mother had come in and taken her to the window, pointing out the stars, and then once she'd calmed a little, sitting by her bed until she fell asleep again.

Gina blinked back a sudden rush of hot tears, horrified at herself. She couldn't be seen snivelling when the CO came out, she told herself; this was ridiculous, and precisely the reason she kept a guard on her thoughts regarding the past. Elsie hadn't even been her real mother, it had all been a lie, and as soon as a girl baby had come along she'd been got rid of. The old feeling came back, the one that made her feel she was shrinking away to nothing, that she was worthless, a nonentity. Suddenly she was a child again, small and alone and bereft.

A door opened and the CO came striding out. Gina's training kicked in, bringing her back from the painful morass of her thoughts. She snapped to attention, saluting and opening the car door for him.

He thanked her and slid inside the back of the car, sounding preoccupied. In truth he could have done without this damn meeting tonight, he told himself irritably, as Gina took her place in the driving seat and the engine sprang into life. He knew what it was about; the week before, one of his men had got into a fight with a local about a girl after drinking in one of the pubs in town and the police had got involved. The local lad had been taken to hospital with a broken jaw and his man had spent the night in gaol before being collected by one of the base's military policemen in the morning. As he understood it, the local had taken umbrage at his girlfriend drinking with the air gunner and had thrown the first punch, egged on by his pals: clear case of self-defence on the air gunner's part. He'd been confined to barracks and given a dressing down, and as far as the CO was concerned, that was the end of the matter. Unfortunately the local in question was also the mayor's son and apparently well known for being something of a bully. In spite of several witnesses corroborating the air gunner's story, the mayor's son was telling a very different tale.

The CO sighed as he settled back in his seat, gazing absently out of the window into the moonlit night. Alexander Baxter-Hughes was a military man from the top of his head to his well-polished boots, and suffered fools badly. He had met the mayor several times and liked him well enough, but it was clear to him the son was a different kettle of fish entirely. Tonight he would have to tell the father a few home truths about the son he obviously saw through rose-coloured glasses, and because Alexander was also a kind man and a father himself, he wasn't looking forward to it.

They had left the camp and were travelling along a country road towards the town, but in spite of the blackout regulations the frost and moonlight lit up the surrounding countryside perfectly well and made driving easier. They had passed through several hamlets and were within a couple of miles of the town when the drone of aircraft registered on Gina. Within moments the sound of air-raid sirens split the night air and in the distance ack-ack guns joined the melee. They were close enough to see the bombs falling, and in her mirror Gina saw the CO sit up straighter.

'Pull over,' he said calmly. 'No sense in driving straight into the thick of it.'

Gina stopped the car and they listened in silence to the scream of falling bombs in the town ahead of them followed by shattering explosions. Gina was just thinking that another few minutes and they would have been right in the centre of it all, when she saw the blazing aircraft coming towards them and a stick of bombs falling which the stricken aircraft had obviously jettisoned. She never really had a clear memory of the next minutes. Deafening noise, a terrific roar, the sensation of the car crumpling as it spun and twisted through the air, and the sound of screaming. It wasn't until a few moments later that she realized the screams were coming from her. The car was lying on its side some distance from where it had been parked but she had been thrown out through the driver's door into a muddy ditch that ran along the bottom of the bank at the side of the road.

She lay stunned for a second or two and then there was an almighty crash somewhere and a column of smoke and flames rose from fields to the left of them where the enemy plane had come down. The sound brought her back to herself and she struggled to get up, aware she was bleeding from a cut to her head as blood blinded her for a moment. Wiping her hand across her eyes, she managed to stand, gasping as pain shot through one of her legs.

The CO's car was on fire as she hobbled towards it, and to her horror she realized he was still inside and that he was moving. As she reached the crippled vehicle that was all twisted metal and burning rubber, she wrenched at one of the back doors, managing to open it enough to reach out to the wounded man as she gabbled, 'Sir, sir, you have to get out, the engine's on fire.'

'I can't, my legs are caught.'

She pushed at the back seat which had moved forward with the impact, wedging the CO's legs between it and the mangled front passenger seat, even as he was saying, 'Leave me. This car's going to be a fireball in a minute. Save yourself, that's an order.'

'I can't leave you like this, sir.' There was no bravado involved; Gina knew she would never be able to live with herself if she left him to burn alive. She pierced her hands on broken glass but didn't even feel it as she jerked and pulled and pushed, and somehow, miraculously, the seat moved two or three inches. There was no finesse involved as she tugged at his trapped legs, and she knew she was hurting him because he groaned before passing out, his head falling onto his chest. Nevertheless, first one leg and then the other was free.

The CO wasn't a small man or slight in build and it took all her strength to haul him out of the back seat onto the ground and then drag him away from the car. The smell of petrol was overwhelming and they were some twenty to thirty yards away when with a fierce whoosh the car did indeed become a fireball as the CO had predicted. Even where Gina was the heat was fierce, but she could go no further. As the adrenaline which had kept her going to that point left her, her injuries and not least loss of blood from the wound on her head and a deep gash in one of her legs finally overcame her. She collapsed by the CO's side as consciousness faded into darkness.

How long it was before she became aware of voices and being lifted she didn't know. Someone was saying, 'They're as cold as ice, get them blankets wrapped round them,' and a different voice was adding, 'Looking at that car they're damn lucky to be alive,' but the conversation was coming from miles away and she gladly went into the blackness again.

The next day she awoke in the sick bay with a WAAF nurse bending over her and smilingly offering her a cup of tea. For a moment Gina had no idea where she was and then it all came flooding back; she winced as she tried to sit up and the room spun.

'Take it easy,' the nurse said gently. 'You've had quite a bang on the head and the MO suspects concussion for a day or two.'

'The CO?' she murmured as the room righted itself. 'How is he?'

'He's been transferred to the RAF hospital in Scarborough,' the nurse said cheerfully. 'His legs were a bit of a mess.'

'But he'll be all right?'

'Oh, yes, thanks to you. He told the MO how you risked your life to get him out. You're the hero of the camp.'

Gina grimaced. She didn't want to be the hero of the camp, not for doing something anyone would have done in the circumstances.

Nevertheless, that seemed to be the way everyone was

determined to see things in the days that followed. She spent three days in the sick bay with such a steady stream of visitors that in the end the MO ordered total peace and quiet for his patient, and when she was finally allowed back to her hut on the third evening all the girls clapped and cheered and threw the inevitable party to celebrate her return. The next day was Christmas Eve, but that evening Gina didn't go to the concert in the NAAFI. Her head still ached on and off, along with her leg, which had been stitched up by the MO and was turning a nice shade of purple. She had bruises and cuts all over and felt exhausted, something the MO said would pass in a few days. He had ordered her to remain in barracks and not to take up duties again until after Christmas, and in truth she was quite happy to remain in bed most of the time. The other girls made sure the stove was burning well and the hut was fairly warm, and she had a hot-water bottle at her feet, several books to read and a couple of boxes of chocolates to work through that she'd been given. It was so different to normal life at the camp that sometimes she wondered if she was dreaming.

It started snowing on Christmas Day and didn't let up for some days, but by the time she resumed normal duties the sky was blue and high even though it was bitterly cold and the snow made the surrounding countryside into a winter wonderland. On the first of January she was called into the CO's office and told by the RAF hierarchy assembled there that she would receive a mention in dispatches and had been promoted to corporal. The CO was making progress apparently, but it was doubtful that he would be back before the end of the month, and when he returned he had requested that she become his personal driver. This would mean she would be taken off general duties, of course. Gina nodded as though she had taken it all in, which she hadn't, not until she got back to the hut and Kitty whooped and hollered and Nancy said, 'Blimey, lass, does that mean we'll have to salute you all the time?'

That night in bed, when all the other girls were asleep and she lay dissecting the day, Gina shook her head to herself in the pitch blackness. With the outbreak of war her life had taken a different path to the one she had envisaged, but who would have thought that after just fifteen months in the WAAF she'd be promoted to corporal? She wasn't quite sure how she'd like being the CO's personal driver, truth be told; she'd enjoyed the variety of driving the RAF trucks and vans and jeeps even though the conditions of work meant she sometimes missed meals and went hungry. But it was kind of him nonetheless. She had only exchanged the odd word or two with him when she had occasionally driven his car in the past, but he seemed a nice man and it was common knowledge his three sons were bomber pilots. That must be a constant worry at the back of his mind. Everyone was still reeling from the terrible attack by the Luftwaffe three nights ago when the Germans had tried to set fire to the city of London. The capital had become an inferno and it was lucky the raid was called off just when the

Luftwaffe seemed to be winning. They'd been told the Air Ministry believed that this was due to the weather unexpectedly deteriorating over low-lying German airfields. It was an illustration of how utterly ruthless the Luftwaffe were and what a formidable adversary.

Gina turned over and hugged her knees up to her chest. Once they were in bed and the warmth from the stove began to die down the hut rapidly became icy cold. It reminded her of her little bedroom at the farmhouse on a winter's night.

Immediately the thought formed she took hold of herself. No thinking of that time, it was too weakening. All day she'd had to battle with herself against the memories and she knew why; it had been one of the officers – well-meaning and smiling – who had remarked that her promotion and being mentioned in dispatches would be something to write home about. A perfectly natural comment, of course, and she knew the officer would have been horrified if he'd known it was like a knife piercing her heart. She had no family to be proud of her, no parents or siblings to care if she lived or died, succeeded or failed.

No, no self-pity. She blinked away the tears and then as Kitty gave a particularly loud snore, smiled to herself. She had this family, these girls who loved her and cared about her. That was enough. Life had to be lived looking forwards, it was the only way.

PART FIVE

Alien Stars

1944

Chapter Seventeen

Gina stood on the deck of the ship, her kitbag at her feet, gazing at the busy dock stretched out before her. Without the sea breeze which had been so welcome the nearer they had got to Egypt from England, the air was desiccated and scorching, and full of a mixture of unfamiliar smells. She sniffed quietly and then turned as a voice behind her said, 'Now you really know you're abroad. I remember this smell from before the war when the wife and I visited Egypt – cheap petrol, Egyptian cigarettes, exotic perfume, jasmine and frying chapattis, and acres of unwashed humanity, of course.'

She smiled at the CO. 'I like it, sir.'

'You won't when you get the full force down there.' He inclined his head at the dock. 'But you'll get used to it.'

'Yes, sir.' If she had spoken what she was feeling, she would have said she still couldn't believe she was in Egypt. When the CO had told her he would be leaving for an overseas posting that was strictly hush-hush and asked her if she wanted to accompany him, she'd had no hesitation in agreeing immediately. That had been some weeks ago, and she had been medicated, lectured and equipped since then, but still had no idea of what the CO had been asked to do, such was the blanket of secrecy surrounding his mission. Not that it mattered. Her job was what it had been for the last few years, acting as his personal driver, and it was something she had found she enjoyed more and more as time went on. He was a fatherly kind of man, at least with her, and they had got to know each other quite well. She had met his wife, a quiet, gentle woman, and his remaining son. His other two boys had died the year before, one in January and the other in August when RAF night bombers had attacked Hamburg, and their deaths had affected him deeply. She'd privately wondered if that was why he'd agreed to get away from anything familiar.

They had travelled by troop ship and Gina wasn't sorry the journey was over. Her cabin, which she had shared with a number of other WAAFs who were signal shift workers on their way to Heliopolis in Cairo, had been very small. It had contained four three-tier bunks and because of the blackout, had been painfully hot and airless. There was always the threat of U-boats too, and at night when it was pitch black any bump or sound was magnified a hundred times.

But she was here now. She followed the CO down the gangplank, the Egyptian sun beating through her clothes and the smells engulfing her as small children popped up around her, clamouring in their own language and trying to yank her kitbag and the small case she'd brought with her out of her hands.

The CO glanced over his shoulder. 'Ignore them,' he said briefly.

It was easier said than done, besides which she felt uncomfortable and churlish, but the CO was striding towards a waiting jeep and she had to hurry to keep up with him. He climbed in beside the RAF driver and she got in the back with their luggage, feeling utterly over-whelmed. The disorder, the heat and not least the noise were unnerving, and she wondered how the other WAAFs were faring; but then the jeep rattled away and she found herself only half-listening to the conversation of the two men as she attempted to take in her surroundings.

She had expected Egypt to be different to anything she had known at home, and the CO had spoken to her about his experiences abroad, but nothing had prepared her for what she was seeing. It wasn't too extreme to say she had stepped into a new world, an exotic, harshly bright and colourful, mesmerizing world.

As they left the teeming furore of Port Said the sights and sounds left her breathless. Brilliant white buildings, sidewalk cafés where old men in flowing robes sat gossiping over black coffees, shaded squares, market-places, endless beautiful minarets dominating the vivid blue skyline, dusty roads and people – countless people. Austere Arabs, market traders with sandalled feet, veiled women of every shape and size and children, children,

children. They swarmed like little ants, somehow avoiding the donkeys and carts, camels, lorries, cars and jeeps and other obstacles, some ragged and barefoot, others slightly better dressed but all seemingly bright-eyed and bushy-tailed.

The play of light and shadow, of deep shade ripped open by streaks of blazing sun, the amazing heat which was like existing in an oven and the strong feeling of an ancient faith and old rites, kept her silent as she drank it all in from her view in the rattling jeep. She was glad she'd thought to bring a good supply of night cream with her, Gina thought as she became damp with perspiration. She'd need to plaster it on every night to keep her skin from drying out; already her face felt tight and slightly sore.

When they reached the RAF camp at Heliopolis, Gina was tired, hungry and thirsty; she had never longed for a bath so much in all her life, but had never felt so alive either. Due to the secrecy surrounding the CO's mission she had been unable to tell Kitty and the others where she was being posted to, merely that it was abroad. She would miss them, she thought, as the jeep rumbled up to the administrative block and the driver cut the engine. And she would especially miss not going to Minnie's wedding. This had originally been scheduled for some months after Norman had proposed, but then he had been sent to North Africa where he had been badly injured fighting Rommel's troops and eventually shipped back to Britain. Broken in body and mind, he had insisted on breaking the engagement, declaring he would not tie Minnie to a life with an invalid who would never be any good to man or beast. It had been then that the scatter-brained, disorganized Minnie had shown her true worth. She had refused to accept that their engagement was over, visiting him whenever she could get leave and talking incessantly about their future together. He had lost both legs and been blinded in one eye when a grenade had exploded, leaving him badly facially scarred, but Minnie had never faltered in her love, and eventually he had conceded to the wedding going ahead but only when he could walk her down the aisle on his artificial legs. After numerous operations this had recently become possible and so the wedding was set at long last.

She was glad for her friend, Gina thought now as she quickly followed the CO into the building where weary fans were moving the thick sluggish air about, but marriage was something she would never want for herself, let alone fight for. Everyone to their own, though. It was what made the world go round.

The CO was met by his counterpart and Gina was told to sit and wait as the two men disappeared into a separate office. A fair-haired WAAF who had been sitting at a desk typing as they'd walked in had been dispatched to fetch coffee for the CO, and when she returned with a tray she'd brought a cup for Gina along with some biscuits. Once she'd delivered the refreshments to her boss she came back and sat down, smiling across at Gina who had devoured the biscuits as she said, 'Hungry?'

'Starving,' said Gina through a mouthful of digestive. 'What's the food like here?'

'Not bad actually.' The girl's stripes showed she was a corporal too, and now she said, 'Our huts are pretty spartan but then what can you expect? And the showers are cold water only but in this heat cold means tepid. There's an old Sudanese called Achmed who speaks English – he's in charge of all the local boys who do the daily labour in camp. You want to keep on the right side of him but don't stand any nonsense. They don't think much of women in their culture from what I can make out, but as long as you let him see who's boss from the start, I've found him all right when there's any problems. Most of the boys are lazy little devils and will get out of anything that needs to be done if they can, always with a smile, of course. They look on working in the camp as a cushy number compared to their normal life, according to Achmed, even when they have to empty the ablutions tank and clean and disinfect it.'

A buzz on her telephone caused the girl to pick it up smartly and say, 'Yes, sir?' into the receiver. 'Of course, sir, right away.' Replacing it, she nodded at the CO's office. 'They're going to be some time and I've been asked to take you round and show you the ropes. Your CO says he won't need you till morning. Considerate, isn't he.'

The girl's tone made it clear her CO wasn't so thoughtful, but Gina just smiled and nodded.

'I'm Pam by the way, Pam Cunningham.'

'Gina Redfern.'

Stepping out into the heat again caused Gina to realize that the fans in the building hadn't been as ineffective as she'd imagined. It was baking hot outside.

'You'll get used to it.' Pam had seen her wince as they had left. 'And it's midday, the hottest time. It's the sand-storms that I can't stand, horrible things.'

As they walked, Pam pointed out this and that, her voice cheery. The covered verandah of the NAAFI was apparently the coolest place in camp and also the nicest, according to Pam. Before any airwomen had come to Egypt, some of the RAF men, feeling far from home, had got together and had tons of soil brought in. They'd made a garden outside the verandah filled with flowers and bushes that gave off exotic perfumes in the evening, with even a couple of trees. Achmed's boys had been assigned the task of keeping the garden well watered.

'You can sit there in the evening with a G and T and pretend you're on holiday abroad and the war's never happened,' Pam said happily. 'Well, except for the fact that everyone's in uniform, of course.'

The accommodation huts that had been built for the WAAFs were not far from the men's but had a boundary fence between them, along with a guardroom and office with sleeping accommodation for two, Pam told her as they approached the compound. Once past the guard-room, Pam opened the door of the nearest hut. There were fourteen iron beds with thin mattresses, and each bed space had a shelf over it with hooks fitted underneath to hang things. Bomb boxes at the foot of each bed stored all other possessions, Pam told her. Above the beds were tall narrow windows of fine wire mesh for ventilation with shutters to close in the case of sandstorms, and a row of electric ceiling fans had been installed in the middle of the room.

'Each hut has its own corporal's room,' said Pam, opening a door to the left of her to show Gina a miniature version of the bigger room, 'and as luck would have it this one's free. Poor Sandra was involved in an accident in town and she's been shipped back home. They think she'll lose her leg.' Before Gina could say anything, Pam added, 'One of the boys has brought your things here already so you can settle in before you meet the rest of the girls in your hut.'

Sure enough, Gina saw her kitbag and case on the bed. Feeling a little awkward that she'd come by the room because of the other corporal's misfortune, she said hesitantly, 'If there was someone else in line for it . . .'

'No, no. Anyway, we've been told that you are your CO's driver and PA and you're here on something very hush-hush so you'll need your own room.'

'Have you?' Gina looked at the other girl in surprise. 'I don't know where that came from. It's true he's here on something for the top brass but what it is I haven't a clue, and certainly I'm not in on it. I'm just his driver.'

'Really?' Pam relaxed a little, sitting down on the bed. 'Oh, we'd all got the idea we had to mind our Ps and Qs round you.'

'Please don't. I'd hate that.'

'We couldn't have kept it up anyway,' Pam giggled. 'The girls here are a nice lot on the whole, all keen to do their bit for King and country, although the two consigned to the pay office moan all the time, saying scrutinizing other people's figures and sums for mistakes is deadly dull and not what they joined up for. You'll soon learn to ignore them, everyone does.'

So saying, she jumped off the bed and opened the door. 'I'll come and take you to the mess later when you've unpacked, and the ablutions are at the end of the huts, by the way. Pretty basic lavatory bucket system and check for snakes and other nasties before you sit down.'

'*Snakes?*'

''Fraid so. One of the girls was a bit tiddly the other night and sat down to do the necessary, only to leap six foot in the air when she got bit on the bum. Fortunately the snake wasn't poisonous, but it was a bit embarrassing having to present her rear end to the MO in the middle of the night.'

Gina stared at the other girl. Was she joking? She didn't appear to be.

'And by the same token, make sure there's no spiders or scorpions in your bed before you turn in. They have a way of getting everywhere.'

Gina gulped. The Nazis were preferable to creepy-crawlies and snakes. 'Will do,' she said weakly.

Once Pam had left, she unpacked, checked the bed and then lay down, needing a few minutes to compose herself.

Somewhere in the distance a radio was playing, and she could hear the faint strains of Glenn Miller's 'Chattanooga Choo Choo'. Since the Americans had come into the war after the Japanese had bombed Pearl Harbour and the GIs had made an appearance in England, half the WAAFs she knew had become enthralled with everything American. For herself, she wasn't so sure. Films like *Mrs. Miniver*, showing Hollywood's idea of Britain under fire with Greer Garson playing an undaunted English middle-class mother rousing the local villagers, seemed ridiculously rose-tinted to her, although even Winston Churchill had said the film was worth a hundred warships as propaganda and it had collected six Oscars.

Kitty had been out with several GIs, so called because their equipment was all labelled 'Government Issue', and there was no doubt that their stylishly tailored uniforms, friendly outgoing personalities and lavish, open-handed gifts made them seem impossibly glamorous to British women. Lucky Strike and Camel cigarettes; precious nylon stockings that took the place of the silk stockings that had long since vanished from the shops; scented soap; chocolate; ice cream and more. Gum-chewing and jeep-driving, and sufficiently well paid to take girls to the best local clubs and restaurants, the GIs were like magnets. It was through them that many British girls received their first lesson in jitterbugging, a dance craze that had spread with such enthusiasm that many ballrooms had had to ban it to protect their sprung floors. The dance was for the uninhibited, like the GIs themselves.

Was it the extrovert Casanova aura about the Americans that repelled rather than attracted her? Gina asked herself now. She wasn't sure but since she had found out about Mark's fiancée his sort of man – the lady-killer type – seemed shallow and facile. She'd told herself on many occasions that she was probably being unfair and such a sweeping generalization of the GIs was unjustified, but it was the way she felt and she couldn't help it. The average British man's summing up of the American visitors – that the GIs were 'overpaid, oversexed and over here' – seemed about right to her. She and Kitty had had many heated discussions about it, but had finally agreed to disagree and the GIs had become a forbidden subject.

Gina stretched, gazing idly up at the ceiling fan as it gently whirred.

Men in general had become a forbidden subject, come to that, she thought with a smile. They were so different, she and Kitty. Kitty was intent on getting every romantic minute she could out of the war and had already set her sights on being a GI bride and ending up in America, where she was sure she would live her days in the lap of luxury.

She sat up and then found her brush and comb, raking through her thick dark curls and restoring them to order. She'd had her long hair cut short to softly frame her face shortly after Mark had died. It had been part of the desire to put that period of her life, with its deep hurt and sense of betrayal and grief, behind her. To shut it up in a little box in her mind and throw away the key.

Gazing at herself in the cloudy mirror on the wall, she nodded at her reflection. She *would* travel and see America one day but not as a GI's wife. She would visit many countries – she was determined about that – perhaps living and working in a few. Why not? She was her own mistress, she had no one to answer to but herself and that was the way she liked it. She could trust herself, but you never really knew what was going on in someone else's mind. If the war had taught her one thing it was that every day was precious and not to be wasted, and it was no good crying over spilled milk. You had to pick yourself up, dust yourself down and get on with things.

The deep blue eyes in the mirror had narrowed with her thoughts, their habitual softness for a moment taking on a hardness that didn't sit well with her. She turned away, shaking her head as though in defiance of the momentary weakness. She had learned from her mistakes, that was all, and it was a good thing. Only the foolish set themselves up to be knocked down again and again, and she wasn't foolish. Not now and not ever. It was as simple and clear-cut as that.

Chapter Eighteen

The next few weeks were ones of adjustment, not least because Gina found the CO needed her far less than he had in England. Never one for sitting twiddling her thumbs, she found the long stretches between driving him here and there boring and tedious, and after a while he realized this. Whatever his mission was, it involved periods of three or four days when he would be absent from the camp entirely, but on those occasions one of the pilots on the base flew him to where he needed to be.

It was after one of these absences that Alexander Baxter-Hughes called her into his office, which had been a warrant officer's until he'd been turfed out for the important visitor from the UK. Gina thought he was going to give her the day's itinerary but instead he said, 'Sit down please, Gina. We need to have a little chat.'

Wondering what she'd done wrong, Gina perched on the chair in front of his desk.

'I have to confess that this hasn't turned out quite as I expected,' he said quietly. 'I thought, knowing your desire to travel in the future, that an overseas posting would be good experience for you, but I hadn't taken into account the nature of my assignment and the visits I need to make elsewhere at times. D-Day as you know was a great success and the Germans are on the run throughout Europe. From my base here I have the task of pulling certain pockets of resistance together and making the Allies more effective in some areas. This war has dragged on long enough, as I'm sure you will agree.' He smiled sadly.

'Yes, sir.'

'British troops landed in Greece yesterday, three and a half years after being driven out by the Nazis. This great day has come about only ten days after British seaborne and airborne forces captured Patra on the Gulf of Corinth and finding little opposition, started to push towards the Greek capital. However, it would be dangerous to assume the Germans will give ground lightly. We know they have been ordered to defend to the death but fortunately not all of them are infected by their Führer's madness and blood lust. As we speak, higher up in the Adriatic a furious battle is being fought for Corfu with British troops, supported by Albanian patriots, attacking the German garrison. But that is by the by.'

He smiled again. 'Having just returned late last night I need to leave for Almaza later today by plane and then elsewhere. I have told the CO here that in my absences you would be available for any duties he might have for you. I take it you would be comfortable with this?'

'Yes, sir. Of course.' Gina smiled back. She wondered

how many COs would be concerned about their driver's feelings, but then theirs was a special relationship. After the accident, when she had saved his life, there were times when he treated her more as a daughter than a lowly WAAF under his command.

As though in confirmation of the thought, the CO leaned forwards and said softly, 'Make the most of the time you're here, Gina. You only have to ask for a few days' leave and it's yours. I understand some of the girls have been to Luxor and Aswan, visited temples, the Valley of the Kings and Tutankhamun's tomb. It shouldn't be all work and no play.'

'Thank you, sir.' She was careful never to take advantage of his continuing kindness but now she said impishly, 'Would you like me to bring you back any souvenirs if I go on any trips?'

He chuckled. 'Please don't. Felicity has got a houseful from my various postings before the war.'

She knew he had been based all over Europe in the past as well as travelling extensively for pleasure with the family. She supposed that was one of the things that made him so perfect for this particular assignment; he knew several countries like the back of his hand as well as having contacts everywhere. His manner as he settled back in his chair told her their talk was over, and she rose to her feet, saying, 'Is there anything else, sir?'

'Not at present, no. I shall be away for a few days until Wednesday, but Gina –' he looked at her meaningfully – 'I meant what I said, have a little fun now and again.' And then he surprised her by adding, 'I know I benefit from your devotion to duty but you're young and life is for living. Now pop over to the duty corporal in the admin office and see if they have anything for you. They know you're available for the next little while.'

Once outside the office she bit her lip. She was glad she was going to be kept busier but as for fun . . . Equally, she would like to see some of the sights of this hot and ancient land. She hadn't really struck up a friendship with any of the WAAFs in her hut but then with her being a corporal and essentially in charge of them she hadn't really expected to. Pam and another corporal, Mildred, however, had made a point of including her in their group in any off-duty time. She knew they had a trip to see the pyramids planned on their next leave, so she might ask if she could accompany them. It helped that Pam had a fiancé in the army and Mildred's boyfriend was in Normandy so neither girl was interested in flirting and carrying on with the RAF personnel on camp, unlike some of the WAAFs. She'd already had a pilot and one of the technicians who worked on the planes asking her out, both of whom she'd refused. Pam had told her she'd already been christened 'the ice maiden' in some quarters, but that didn't concern her. In fact, she welcomed it.

As she stepped out of the building the heat wrapped round her like a stifling blanket. It was October now, and although the temperature in the day was still in the high eighties, the nights were cooler than when she had first arrived. She walked across the dusty compound to the admin office and as luck would have it, it was Mildred on duty.

Mildred looked up as she entered, smiling and saying, 'Oh, it's you. Pleased you won't be kicking your heels most of the time when he's not here, I bet. Well, I've got a supplies pick-up today – you'll need to take one of the trucks and a couple of Achmed's boys with you – and tomorrow there's a longer journey if you're up for it. We've got a house in Alexandria that's been taken over as a leave centre for WAAF in the Cairo area and it has to be checked every two weeks. I'll give you the details tomorrow. It's a twelve-hour journey and no one likes doing it.' She raised her eyebrows at Gina.

'That's fine. I don't mind.' Anything would be preferable to the last weeks with little to do.

'There's a regular fortnightly convoy making the eighty-mile trip to a maintenance unit near Alexandria from our camp, so we always go with them. The MT officer, Warrant Officer Proby, drives the first lorry and the other drivers are German prisoners of war. You'll wait while they do whatever it is they do at the maintenance unit and then all drive on to the house. They bunk down in a converted building in the grounds and you stay in the house for the night, then make the return journey the next day with them. OK?'

Gina hesitated. 'German POWs?'

'Oh, they're fine,' said Mildred airily. 'They're accompanied by guards, of course, although they're not really needed, the guards I mean. The drivers they choose are all hand-picked and chosen for their cooperation as much as the driving and the work they do at the unit.'

'Right.' She had seen a number of German POWs since she had been at the camp, one or two helping the RAF technicians working on a couple of German Junkers 52s that had been brought in among other things. They all seemed very stiff and correct and unsmiling but not hostile, and although they were contained in a secure unit at night, in the day their guard was minimal. If there was one quality they seemed to share it was resignation.

Anyway, there would be no reason for her to come into contact with any of the POWs, she told herself as she left the office and made her way towards one of the RAF trucks in the distance, the keys of which Mildred had given her. And that was tomorrow anyway. For now she had a couple of Achmed's boys to control, and if they were anything like they usually were, she would need all her wits about her.

The next morning she reported to Warrant Officer Proby, a tall thin-faced man in his late forties, and was already sitting in the cab of the truck when the German POWs were marched into view. The four men were all young – even the oldest appeared no more than twenty-five or so, and the youngest only about eighteen with a baby face and a shock of fair hair. It was as they walked past her truck that one of them glanced at the cab and their gaze met. The piercing blue eyes in the tanned face held hers for a moment and then he was gone, but she was left reeling internally from the contact with a gaze that had all the warmth of frozen seawater. She couldn't have said whether he was tall or short, thin or fat, good-looking or ugly, but his eyes were unforgettable and coldly beautiful. She shivered suddenly, even though the inside of the cab was sweltering.

She was glad once the convoy got on its way and she had to concentrate on her driving. She had been warned that the journey would be exhausting, slow and unpleasant on the gravelly desert roads with big potholes and other hazards, and this was true, but she found the landscape had its own beauty too. High dunes and low ones, sand drifts and sand shadows, and smooth rippling yellowy beige sand coating whatever it could. She supposed to the men and women who did this journey often it was just something to endure and get through, but in the desert, of all places, beauty was in the eye of the beholder, she reflected. Even the blinding sunshine, hot and white, had its place. However, by the time they reached halfway on the journey she was glad when the convoy halted at what the warrant officer had described before the trip as Ali's pub. In truth, the building was nothing more than a wooden hut where a wrinkled, toothless old Arab sold warm beer and lemonade.

She climbed gratefully out of her truck and joined the others, accepting a drink from the warrant officer with heartfelt thanks. He grinned. 'The first time you make this journey is always the worst, but imagine what it was like in days gone past when slaves of the ancient Egyptians were herded in human caravans for mile upon mile.'

'I can't.' She shook her head and took a long gulp of the warm and somewhat flat shandy. It tasted like the nectar of the gods. 'It's too awful.'

'Aye, well, that's man's inhumanity to man for you.' He cast a hard glance at the group of POWs drinking their beers some distance away, silent and heads down. 'But them Egyptians were nothing compared to the Nazis, and they call themselves civilized and the master race. I hope the lot of 'em burn in hell.' The warrant officer had lost his two brothers in the war, and his wife and one of his children had been killed when a bomb had scored a direct hit on their air-raid shelter.

Gina said nothing. She had the feeling the POWs could understand every word although they just continued to sip their beers without looking up or glancing around.

'What they found in the Majdenek concentration camp in Poland in August beggars belief. Prisoners from all over Europe, one and a half million they reckon, gassed to death, their bodies stripped of all possessions and then burned to ashes. They say the clothing and valuables were sent to Mother Germany and the ashes used as fertilizer. Children, babies, they didn't care.' The warrant officer took a shuddering breath and brought a packet of cigarettes out of his pocket, offering Gina one and then lighting his. He took a deep drag, shutting his eyes for a moment and then blowing smoke out through his nostrils. 'Sorry,' he said. 'I didn't mean to go on.'

'It's all right.'

'We do the right thing, abide by the Geneva Convention

and the rest of it and them devils are cocking a snook at us, laughing at us they are.'

'I don't think all Germans are like the ones in charge of the death camps and so on,' Gina said quietly.

'No? Well, you've got more faith in 'em than I have, I tell you straight.' He slugged back the last of his beer, wiping his mouth on the back of his hand, and as he did so Gina happened to look up and find that same pair of piercing blue eyes fixed on her. She froze, this time taking in that the man in question was tall and lean with hollowed-out cheeks and hair the colour of the desert sand. His gaze dropped almost immediately and he half-turned but she continued to stare for a moment or two more, unnerved again by the encounter.

The warrant officer had noticed nothing and after another two drags on his cigarette he said, 'If you need to go it's behind there,' nodding towards a matting fence a short way from the hut. 'Just a pit in the sand but we've still got a long journey in front of us.'

Gina swallowed hard. She had seen some of the men disappear behind the rickety fence and emerge again and had half-guessed it was the only toilet facility, but having it confirmed was dismaying. She had imagined her days in the WAAF had hardened her to all things intimate, but being the only woman in this small company of men was something else. Highly embarrassed, she murmured, 'I'll – I'll be all right.'

'You won't,' he said flatly. 'Go on, I'll make sure you're not disturbed.'

Feeling as though umpteen pairs of eyes were boring into the back of her head, she handed the warrant officer her empty glass and walked towards the matting fence. It was worse than she could have guessed behind it, smelly, with so many flies buzzing that the air was black with them, but she would never hold her bladder until they reached their ultimate destination. Telling herself not to think about it she did the necessary, her cheeks burning with more than the sun's heat when she emerged again. Mercifully, not one of the men looked at her as she walked to her truck and climbed into her cab, and within a few minutes the convoy moved off. She could see why the other WAAFs didn't want to do this duty, she thought ruefully as the vehicles rumbled and bumped along. Mildred hadn't mentioned this last little nicety to her.

By the time they had stopped at the maintenance unit and then carried on to the house in Alexandria it was late evening. The men disappeared to their quarters in the grounds of the house and she was met by a small Egyptian woman who was apparently the housekeeper and had a meal waiting for her. What the men ate she wasn't sure, probably RAF rations. She had a quick bath in lukewarm water and washed her hair with the bar of soap she had brought with her, and then went downstairs to eat, feeling completely drained. The meal was simple but filling, and afterwards she worked through the checklist Mildred had given her. There were no other WAAFs staying at the house at the moment, but some would be arriving within a day or so.

The six-bedroom house was surprisingly airy and cool, surrounded by a generous amount of land all enclosed by a high fence. From the bedroom windows the grounds at the back appeared something of a wilderness and she couldn't see the men's quarters, but to the sides of the building and in front there were flower beds and palm trees and a couple of fountains tinkling away. It was very pleasant, an oasis, and Gina could see why the RAF had seconded it for the airwomen's use as a leave centre.

It was past midnight when she finally got into bed in the smallest of the bedrooms. The cotton sheets were crisp and white, and the mosquito nets shrouded the bed in protection, but an hour later she was still wide awake. Her body felt tired from the strain of the journey but her mind was racing – although she wasn't quite sure why. After another ten minutes she gave up the battle for sleep and slid out of bed, stuffing her feet in the fluffy mule slippers which had been a present from Kitty and looked somewhat incongruous with the severely mannish service pyjamas. Padding downstairs to the kitchen, she made herself a cup of coffee and then decided to drink it outside, opening the front door and stepping out into the cool air.

It was a moonless night, but the brilliance of the stars in the indigo sky made shadows sway and move in the slight breeze as she stood for a moment in the scented garden. It was so very different to England and anything she had known before, she thought, drinking in the heady perfume of bougainvillea and a hundred sweet blossoms she didn't know the name of. So very different to the camp, if it came to that. Even the stars seemed alien – brighter, more dazzling and radiant. She breathed deeply, and then as the tinkling of the fountain permeated the stillness she wandered away from the house, the smell of the coffee mingling perfectly with the scents of the garden.

It was as she reached the stone fountain that a shadow beside it moved, causing her to start and almost scream. Coffee slopped down her pyjamas but in the next moment a deep voice said, 'Do not be frightened, you are quite safe, *Fräulein*.'

She froze, and it was only afterwards that it dawned on her it would have been more sensible to run back to the house. 'Wh-what are you doing here?'

'Enjoying the night air.'

As the man stood to his feet she realized it was the same POW who had so unsettled her in the day. Now he was so close she realized he was six foot or more, his chiselled features and blond hair very Aryan.

'Are you allowed to be out here by yourself?' she asked shakily.

He shrugged. 'Of course not.'

'Oh.' She stared at him, taken aback. He smiled, and she drew in a breath at the way it transformed the stern, rather aristocratic face.

'I promise you I will not try to run away,' he said with grave humour. 'Where would I go?'

'You shouldn't be wandering about, though.'

'I am not wandering.'

This was true but it was hardly the point.

'I wanted to smell the air and see the sky,' he said gently. 'That was all.'

Now the initial shock was over she found she wasn't frightened which was strange, all things considered. He was the enemy, after all. She frowned. 'How did you leave your quarters without anyone seeing you?' Someone had slipped up somewhere.

'Everyone had fallen asleep.' He spoke perfect English but with a marked accent. 'Including the guard on the door. I simply walked out.' He smiled again. 'This is very bad, yes?'

'Well, yes.'

'But I will return shortly and then all will be well, unless you wish to inform the warrant officer of my escape? I think he would be very pleased of an excuse to shoot me.'

She ignored this. 'I'm sure if you were going to escape you would have done so straight away,' she said matter-of-factly, 'rather than sitting in the garden.'

'This is true.' He nodded seriously, but she had the feeling he was laughing at her. And then he said softly, 'Have you noticed the stars, how they shine? If they could speak, what would they say when they look down at the world and what is happening?'

Again she was totally taken aback. She had realized he had been sitting on a small stone bench to one side of the fountain and now she sat down herself, even though she knew she shouldn't. 'I think they would say they are very sad.'

'I agree.' He looked down at her. 'May I?' he asked, indicating the space beside her, and when she nodded he sat down carefully, making sure their bodies did not come into contact. 'Yes, they would be sad,' he said quietly.

'Are you? Sad about the war and everything, I mean?' She had no idea why she was talking like this with a man she didn't know and who was a German to boot, but ridiculously, it seemed perfectly natural.

He didn't answer this directly. What he did say was, 'My country has been destroyed from the inside out and is in the grip of something so terrible, so evil, that I find it incomprehensible.'

'But—' She hesitated.

'Yes?'

'If you feel like that why did you fight for Hitler? You must have believed what the Nazis were doing was right, surely?'

He sat without speaking for some twenty seconds or so. And then he turned and looked at her. Even in the shadowed night his eyes pierced her, their blueness almost black in the darkness and his stern mouth tight. And then his face relaxed as he shook his head. 'It is difficult to explain.'

'Please try.' Even as she said it, she wondered why it was so important that she understood.

'I will need to start at the beginning and it will be a long story. You must have your sleep, *Fräulein*.'

'No, I want to hear.' She felt it was crucial, the most important thing in her life that she heard what he had to say – which like everything in this crazy scenario made no sense at all.

'I am twenty-three years old and when I was thirteen what can only be described as an extraordinary series of social and political events took place in my country,' he said quietly, leaning forward now with his hands on his knees and staring at the ground. 'With the death of Paul von Hindenburg, our president, Adolf Hitler became Führer and the Third Reich was conceived. The Führer acted quickly to seize total power, appointing loyal men to various positions within his new government and replacing all labour unions with the Nazi-controlled Deutsche Arbeitsfront, the German Labour Front,' he explained quickly. 'In addition to this, the Führer outlawed all other political organizations and soon the press, the economy and all activities of a cultural nature were placed under Nazi authority. Can you understand what that meant?'

He raised his head and as he looked at her she swallowed hard, finally accepting that she found this German who was the enemy of her country the most attractive man she had ever met. It wasn't that he was particularly good-looking – there were dozens of men on the base who were far more handsome than he was – but there was something about him, something indefinable that drew her like a magnet.

'No, I can't understand what that meant,' she said, after a moment when she had to clear her throat.

'It meant that one's livelihood depended on absolute

political loyalty to the Führer, particularly those who were wealthy or had influence. Anti-Nazis were rounded up and transported to concentration camps where most of them received the death sentence. A massive propaganda campaign finished democracy in my country and at the same time huge specially staged rallies took place. Everyone supported the Führer, or at least that was how it seemed to me as a boy at that time. My father and mother had suffered like many German families as a consequence of the First World War, and at first they were excited about this new order. The name Hitler was mentioned many times in our home and my sister, Kirsten, and I were told the Führer's vision and that what he offered by the way of prosperity would mean a better standard of living. We were not poor – we lived in a nice house in the Mitte district of Berlin and my father was an architect – but I suppose it is human nature to always want a bigger house, a bigger car, more money, yes?'

'Yes, I suppose so.' She was fascinated by what he was saying, her coffee stone cold. 'People are rarely satisfied with what they have.'

'This is so.' He inclined his head in a short sharp nod and for a second he was very German. 'There were many working-class ordinary Germans who blamed Jews for the unemployment and poverty that existed after 1920. This was because they had been listening to the Führer. He exploited their fears to further himself politically, although as my father said, many factories, workhouses and businesses in the streets *were* under Jewish ownership.

When men lost their jobs they blamed their Jewish bosses, and the Nazis took advantage of this. At my school Jewish children became the subject of ridicule and violence from some of the other pupils, and we were not allowed to talk to them as our teachers insisted it was forbidden.'

He raked back a lock of his blond hair from his forehead in what was almost a despairing movement, obviously remembering things he would rather forget. Softly, she said, 'Did you feel like that about the Jews?'

'My father and his partner employed a Jewish assistant, Wolfgang, and his children were the same ages as myself and my sister. We had grown up with them and enjoyed meals at their house and they at ours, that kind of thing. Their being Jewish did not register on myself and Kirsten. Otto and Hannah were our friends and as much a part of our family as our cousins, I think. They spoke no Yiddish or Hebrew and religion was never discussed. The family were not devout and they seemed just like us.' He paused. 'Of course, they *were* just like us,' he said quietly, 'but they were also Jewish. Within a few months of the Führer's rise to power my father was told to dismiss Wolfgang from his service. Kirsten and I were told not to talk to Otto and Hannah and forbidden to mention the family again. We were respectful children, we obeyed our father without question.'

He leaned forward, his head drooping. For a brief moment she had the urge to reach out and put a hand on his shoulder. It shocked her so much she almost got up and went back to the house. Almost.

'One day at school a group of girls singled out a Jewish girl, pulling her hair and tearing her clothes and slapping her. As she lay crying on the ground they spat at her and shouted "*Jüdin*," over and over. The Jewish girl was Hannah and my sister was one of the girls who tormented her. When I found out, I asked my sister if this was true. She said, but of course, as though it was nothing.' He shook his head. 'Kirsten was a good Aryan child, you see.'

He stood up, letting the water from the fountain trickle through his fingers, his back to her. 'You have no idea of what it was like in my country at this time, the encouragement of hatred towards anything Jewish.'

She didn't know what to say. Sitting here in this quiet perfumed air, with the peace of the Egyptian night surrounding them, made what he was saying all the more terrible somehow. How could such things have been allowed to happen? And worse, much worse. With the dictatorial control of the Third Reich in place, even children like this man and his sister had been had become victims of Nazi propaganda and ideology.

'I told my parents what had happened and I could see that they were shocked and upset, but they dared not take Hannah to task in case she said something about it at school. Jewish sympathizers had a way of disappearing suddenly.'

He sat down beside her again but as before was very careful not to touch her. 'I, like all the boys I knew, was a member of the Jugend by this time, of course, the Hitler

Youth. It was expected. But we boys did not object. It was exciting with the sports and comradeship and military emphasis, but of course we did not realize that the youth were to prove such an important factor within the social fabric of Hitler's new Germany. How could we? In the beginning much of what the Führer was offering appeared attractive and exhilarating. I remember a Sunday in September in 1936 when I was fifteen years old and the ceremony of the Hitler Youth was held in Nuremberg. Thousands came from all over the Reich to attend, and starting from the early hours of the morning huge columns of boys and girls marched into the stadium like soldiers. Kirsten had joined the Jung Mädel by then and she also marched that day. This she enjoyed very much. Too much, I think. It was a warm day and the girls wore their uniform of white blouse, black tie and navy-blue skirt, each regiment wearing the cloth arm patch of its particular borough of origin, stating the town or city. The photographers there concentrated on the girls that day but everyone, even the foreign press, was saying that nowhere else in Europe could boast of creating such an admirable institution as the Hitler Youth. The sheer discipline and strength were outstanding.'

He turned to her. 'Can you imagine how it felt to be part of such an organization? The pride that we as young people experienced? The feeling of oneship? It was—' He paused, murmuring, 'What is the word?' Then he said, 'Ah, yes, intoxicating. It was intoxicating.' He made a sound in his throat, a harsh sound, before whispering almost to himself, 'Such manipulation of innocent minds, such brilliant exploitation.'

For more than a minute they sat in complete silence. His stern profile could have been that of a man three times his age. Gina didn't know what to say – she felt at a complete loss – but when the silence became unbearable she said quietly, 'You speak very good English.'

'Yes, this is so.' Her words brought him out of the reverie he'd fallen into. 'My father made sure I had an excellent education.'

'Kirsten too?'

'Not in the same way, no. My father was of the opinion that women are unable to think logically or reason objectively and are governed by their emotions. In his view Kirsten was destined to be a wife and mother. This fitted perfectly with the Führer's opinion on such matters. Before the Nazis came to power women in my country had the vote and there were thirty female Members of Parliament. The Führer threw out all the women MPs, removed women from clinical practices, positions within the civil service and the teaching profession. They were also banned from law courts as judges, lawyers and even jurors.'

Gina sat bolt upright. 'But that's archaic. Surely they objected, the women I mean?'

He sighed. 'The issue of male supremacy and domination over women in the Third Reich was very clear, and therefore the standing of young males and men as masters was never questionable. Perhaps some women objected,

I do not know. All I *do* know is that for most women and young girls their destiny was to form one half of the gene pool of the Aryan Race and fulfil their role as child-bearers. Mothers of large families were given financial benefits and awards, and could earn themselves an audience with the Führer himself for producing children for the state.'

'But that makes girls and women second-class citizens. Didn't they *see* that?'

He shrugged. 'I can only speak for Kirsten and she did not. Her time was divided between going to school, coming home and helping my mother and learning how to run a home and, most importantly, being part of the Jung Mädel and later the Bund Deutscher Mädel for older girls. Kirsten is very fair-haired and has blue eyes and a milk-white skin – she was told she was special on numerous occasions, a perfect German maiden, and this she liked very much. The strict regime of the Jung Mädel with hard physical exercise and political commitment seemed made for her – she was an excellent athlete and took place in the Youth Olympiad in Tokyo. Her proficiency was quite outstanding in many respects. She earned many medallions and awards. The Jung Mädel was her real family, I see this now. She embroidered a – how you say – a picture, a . . .'

'A tapestry?'

'Yes, just so, a tapestry, and hung it above her bed. It was the motto of the organization, "Be faithful, be pure, be German". Our maidens were called upon to be beautiful, supple, radiant, strong and athletically graceful, and to regard Jews, Slavs and Gypsies as subhuman and grotesquely inferior.'

Somewhere in the distance a dog barked. He turned his head and looked at her, his fair hair a halo in the shadows. 'This new order, it is hard to explain how it was to someone who has not grown up under it. We were told as youngsters that the Jew was a kind of monster who would destroy us if we did not force him out of our homeland, and the films we were shown, the books we were told to study, covered a whole range of anti-Semitic issues. The Führer's *Mein Kampf* became the Hitler Youth bible. Even then I found this hard to reconcile with the memories I had of Wolfgang and his family, but I had no one to speak to of my misgivings. Nonconformity was not an option. Kirsten and I were now group leaders within our respective organizations; she embraced this wholeheartedly, I less so. My intellect was already rebelling against what I was asked to accept as 'normal'. Unbeknown to me, my parents, especially my father, were becoming disillusioned with what Nazism really meant, the hate-filled orations, the brutality and blind allegiance to the Führer, the systematic and insidious influence and re-education the Hitler Youth organizations had over their members, which purposely took the place of parental authority. My father and my mother kept this to themselves, though – it was too dangerous to speak of, even in their own home, or perhaps especially in their own home. By now, at the outbreak of the war, Kirsten was

– what is the word – ah, yes, betrothed to a high-ranking Nazi officer in the SS. She was eager to embrace the Nazi regime which celebrated female domesticity and rewarded prolific childbirth.'

He paused. 'But I am boring you with this talk of myself and my family, *Fräulein*. This is rude of me, yes?'

'No, no, of course not,' she said quickly, probably too quickly, she acknowledged uncomfortably, but she wanted to understand all there was to know about Nazi Germany. Immediately her conscience smote her. Nazi Germany? a little voice in her mind probed. Nazi Germany be blowed. It's him you want to understand.

He stood up, and for a moment Gina thought he was going to walk away. Instead he said softly. 'I have been remiss. I have not introduced myself, *Fräulein*. My name is Josef Vetter and I am at your service.' He clicked his heels together as he spoke and bowed his head once in a sharp movement.

She hesitated for a moment. She could feel the colour hot in her cheeks and hoped the darkness hid it. 'Gina,' she said, willing her voice not to tremble. 'Gina Redfern.'

'Gina.' He smiled and her heart thudded. 'This name suits you, I think. Yes, it is a good name.'

'Thank you.' She didn't know what else to say. 'I think Josef is a nice name too.'

There was a quirk to his lips as he said politely, 'Thank you,' in return, before sitting down beside her again. 'It is my father's name, and his father's before him. This is the way in England too?'

'Sometimes.'

'And with you perhaps? Gina is your mother's name?'

She froze, and she knew he must have noticed her body's immediate reaction because when he next spoke his voice was stiffly formal as he said, 'Forgive me, *Fräulein*. I did not intend to take liberties. I will leave you now.'

'No.' Her hand went out to restrain him and stopped in mid-air. 'No, I'm sorry, it isn't that. Really.'

He had half-risen but now sank back on the stone bench. Quickly she said, 'It's just that I never knew my real mother and I have no idea what her name was. She – she gave me to a family before she died, that's all I know.' Part of her couldn't believe she had just told him that, something she hadn't confided to her closest friends. 'They, this family, put me in—' She couldn't bring herself to say the workhouse even though being German he might not be aware of the stigma attached to such places – she had no idea if they had workhouses in his country. So instead she said, 'In an institution when I was nearly six years old. Until then I thought they were my real parents.'

He was visibly shocked. She didn't know what she had expected him to say, but when he spoke his voice was warm and soft, the somewhat clipped, cold intonation completely absent. 'That was cruel beyond belief. You have suffered greatly, Gina. May I call you Gina?'

She nodded, unable to speak for the lump in her throat.

'There is a saying in my country that does not translate well into English but basically it's that suffering and pain bring forth character. It is commended as a good thing. I do not believe this is so all the time although it would be comfortable to think so. I think suffering and pain can break a person and what remains becomes a hard core that can blight and cripple a life. This is not the case with you.'

Surprise caused her eyes to open wider. 'What makes you say that?' He didn't know her from Adam.

'Because the eyes are the window of the soul and your soul is still gentle and forgiving.'

She stared at him. His words had utterly amazed her. Nothing about him was what she would have expected from a German, a Nazi, the enemy. She drew a deep breath and for a moment wished she had never sat down and talked to him this night, and then in the next breath knew that she was glad whatever the outcome.

Somehow she managed to say, 'You can't know that.'

'I disagree.'

'But how? I mean, how do you know?'

'Because I have sadly seen the other side to this particular coin, yes? With the hardening of one's soul comes a deadness in the eyes. It is a great tragedy, the more so if the pain and suffering were undeserved.'

She shook her head, lowering her gaze. 'I'm not as saintly as you make out.'

'Did I give the impression I thought you were saintly? Then forgive me. I did not mean to and I do not think you are a saint, Gina Redfern.'

She heard the smile in his voice and it was there on

his face when she looked up. In spite of herself she smiled back and then they both laughed softly. It was in that moment that she knew things would never be the same again.

Chapter Nineteen

Dawn was breaking when she finally went back inside the house; they had talked the whole night away. She had told Josef about her childhood before and after the cottage homes, about the farm, her brothers, James who she had thought to be her twin, her mother whom she'd adored and her father whom she'd hated.

His brow had wrinkled when she had related the happenings of the night she had been taken from the farm by her father. 'But how do you know that your mother wished for you to leave?' He had shaken his head. 'This does not make sense with the woman you have described. It does not ring true to me. With the man you thought to be your father, yes. I can see he would do such a thing, but not her.'

'She didn't come and find me though, did she,' she'd argued.

He had continued to stare at her, his face troubled. 'Perhaps she tried but did not look in the right place.'

'You mean he didn't tell her where he'd taken me?'

'I do not know what I mean, only that love such as this woman displayed to you cannot be cut off so abruptly.'

She hadn't wanted to pursue this and had moved on with her story, but once back in the house his words had returned to her as she made herself breakfast. She worried at it like a dog with a bone before putting it out of her mind. She couldn't allow herself to go down that road, to hope, and it really didn't matter after all this time. The past was the past, and furthermore she was a different person now. She had no way of knowing what was true and what wasn't and she never would, and to open up the old wounds was too agonizing. Even now. Which gave the lie to the fact that it didn't matter.

Suddenly cross with herself, she growled, 'Stop it, just stop it,' and carried the bowl of fresh fruit over to the window where she ate it, gazing out of the window and refusing to think about anything at all. That didn't last long. Josef Vetter wouldn't let it.

She groaned to herself as she plonked down in a chair. She liked him. She liked him very much. Josef Vetter, a Luftwaffe pilot who had probably shot down a number of her own countrymen. But he wasn't a Nazi, not from what he had told her, and she believed every word. Which was strange, because she couldn't think of another man she would trust apart from maybe the CO.

Josef had told her about his privileged childhood during which certainly, in his very young days, he had been cocooned in a small elite world where the things happening outside it had made no impact on him. The Hitler Jugend for boys had been in existence since 1926 and in creating his youth movement, Hitler had viewed himself as the architect of a new generation of German boys and girls, from the very young to those in their teens. But Josef had said that at first things had been much more low key. It had been during the mid-1930s, when the Führer had defiantly crowed to the outside world the pride he had for his youth, that it had become more apparent to Josef that all was not as it seemed. He'd repeated to her the Führer's boast at a rally: 'The youth who graduate from my academies will terrify the world.' At the time this coincided with programmes to mobilize his workers and re-arm Germany, and the plans he'd put into effect to rid the Fatherland of undesirable racial elements by introducing discriminatory laws against Jews, Gypsies, Communists, Jehovah's Witnesses and anyone with a black or brown skin.

'I confess I tried to ignore my misgivings,' Josef had told her quietly. 'We were told that as good German boys and girls we had certain obligations to fulfil for our country and must obey the new German order in the name of Adolf Hitler, our Führer, without question. I was not anti-Jewish – how could I be when for a large part of my childhood I had called Wolfgang and his wife aunt and uncle, and played with their children as part of my family? But I obeyed the new edicts and while I would not have physically harmed anyone regardless of their race or religion, nor did I speak out against such things.'

'But you were just a boy,' she had protested. 'It must have all been frightening and confusing.'

'I was aware that the veneer of civilization that keeps hatred and prejudice at bay had been stripped away, that is for sure. Gangs of Nazi thugs owned the streets in Berlin. They drove around in trucks, flashing their guns and their swastika armbands and hooting at pretty girls. If they wanted to pick one of the "undesirables" up and beat them senseless they did so with impunity. Anyone who resisted them was beaten or killed or taken away to Dachau or Buchenwald or some other concentration camp. Looking back, I can see that my father was getting increasingly worried about the Nazi regime. One of our neighbours was reported to the authorities as having illicit books in his house, books that were not in line with the Führer's ideology in other words, and music written by Jewish composers and playwrights such as Mendelssohn and Reinhardt. Their house was searched by the Gestapo and Hans and his wife were taken to Stuttgart. That was the last we saw of them. For days my father would suddenly say, "For a few books and some music, for a few books and some music." He hoped they would come home after being questioned but this was not to be.'

After joining the Luftwaffe he had told her he was rarely home on leave, but Kirsten had married her SS officer and lived close by. 'I felt comfort from this. I thought she would take care of our parents.'

He had stopped here, and the look on his face had made her say, 'What is it? Did something happen to them?'

'They had been to the cinema and saw a *Wochenschau* – a newsreel – of Jews being herded into a camp. "These people are murderers," said the announcer. "Murderers finally meeting with the punishment they deserve." To my parents' horror they recognized Wolfgang among the prisoners. The next day Kirsten came to visit for an hour with her little ones. My father told her what they had seen. He made the mistake of saying Wolfgang was not a murderer, that he was a good man. Kirsten told this to her husband. The Gestapo came in the middle of the night and my parents were taken to a death camp.'

She had drawn in a shocked breath. 'She can't have expected her husband to do what he did? She must have been filled with remorse.'

'This is not so. When I found out, I obtained a twenty-four-hour leave and went to see her at her home. She was not, as you say, remorseful and it became clear she had known exactly what she was doing. She was—' He had shaken his head, his long, finely boned hands clasped together, the knuckles showing white. 'She was proud, I think. Yes, proud. She talked about the greatness of the Führer, of what a fine man he was. A lover of little children, a patron of the arts, and the future that lay ahead for Germany because of his inspired leadership. World domination. Had I seen the newsreels of Hitler marching triumphantly through those countries he'd taken? What glorious days lay ahead when we would finally enjoy world leadership which the demonic Jews had snatched from us in the past with their duplicity and cunning. I looked at her, at her chubby little fair-haired boy and the pale-skinned baby in her pram, and I knew I no longer had a sister or nephew or niece. My family was gone, destroyed. I walked out of the house and the next day I made sure I was shot down. I wanted to die, to join my parents in whatever is beyond this world. Of course, we do not always get what we want, or deserve.'

Rising from the chair, Gina made herself a cup of coffee which she drank black and strong even though, funnily enough, she didn't feel tired after her sleepless night. Confused and torn by her feelings certainly, but not tired. In fact, she had never felt so wide awake. When they had parted, as the first tentative rays of an Egyptian dawn had begun to steal across the dark sky, there had been no mention of their conversing again. He had clicked his heels together, lowering his head in the short nod she'd seen before and making no effort to touch her as he had said, 'Thank you for your company, *Fräulein*.'

She had wondered for a moment where the 'Gina' had gone to but had just said quietly, 'Thank you for yours, Josef.'

The piercing eyes had travelled over her face and for a moment she had thought he was going to say more, but then he had turned and walked away. That last look had made her tremble inside. She shook her head at herself now, despair warring with the desire to see him again even though it had only been an hour or so since he'd left her. She knew why he had returned to such cool formality in that last minute or so, of course. He was a

German POW and she was an English WAAF; a friendship between them was impossible. She remembered the bad feeling in the Channel Islands after they were invaded four years ago and some of the impressionable girls there went out with German soldiers, attracted by their good looks and generosity. The girls were dubbed 'Jerrybags' by other islanders and had suffered abuse and ostracism, which she could completely understand. At the time she had been horrified that nice girls could behave in such a way. But this was different.

Immediately the thought came, she bit her lip. Hark at herself. The main issue was the same. Josef was German and she was English, and their countries were at war. All right, so he had lost faith in Hitler and had never really been a Nazi from what she could make out, not in any real sense, but the fact remained that he had flown in the Luftwaffe and bombed her countrymen. Or tried to. Whether he'd actually killed anyone they hadn't got on to.

Stop it. Enough thinking. She finished the last drop of coffee and washed up the breakfast things angrily, annoyed at herself and the position she found herself in. It was her own fault. She nodded at the thought as she got dressed. Totally her own fault. She should have gone back into the house the moment she realized he was one of the POWs – any sane sensible woman would have done just that. What had she been thinking? She must have been mad. Thank goodness he clearly wasn't going to make anything of the hours they'd spent together; his last words to her had been evidence of that. He probably didn't even like her, as a woman, that was. And then she recalled the look in his eyes before he had walked away and her heart jumped in her chest.

The journey back to camp was without incident. The drivers had all been waiting in their trucks when she had joined them and she had purposely not looked for Josef, climbing into her vehicle after a brief 'Good morning' to the warrant officer. When they reached the halfway house of Ali's so-called pub, she made her visit to the foul little pit before accepting the shandy the warrant officer bought her and taking it back to her cab to drink. She looked neither to the right nor to the left, but nevertheless she knew exactly where Josef was standing drinking his beer.

All the way back she studiously kept her mind on her driving, fighting the darts about the night before that her mind threw at her if she relaxed for a moment. After parking the truck she made her way to the administration office, where Mildred greeted her like a hero returning from battle.

'How was it?' she asked sympathetically. 'Rotten assignment by all accounts but you've done your stint now. I'll get someone else to do the next one if I can, OK?'

She didn't have to think about her reply. It had been there all the time on the way back to camp, she realized, as she said, 'I enjoyed it, actually, makes a nice change from the normal run of things. And I'd be happy to do it as long as I'm here and the CO doesn't need me for anything.'

'Really?' Mildred looked surprised but delighted. 'Thanks, that's great. I'll take you up on it if you're sure.'

'Quite sure.' And she was.

Josef had watched her as she had walked across to the office, and it was only when the door closed behind her that he turned away. She had not looked at him once today, not even a glance. He would have known – he had not been able to take his eyes off her. But this was good, that she felt nothing for him, that she could dismiss him so easily. Anything else would be dangerous for her. He understood that – with his head. His heart, he was finding, was a different matter.

Later that night in his bunk, he lay with his hands behind his head, wide awake as his fellow POWs snored around him. They were a nice enough bunch on the whole, he reflected, Luftwaffe pilots like him who had only really wanted to fly their planes, the war coming second to the joy of being in the air. There was one man, Werner Felgentreu, who he did not like, however. He glanced across the dark room to where the man was sleeping. Werner was committed to Nazism in its every possible form and even now did not believe that the Fatherland would lose the war. He was saturated with Nazi politics and ethos and believed that one day the Germanic Aryan race would inherit the earth. It was his attitude to women that really caught Josef on the raw, though. Even German maidens Werner regarded as chattels, fit only to satisfy men's lust and produce children for the Fatherland, and as for those from different nations, his language and crudity regarding them had made others besides himself take the man to task. And he had seen Werner watching Gina today, seen what was in the man's face.

His hands clenched into fists and he moved his arms down by his side; otherwise he lay still and stiff, years of military training enabling him to control himself when what he really wanted to do was to fly across the room and take Werner by the throat. He smiled grimly. Perhaps this woman was accomplishing what even Kirsten's betrayal had failed to do and was sending him mad? Certainly it was madness to feel the way he did about her, something he was sure she would not want. She had been kind to him, that was all. It was clear it was her nature to be kind in spite of the wrongs she had suffered as she was growing up.

He shut his eyes, willing himself to relax, but the image of Gina was too clear on the screen of his mind, producing feelings he could well have done without. He had slept with three girls in his life, one a childhood sweetheart whose family had moved away when she and he were seventeen years old. The night before she had left Mitte they had consummated what they had seen as their great love, but within a very short time their letters to each other had become spasmodic before dwindling away altogether. The other two women had been brief affairs, brought about by the war and the need to make the most of every minute as much as anything else. He liked women and he had been attracted to many in his time, but he had never experienced anything like the bolt of lightning that had hit him when he saw Gina. His logic told him love at first sight was a myth put out by poets and writers of women's magazines; how could you fall in love with someone without knowing the first thing about them? Instant attraction perhaps, though that was an entirely different thing. But then he had talked to her.

He groaned deep in his throat, turning on his side and telling himself to go to sleep. He had been awake for over twenty-four hours now and he was exhausted, but only in his body. His mind he didn't seem able to shut down.

He lay there, willing his breathing to become deep and steady, but still his mind was uncharacteristically chaotic. His imagination played images of his parents, how they'd once been, of them terrified in the death camp, and of Kirsten that last day he had seen her, so proud, so obsessed, so full of venom and hatred. Nonconformity had been a very dangerous path to take as he and Kirsten were growing up and he had always excused her enthusiasm for the Führer and the new regime by thinking at bottom she was like him, appearing to go along with Nazism but deep down keeping her inner self untouched by the excesses that had grown more brutal and violent as time had gone on.

Were his sister and her children still alive now? Their last meeting had been in spring the year before and he knew that within months Berlin had sustained a series of relentless heavy raids by the RAF and USAAF. One of his fellow POWs had been fighting in the battle and he had said that while the Luftwaffe had been successful in intercepting the enemy bomber formations by both day and night and inflicting heavy casualties on the attackers, it had taken its toll. Thousands and thousands of high-explosive bombs had set Berlin on fire and he spoke of a pall of smoke hanging over the city which blocked out the light for days on end.

'And still they came,' Franz had said grimly. 'Over and over again, they were unstoppable. There was not one part of the city that escaped the bombs.'

If Kirsten had been killed, he would not grieve for the person she had become, but for the little girl he had played with as a young child, he told himself. And for her little ones, yes, he would grieve for them until the day he died, little Robert with his chubby dimpled knees and the baby, Bärbl, so tiny and perfect. He did not wonder if his parents were alive. He knew they were not. He felt it in his bones.

He must have drifted off to sleep eventually, because when he awoke with a start some time later it was from a dream so vivid that for some moments he could not reconcile where he was. It had been a beautiful summer's day in the dream, hot but not like the intense heat of Egypt. He and Gina had been walking in a lush, gold-toned landscape, like the paintings by Schmid-Fichtelberg or Herman Urban that his mother had loved because they made Germany look like the Elysian Fields. They had been holding hands, and she had been wearing a soft, colourful dress; her hair had been longer than it was now, flowing down her back in rich waves and curls.

'Look up into the sky,' he had said to her, and it had been a deep clear cornflower blue. 'You see those birds swooping and gliding with not a care in the world? They are glad because they are free, free to go where they please and do what they want to do. They are not hampered by what man thinks of them, of being conformed to a pattern. Fly with me, Gina. Fly away with me now.'

He had begun to run, pulling her with him, and the next moment they had risen into the sky, soaring over the fields of gold, over rooftops and rivers and farmsteads and on still, until they reached the rich blue of the ocean.

And then he had woken up.

Chapter Twenty

During the next months, Gina found herself existing from one visit to the house in Alexandria to the next. Each time she was there, by unspoken mutual consent, she would go out into the garden once she was sure everyone was asleep, and Josef would be waiting by the fountain. The first time she had done this after their initial meeting she had wondered if he would come, but he had already been sitting on the stone bench and his presence had caused her heart to start hammering so loudly she was sure he must have heard it.

They talked of everything and nothing, of big things and little things, of their pasts and the present – but never the future. She kept nothing back from him which both amazed and terrified her, and after each such encounter told herself she wouldn't be so foolish as to risk another clandestine assignation, although the fact that they never actually arranged to meet meant they could say this in all honesty if they were discovered one night. But come the next time the magnetic pull he exerted had her slipping into the garden, regardless of the danger.

She knew she loved him. It hadn't been a sudden revelation, it was as though from that first night the knowledge
had been there, however much she'd tried to fight it. She
also knew he loved her – it was in his every look, his every
expression although never in his words. How she could
ever have thought his eyes were cold, she didn't know.
Every time they held hers they glowed with such warmth
that she felt weak at the knees. But to speak of their feelings would have let down the barriers that needed to stay
in place, at least until the war was over. And it wasn't over
yet. The CO had told her there was now no doubt the
Germans would be defeated, but still the maniacal rants
of the Führer went on as he refused to accept the inevitable.

Shortly before Christmas she went on the trip that Pam
and Mildred had arranged to see the pyramids. It was
enjoyable, but their time was overshadowed by the death
of Glenn Miller the week before and it was all Pam and
Mildred seemed to talk about. Colonel Miller and two
companions had been on a routine flight to France where
his band had been due to play when the plane had been
lost; no distress call had been heard and no wreckage found.
It seemed impossible that the man who had given the world
'In the Mood' and 'Moonlight Serenade' had died so
suddenly, and in spite of all the bombing and loss of life
and devastation the war had caused, this event touched
everyone, possibly because the band leader's songs had been
such a morale boost in the midst of hardship and suffering.

When Gina got back to camp after the trip, she found
a letter waiting for her. This wasn't particularly unusual;

she corresponded regularly with Kitty and Minnie, the three of them eager to keep in touch. What was unusual was that she didn't recognize the writing and furthermore, it looked as though the letter had been forwarded on several times. From what she could make out, the original address had been the cottage homes, then the hotel where she had worked for a while, followed by the picture house and finally the WAAF, where again it seemed to have done the rounds.

She took the letter back to her room and sat down on the bed, wondering if perhaps Peggy or Ethel or Vera or even the twins had tried to make contact with her. It had to be one of them; no one else apart from Josef knew about her childhood in the workhouse. She stared at the envelope, her stomach churning slightly at being confronted so unexpectedly with the period in her life she had tried to put behind her.

She slipped off her jacket and loosened her tie; the small room was muggy and although the shutters covered the window they did not fit perfectly and small chinks of sunlight filtered through, brilliantly bright. Today was Christmas Eve, but in this land of Allah it didn't feel like it. They'd tried to have fun on the trip, singing carols and songs like 'Mairzy Doats' and 'This is the Army Mr Jones', but most of the time she had been thinking of Josef. The next trip to Alexandria should have been due a couple of days ago, but because of the planned festivities for Christmas it had been put off until the day after Boxing Day. She'd had a hard job hiding her disappointment. She caught glimpses of him now and again but that was all, and even if they passed quite close there was no chance of a few words or even a smile. She knew men like the warrant officer would make Josef's life hell on earth if they caught a whiff of their – albeit platonic – relationship, and she couldn't risk that, besides which the personal driver of a CO consorting with the enemy would go down like a lead balloon.

Running a hand through her short curls, she picked up the envelope again, turning it over once or twice before she told herself to bite the bullet and open the darned thing.

Inside were three sheets of lined notepaper and she could see the writing was big and babyish like the envelope. The first words took her breath away and caused her to drop the letter as though it had burned her: '*My dear bairn*'.

My dear bairn? She had sprung up from the bed and was now standing pressed against the wall, her hand over her mouth and her eyes wide with shock. The blood had rushed to her head and she felt sick and dizzy. For a moment she thought she was going to faint and told herself she mustn't, she mustn't pass out. Gradually the nausea faded, along with the dizziness, but she still couldn't bring herself to move.

Outside, she could hear Achmed scolding one of his boys; this was a regular occurrence umpteen times a day and right now Gina found it reassuring in its normality. After a further few moments she forced herself to walk back to the bed, sit down, and pick up the sheets of paper. Her heart was trying to break out of her chest, thumping so hard it actually hurt, but at least the horrible feeling of faintness had receded.

She had to read this. Whatever this letter contained, she had to read it, she knew that, so she might as well get on with it, she told herself shakily. Smoothing the first sheet of paper out, she took a deep shuddering breath and began to read:

My dear bairn,

I am praying this will reach you in these uncertain times in which we live, and that if it does you will find it in your heart to forgive me. I knew nothing of what my husband did, that is the first thing to say and you must believe me. How could I have suspected such wickedness? Even now I can scarcely believe it. When I think of the grief that sent me half mad but more than that, what you have suffered at his hands, it is a good job he is dead. But I am getting in front of myself here and I must start at the beginning.

When we found you gone the morning after Betty was born Kenneth said you had run away because of her being a girl. We searched far and wide, or at least the lads did. Knowing what I know now I doubt Kenneth did anything. He told me he'd contacted the police and other folk in authority but I think that was a lie. The weather being so bad and the rivers swollen, in time I

*accepted the inevitable, that you had got lost and
perished. But still I prayed every night for a
miracle, that by God's grace he would return you
to me, my precious bairn, the light of my life.*

The tears were blinding her now and she couldn't read
on for some minutes, falling across the bed in a paroxysm
of weeping that could easily have turned into hysterics if
she had let it. Eventually she rolled over and reached for
a handkerchief, drying her hot wet face and blowing her
nose. Her hands were trembling when she picked up the
letter again and nothing existed but the words on the paper:

*Kenneth got ill some months ago, a growth in
his stomach the doctors said. He had a terrible
time of it even with the medicine they gave him to
dull the pain. It was on his deathbed he told me
what he'd done, afraid to meet his Maker with it
on his conscience, I think. I couldn't do what he
wanted and forgive him, lass, I just couldn't. The
loss of you took all the joy out of my life and it's
never come back, he knew that, and to do that to
you, an innocent little bairn. I've been beside
myself thinking of what you must have gone
through after what he did and what he told you.
He was a hard man, stubborn and ruthless at
times, but never would I have believed he was
capable of such evil cruelty.*

Gina shut her eyes for a moment. He *had* been evil and cruel, but then look at what Hitler and his Nazis were doing, the Japanese too. Man's capacity for wickedness was every bit as great as his capacity for good and she had long since stopped seeing the world through rose-coloured glasses – from the age of six, in fact. Picking up the second sheet of paper she read:

It is true, my bairn, that I didn't give birth to you, but in every other respect I am your mam. The bond we had between us was stronger than anything I've ever known and you've always had my heart in a way no one else has. Perhaps that's what Kenneth couldn't stand, I don't know. When you were born you weren't breathing and it was me who got you to take a breath, so in a way you could say I gave you life. That's what I told myself when I kept you anyway, to quieten my conscience maybe. But as to your mam, the lass who gave birth to you, it happened like this. We found her one night in the barn, in the middle of a blizzard it was, but where she came from or what had led her to us I don't know. All she could say was that you were to be called Gina, after her own mother, before she passed away. She was a bonny lass but very young, no more than fifteen I'd say, but nice, a good girl. I feel sure she was sinned against rather than a sinner.

Gina had to stop reading again to wipe the tears from her eyes. '*Sinned against rather than a sinner*'. For a young girl such as her mam had described to turn up at the farm, remote as it was, in such weather, she must have been thrown out by her parents. Or from her place of employment, perhaps? Whatever the case, someone had treated her abominably which had resulted in her losing her life. The poor, poor girl. She couldn't think of her as her mam – her mam would always be Elsie – but this girl had been the means of giving her life and she had died so young. Outside in the compound, she could hear one of the dogs that the Royal West African Frontier Force had to help them guard the camp. It was barking but the sound meant nothing. Her mind and every cell in her body was concentrated on the letter that had come like a bolt out of the blue.

She read on:

> I took you for my own bairn, lass, and with
> James having just been born, it was easy to say
> you were his twin. I didn't want the authorities to
> have you and you be put in the workhouse
> nursery, but it was more than that to be truthful.
> I loved you from the minute you were born and I
> knew you were God's gift to me. My daughter,
> my tiny storm child. Your poor mam had gone,
> nothing could be done for her but I felt then, and
> I've always felt it, that she gave me her blessing.
> She loved you, Gina. It was in her eyes as she

held you and looked at you for the first and last time. And then she just closed her eyes and she was gone. After Kenneth had told me what he did, I went straight to the cottage homes the next day to ask for their help. I spoke to the master, a Mr Preston, and he agreed that if I wrote a letter to you addressed to the cottage homes he would see to it that it was forwarded to your place of employment. That was all he was prepared to do. I tried to speak to some of the other staff but no one would say anything. It was like hitting my head against a brick wall, lass. So I wrote this letter and covered it in prayer, asking God to let it find you. If you can find it in your heart to let me know you are all right it would mean the world, my bairn. I love you, my precious Gina. I have never stopped loving you, not for one minute.

Your mam xxx

She sat on the bed, hugging herself round her middle and rocking backward and forward for some minutes with her eyes shut. The great lonely void that had been inside her since she was a child had filled so suddenly it was painful and achingly bittersweet. Her mam, her mam. She reached out and stroked the handwriting. Her mam had written this. She pressed one of the sheets of paper to her lips. Her mam had wanted her, she loved her, she always had.

Another storm of weeping took hold and it was a while before she could pull herself together. There was a bottle of water on the small cupboard beside her bed and she tipped some of the liquid onto her handkerchief, bathing her face, before lying back and letting it rest on her swollen eyes. She needed to look as normal as she could before she went to the NAAFI later for the carol concert that was being held. Tomorrow morning a film show was being put on – Bing Crosby and Marjorie Reynolds in *Holiday Inn* so no doubt everyone would be singing along with 'White Christmas' – and in the afternoon Squadron Leader Fletcher had organized a concert party which involved airmen and airwomen. Sketches, songs and a couple of comedians, along with a row of WAAFs in the chorus line, would no doubt bring the house down. This was going to be followed by a dance. She had been looking forward to the festivities but now all she wanted was to show Josef the letter and tell him he had been right – her mother hadn't been party to her being taken away and put in the workhouse.

She sat up and looked at the address on the top of the letter. It began '*Cowslip Farm*'. She had never known the name of the farm; she had been so young when she'd lived there she didn't suppose it had registered on her. Now she knew the name and the address. Her heart raced. Once she was back in England, whenever that was, there was nothing to stop her going to see her mam. A sudden joy flooded her, violent and strong. She wanted to dance and shout and scream but she did none of these things. Instead she sat perfectly still, her eyes wide and looking into the future. Miraculously, yes, miraculously, her mother had been returned to her, and that meant James and her other brothers too. Oh, she knew they weren't her flesh and blood but that was unimportant, the biological side. They had loved her and she had loved them, and but for the man she had thought was her father, her life would have been with them all. There would have been no cottage homes, no Mrs Bainsby, no master and mistress. She would have lived in the farmhouse and slept in her little room under the eaves. She would have been happy. Her mother had said she couldn't forgive him, and neither could Gina. In fact, she hated him more than ever even if he *was* dead. Folk always conferred sainthood on the departed no matter how foul the person had been in real life, saying it didn't bode well to speak ill of the dead. Well, she didn't care about that. She hated and loathed him, and she hoped he was burning in hell right now.

The fierce pain and hate had swept away the joy and she sat for a few minutes more, telling herself to calm down and breathe deeply. After a little while she brushed her hair and tidied her clothes and then looked at her reflection in the speckled cloudy mirror. Her eyelids were swollen but apart from that she didn't look too bad, and with the sand and dust everyone had itchy irritated eyes now and again.

The carol concert went well and she caught a glimpse of Josef sitting with the other POWs at the back of the room, a couple of the Royal West African Frontier Force

– all six-foot-tall West Africans – standing behind them. She would have given the world to have a few minutes with him but it was impossible. The POWs were treated well on camp – too well, according to the warrant officer who accompanied them on the maintenance trips and would have gladly seen them all in chains and starving – but it was because of men like him that she dared not risk even a smile in Josef's direction. And in one way she couldn't blame the warrant officer and others of the same mind for how they viewed the POWs. Reports were coming in thick and fast about Nazi death camps, the inhuman treatment of British and Allied servicemen, and the utter devastation of Poland at the hands of the Nazis. But Josef wasn't like that, and she knew some German men and women had chosen death rather than becoming part of the Nazi regime, while others had risked their lives and those of their families to help Jews or even hide them in their own homes.

She couldn't sleep that night. She knew every word in her mother's letter off by heart now, she had read them so often, and lay in bed thinking about her early days at the farm and imagining herself walking through the same fields and being at home once again. Of course, it would be different, she knew that. The lads were all grown up now and there was the daughter too. She didn't know how she felt about her, and so it was easier to shut her mother's natural daughter out of her thoughts.

Christmas Day brought an exchange of inexpensive presents with Pam and Mildred, little things the girls had bought at the local bazaars and shops. She sat through *Holiday Inn*, her mind anywhere but on the film, and she endured the concert party in the afternoon in the same way. What she really wanted was to be able to sit quietly and think about her reply to her mother, but first she wanted to discuss everything with Josef. It was strange, considering they had never even kissed or spoken of love, but this situation had forced her to recognize what she had known for some time, that Josef was the most important person in her life and always would be. And that was frightening in itself. She had no idea how the future would pan out when the war was over or even if Josef actually envisaged being with her, to be fair, but however things worked out it was going to be difficult and problematic in all sorts of ways, not least because a love match between a German man and an English woman so soon after the war would be viewed with hostility by practically everyone.

Did that bother her? she asked herself as she got ready for the dance in the evening, and she found she could say in all honesty that it didn't. All that mattered was Josef. But of course, she was way ahead of herself here; he hadn't mentioned the future and although she knew he cared for her it might not be enough for him to contemplate a serious relationship. Her heart began to thud hard at the thought of what that would mean; being in his arms, in his bed, marriage, perhaps even children.

And then she spoke out loud as she told herself, 'No more. No more thinking along those lines.' One day at a time, that was all she could contemplate for now.

Chapter Twenty-One

The trip to Alexandria seemed to take forever, but at last she was once again ensconced in the light and airy house. The evening sky had been extraordinary, pink clouds with scalloped edges standing, each one separate, against the horizon, and she had sat watching it get dark on the flat roof of the house where there was a table and chairs and some potted plants. Over the last weeks the weather had been cooler, softer, although still very warm, and tonight there was actually a chilly breeze, or chilly in comparison to how it had been when she'd first arrived in Egypt.

She waited until past midnight before quietly venturing outside into the scented garden and making her way to the fountain. Josef was waiting for her on the stone bench and rose immediately he saw her, giving the little bow and nod of his head that was so very German. Tonight a full moon turned his fair hair silver and she could see his chiselled features clearly in the moonlight as she sat down, a moment before he joined her, his long legs stretched out in front of him.

He smiled at her, saying, 'It seems to have been a long time since we were here last, do you not think?'

She did, but eager to show him the letter, she drew the envelope out of the pocket of her dressing gown, and said, 'I've had this from home. From – from my mother.'

'Your *Mutter*?' He stared at her in amazement. 'How is this so?'

'You were right, she did look for me. She had nothing to do with my father taking me away. Read it.'

He took the letter from her but didn't open it immediately; instead his gaze ran over her bright face and glittering eyes. This meant the world to her, he could see that, and her transparent vulnerability swept away the rigid self-control he normally brought to bear when he was close to her. Before he knew what he was doing he took her into his arms, kissing her as he had wanted to do from the first moment he had set eyes on her.

When he raised his head they were both breathless, and he kept hold of her as he muttered, 'Forgive me, I should not have done that.'

'I'm glad you did.'

She was half-laughing, half-crying, and when she reached up to him and placed her lips on his he groaned before pulling her on to his lap and kissing her again, this time muttering endearments as he covered her mouth, her nose, her cheeks, her ears in tiny burning kisses that set her whole body aflame.

It was some minutes later before he found the strength to stop, murmuring, 'Gina, Gina, this is madness.'

'I love you.' She didn't care that she had said it first.

He bowed his head, shaking it slowly. 'You must not say that, it is too dangerous for you. Even your CO would not be able to protect you if our association became public. You understand this?'

She ignored that, saying, 'Do you love me?'

He should deny it. He should get up and go back to the barn and never meet her like this again. Instead he murmured, 'With all my heart and soul.'

'Then nothing else matters.'

'I wish this was so.' He sighed, gently disentangling her arms from around his neck and setting her back down beside him on the bench. 'But our countries are at war and I am your enemy. You would be reviled by everyone who knows you and disciplined severely. You know this is true, my Gina.'

The words 'my Gina' were sweeter than any love song. 'You are not my enemy,' she said softly. 'You never could be.'

He reached out and touched her face in the lightest of caresses. 'But the facts remain as they are, and I will not see you disgraced. I should not have allowed things to get to this point but where you are concerned it seems I'm not the man I thought I was. I am weak.'

'Josef—'

'No, Gina.' He straightened himself and picked up the letter that had fallen on the bench, biting his lip before saying, 'With your permission?'

'Of course, I want you to read it.'

He read it through twice before raising his head and looking at her, his eyes as well as his mouth smiling. 'I do not know your mother but I feel as though I do and it is clear you are – how do you put it – the apple of her eye, yes? What do you intend to do?'

'Write back and tell her I'll come and see her when I can although when that'll be, I don't know. It's ridiculous but I didn't even know the farm was called Cowslip Farm. It's a bonny name, isn't it.'

'It is charming.' He was having great difficulty in not taking her into his arms again. 'And it is good you have the address, but more than that your mother's heart laid bare. Has it helped? To know she knew nothing of what her husband had done?'

Gina nodded. 'But how could he have been so wicked, Josef? Not just to me but to her too? He must have seen how she was suffering but he let her believe I was dead. Why did he hate me so much?'

'I don't suppose you will ever know why, but hate has its own life force, like love. The one to bring joy and harmony and the other devastation.'

'I was only a small child, though, that's what I've never been able to understand. It's never made any sense.'

'Sense goes out the window where hate's involved. I remember when I was a boy and the Nazis burned a mountain of books at the University of Berlin. My sister and I did not understand why my father was upset – to us it was an exciting spectacle – but my father saw the hate behind it.'

She stared at him. 'Strange, isn't it,' she said softly. 'How one man or an ideology can so influence a nation. And he, the man I thought was my father, he changed the lives of those around him with no remorse or feelings of guilt.'

'You don't know that for sure.'

'I do. Like my mam said, it was only his fear of dying without having confessed and getting absolution from her that made him tell her what he had done. He didn't feel sorry, not really, and he didn't care about her feelings or me. I find that unforgivable. I hate him. I shall always hate him to my dying day.'

Josef said nothing, his blue eyes on her flushed face.

'I'm entitled to hate him, surely?'

'It is understandable,' he said at last.

'But you disapprove?' She felt terribly hurt.

'It is not a question of disapproving.'

'I think it is.'

'No, no.' He swore softly in his own language. He had upset her and that was the last thing he wanted to do. 'I am concerned for you, that is all. Hate changes the best of people, it is a malignant emotion, this I know. Holding on to it, however justified you feel, will hurt you. It is like the fungus, you know?'

'Canker? Is that what you mean?'

'Yes, yes, just so, the canker. A destructive disease, an open wound, a corrupting influence. Just as trees and plants and even animals can be consumed by canker, so can the mind. Believe me, Gina, I have witnessed this, I know it is so.'

She felt he was talking about Kirsten but she wasn't like his sister, she thought hotly, hating a whole race of people. She just hated the man who had treated her so cruelly and she wasn't going to apologize to Josef or anyone else for it.

'Well, I do hate him,' she said passionately, 'and no one would blame me for it if they knew what he'd done.' No one but you.

'I have upset you and that was not my intention,' he said very softly, 'not on such a joyous day when you have heard from your mother. Please forgive me.'

She sat, willing herself not to cry, quite unable to speak.

'I love you and to me you are perfect.' He brushed a strand of hair from her forehead, his blue eyes troubled. 'Do you know this? Because it is true.'

'Even if I hate Kenneth Redfern?' She had made up her mind she would never refer to him as her father again; he wasn't, for one thing, but even more he didn't deserve such a title from her.

'Even then.'

She sniffed, and this time when he enfolded her in his arms, he made no attempt to kiss her but just sat quietly holding her close.

After a few moments she said, 'Do you realize we've just had our first quarrel?'

He turned her head up to him and kissed the tip of her nose. 'Not a quarrel.'

She smiled. 'What then?'

'A meaningful discussion.'

'Do you think we'll have lots of meaningful discussions when the war's over?' There, she had said it, she had mentioned the future.

Now he chuckled and she was captivated by the softening of his stern mouth. 'Of course, but I think you will be the *auslösen*.'

She frowned. 'What's that?'

'In English I think the trigger element.'

She pushed against him. 'Are you saying I'm argumentative?'

'You are the most wonderful, beautiful, amazing woman in the whole world, that is what I am saying, and you know your own mind. I like this. It is good.'

They sat quietly for a while, the night-time sky adorned with blazing stars hanging from the indigo depths like brilliant lanterns. She wished they could stay here like this for ever, under these alien stars where the past and the future didn't count and only the present mattered, just two people who wanted to be together. Of course, real life wasn't like that. But at least they would have a few hours together tonight.

She had no sooner thought it than a voice out of the darkness called Josef's name. He shot to his feet. 'That is one of my friends,' he whispered urgently. 'If any of the guards awoke, I told him to say I was feeling unwell and had gone to sit outside. If I don't return immediately they will assume I am trying to escape.'

'Go, go.' She didn't have to think about it. Grabbing the envelope with one hand, she pushed at him with the other.

He gave her one brief scorching kiss and then he was gone, calling out reassurances to the guards as he went. She sped back indoors like a silent shadow, shutting the front door behind her and then standing with her back to it and her hands to her chest. Her heart was thudding violently but there were no shouts or gunshots, simply silence. She knew the two guards who had accompanied the POWs and they seemed nice, reasonable men, unlike the warrant officer who she knew would shoot first and ask questions later. After a few more minutes she crept up the stairs to the bedroom she used and sat on her bed, shaking slightly. She would have loved a cup of coffee, but just in case the warrant officer suspected anything and came snooping to see if she was up and about, she stayed in the upstairs room.

It was going to be another two weeks before they would have the chance to meet again. An eternity. She got into bed, the crisp cotton sheets cool against her hot skin. She was too agitated to sleep, her thoughts flying here and there and all about Josef. She was well aware that their relationship had entered a new phase; they were committed to each other now. Perhaps they always had been from the moment their eyes had met, but with the declaration of their love for each other there was no going back. Not that she would ever want to. Whatever happened, whatever it took, she wanted to be with him for the rest of her life. She had never imagined in her wildest dreams she could feel like this about a man; it made the emotion she had felt for Mark a weak shallow thing by comparison. And when Josef had kissed her . . . She sat up in bed, hugging her pillow to her. Oh, how would she survive two weeks without being in his arms?

She must have eventually drifted off to sleep because when she opened her eyes bright white sunlight was pouring into the room and there was a tooting of horns outside. She'd overslept. Leaping out of bed, she shouted through the window that she would be ready in a moment and hastily bundled her things together after a bracing wash in cold water. Once dressed she felt more in command of herself, and forgoing breakfast she met the convoy outside, refusing to let her eyes wander in search of Josef.

The first half of the journey was uneventful, and when they stopped for the customary refreshments at Ali's pub she was relieved to see Josef standing with the other men, apparently relaxed and at ease. Warrant Officer Proby again bought her a shandy and stood with her drinking his beer, his eyes on the group of men some yards away.

'Had an incident last night,' he said flatly. 'One of the damn Krauts taking the mickey. Things need tightening up a bit.'

'An incident?' She opened her eyes wide. 'What happened?'

'One of 'em decided a nice little stroll in the garden was in order. According to him he wasn't feeling well and wanted some fresh air.'

'And you don't believe him?'

'He didn't try and escape so I wouldn't say I don't

believe him, but what the hell the guards were doing I don't know. Well, I do. Sleeping on duty, that's what. Heads will roll when we get back to camp, believe me. They're POWs, for crying out loud, and this isn't some friendly Sunday-school picnic. If one of 'em gets away on my watch, it's me who's hauled up before the CO.'

'But no one did get away.'

'Not this time, no, and I'm going to make damn sure they don't in the future.'

She nodded. 'What will happen to the POW in question?'

'Him? Nowt this time. According to the guard he was only a few feet away sitting taking his ease, cheeky blighter. Cocking a snook at us all, more like. I shall be keeping my eye on him in particular and if he so much as sneezes I'll be on him like a ton of bricks. I wouldn't be surprised if he was doing a recce to see how easy it'd be for him and his pals to escape some time. Well, they can try, but a bullet in the back of the head might bring 'em up short. They think they're superior to us you see, master race and all that.'

He was fairly quivering with the force of his hatred, his lips drawn back from his teeth and his eyes narrowed into slits. For a moment Gina wondered if he was unhinged. And this was the man who was in charge of Josef and the others. She felt a deep gripping fear that choked any reply she might have made.

'I'll have him one day, sure as my name's Arthur Proby, the one who tried it on last night. He won't be going home to his damned Fatherland, not if I have anything to do with it.' He finished his beer in a couple of gulps, wiping his mouth with the back of his hand, before saying, 'You all right? You don't look too good if you don't mind me saying.'

'I didn't sleep too well last night.' She shrugged her shoulders as she forced her voice to sound casual. 'The bed's too comfortable if anything – I've got used to the service ones.'

'Yeh? Me, I can sleep standing up if I have to.' He pulled his cap further over his eyes before saying, 'We'd better get this show on the road again. I want them beggars back at camp as soon as possible, I've had enough go wrong this trip.'

He strode off, barking orders right, left and centre and clearly still in a foul mood. Gina glanced across to Josef, hoping to catch his eye, although how she could warn him to be extra careful from now on she didn't know. He was already walking towards his truck anyway and had his back to her. She'd have to find a way of talking to him in the next little while, she told herself as she climbed into her vehicle. She might be doing Warrant Officer Proby a disservice, but she wouldn't put it past him to manoeuvre Josef into a situation where he could shoot him and claim he had only been doing his duty.

As the convoy trundled into the camp later, any chance to even mouth a warning to Josef was impossible. The POWs were marched off as soon as their feet touched the ground, besides which Mildred shouted across the compound to her as soon as she jumped down from the cab.

'Your CO wants you to go straight to his office,' Mildred called. 'He's been waiting for you to get back.'

Her mind full of Josef and the danger he was in, Gina didn't even wonder what the CO wanted, but once she was standing in front of him and looked at his face she knew it was of some importance.

'I'm sorry for the short notice, Gina, but I need you to be ready to leave in an hour.'

'Right, sir.' A trip into the town maybe?

'We're flying to New Delhi so don't forget anything. There'll be no way of retrieving it.'

She stared at him. He had been sorting papers on his desk but now he looked up at her almost absent-mindedly, his thoughts clearly elsewhere. 'All right?' he said distractedly.

'You said New Delhi, sir?' She almost said, 'New Delhi, India,' but of course that was what he had meant.

'Yes.' And then his expression cleared, and he smiled. 'Oh, I'm sorry, I should have explained. The powers that be want me out there pronto so if there's any goodbyes you need to make . . . ?'

'Goodbyes?' For a moment she thought he knew about Josef.

'To the other girls?'

'Oh, yes, sir. Of course.'

Alexander looked at her more closely. Gina didn't seem herself today, but then the trip to Alexandria was always tiring. 'This has come as a bit of a surprise to me too,' he said, his gaze returning to the papers on his desk, 'but it seems Intelligence in Delhi has requested my assistance, so –' he shrugged – 'we're on the move again.' He knew what it was about, of course, the Japanese campaign in Malaya. He would be working on the proposed Malayan invasion, which was still some time away. 'I'd like you back here in an hour, Corporal.'

The formality told Gina she was expected to leave but nevertheless, she said, 'Do I take it we won't be returning here, sir?'

'That's correct.' He didn't look up. He still had a hundred and one things to do and in truth he would have appreciated more time to prepare, but that was the war – and the RAF – for you.

Gina left the office in a daze. Once back in her little room she pulled her things together, which took all of ten minutes, and then plumped down on her bed. She needed to write the letter to her mother, but all she could think about was how on earth she was going to let Josef know about the new posting. They hadn't even had a chance to say a proper goodnight the previous evening and who would have imagined that last rushed kiss was goodbye? How was she going to keep in contact with him if she left for India? Her thoughts whirled chaotically. Could she write a note and ask Mildred to pass it on? Immediately she knew the answer. It would be far too dangerous for both of them if their relationship became known, but especially for Josef. What if Proby found out?

And she had no confidence Mildred would help her – she might think it was her duty to pass such a note to her superiors, Josef being German.

Picking up her kitbag and suitcase she went outside and into the main camp, hoping the POWs might be around. They weren't. Neither did they materialize before the hour was up.

Even as they walked to the plane that was going to take them on the first lap of the journey to India, she was glancing over her shoulder, absolutely beside herself but fighting not to let it show. She had never felt so helpless and panicky in all her life. It couldn't, mustn't, end like this. What would he think if she simply didn't turn up when the convoy next left for Alexandria? But his post would be inspected if she wrote to him; she couldn't risk getting him into trouble and the letter might not reach him anyway. And what about Proby and his threats?

For a crazy, frantic moment she almost threw down her kitbag and suitcase and raced back into the camp to find him; only the repercussions of what such a reckless act would mean for Josef stopping her. And then they were boarding, the plane door closed and the Dakota took off. It was too late. She sat frozen with disbelief and bewilderment, a part of her mind listening to the CO's conversation with the other couple of RAF officers who had accompanied them, and the other part silently screaming.

*

By the time the long, exhausting journey was over Gina had lost track of how many times they had slept, eaten, changed aircrafts, washed and bedded down for a few hours at this airbase and that en route and shown their documents to officials. They arrived in New Delhi to a temperature of over a hundred degrees, flies and more flies, and the sights and sounds of a new and amazing country that was different again to Egypt.

Once in the camp the heat was even worse, in spite of coolies throwing water at bamboo screens to try and cool the air. Fans just moved the scorching air around and her tin bath was full of warm water. They ate the evening meal of rice and some sort of fish on the mess verandah, the flying foxes dark shapes that flitted from tree to tree. All Gina could think of was Josef and she had never felt so miserable and worried in her life, her anxiety made all the worse because she had to hide it from everyone.

She went to sleep that night under the mosquito net with her mind buzzing louder than the insects outside and her heart one big ache. This war, she thought fiercely just before exhaustion overtook her. This wretched, foul war. It had separated her and Josef as effectively as death itself and she had no idea if they would ever meet again. She had found the one man in the world she could love and have a future with, and she had lost him. Not only was he a German POW and she a British WAAF, but he was in Egypt and she was in India. If they both survived the remaining days of the war, all she knew was that his name was Josef Vetter and he had lived in Berlin before joining the Luftwaffe. Now Berlin was a bombed-out city full of dead and dying people and Josef had been almost sure his sister and nephew and niece wouldn't have survived.

She turned over in the hard, rickety bed trying to get more comfortable. Josef knew her name, of course, and that she hailed from the north of England originally, but that wasn't much to go on. It was a mess, such a mess, she thought angrily. And who would help two people from different sides of the conflict find each other anyway? With so much bitterness and heartache? She couldn't see Warrant Officer Proby ever forgiving and forgetting, and there would be plenty like him.

A thick blanket of sleep was descending now and she didn't try to fight it, weary in mind, body and spirit. If she had been a normal WAAF and not attached to the CO she might have been able to stay in Egypt until the end of the war, or at least she and Josef could have planned for a rendezvous somewhere in the future if they'd had time to say goodbye. Josef, oh, Josef.

She went to sleep with his name on her lips.

PART SIX

Cowslip Farm

1946

Chapter Twenty-Two

The last couple of years had been ones of mental turmoil for Gina. At times she'd felt as though she was two different people in the same skin.

As the Reich's final days had played out, the full horror of the Nazi death camps had unfolded, and fury and revulsion against the Germans had risen to new heights. The Allies had known of the existence of the concentration camps for years, but no one could have guessed at the extent of the barbarity. What had emerged was the awful truth about a cold-blooded and systematic attempt by the Nazis to destroy an entire section of the human race, and along with this the inhuman treatment of Allied prisoners in German POW camps was revealed.

Gina had been as appalled as everyone else, but in the outrage people seemed to forget that some German men and women had given their lives to protect and help the Jews and to fight against Hitler's madness. She knew Josef would not have been capable of cruelty in any form, and hadn't his parents paid the ultimate price for criticizing the Nazis? So when some of those around her branded every German man, woman and child as monstrous and sadistic, she found herself torn to pieces inside.

Berlin had been crushed in a storm of blood and fire in the last days of the war before the Germans had surrendered, and even though she knew the Allies were doing what they had to do, she thought of Josef all the time and how he must be feeling, knowing his childhood city was no more. Even when victory celebrations had resounded in battle-weary Europe, she couldn't get excited. For one thing, the war was far from over where she was in Delhi with the Japanese still to be defeated, and for another, with so many millions dead, dying and injured, and such devastation in Britain and other countries, victory was bittersweet.

As it happened, the planned Malayan invasion did not take place due to the dropping of the atomic bombs on Hiroshima and Nagasaki, after which Japan surrendered. When the news had come through during the night, everyone in the camp had turned out into the parade ground. A huge bonfire had been lit and they had all danced and sung until the early hours of the morning. Gina had joined in the celebrations. It had not been Josef she had been thinking about so much as Mark, who had given his life for this day, the final end to the war. Her feelings towards him had mellowed over the last months since meeting Josef and now she remembered the good times they'd had and how sweet he had been to her, rather than holding on to and nursing the pain of his deceit about his fiancée.

She had written to her mother soon after arriving in India, a long letter telling her how much she loved her and exactly what had happened in the immediate aftermath of being taken from the farm and then the years following, right up to the present day. She had asked after the lads and Betty but hadn't mentioned Kenneth Redfern once. There were some feelings too extreme to commit to the written page. The letter she had received back had made her cry, it was so full of love and longing and regret. Elsie had begged her to come to the farm as soon as she was able, but Gina had known that wouldn't be soon. The demobilization of the WAAFs had begun in the last months of the war, and she knew from letters she received from Kitty and Minnie that the RAF had begun organizing educational and vocational training courses to allow personnel to catch up on pre-war skills, or to ready themselves for new ones, in preparation for leaving the service. Of course, her situation in India was different, particularly as her CO had been asked to oversee what he called 'mopping-up work' which meant they had been called upon to stay in Delhi for the immediate future, but she had read with interest Kitty's positively ecstatic account of the John Lewis shops in London giving a fashion display to WAAFs on what to buy with their clothing grants. Kitty had apparently tried on fabulous clothes which she knew she couldn't afford and had had the time of her life flirting with the John Lewis manager.

Minnie's take on things had been more down to earth. She had attended mothercraft courses because she was determined she and Norman would start a family as soon as possible, and talks on budgeting housekeeping and other such practical issues, including the best way to spend her forthcoming gratuities and clothing coupons to make them go as far as possible.

The letters had been oddly comforting to Gina. Over fifty million people had been killed in the war worldwide, only one fifth of whom had been combatants, and countless numbers had been maimed for life, but Kitty and Minnie were still exactly the same. Whereas she knew she, herself, had changed in all sorts of ways compared to the outwardly confident, inwardly troubled and damaged girl who had joined the WAAF. Part of this had been due to the fact that she couldn't have endured some of the hardships of service life unless she had opened her heart and let Kitty and Minnie and other wonderful friends in. There had been happy days and very sad days, but they'd shared them together. She had survived the fallout after Mark's death and despite herself found the courage to love again, which had been both the greatest joy of her life and the most crippling pain because she didn't know if she would ever see Josef again. But it had been hearing from her mam that had made her whole again in a way nothing else could have done.

She'd had several letters from Elsie now since that first one and each was precious beyond words, coating her sore heart with a balm that soothed and healed.

She worked hard with the CO after the war with Japan was over, not just assisting with the mountain of paperwork and red tape his commission involved but also taking statements from some of the RAF men who had been in the Japanese POW camps when they arrived in Delhi to convalesce before being shipped home. Part of this involved making lists of men who had not survived the terrible conditions, a sad task. Some of the survivors would show her a small item like a button or a cap badge they'd saved from the uniforms of their dead friends in order to take it back to the deceased families, and in private she shed many a tear. And all the time, no matter what she was doing or who she was with, she thought of Josef.

Where was he, what was he doing, was he even still alive? She had written to Mildred after Japan had surrendered, a friendly casual letter, but in it she had asked what had happened to the German POWs at the camp. It had been a long while before she had received a reply; apparently Mildred and some other WAAFs had been sent home to England not long after she had been posted to India. Mildred had told her she had no idea of what had become of the POWs, just a few words in a long letter that had been mainly concerned with Mildred's upcoming marriage to her childhood sweetheart who had survived the war unscathed.

It was during the week before Christmas, more than fifteen months after the formal document ending the war with Japan was signed on 2 September 1945, that Alexander told her she was being demobbed at last and that they were going home in the New Year. 'You've been an enormous help to me in every way,' he said with a warm smile, 'and I shall miss you. You must keep in touch, Gina.'

She had promised she would, even as she had wondered if he would still want to keep contact if he knew she was in love with a German POW she'd met in Egypt. The CO was kind, and had an unusually gentle manner for a military man, but he had lost two of his three sons to the Luftwaffe.

Over the next little while they worked together clearing any loose ends and packing masses of documents which would accompany the CO to England and his new job in Intelligence. Gina had her last medical, filled in umpteen forms and waded through the inevitable red tape, but then at last, in the first week of February, she was ready to make the journey to England with the CO. Her feelings were very mixed. She had written to Elsie once she had known she was being released from the WAAF and had received a letter back declaring she must come and stay at the farm as soon as she was able. And she wanted to, she wanted to so much, but feverish anticipation warred with anxiety about what it would be like to be there again after so many years. Elsie had told her that Edwin and Larry had both volunteered in the first days of the war, surviving Dunkirk, then the Balkan Campaign and finally the conflict in North Africa before returning to England at the end of the war. James and Robin had remained at home working on the farm but it had been Robin out of the four brothers who had met an untimely death, succumbing to a bout of pneumonia in the winter of 1942 when he was just twenty-three years old. Even though she knew she had no blood tie with the lads she still thought of them as her brothers, and she had grieved for the young boy she remembered. And then, of course, there was Betty. She wasn't sure how she felt about her.

On arriving in England, the first thing that hit her when she stepped off the plane the RAF had sent for the CO was the cold drabness of the scene in front of her. No colour, no warmth, none of the vibrant chaos of India with its rich smells and noise, just a bleak airfield, freezing sleet falling from a grey laden sky and a bitter wind that cut straight through her service greatcoat.

The CO had kindly arranged for a car to take her to Wythall near Birmingham where she would officially be demobbed rather than her having to take the train, and he had also paid for a room at a hotel in the area for a week, while she got her bearings, as he had put it. She'd been overwhelmed by his generosity and quite tearful as she'd made her goodbyes, the more so when she opened the envelope he'd pushed into her hand at the last moment before shutting the car door and waving the driver on. It had contained a cheque for a huge amount that had made her eyes widen, along with a short note which had read:

My dear Gina,
   This is just a small token of my continuing debt to you, not just for saving my life all those years ago but for your support and loyalty ever since.

As you know, Felicity and I were not blessed with a daughter, but I like to think that if we had been she would be just like you. I meant what I said about keeping in touch, my dear, and I wish you well in civilian life. If at any time you would like to consider a career in the air force, be assured my door is always open. All you have to do is knock! Bless you, my dear, and may you find great happiness in the future.

Yours fondly,
Alexander

She had gulped and sniffed her way for the next few miles, totally taken aback by the cheque but more so from his sentiments. She had known he held her in some regard, and certainly he had treated her differently to anyone else, but to know he was so fond of her meant more than anything.

She had stayed overnight at the very nice hotel Alexander had booked before going to get demobbed the next morning. Another medical had ensued along with a whole host of papers to send her into civilian life: food ration cards, clothing coupons, a twelve-pounds-ten-shillings clothing allowance, ration money and two months' leave with pay she was apparently owed.

Still in uniform, she returned to the hotel somewhat bemused and lost, going up to her room and sitting on the bed in a daze. A hundred and one memories of her time as a WAAF flooded her mind: kit inspections and domestic evenings; Kitty meeting her beaus behind their barracks; Minnie dropping everything that could be dropped and not knowing her left from her right; Mark and their evenings spent at the village pub with the others; Egypt and Josef; India and the heat and flies and exotic food. Now it had all come to an end and although she'd had time to prepare herself, it seemed so sudden and final. From childhood she had learned the hard way to adapt and take care of herself, and although she had weathered the life at the cottage homes with Peggy's help, it hadn't been until she'd joined the WAAF and met Kitty and Minnie and the others that she had known what true companionship and friendship were. She would always remain in contact with them, she knew that. Their friendship had been born in the laughter and sorrows, the victories and traumas, the shared experiences that no one else could possibly understand. And it was good that she had such wonderful friends, but she wanted more. She wanted Josef.

Over the next days she was grateful for the CO's foresight in providing her with a breathing space before she ventured properly into the outside world. Much as she wanted to fly to the farm and see her mother, mentally she had to prepare herself for whatever might happen.

In many ways, despite the awfulness of the war and the danger they'd been in at times, she and the other WAAFs had led a strangely insular life in a small world of their own with its support mechanisms, rules and hardships. She hadn't realized until now how tight and close a community it had been.

Their Air Force Blue had united them. It had created an unbreakable bond. The nights dancing to Glenn Miller, sharing make-up and doing each other's hair, eating cakes and biscuits from home on Domestic Nights and drinking tin mugs of gin or wine some of the girls smuggled in had been good. All of it. More than good, in hindsight.

She made a couple of shopping trips for clothes so she could fold up her uniform for good, and as she did so she became increasingly aware of the grumblings about rationing from ordinary men and women. The transport strike in January hadn't helped things when troops had had to be called in to move food and maintain essential supplies, causing huge queues outside food shops, with irate housewives shouting the odds. Towards the end of the month the fresh meat ration had been reduced and in a gloomy review the government had predicted a cut in bread rations and no increases in supplies of bacon, eggs or fish, with beer production cut by fifty per cent. She hadn't expected it to be like this, she acknowledged to herself, which was perhaps naive in hindsight, and it added to the growing feeling of not belonging. And it was so cold, so bitterly cold after the heat and light of Egypt and India.

But soon she would see her mam. She hugged the thought to her each night in bed. She could hardly wait for that.

Chapter Twenty-Three

Elsie stood with her hands on her ample hips, looking across the farmyard. It was not yet dawn and the yard was a sea of frozen ridges, some a foot high, and perfect for breaking an ankle, she thought irritably.

The snowstorms mixed with sleet and rain of the last three months had turned the farmyard into a quagmire of mud which had got trodden into the house no matter how she'd tried to keep it out; she insisted everyone took their boots off on the kitchen doorstep and changed into their slippers, which she always left in a row just inside the doorway. But February had seen a marked change in the weather as temperatures had dropped like a stone and thick white frosts during the night hadn't melted during the day. She'd been glad the mud was a thing of the past, but at the same time the bitterly cold conditions brought their own problems.

Never satisfied. She nodded at the thought, glancing up into the dark sky from which a few desultory snow-flakes drifted, dancing in the frosty air. But then to be fair, sinking up to your armpits in stinking mud every time you stepped outside, or risking life and limb on the ice every time you had to see to the animals wasn't much of a choice. Still, that was farming for you.

She sniffed the air. The forecast was for snow, lots of snow, and she could smell it. They were going to be in for a right packet, that was for sure.

She sighed, flexing her shoulders and telling herself to count her blessings, as she often did when what she called 'the blues' took hold. She had never suffered with depression before Gina had disappeared, but since that time it had been a daily battle although some days were a lot better than others. She didn't think it would ever truly lift until she saw her bairn again, but she was having a hard time believing that would happen. She wasn't sure why. Gina had said in her letters that she would come to the farm and in her last one, when she had said she was being demobbed, she'd mentioned it again. But perhaps she was finding it hard to believe because it meant so much?

Elsie shivered and, suddenly realizing she was chilled to the bone, turned from the doorstep into the snug warmth of the farmyard kitchen where the massive range was kept going day and night. The rest of the household were not yet up – she often rose half an hour or so early to have her first cup of tea in peace and quiet – and now she walked across to the range where she had left the tea mashing and poured herself a cup, nice and strong, the way she liked it. Sitting down at the scrubbed kitchen table, she let her mind wander again.

She could still scarcely believe what Ken had done that night so long ago, taking the bairn and leaving her at the workhouse doors and then lying to her for years. And she had no doubt she would never have known the truth but for his fear of dying without confessing his sin. It had been wicked, she couldn't think of it any other way, and *he* was wicked, evil. She'd said as much to the lads and Betty, and she knew the lads had understood and even agreed with her, but Betty was a different kettle of fish. It was funny, all the years when she had longed for a daughter, but Betty had never really been hers. She was all her father's. If Ken had ever really loved anyone, it was his daughter. He had spoiled her rotten from the day she was born and in return she had been devoted to him. He couldn't do any wrong as far as Betty was concerned. And even when the truth about Gina had come out on his deathbed, Betty had defended him to the hilt, saying he'd acted for the best for the rest of the family. It had been Betty who had tended to him for the last couple of days of his life, because Elsie hadn't been able to look at him or go in the bedroom. Betty would never forgive her for that – she'd made her feelings very clear.

Elsie shook her head to herself. Her daughter even looked like a female version of Ken, big and hefty with gimlet eyes under bushy eyebrows and a head of coarse, wiry black hair. So different to her fairylike, bonny Gina. And then she chided herself as she'd done in the past when the same thought had surfaced, telling herself that Betty did the work of two men round the farm and of all the bairns understood what was needed. And it hadn't been easy over the war years with the twins away at the front and then her Robin passing so suddenly, bless him, and Ken constantly at loggerheads with the local War Agricultural Committee. She had seen eye to eye with Ken about that. As far as they could tell, the committee's sole purpose was to tell farmers how to do a job they had been doing for generations, but their powers had been considerable. Telling a farmer what crops to grow, how to manure them, what animals to keep and what labour they had to employ, and always with the threat of eviction held over their heads if the farmer didn't play ball. They'd heard of a farm a few miles away where that had happened, and the farm had been let to someone else with no appeal possible against the decision. But fight as he had, Ken had been forced to plough up grassland for crops of grain, sugar beet, potatoes and vegetables, accept land girls on the farm and in the later years of the war POWs too.

She finished her cup of tea and poured herself another, setting the pan of porridge she'd left soaking overnight on the range and slicing thick slices off a side of bacon ready to start frying once the milking was done. Then she sat down again with her cup of tea but didn't drink it immediately, staring pensively across the kitchen.

She was glad the war was over, of course she was, and it meant Edwin and Larry were home again and in one piece too, praise God, but their return had thrown up all sorts of issues she hadn't expected. Mainly caused by Betty, she had to admit. Her daughter seemed to think she could order her brothers about like she had the land girls, which hadn't gone down at all well with the twins. There were daily arguments and sometimes the atmosphere was so thick at mealtimes you could cut it with a knife. And of course, Edwin and Larry had changed from the easy-going, untroubled lads they'd been before the war. You couldn't go through what they'd been through and see what they had seen without it having an effect.

They were both courting too, Edwin with a young widow whose husband had been killed in the last year of the war, and Larry with a farmer's daughter. They'd be wanting to get wed soon, that was only natural after all, and they deserved a settled family life after the last years. If it wasn't for Betty's attitude no doubt her lads would have been happy to bring their wives here to the farmhouse to live, but as things were, they would each need their own place.

Her brow wrinkled and she ran her hand across her forehead in a weary gesture. Since the end of the war the government had begun to shift the emphasis slowly back to livestock. It was going to be that way in the future – the writing was on the wall – and that was fine. They still had their big dairy herd, but they'd have to build up their stock of pigs and poultry again. Already there was talk about more mechanization even for the smaller farms like theirs, and supplanting horses with tractors and so on. There was so much to think about, so many decisions to make, and with Betty strutting about half the time like the farmyard cockerel and driving Edwin and Larry mad, along with the two burly farmworkers who they had taken on once the last of the POWs had left, life at the moment seemed one long round of petty squabbling and sudden bust-ups. She couldn't afford to lose Edwin and Larry and this farm was their birthright, after all, but she didn't know how much longer they would tolerate their sister's bossiness. She was a chip off her father's block all right, was Betty.

As though the thought had brought her downstairs, Betty walked into the kitchen dressed for the milking in a thick jumper and men's trousers. It was bang on half-past five, and Betty's voice reflected her impatience as she said, 'Aren't the others down yet? The cows won't milk themselves.'

Elsie didn't respond to this. Instead she said, 'Have a cuppa before you go out, lass. It's enough to freeze your lungs out there this morning.'

Betty took the cup of tea Elsie gave her without thanks and remained standing as she drank it, scalding hot, straight down just as her father had used to do every morning. Putting the empty cup on the table she said, 'You'd better give 'em a shout if they're not down in a couple of minutes. I'm not doing the milking by myself.' Being a Sunday, it was the farm labourers' day off.

'They'll be down in a minute, don't fret.' Elsie tried hard to keep her irritation from showing. That was the thing with Betty, she could get under your skin quicker than anyone she'd ever met.

Betty made a sound in her throat that could have meant anything and stamped out of the kitchen, leaving Elsie biting her lip. This would set the tone for the day now Betty was in this mood. No one would be able to do anything right. James was used to her and let anything she said or did roll off him like water off a duck's back, but Edwin and Larry met her head on every time.

As she had expected, within a couple of minutes all three lads were downstairs and after a quick cup of tea marched off to the cowsheds where the cattle had been brought in for the winter from the fields. She had told them Betty was already out there, receiving raised eyebrows from the twins that spoke volumes and a grin from James that said he knew what was in store and didn't give a hoot. All her lads had been born with the same taciturn nature as their father, but of the four, James had always been the least dour, possibly, she suspected, because for the first six years of his life he'd had Gina to tease or cajole him out of his solemnness. He had certainly missed her the most and had been inconsolable for months after her disappearance, frequently wetting the bed and having screaming nightmares that had woken the whole household. Knowing what she did now, she had often wondered if Ken had regretted what he'd done when he'd seen the effect it had had on her and James, and to a lesser extent the three older boys.

Out in the cowsheds Betty was quietly crooning to the cow she was milking when her brothers walked in and didn't acknowledge their arrival by so much as a flicker of an eyelash. She had a way with the cattle, even the most awkward ones, and could get them to let down their milk immediately. She loved them, that was the thing, and she felt they knew it. She was fond of all the animals and the two farm dogs were devoted to her. From a little girl she had much preferred animals to people, her father being the exception because she had worshipped him. Animals didn't judge you and find you wanting, or call you names because you weren't dainty and pretty like most of the girls. Her school days had been torturous at the hands of the other children, and she had hated every minute, only the fact that the farm and her da were waiting for her every evening enabling her to endure them. She had been born to be a farmer, she knew that, and the hard work and long hours didn't bother her an iota. Like her father she had bitterly resented the necessity for land girls coming on to their farm, all the more so because she knew they had sniggered and talked about her, calling her 'Master' Betty behind her back. The Italian POWs they'd had to take she had loathed for a different reason. At least the land girls had worked hard but the Italians had been lazy and apathetic and it had been an uphill struggle to get them to do the work allotted to them.

The stars were still shining after the morning milking was over and the business of washing out everything that had been in contact with the milk was finished. The four of them left the cowsheds together, united in their ravenous hunger if nothing else. It was beginning to snow more thickly, big fat flakes that settled on the frozen ground and made the ice underfoot more treacherous.

Their breakfast of porridge, home-cured bacon and

eggs and toast was eaten mostly in silence, with just Elsie putting in the occasional word now and again and fetching more toast and blackcurrant jam to the table. Once it was over Elsie disappeared off to the dairy, and Betty and the others to their various jobs outside. Before the war Betty had usually helped her mother in the dairy but when the land girls had arrived, Betty had designated one of them for the job. She'd always hated working in there, much preferring to be with her father and the animals, and once the war was over had flatly refused to return to the old system. Elsie hadn't argued. She could just about manage by herself and Betty had always been so sullen and resentful when she'd had to do dairy work that Elsie would rather struggle through than have her daughter huffing and puffing and banging about.

Edwin and Larry were building a new pigsty after the old one had finally collapsed a few days before and were nearly finished, which in view of the weather forecast was fortunate, and James was hedge-cutting, a useful winter job when the rock-hard ground made it hard to work on the land. Betty had gone straight back to the cowsheds, where she would be with the cows until lunchtime. When Edwin and Larry had come back from the war she had made it very plain that seeing to them was her job and that she required no help unless she asked for it. Once inside the sheds she opened a bale or two of oat straw and threw a great armful to each cow, after which she got down to the warm work of cleaning out, with shovel and brush and a wheelbarrow to cart the old manured bedding to the midden. Then she gave the animals a fresh bedding of wheat straw which they invariably began to eat, their long-lashed brown eyes watching her as she worked.

As a youngster she had wanted to name each of the cows and her father had indulgently given in to what he had seen as a temporary whim, but she knew he'd been amazed at her ability to pick each individual cow out of the herd and recognize them as easily as people. Even the most frisky cow, like Buttercup, would let Betty rub her nose and pet her, and now, as she shovelled the small pieces of turnip she'd put through the root-chopper into their feeding troughs, their soft moos of pleasure made her smile.

Once each animal had had its fair share, she climbed up into the loft above the sheds and pitched hay down on to the floor while the cows bellowed and stamped and stretched out their long tongues in the hope of catching a floating wisp of hay.

'You're greedy girls, all of you,' she chided softly, in a voice so gentle her brothers would have been amazed if they had heard it. 'What am I going to do with you, eh? You'll be so fat you won't be able to waddle out to pasture after the winter.'

She knew her father had always been relieved when the time had come in the spring to turn the cows out to pasture, and for her part she loved seeing them kicking up their legs and rollicking about after the long months of being kept inside with only the cobbled yard adjoining the cowsheds as outside space. But – and she would rather be hanged, drawn and quartered than confide this to a living soul – in the summer she missed the closeness of caring for the cows. It was an enormous amount of work, and now, once she had had her lunch in the house, she'd be back to prepare them a meal consisting of a few hundredweight of potatoes mixed with a little corn and then a little hay. After that she'd be able to get on with something else while her charges chewed the cud and dozed the afternoon away until it was time for the evening milking at four, and another meal of turnips and corn. One more meal at seven o'clock and then they settled down for the night, their great heads tucked round and pressed against their sides.

Once down from the loft she stood for a moment or two surveying her 'ladies', as she secretly called them, and then left the warmth and smells of the cowsheds, gasping slightly as the bitter cold wind took her breath away. A good inch of snow had settled during the morning and before going into the house she made her way to the pigsty to check on how Edwin and Larry were doing. They had worked without stopping all morning, conscious of the worsening weather, and had just finished the large new sty which Betty had to admit she couldn't find fault with. In typical fashion she didn't say this, however, merely nodding at them as they walked towards her and saying, 'The hay barn roof's got a leak at the far end. You'll be able to get on with that now you're finished here.'

'We know what needs to be done as well as you,' Larry said sharply.

'All right, all right, I was only saying.'

'Well, you don't *need* to say. We all pull our weight – it's not only you who works from dawn to dusk.'

Betty made a face but said nothing more. In truth, the twins' ill-humour made her feel better; she liked to needle them when she could. They had come back from the war expecting to lord it over her and she wasn't having any of it. She'd said this to her mother who had denied it vehemently but then her mam was always on anybody's side but hers.

The mouth-watering smell of Elsie's Sunday roast met them as Betty opened the kitchen door, and not for the first time she reflected she was glad she'd been born on a farm rather than in a town or village. Rationing was biting worse than ever, according to the papers, despite the fact that they had won the war. There had been a huge hoo-ha in May the year before when the government rationed bread for the first time because, apparently, of the growing threat of a world famine. The newspapers had predicted Britain would soon be back to wartime austerity or worse, which had caused an outcry, but then the nation had accepted what they couldn't change. That was the trouble with the working class in Betty's opinion; they went along with what their supposed 'betters' said without fighting back. No gumption, as her da would have put it. Well, she had gumption, and no one was going to talk down to her, never again. She had been eleven years old when war had been declared and had already been working as hard as any man on the farm, better than most, her da had said. Once she had left the misery of school and joined her da full-time, she'd been his right-hand man, and there was nothing she didn't know about running a farm.

Once she and the lads had washed and cleaned up they sat down at the table and tucked in. Her mam was a good cook, there was no doubt about it, whereas she herself had no interest in playing housewife. She was a disappointment to her mam, she knew that. Oh, her mam had never said, not in so many words, but she knew nevertheless. She wasn't Gina, that was the thing. She glanced across to the range. Above the long oak mantelpiece, hanging on the wall, was a framed picture of a cornfield with two people, a woman and a smaller figure, smiling. It was a child's drawing and it had been done by Gina when she was five years old. The woman was her mam and the child Gina. After Gina had gone missing, Larry, who was good at woodwork, had framed the picture for their mam and she'd put it high up on the wall where it was safe.

Betty stared at the picture. She had always hated it. Hated the way her mam would stand in front of it for minutes at a time, often turning away with tear-filled eyes; hated the way her mam's face would change, becoming filled with longing and pain and love and other emotions she couldn't name. Hated the fact that she knew whatever she did or made or drew, it would never be as precious to her mam as that drawing of a cornfield and two stick-like people with big smiles on their faces.

After the truth had come out about what had happened to Gina and the part her da had played in the child's disappearance, which was shocking, she admitted that, she had really thought her mam was losing her mind for a while. In fact, she wouldn't have been surprised if her mam had tried to do her da in, which was why she had sat with him for the last forty-eight hours of his life, only leaving the bedroom to visit the privy.

Her mam, beside herself, had gone flying off to the cottage homes, demanding to know what had happened to Gina and causing a right old barney. After they'd agreed to take a letter for Gina from her, her mam had barely eaten or slept for weeks, going about her duties the same as ever but with hardly a word to anyone. It was as though she was eaten up inside and they'd all been frightened for her because she was fading away in front of their eyes. And then, after months, the letter with the strange postmark from abroad had come.

Betty forced her gaze away from the picture and continued eating her meal although now she was barely tasting it. The lads had been glad for her mam, she knew that, and she supposed she ought to be, but she'd been filled with such rage she'd had a job to conceal it. It wasn't that Gina had written back or even what she'd said, her mam having read the letter out to them all, no, it was the look on her mam's face, her whole persona, that had made her so angry. She had been like a different person, a *new* person, as though she had shed a skin and revealed her true self, a younger, brighter, joy-filled self.

'Betty?'

Her mam's voice interrupted the dark thoughts and as she looked up, she saw her mam hovering with the roast potatoes.

'I asked you if you wanted some more but you were miles away, lass. Is everything all right?'

She nodded, her voice abrupt as she said, 'Aye, why wouldn't it be?', waving away the dish of potatoes as she spoke. She knew that one day this Gina, this beautiful angel, this amazing creature who was barely human and beyond compare, would come to the farm and she was dreading it with every fibre of her being. The farm was her home, *hers*, the one place in the world where she felt safe and secure and happy. She knew every inch of it, loved every blade of grass, every animal, and if this girl from a world before she was born came here, everything would be spoiled. She knew it.

Would Gina want to stay here for good? The thought was not a new one and every time it surfaced her stomach turned over and she felt physically sick. Her mam would want that, the lads too, especially James. Gina and James had been brought up as twins for the first few years of their lives, and she knew her brother had been broken-hearted when she'd disappeared. She still found it difficult to reconcile in her mind the man who had spirited away a small child to the horror of the workhouse with her da, her gruff, impatient but lovely da. But she trusted him. He'd told her, racked with pain as he'd been, that he'd known it was the best thing for the family and so she had to believe that. Gina had been nothing but trouble, he'd whispered, causing them to fight among themselves and dividing the house down the middle.

'She was sly and manipulative and cunning,' he'd murmured, gripping her hand with a strength belying the fact that he was at death's door. 'We'd taken her in out of the goodness of our hearts but we'd nursed a viper to our bosom. I couldn't let that continue, lass. I couldn't.'

And now the viper would come to her home, her beloved farm, and she would be older and even more cunning than she had been as a child. Betty drew in a ragged breath. But she wouldn't be fooled. Her mam and the lads might fall all over Gina when she arrived, but this was one person who had Gina's measure and she would find a way to bring her down. Or her name wasn't Betty Redfern.

Elsie had been restless all afternoon. She had plenty to do – there were always lots of jobs on a farm – but usually on a Sunday they all sat and dozed in front of the fire in the sitting room for an hour or two, stuffed to the gunnels after the Sunday roast. But today for some reason she couldn't relax.

It had stopped snowing while they ate lunch but within the hour had started again and now it had turned into a blizzard. Pulling on her coat and boots she went and marshalled the hens into their coop and then checked on the pigs in their new sty. The lads had done a first-rate job and there was ample shelter for the pigs, along with fresh straw for their bedding. She didn't need to check the cows – she knew they would be all right. Betty would rather starve herself than let the herd go hungry.

This thought brought a brief pang of tenderness followed by the rueful reflection that if only her daughter would treat her brothers as kindly as she did the cows, life would be much easier all round.

Walking into the big hay barn, she stood just inside looking across at the spot where Gina's mother had lain that winter's night so many years ago. In the months following the child's disappearance she'd come in here often to stand where they'd found the girl and beg her forgiveness for not looking after her baby properly. Gina's mother had entrusted the bairn to her and she'd let her down – her baby had still died in childhood, she had cried out to the rafters in an agony of grief. She had blamed herself for leading Gina to believe the new baby would be a boy, for not making more of the bairn when she'd come with the lads to see Betty, for not understanding how Gina must have felt – oh, a hundred and one things. And Ken had stood by and watched her grieve.

She sat down on a bale of hay, pulling her shawl more closely round her shoulders. On the day of his funeral she had told the parson what Ken had admitted as he was dying. He had been shocked, she had seen that, and he hadn't tried to make excuses for Ken, not exactly, but he had talked about forgiveness and other stuff she hadn't been ready to hear. She still wasn't ready, come to that. She supposed a parson had to say what he'd said – it was part of his job, wasn't it – and he had been kind when Robin had died, but she hadn't been back to the church since. She prayed to God about it and she didn't know if it was Him talking to her or her own mind, but something kept reminding her of how Jesus had prayed on the cross when they were crucifying Him, 'Father, forgive them, they know not what they do.' But Ken *had* known what he was doing, that was the thing, and not only that but he could have put it right at any time, he could have gone and fetched Gina and brought her home. But he hadn't.

After a little while Elsie rose wearily to her feet. She needed to make a pot of tea and wake them up; it would be getting dark soon and there were jobs to do before nightfall.

She was just closing the door of the barn when she saw the white-coated figure standing some distance away. She peered through the whirling snowflakes, blinking, before taking a stumbling step forwards and then another, her heart racing and making her head spin.

'Gina?' Suddenly the years fell away and there was her bairn, a full-grown woman now but still her bairn.

Gina dropped the suitcase she was holding as Elsie reached her, her heart flooded with such emotion that she couldn't have spoken. Her mam was the same, just the same, and as she felt herself enfolded in Elsie's arms the familiar smell of lavender from the dried bunches Elsie had always placed amongst their clothes took her straight back to childhood. They hugged and cried, incoherent words and endearments mixed with kisses, two women in a white landscape where nothing mattered but this moment, this wonderful, longed-for moment of reunion.

It was some time later when Elsie took Gina's face in her work-worn hands, saying softly, 'Let me look at you, hinny. By, you're the most beautiful sight in the world. Funny how a storm gave you to me and now one's brought you back home.'

'Oh, Mam.' Tears were still welling in Gina's eyes and now she gave a shaky smile, gulping before she could say, 'I've missed you so much.'

'Me too, lass. Me too. When you went something died in me – it was like all the joy in the world had been sucked away. And it never came back, not till now, that is.'

She had been wrong about her mam being the same, Gina thought, as she looked into the dear face. There were deep lines of pain grooved in her face that hadn't been there before and her hair was nearly white. She was older and of course she had expected that, but not the suffering that was so visible in her mam's eyes.

'I love you, Mam,' she whispered, a catch in her voice. 'I love you so much.'

'And I love you, hinny. More than you'll ever know.' For a moment Elsie looked as though she was going to cry again but then she pulled herself together, saying, 'Look at us, standing and getting chilled to the bone, and you must be frozen after your journey. How did you get here, lass?'

Gina picked up her suitcase and then slipped her arm in her mother's, not wanting to let go of her yet. She had left Birmingham on the night train the evening before and had been travelling for nearly twenty-four hours, changing trains at numerous stations and experiencing delay after delay because of the severe weather conditions. When she had finally arrived in Gateshead she had thrown caution to the wind and hired a taxi to bring her the last sixteen miles or so to the farm, but once they'd had to turn off the main road on which they'd been travelling the driver had flatly refused to go any further. He knew the farm, he'd told her, and all she had to do was to follow the country lane ahead of them for a couple of miles or so before she came to a track on the right with a sign for Cowslip Farm. If she kept on that for another mile the barns and the farmstead would come into view. He couldn't risk getting stuck out here with the weather worsening by the hour, he'd been daft to try in the first place. She was welcome to come back to Gateshead with him and find a hotel for the night if she didn't fancy a walk, but that was the best he could offer.

'By train and taxi,' she said, answering her mother's question, 'and then I walked the last bit.'

'Eh, lass, you never did. You could have fallen down and no one would have found you.'

'But I didn't.'

'No, you didn't.' Elsie stopped and pulled Gina into another bear-hug before they carried on towards the farm-house.

The snow was making it difficult to see clearly but Gina was recognizing the layout of the farm as they walked. When they reached the house her heart jumped and then began to pound like a sledgehammer. She knew Kenneth Redfern was dead, she knew he couldn't hurt her any longer, but it didn't make any difference. For a few moments she felt like a little girl again, frightened of the man she called her father and yet defiant against his harsh treatment of her at the same time. He had been all powerful in her childish understanding, a tyrant against whom she couldn't win. And then Elsie drew her into the warm bulk of her, saying softly, 'Welcome home, my bairn,' and the spectre of Kenneth Redfern faded.

It was quiet and beautifully warm in the kitchen when they entered, the heat causing Gina to shiver, and immediately Elsie said, 'You're frozen and no wonder, and your boots are wet through. Get them off, hinny, and sit by the range with your feet on the fender like you used to do as a bairn, do you remember? Here, give me your coat and hat, that's right, and I'll put the kettle on for a cup of tea. You need something warm inside you.'

As Elsie bustled about Gina sat in what she remembered was her mam's rocking chair, her feet dutifully on the fender as instructed, and gazed about her. Here, at least, nothing had changed. It was exactly as she had pictured it so many times when she had been in bed in the cottage homes. She glanced above her and said, 'That picture, Mam?'

'Aye, it's yours, hinny.' Elsie stopped her scurrying, her voice thick as she murmured, 'It's more precious than any of these works of art they talk about these days.' Drawing one of the hard-backed chairs from the table close to the rocking chair, she sat down. 'I'm sorry, I'm so sorry for what he did, lass.'

'You've got nothing to be sorry about.' Gina reached out and took her mother's hands. 'You didn't do anything wrong.'

'I should have known. Somehow I should have guessed what he'd done but who could even imagine such a thing?'

'No one could, Mam.' Gina was desperate to alleviate the pain in her mother's face. 'No one could imagine that.'

'No.' The syllable trembled as it passed Elsie's lips. 'But I should have, nonetheless.'

'That's not true. That would have made you like him, don't you see? To even conceive of such a possibility would be beyond the scope of most people's minds, good people, and you are a good person, Mam. He was responsible for what he did, him and him alone.'

There was a long pause that went into ten seconds before Elsie whispered, 'I've never looked at it like that before.'

'Well, it's the only way to look at it. What some of the SS guards did in the concentration camps, both men and women, wasn't within the scope of normal people's minds. They'd lost their humanity and something had taken them over. To a lesser extent it was the same with him.' She couldn't bring herself to say his name. 'You couldn't have known so don't think like that.'

'Oh, lass.' Elsie gripped Gina's hands now, her bottom lip trembling. 'All them lost years.'

'Don't dwell on them. It's now and the future we've got to think of, all right?'

Elsie gave a wan smile. 'It should be me saying all this to you, hinny.'

Gina smiled back. 'I don't know about that, but what I do know is that we've found each other again.'

'Aye, praise God. And you'll stay? Here at the farm I mean, with me?'

Gina hesitated. Now wasn't the time to say she had no idea how her coming back here would work out. It would have to be a day at a time, she knew that, because there wasn't just her mam and her to consider. She had been gone for so long for one thing and she knew she just couldn't slot in as though she'd never left. There were the lads too, they were grown men now and bound to be different to the boys of her memories. And, perhaps most important of all, there was Betty, her mam's natural daughter. Flesh of her flesh. She had no idea how Betty would view her turning up. Quietly she said, 'I'd love to stay if that's all right?'

'It's your home, hinny. You don't have to ask.'

And then there was a creak and the door from the hall opened, and standing in the aperture was Kenneth Redfern.

Chapter Twenty-Four

Gina lay in the darkness, a hot-water bottle at her feet, listening to her mother's gentle snores. After her husband had died, Elsie had cleared their bedroom of the double bed and replaced it with two twin beds. She'd told the lads and Betty it was because the bed was old and tired and the mattress sagged, but really she couldn't have slept in it again after the shock revelation about Gina. She wanted to cut Ken out of her thoughts as much as possible and a new bed was somehow symbolic of this. She had thrown out the two chairs by the window that had been in the room since she got married and which had been there from Ken's parents' days, and sold the big mahogany wardrobe and matching dressing table, buying smaller and less well-made ones for the money, but she didn't mind about the inferior quality. She wanted the room completely changed. She had whitewashed the walls, made new curtains and a clippy mat for the side of the bed, and only after that had begun sleeping in the room again. Until then she'd slept on the sofa in the sitting room.

She had told Gina all this when they'd taken her case up to the room and in truth all Gina recognized from her childhood was the pretty tiled fireplace with its black-leaded grate. She could completely understand her mother's feelings; there was nothing remaining of Kenneth Redfern in this, her mother's little sanctuary.

Gina turned over in bed, unable to sleep with her head buzzing from the events of the day. The fire in the grate took the chill off the room but it was still cold, although snuggled as she was under the heaped blankets and thick eiderdown she was as warm as toast.

It had only taken her a moment to realize the tall grim figure standing in the doorway dressed in a dark jumper and trousers wasn't Kenneth Redfern, but it had been a shock nonetheless and she knew her face must have reflected this. It hadn't been the best of starts to meeting the girl Elsie insisted on introducing as her sister, although it would have needed a huge stretch of anyone's imagination to think they were in any way related. Edwin and Larry and James had followed on Betty's heels and that, too, had been awkward but in a different way. They were grown men now and she was a young woman, and their clumsy pecks on her cheek had spoken of their embarrassment. It had been James who'd finally broken the ice when he had grinned at her and said, 'Who would have thought my little twin sister would have grown into such a smasher, eh?' and everyone had laughed and started talking. Everyone except Betty, that was.

The big log that Elsie had placed on the fire as they'd

gone to bed shifted slightly, sending a shower of sparks up the chimney and flickering shadows onto the whitewashed walls. The curtains at the window were open and it was still snowing heavily outside. If she hadn't persevered and made it through to the farm today she doubted she would have been able to in the next few days. There had been lots of times when she was a child that they'd been cut off from the outside world for days and weeks at a time, but she had never minded. The farm was self-sufficient and it had been fun making snowmen with James once their chores were done or having snowball fights with Larry and Edwin and Robin. Poor Robin. She tried to picture him on the screen of her mind but could only remember that he'd looked a lot like the twins. It was James who was less a Redfern than the others – he had Elsie's softer features to some extent and his manner was more his mother's – whereas Betty . . .

She bit her lip in the darkness. Betty *was* her father from what she could make out, not only in looks but temperament too. And Betty didn't like her. It had been as clear as the nose on her face. Kenneth Redfern's face.

Her mam had noticed this too. Once in bed and before Elsie had settled down for sleep, she'd said softly, 'Don't mind Betty, lass. She's the same with everybody, bless her. It's just her way and it's best to ignore her moods like James does. Larry and Edwin always rise to her bait no matter how much I tell 'em to take no notice.'

She had murmured something in reply, she forgot what, but she had known it was more than Betty's normal antagonism with her brothers. Betty had looked at her the way Kenneth Redfern used to. She lay worrying about it for a while before telling herself that there was nothing she could do. If Betty was determined to hate her at first sight, without even getting to know her a little, then the die had been cast. The girl made her flesh creep if she was being honest – she looked so much like her father – so she would try and stay out of her way while she was here but she wouldn't kowtow to her.

Having settled that in her mind, she turned her thoughts to Josef as she invariably did once she was in bed at night. She knew from her work with the CO that many German and Italian POWs had been set to work in the countries in which they were being held, and others had been shipped back to their country of origin. She had seen confidential reports about the rape, torture and killing of German men, women and children by the victorious Russian forces when Berlin had fallen, some of the atrocities every bit as disturbing as the horrific things the Nazis had done, and prayed Josef hadn't fallen into Russian hands after the war. On paper, Britain, France, America and Russia had agreed to divide Germany into four zones of occupation, but it had become apparent that the Russians treated the Germans very differently to the three other Allies. German soldiers had been transported to Russia and sent to labour camps, and in the large Soviet zone to the east many of the German population had been forcibly expelled from their homes, creating some ten million refugees. Berlin had been left as a city without infrastructure and in a state of complete turmoil when the Red Army finished with it, and by the time the first American forces had arrived, a month after occupation by the Russians, the people had been shattered and terrified.

She hated to think of Josef trapped in a country where there was little food, many homes still in a state of disrepair and without adequate fuel for even the most basic of heating facilities, and where people were freezing to death every day. According to the newspapers, the Soviets had dismantled and removed nearly seventy per cent of Berlin's industrial capacity, and lots of cities in Germany had also suffered some seventy per cent ruin with the remaining population crammed into what buildings remained intact, often meaning four families having to live together in a small single apartment.

Gina thought of the stories that filtered through from the observers in Germany; of children scouring the streets and ruins searching for small pieces of coal, and families selling what few possessions they had in order to buy a few potatoes to eat. All over the land, gangs of any able-bodied men, girls, boys and women had been organized into clearing-up groups to remove the detritus of war, but with this winter and the two before it being so harsh, people were collapsing where they stood. The US Red Cross were making valiant efforts to prevent the misery by distributing blankets, clothing and care parcels, and the British were also helping, but things were still desperately dire. If Josef was still alive, *if*, then he could very possibly be in the midst of all that, knowing he had lost everything – his home, his parents, possibly his sister and her family too. *And it wasn't his fault.*

Her hands clenched into fists for a moment and she had to make a conscious decision to relax them. The nightmare world created by the twelve years of National Socialist rule under Hitler had brainwashed so many of its youth; children had been taught nothing of the outside world and its many differing races and cultures, only what Hitler and his Nazis wanted them to know. The indoctrination had been brutal and thorough. The youth of Germany hadn't realized it was happening because Hitler's regime was all they'd known, and those adults who opposed the Nazis had been disposed of with a ruthlessness that reflected what was to come. The Nazis had murdered many ordinary Germans but she doubted if people were ready to see that side of it. Would she have been, in all fairness, if she hadn't fallen in love with Josef? Probably not, she admitted ruefully.

She had told her mother and the others about her WAAF life over the evening meal, trying to make it as humorous as she could and skating over any sad bits. She hadn't mentioned Mark or Josef, it hadn't been the time, but she intended to confide in her mother at some point when they were alone. She hoped Elsie would understand about Josef, but if she didn't it would make no difference to the way she felt about him. Josef was a part of her, always would be, and the only man in the world she could ever truly love and contemplate spending the rest of her life with. It was as simple as that.

The opportunity to confide in Elsie came earlier than Gina had anticipated. She hadn't slept well, there had been too much on her mind, and it was still dark and very early in the morning when she awoke from the light doze she'd fallen into and decided to go downstairs to the kitchen and make herself a hot drink. She slid out of bed, drawing in her breath as the cold hit her after the warm cocoon under the blankets, and began to pull on the thick jumper and pair of dungarees she'd bought specially for her visit. She thought she'd been as quiet as a mouse, but just as she pulled her jumper over her head, Elsie said, 'What is it, lass? You all right?'

'I'm fine, Mam, go back to sleep. I'm just going to get a drink, that's all.'

'I'll come with you, hinny.'

As they walked downstairs together Gina found herself marvelling, as she had the day before, how easy it had been to slip into the old close relationship with Elsie. Their bond was as solid as it had ever been and it was a balm to her soul, and although she knew it was mean of her she was glad Elsie didn't have the same intimacy with Betty. It had only been in the hours since she had got home that she had realized deep down she had been frightened she'd been usurped in Elsie's affections by her mam's natural daughter. She could have understood it, of course she could, and the green-eyed monster was an awful thing, she had to admit, and it wasn't something she was proud of, but nevertheless she was relieved. In fact, relief was a weak word to describe how she felt.

Once in the kitchen Elsie made them both a mug of milky cocoa and put out a plate of her ginger biscuits. These were traditionally sold as 'fairings' at the seasonal fairs which toured the towns and villages of the north in spring and autumn, and when she was a little girl Gina had thought they were called fairies, something Elsie now mentioned as she said with a smile, 'Help yourself to a fairy, hinny.'

Gina smiled back. 'You remembered.'

'There's not a thing I've forgotten about you, lass.'

Gina sipped the frothy cocoa. Again, the taste took her straight back to childhood. No one made cocoa like Elsie. Whether it was the rich creamy milk from the cows on the farm she didn't know, but it tasted wonderful. She ate one of the biscuits before she said, 'Mam, there's something I need to tell you.'

'Oh, aye?'

'You might not like it.'

'Whatever it is, it'll be better out than in.'

'I met someone, a man, when I was in Egypt. He was a POW. A German POW. We – we fell in love.'

She saw Elsie exhale. 'Is that all? I imagined all sorts of things from the look on your face.'

'You don't mind?'

'Lass, I was thinking someone had hurt you, there have been such awful things done in this war.'

'But he's a German.'

'Aye, and if you love him a nice bloke, I bet. Tell me about him.'

She did. They talked for an hour or more and she told Elsie about Mark too. She hadn't really mentioned the cottage homes the day before or the night that Kenneth Redfern had taken her from the family home, but after Elsie had made them both another mug of cocoa, she said, 'The night Betty was born? What happened exactly? I'd like to know but don't tell me if it's going to upset you, hinny.'

'It won't upset me. He came to my room in the middle of the night when I was asleep and carried me outside. I tried to fight him, to cry out, but I couldn't. He was too strong.'

'Of course he was, the wicked so-an'-so.'

'I can't remember much about the journey now except it was cold and I was frightened of being thrown in the river. He threatened that, to keep me quiet, I suppose. And then he left me at the gates of the workhouse and disappeared.'

'Did he hit you, lass?'

'Once, out in the farmyard, and he shook me later, I remember that, and after that it's a blur. I think I must have had concussion or something because I was ill for a while, and after I was a bit better they transferred me to the cottage homes.'

'Did he say why he'd done it?'

'He said you'd taken me in when my mother died but now there was no room for me because of the new baby and you both wanted me gone.' In spite of herself, Gina's voice trembled.

'The swine, the lying swine. To tell you that, to make out I was part of what he did.'

'I didn't believe it, not at first, but then after a while when you didn't come . . .' Gina's voice dwindled away. She took a deep breath. 'I became resigned, I suppose.'

'Oh, lass, lass. What you must have gone through.' Elsie was weeping again, and so when she asked, 'What was it like in the homes, was it bad?' Gina reached out and took her mother's hands.

She had to lie now and make it convincing. Her mam had been through enough and the truth would only hurt her more and what good would that do? Her mam knowing couldn't alter the past and it would only prey on her mind. 'It wasn't home,' she said softly, 'and I missed you so much, but I made some good friends and that helped. We were fed well and received an education. It could have been a lot worse.' She needed to change the subject and because she wanted to know, she said quietly, 'The night I was born? Did my mother say anything other than what my name was to be?'

Elsie shook her head. 'She was in a poor way. I don't know how she had managed to drag herself into the barn. Whoever it was turned her out has her death on their heads, that's for sure. Something makes me think it wasn't her own folk, her mam an' da, who did that. She wanted you named after her mam for one thing. And I don't think she was from these parts, there was an accent to her voice like a foreigner might have. Only slight but it was there.'

She had to ask. 'What did she look like?'

'She was bonny, lass, beautiful. She looked a lot like you except her eyes were brown, not blue.'

'What – what happened to her, after she died, I mean?'

Elsie took a deep breath. She had known this moment would come and she prayed her lass wouldn't hate her for what she was going to say. And she couldn't blame Ken for this; it had been her idea and hers alone. 'I knew if the authorities found out about your mam and that you weren't mine they'd put you in the workhouse orphanage so we had to get rid of the – the body.'

'She's buried somewhere on the farm?' Gina asked, and the hope in her voice was like a dagger in Elsie's heart.

'No, lass, I'm sorry. We couldn't risk the farmhands coming across her and the weather was too bad to dig a grave, so we did what I believed was the only thing we could do and gave her a water burial.'

Gina's brow wrinkled. 'I don't understand.'

'The river, lass. We let the river take her.'

Gina stared at Elsie, shock on her face. For a moment she didn't know how to respond. Then she said, 'Did anyone find her?'

'Not that I heard, no, lass.' Elsie swallowed hard. 'We were snowed in for weeks and with the weeds and debris in the river and trees being blown down it's possible that – well, that she . . .'

'Never surfaced,' Gina finished for her. She sat for a

moment, thinking. 'Perhaps she would have liked that better, to be free in the water rather than buried in a hole in the ground.'

Elsie watched her face, scarcely breathing.

'Yes, I think if she was so young she wouldn't have wanted to be put under the earth.' She was bitterly disappointed there wasn't a place where she could know her mother was, stand and grieve for her and pray, but she'd come to terms with that. Her reward for not letting her disappointment show was the look of relief on Elsie's face when she glanced up at her. 'When the weather's better will you show me where she went into the river?'

'Of course, lass, anything. I've often gone there myself and said a prayer for her. She was nowt but a slip of a girl and she was taken too soon.'

Gina nodded. 'Do the others know about everything?'

'Not everything, no. Ken told them when he was dying that we'd been asked to take you in because your parents had died and there was no one else who could look after a baby. When they asked me about it I said it was an old friend of the family who came to see us with you and who asked if we could help. I said we'd since lost touch with them.'

Gina nodded. So many lies. But all done for the best, as Elsie had seen it. And perhaps it had been. But with her mother vanishing so completely and the authorities being unaware of it, it was far too late to ever discover who she had been.

'I'm sorry, lass.'

Elsie's voice brought her back to herself and Gina reached out her hand. 'You saved me that night, Mam. You said yourself I wasn't breathing and that I was tiny. I wouldn't have survived if it wasn't for you. And I had a wonderful life here before he took me away.'

Elsie sniffed and nodded. 'No one could have loved you more than me, hinny.'

'I know, really I do.'

The clock on the kitchen mantelpiece struck the half-hour and as it did so they heard someone coming down the stairs.

It was half-past five and a new day was starting.

Chapter Twenty-Five

The snow which had begun in earnest the day Gina had arrived at the farm did not let up for the next few days, and it soon became clear that Britain was in the grip of one of the worst winters ever recorded.

Heavy snowstorms and blizzards and sub-zero temperatures combined with a serious fuel shortage brought the country to its knees. Power cuts, twenty-foot-high drifts and relentless winds left thousands of homes without heat or light, and the RAF began dropping food for stranded villagers and their animals in some areas. Isolated country houses displayed sheets as a distress call, and as the weather continued to worsen still further, whole towns were cut off and essentials such as milk and bread ran out.

On Cowslip Farm, however, life continued fairly normally. The modern conveniences of gas and electricity hadn't yet reached them, and Elsie always made sure they were well stocked up with oil and candles for the winter months as a matter of course. The log store was stacked to the rafters with enough wood to see them through to the spring, along with sacks of coal in the coal hole. Fortunately, the well from which they drew their water wasn't reliant on such a fickle thing as the weather. The farm was used to harsh winters, and although this one had all the makings of a particularly bad one, they took it in their stride.

The lads were kept busy day and night clearing the fresh snow that fell with relentless determination from the yard and other areas of the farm, ensuring the hens and pigs were safe and dry and that the route to the cowsheds was always open. Betty saw to it that her precious charges were not inconvenienced in any way and it was doubtful if her 'ladies' even noticed the horrific conditions.

Gina and Elsie worked in the dairy and in the house, making sure three hot meals a day were on the table along with plenty of snacks and hot drinks to thaw out the others when they came in from outside, and that the range and the fires in the sitting room and bedrooms were kept going twenty-four hours a day. The clothes line strung across the kitchen ceiling and Elsie's huge wooden airer were always full with sodden coats and hats and trousers, and each night saturated boots were lined up in front of the range to dry out for morning. It wasn't the battle against the elements that concerned Gina, however, as much as the unspoken conflict between herself and Betty. Elsie's daughter never spoke directly to her; her every look was a glare and if Gina said something to her it was ignored unless Elsie was present, when Betty would mutter a grudging answer. Gina knew the lads had spoken to Betty and according to James

had received short shrift with her telling them in no uncertain terms to mind their own business. Gina wasn't
concerned for herself; Betty's antagonism was annoying but
she'd encountered much worse in the past. What did bother
her was the fact that her mother might be upset. And so
when she had been at the farm for a full two weeks, she
took the bull – or in this case Betty – by the horns.

It was the last couple of days of February and the big
freeze showed no signs of releasing its grip on a beleaguered
Britain. The day had begun like the ones before it with the
lads up at five in the morning to begin clearing the snow,
and Betty coming down half an hour later and stamping
off to see to the cows. The day before, Gina had tackled
the household's washing, pounding away with the poss stick
in the big tub in the scullery for what had seemed like
hours, and then putting the sheets and towels and pillowcases through the mangle along with some of the other
items. The ceiling of the kitchen had looked like the sails
of a ship by the time the sheets and pillowcases were hanging
from the line across it, and the clothes airer was full too,
damp steam rising like a mist. There was far too much
stuff to dry in one go and she had another huge pile of
clothes and what have you waiting in the scullery until the
first lot was dry enough to iron. It had been exhausting
work, and how Elsie managed to do this and cope with
running the household, cooking meals and working in the
dairy, Gina didn't know. It was too much and although she
knew Betty wouldn't like it, she intended to tell her so.

Once breakfast was over and everyone had disappeared

to their various jobs, Gina made the excuse that she needed to go to the privy and slipped outside, making her way quickly to the byres. Betty was opening up a bale of oat straw as she walked in and paused, straightening as she stared coldly without speaking.

'I need a word with you.' It still amazed Gina that Betty looked so like her father, not only looked like him but seemed the very personification of the farmer in every way. When she received no reply, she went on, 'All the work that Mam has to do in the house and the dairy is too much for one person, especially now she's getting older. When I leave she'll need help or she'll make herself ill. I know you and the lads have your work cut out with everything outside, but I'm sure a woman from the village could come for a few hours each day.'

Betty's eyes narrowed. 'So you *are* going to leave then?'

Gina stared at the other girl. It was as though Betty hadn't heard anything else she had said. 'At some point, yes.'

'Not the easy ride here you thought it'd be?'

Gina ignored this, saying, 'And that's the other thing I wanted to talk to you about.'

Betty's brow furrowed and Gina watched as her chin pressed into her neck. She clearly didn't understand what Gina meant but wasn't about to ask.

'Your opinion of me doesn't bother me in the least except for the fact that you seem determined to upset Mam by showing at every opportunity how much you dislike me. It's unnecessary and childish and has to stop.'

Betty gazed at her; her whole attitude shrieked incredulity. No one had ever spoken to her like this. She'd had her ups and downs with the lads, but she knew her arguments with them had been because she provoked them and she had always been in control. It took a moment for her to be able to say, and more weakly than she would have liked, 'Don't you tell me what to do.'

'Someone has to.' Physically, Betty made two of her being so tall and big but she had made up her mind she wouldn't be intimidated by Kenneth Redfern's daughter. It helped that she could see nothing of Elsie in her, and now she said, 'If you've got any feeling for Mam at all you'll stop being so awkward and nasty in front of her. It serves no purpose except to make everyone uncomfortable. I know you don't like me, but you don't have to prove it every minute, all right? Just act your age.'

'How dare you!' Betty's temper, so like her father's, was blazing now. 'You come here acting like Lady Muck and tell me what I can and can't do? Well, I've got news for you – you don't belong here. You've caused nothing but trouble since the day my mam an' da took you in, and you're still causing it. Now I've met you I can understand why Da did what he did. Oh, aye, I can. He called you a viper and that's what you are, a snake, a viper in the midst of us.'

Stunned as she was by the sheer venom, Gina retained her composure. Her voice low, she said, 'You aren't a stupid person, Betty, so don't act like one. I was just coming up for six years old when your father took me away in the middle of the night and then made up a pack of lies to conceal what he'd done. He knew it would break Mam's heart but he didn't care, not as long as he got what he wanted. He was a liar and a coward, and only a monster would do what he did, so don't pretend you don't know that. I could never do anything right, as far as he was concerned, from when I was a baby and that's the truth of it. He'd made up his mind he didn't want me and that was that.'

'You caused him and Mam to be estranged when he was dying and he died miserable because of it.'

'Anything he felt he brought on himself.'

'He was a good man, my da, whatever you say, and what are you anyway? Some man's flyblow, that's what. My da told me you'd been born the wrong side of the blanket and your mother no better than she should be.' Betty's face was a fiery red, her breath coming in gasps between the poisonous words. 'Well, you might think yourself the cat's whiskers with being bonny an' all, but I see through you even if the others don't. You're bad and woe betide anyone who gets mixed up with you.'

Such hate. Gina looked into the mannish face and it really was as if Betty's father was standing there. She was trembling inside but somehow she managed to conceal it from the angry girl in front of her.

'I take back what I said about you not being stupid because only a stupid person could know the facts and not accept them for what they are. He was your father and you loved him, I understand that, I can even admire your loyalty, but the truth is the only person who was bad was your da. What he did was unforgivable and cancels out him being a good father to you, at least in my book. Because you were a girl he thought he could get rid of me like an unwanted parcel and substitute a replacement more to his liking. It was cruel and wicked to me and actually quite insulting to you, but you don't want to see that, do you. You want to hang on to this image you've got of him rather than see him for what he was and still love him in spite of it. You're a coward, Betty, like he was.'

She turned, and she wouldn't have been surprised if Betty had sprung on her from behind, such had been the look of rage on the other girl's face, but then she was walking out of the cowshed and into the piercing cold outside. She stood just beyond the door, taking great gulps of the icy air. Before she had gone into the cowshed she had hoped that in some way she and Betty might reach a compromise where the other girl could at least tolerate her while she was here. Now everything was ten, twenty, a hundred times worse, which wouldn't help Elsie at all. Her mother had enough to contend with. Elsie had confided to her a few days ago that the farm was not doing well; Kenneth Redfern hadn't been a forward thinker and had fought change while he'd been alive, unlike some of the other farmers hereabouts. The lads understood they needed to modernize, she'd told Gina, and get electricity to the farm so that the cows could be milked by machine and they could increase the herd; but this would cost money and Betty was chary of taking a loan like her father had been, and she had worked on her brothers until they, too, were nervous about it.

'Nothing stays the same, that's the thing, lass,' Elsie had said quietly. 'Ken didn't understand that and neither does Betty. I've told her a farm's not a mausoleum. Old Jed Lyndon, him who has the farm in Chesterwood the other side of Hexham, told the lads on market day that there's grants and technical advice to be had from the government now the war's over. Kenneth always wanted this to be a dairy farm first and foremost, like his da and granda afore him, and Betty's the same, but that doesn't mean we have to carry on exactly like before, now does it?'

Gina had agreed, saying no, it didn't. She'd been surprised and impressed with how clearly her mother saw the future. Usually it was the young folk who embraced change.

Now, as she stood in the thickly falling snow, she recalled a conversation she'd had with Larry the day before when he had come into the scullery where she had been working and offered to peg the sheets on the kitchen line for her. She'd taken the opportunity of broaching the subject of Elsie's workload with him, asking if Elsie always did the washing and ironing as well as the dairy work and seeing to the meals and other household needs, although she'd known the answer. He had nodded, looking sheepish.

'Me an' Ed have told Betty over and over till we're blue in the face that she ought to help Mam inside, but she's having none of it.'

'Couldn't you and Edwin and James help Mam if Betty won't?' she'd asked point-blank.

'Mam wouldn't have that. She says washing and ironing and inside jobs – and she includes the dairy in that – are women's work.'

Gina had stared at him in frustration. She didn't doubt what he said was true, she could almost hear Elsie saying it.

'Of course, the ideal solution would be for my Lucy to help when we're married. She'd only be doing what she does now on her da's farm, but I'm loath to bring her here in all honesty, Gina. Not to live cheek by jowl with Betty. We'd have no privacy and it wouldn't work. Ed feels the same about his lass.' He had shaken his head. 'I dunno what the answer is, I don't straight. Da left the farm to me an' Ed and we don't want to leave or sell it, and it wouldn't be right to throw Betty out and there's Mam and James an' all, but we're thirty-one years old. We both want to be wed afore we're too much older.'

'If you and Ed could see yourselves staying here for ever would you be more inclined to do what Mam's talking about and look to getting grants and a loan and everything?'

He'd nodded again. 'Aye. But like I said, can you imagine our two lassies rubbing shoulders with Betty every evening and how it'd be? Murder for everyone, that's what. Lucy and Ava, Ed's lass, get on well with Mam when they've met her in the past but it wouldn't be like having their own place for either of them, would it. Not like proper married life where you can shut your own front door when the day's done. But don't say nowt to Mam.'

Gina lifted her head that was already coated in a layer of white and gazed up into the thousands of snowflakes. The idea that had been germinating after her talk with Larry had taken root in the last few minutes after her run-in with Betty. She'd been hoping for a different answer to the problem, she had to admit, but having seen Betty at her worst she knew there wasn't one. Larry was quite right, he and Ed and their future wives would need their own place, but the idea of the farm being sold and the family breaking up would destroy her mam, she knew it would. She would be left living somewhere with Betty, an angry, bitter, resentful and vengeful Betty, no doubt. And her mam wouldn't be around any bairns Ed and Larry might have, not like if her sons were living at the farm. Elsie would wither and go to an early grave. And there was James too. Farming was all he knew and this was his home. She knew they weren't twins, that they were no relation at all, but even now she felt as though they were and she loved him nearly as much as her mam.

But she would have to keep her fledgling idea to herself for now until the weather improved and she could make the journey into Hexham and take advice. She needed to understand what was possible and what was not, pull facts and figures together before she mentioned what was on her mind. It might work, it might not, but it was the only way she could see that her mam would remain in her home with all her children around her, future grand-children too. And her mam deserved that. She was the best of women and had worked her fingers to the bone all her life, but more than that, she had taken a tiny orphaned baby to her heart and saved its life, and in so doing had suffered much grief and heartache.

Decision made, she tramped through the snow to the farmhouse. She opened the door, relishing the warmth and comforting smell of the meat roll Elsie had already got steaming on the range for lunch in another two or three hours.

The atrocious conditions continued for the next few weeks. Non-stop blizzards stopped all shipping in the Channel, creating a new threat to food supplies, and fishing fleets were kept in port. Air travel was in chaos and troops had been called in across the country, along with hundreds of prisoners being enlisted in the north to help with snow clearance. Road and rail transport all but ground to a halt, and in any public houses that remained open the customers learned to drink by candlelight as they discussed the fuel crisis. In March and April as a thaw set in a new hazard presented itself, that of severe flooding. Homes were made inhabitable, two million sheep – a week's meat ration nationwide – were killed, and hundreds of acres of wheat were damaged. On the farm, the battle with acres of mud recommenced but this time Elsie didn't mind so much. She had Gina home for one thing, and in comparison to that nothing else mattered. It also meant spring was round the corner, albeit a late one this year.

It was in the middle of April that Gina asked if she could accompany Larry and Edwin when they went to Hexham for market day. She was purposely vague about the reason, saying that there were some loose ends concerning her time in the WAAF to be sorted and that she needed to open a bank account now she was back in England.

Amazingly, and she hadn't expected it, Betty had been more civil to her in front of Elsie since their conversation in the barn so something of what she had said to her had got through. If Elsie wasn't around though, Betty was openly hostile. James had apparently challenged Betty about it which had made things worse when Betty had rounded on him, saying his loyalty should be to her, his sister, not Gina who was nothing to him. In front of Elsie everyone put on a fairly good act, however, which was all Gina was bothered about. She didn't plan to stay at the farm for ever; she intended to try and track down Josef at some point and find out what had happened to him, but she had to admit she didn't know where to begin and for the time being she felt she owed it to Elsie to spend some months with her.

So far April had been a month of unfolding buds, of warmth and cold, sunshine and showers and blustery winds, but today, although the sunshine was without the heat of summer, the sun was radiant in a deep blue sky without a cloud to be seen. Gina sat between Edwin and

Larry on the cart's plank seat and as they trundled along country lanes, the horse clip-clopping in front of them and clearly enjoying her day out, Gina felt more at peace than she had since arriving at the farm. Not happy, because how could she be happy not knowing if Josef was dead or alive, but the day before Elsie had shown her the spot on the riverbank that had been her mother's last resting place of sorts and since then she had felt she had somewhere to mourn her. She had spent some time there by herself amid dappled shade from the age-old trees growing both sides of the bank, talking to the girl who had given birth to her and weeping softly for her tragic end at so young an age. It might have been her imagination, but she'd felt a strong sense of her mother's presence after a while, a feeling that all was well with her soul, and this had not left her overnight. She didn't try to analyse it because she feared in so doing the feeling might slip away; instead she thanked God for it in her heart and asked Him to tell her mother how much she loved her and wished she could have known her.

The journey along country lanes was a pleasant one and when they reached the outskirts of Hexham it was just before midday. Gina arranged to meet Larry and Edwin in two hours' time in the marketplace where they parted company; the two men having farm business to see to and Gina going straight to the bank, which was just a stone's throw away. There she had a very satisfactory meeting with the manager, who was delighted with her deposit of the CO's cheque and who personally took charge of the formalities involved with opening an account. Her next visit was to the town's building society, but as the manager had gone to lunch she was told to return in an hour. She spent the time talking to a solicitor who fortunately was able to see her without an appointment, and by the time she returned to the building society her head was buzzing with facts and figures. Her last call before she met Larry and Edwin was to a small builders' yard the solicitor had recommended, where she had an informative and helpful conversation with the owner and one of his sons.

She was late meeting Larry and Edwin, apologizing profusely when she found them waiting for her, but as they'd lubricated their business with two or three beers they were in a mellow mood, merely teasing her a little about her lack of packages after her jaunt into town.

'Mam always says she hasn't got much to buy and then she comes back with her arms full,' Edwin said fondly.

Gina smiled but didn't reply, and on the way home she didn't say much, her mind absorbed with the hundred and one things she had to think about after her excursion. Fortunately Edwin and Larry weren't given to chatter so her silence went unnoticed, and once back at the farm they all separated to get on with their respective work, Larry and Edwin outside and Gina to the dairy.

She made one more visit to Hexham a few weeks later, this time with James who was taking the cart in to bring home some materials he needed to repair the bull's winter enclosure, which was the worse for wear. Dairy breed bulls were notoriously less good-tempered than beef-bred bulls and Barney was no exception, and they couldn't take the risk he would finish the job of kicking down his enclosure come winter.

It was after this second visit in the third week of May that Gina asked for a family assembly. After the dire winter May had burst on the scene in a profusion of scents and colour. In the farm's orchard at the rear of the barns snow-like pink and white blossom loaded the boughs of apple and cherry trees, and in the hedgerows stitchwort, white dead-nettle, speedwell and other flowers perfumed the fields and lanes. New life was everywhere and in Bluebell Wood where she had fallen asleep by mistake all those years ago, the blooms that gave the wood its name reflected the deep blue skies in a carpet of dazzling colour.

Gina had been working in the dairy most of the day, but she had managed to escape and spend a few minutes by the riverbank, asking her mother's blessing on what she was going to say to the family tonight. She had sat quietly, watching a young cuckoo in one of the trees overhanging the river being fed by its foster parents as it sat on a branch demanding food. She'd never forgotten Kenneth Redfern calling her a cuckoo in the nest when he'd been arguing with Elsie one night. She'd only been five at the time but something in his voice had burned what he'd said into her memory. The fledgling's foster parents were sparrows and the cuckoo was already three or four times their size, its beak gaping as it cried to be fed and the poor sparrows worn out by the voracious interloper.

That was how Kenneth Redfern had seen her, she'd thought bitterly. An intruder, a trespasser who'd infiltrated his family uninvited, who'd been foisted on him by circumstances. And he'd hated her for it, resenting the very air she breathed and every mouthful of food she'd eaten that should have gone to his flesh and blood. But Elsie and the others *were* her family, even if no Redfern blood ran in her veins. It wasn't the biological act of giving birth to children that made a family, it was the years of nurturing, of love and devotion and sacrifice that created a bond that formed a family. The sparrows were doing their best to raise their enormous foster child and would continue to do so. Kenneth Redfern could have learned a lot from the birds, tiny as they were.

That night during the evening meal, she waited until everyone had got started on the baked jam roll and custard before she said, 'Once you've all finished I'd like us to go through to the sitting room for a few minutes. I've got something to say.'

Betty had raised her eyebrows, sending her a venomous look behind Elsie's back, but keeping her voice pleasant as she said, 'Sorry, got too much to do.'

'No, you haven't, Betty, not so much you can't spare a few minutes.' The cows were outside in the fields now, enjoying grazing on new grass and chewing the cud at their leisure and the evening milking was over. 'It's important.'

Betty gave an exaggerated sigh but protested no more,

and after the pudding was finished they all went through to the sitting room where despite the mild evening a fire was burning.

'Well, lass?' Elsie plumped herself down in one of the easy chairs and stretched her aching legs. Her feet were tending to swell come evening these days but she never drew attention to it. She had been feeling her age for some time but things had eased considerably since Gina had come back; in fact she wondered how she'd managed before. 'What is it you want to say?'

The others sat down too, Betty on a hard-backed chair just inside the doorway which was the furthest point away from Gina, who was standing in front of the fireplace. Gina glanced round at the lads and Elsie. This was her family and although what she was going to do might seem crazy to some people, she had no doubt it was the right thing. It would have been nice to keep the money the CO had given her and it would have cushioned the difficulties involved in travelling to try and find Josef, but she was young and able and she would work her way where she needed to go.

'I've been thinking about the future of the farm,' she said with no preamble. 'I know Edwin and Larry want to get married soon but as things stand there would be no room for their wives, and in the future a growing family, in the farmhouse.'

She saw Larry looking at her anxiously. He'd confided how he and Edwin saw the future with all its difficulties in confidence, and he didn't want Elsie worried or upset.

'A solution to this would be building two extensions, wings if you like, on the house as it stands now. Perhaps a sitting room and kitchen downstairs and three bedrooms upstairs with a bathroom for each wing, something like that. It would mean one of the bedrooms in the current house could be converted into a bathroom because one is badly needed here, along with electricity and a proper water supply to the farm.'

Everyone was looking at her as though she had taken leave of her senses but it was Betty who said, her voice dripping scorn, 'And how do you suggest we find the money for all this? It doesn't grow on trees, you know.'

'No, it doesn't grow on trees.' Gina ignored the sarcasm. 'For certain improvements there are grants available and now is the time to take advantage of them while the government is still grateful for the effort farmers put in during the war to feed the nation. I think we're all agreed that this farm is essentially a dairy one and that crop growing, although necessary, is secondary to the cattle? That being the case we need to look to increasing the herd—'

'Hang on a minute,' Betty interrupted, her voice aggressive now. 'I've got enough on my plate with how things are at present, thank you very much. We can't afford to employ any more than the two labourers we have now.'

'You wouldn't need to, not initially, until the herd increased. The cows would be milked in a milking parlour built next to a new dairy with stalls to accommodate the cows while they were being milked by releaser machines;

the milk would be piped straight into the dairy for processing and the first batch of cows then moved out of their stalls and the next batch moved in. It's happening already in various parts of the country.'

'And why do you think I'd want that?'

'It's called progress, Betty,' Edwin put in succinctly. 'All right?'

'Well, I don't want that sort of progress.'

'Without it this farm will slowly die.'

Betty glared at her brother. 'Says who?'

'Me, and Larry too, and don't forget it's us that own the farm. We can actually do what we like with it.'

It was the last thing Gina had wanted him to say, knowing how it must rankle with Betty and possibly James too, but Kenneth Redfern had been of the mind that the farm was passed down to the oldest son, or in this case sons, as it had been done for generations. She saw Betty's face change from an angry red to white as the blood drained.

'I see, so that's how it is? I've got no more say than one of the hired hands?'

'Of course not, you know we take your opinion on board about everything.'

'Can I just say something?' Gina desperately tried to pull the meeting back on track. 'Some of these changes could be done with the aid of a grant and so on, but some couldn't, or not much of one. I was given some money by my CO when I left the WAAF – we were in a bomb explosion and I saved his life but that's another story. Anyway, he was grateful and it's a large amount, more than I'd ever need. I propose we use that to build the two wings to the house. I've been to a builder and if you three lads muck in and help, the vast majority of the work can be done for the money I have. It'll be hard graft, you'll be labouring for the builders, but it'll help keep the cost down.'

Elsie, who had been listening with growing amazement, sat up straight in her chair. 'You can't give away money that was meant for you, lass.'

'I can actually, Mam, and I want to.'

'And what's in it for you? What do you want?' Betty's voice was more in the form of a snarl.

Gina looked at the girl who was the living embodiment of Kenneth Redfern and never had she seen the situation so clearly. Somehow this had to stop, this hatred that had come from Betty's father and poisoned her as surely as a drug injected into her veins. They would never like each other, she knew that, but if there was some common ground at least it would make life easier all round. Quietly, she said, 'What's in it for me, Betty? To see Mam happy, that's what, and you others too. Farming is in your blood, I know that, all of you, and to make this farm succeed as it could you need to work together. Larry and Edwin having what would be in effect their own separate homes here in the farmstead would be part of that. It would mean their wives could work with Mam in the dairy for one thing, and once they'd learned her way of doing things they could even take it over completely if she wanted them to as she got older. But the way your father left things is to my mind wrong.' She looked directly at Larry and Edwin. 'I'm sorry, but it is. To cut James and Betty out of this place when they work as hard as you two just doesn't seem right or fair, and I'd like you to think about that. If you four had equal shares, like a cooperative, I suppose, wouldn't you all be working towards the same goal knowing a quarter of the farm was yours?'

Larry and Edwin stared at her, their faces a picture.

Without giving anyone a chance to speak, Gina went on, 'If I put my money into the farmstead that's what I'd like to see done. Legally, with a solicitor, I mean. You two have said yourselves that Betty is the best dairy farmer by far around here with the way she handles the cows and cares for them, and James works like a Trojan every day for you. Why shouldn't their labour be for themselves too, knowing they've got a stake in the farm? A solicitor could arrange things so no one could sell their share without the others being able to buy it first, not that I think that would be necessary because I know the way each of you feels about Cowslip Farm and your heritage. But it would be a safeguard, that's all.'

She hadn't glanced at Betty in the last few moments. She had no idea how the other girl would react to this proposal, or Edwin and Larry for that matter. Betty was quite capable of telling her where to stick her idea and that she wouldn't be patronized by Gina, she knew that, and Larry and Edwin might be loath to let half of the farm fall out of their grasp, even if it was to their brother and sister. But to her mind, the twins' half would grow into something that would be worth much more than the whole farm was at present, so financially they wouldn't lose out, added to which they'd still be living with their wives and children in the home they loved, doing what they'd been born for, and with their mother and siblings fully on board.

There was silence for a moment and then it was Elsie who said, in a small voice, 'But what about you, lass? Wouldn't you want a share too? This is as much your home as it is the lads and Betty's.'

Gina smiled at Elsie, a sad smile. She didn't want to upset her, but the truth was the truth. 'But it's not, Mam, is it. Not really. Let's be honest. I couldn't love you more if I was your biological daughter, I know that, but I also know that farming isn't in my blood in the same way that it is in Larry and the others. Coming back has proved it to me. I love being here with you but I don't think I could settle permanently and it wouldn't work anyway.' Her gaze flashed to Betty for a split second but the other girl was sitting staring down at her hands on her knees.

'You're not leaving?' There was a note of panic in Elsie's voice.

'Not for a while. It'll be all hands to the plough for the next months if you all decide you want to go ahead with what I've suggested. And it is only a suggestion, let's be clear about that. But with a bigger herd and better facilities there's no reason why selling the dairy produce and eggs and vegetables and the like should be confined to market days. There's lots of high-class hotels and businesses and shops in Newcastle, for instance, as well as Hexham, and a delivery service to them as well as some of the small towns and villages hereabouts could be lucrative, as well as selling milk to the commercial dairies. I agree with Larry about the farm progressing or beginning to die, though. Everything is going to change now the war's over. I'll leave you all to have a chat but there's no rush to make any decisions. I know this has been a bit of a bombshell.'

She bent down and kissed Elsie, and as she made to walk out of the room James caught hold of her, his voice husky as he murmured, 'Thanks, sis. I dunno what will be decided but thanks anyway.'

She smiled and continued out of the room, but once in the hall dabbed at her eyes. His 'sis' had meant more than he would ever know. She continued into the kitchen, making herself a cup of cocoa before sitting down at the table. In spite of herself a smile touched her lips as she recalled the look on Edwin and Larry's faces when she'd put forth her proposal. But the ball was in their court now. The alternative to her suggestions probably meant that the twins would follow through at some point with what Larry had intimated, meaning the farm would be sold and the family dispersed, but if that was the case she had done all she could to prevent it. Should that happen, then she would use the CO's cheque to buy her mother a little place somewhere and stay with her for a while to see her settled before she started to search for

Josef. Probably Betty would stay with Elsie, maybe even James, although she doubted that.

She sighed, then straightened her shoulders. Tomorrow she would begin making arrangements to pay a visit to Minnie and then Kitty in the next few weeks now the weather was better. When the postman had been able to finally get through to the farm after the big freeze he had brought a couple of letters from each of her friends, inviting her to come and see them when she could. Minnie was living in wedded bliss in Yorkshire, and Kitty had got herself a job at a fancy hotel in Blackpool as a receptionist and already had the young manager in her sights. No doubt the visits would be as different as her two friends were, but equally enjoyable.

Would she tell them about Josef? she asked herself as she sipped the milky cocoa. She felt Kitty would understand but she wasn't so sure about Minnie, not with her Norman being so badly injured in the war. She'd have to see. She didn't want to be insensitive but her love for Josef was part of her now.

'Please be alive,' she whispered into the quiet room, the subdued murmur of voices from the sitting room barely impinging on her mind as she pictured him as he'd been the last time she'd seen him. 'Even if you don't love me any more, even if you've found someone else, be alive.'

PART SEVEN

Seek and You Will Find

1948

Chapter Twenty-Six

The tall, blond man who had just got out of the taxi at the bottom of the track that led to Cowslip Farm looked much older than his twenty-seven years. His naturally pale skin had the tinge of greyness that spoke of illness, and the livid scar that ran down from his forehead, across his eyebrow and part of his cheek, stood out all the more because of his pallor. It also had the effect of pulling his right eyelid down slightly, giving him a faintly sinister look.

Josef paid the driver and then stood breathing in the warm June air that was full of the essence of summer. Towering elms and oaks cast heavy shadows over the leaf-bound lane whilst in the distance, hills were obscured by a trembling heat-haze. It was a beautiful day, quiet and peaceful, and on the journey he'd seen the spring-sown crops and ears of barley and corn in the fields, and cows lazily chewing under any shady trees they could find. Everything was tranquil, as though the war had never happened, and yet in his old home city of Berlin the Western Allies were carrying out round-the-clock airlifts to beat the Russian blockade. The population was starving as the Russians put on the squeeze, having banned any movement of food from the Soviet areas into Berlin and blocked all surface transport.

The world called the Nazis monsters, Josef thought, and they had been, some of them, but the atrocities committed by the Soviet incursions into Berlin in the last days of the war, particularly against German females, had been every bit as bad as the crimes of the Nazis. But the world had drawn a veil over the Russians' grotesque behaviour because they were on the winning side and they were always quick to mention Stalingrad whenever issues of atrocities were raised.

He sighed deeply, shutting his eyes for a moment against the images in his mind, pictures that came to torment him whenever he let his guard down. Bending, he picked up the small brown suitcase that contained all his worldly possessions and then straightened, staring at the hand-painted sign on a large piece of wood that read 'Cowslip Farm'.

He was here, he told himself, flexing his shoulders. Against all the odds, he was actually here. He had memorized the name and address from the letter Gina had shown him from her mother, but there had been many occasions over the last three years when he had doubted finding her. And if she was here at the farm, or if her mother knew where she was, would she want to see him? Theirs had been a brief love affair and she might feel differently about him now. She might have changed.

He sighed again. He had changed. He touched the scar that distorted his face. And not just physically. But in one respect he was the same, in what he felt for Gina.

He stared up the long wide track that wound into the distance, his heart beating faster than normal. He could have asked the taxi driver to take him right to the farmhouse itself, but he'd wanted to walk the last part of what had been a tiring journey over the last couple of days, to take his time absorbing where she had been born. That and the fact that he needed to prepare himself now the time was here for whatever reception he might receive.

Telling himself that faint heart never won fair lady, he made himself start walking. The sun was beating down and on one side of the drystone walls bordering the track he could see cows meandering in a thickly grassed meadow, and on the other crops waved in the warm breeze. It was a while before the farmhouse came into view round a bend in the track, and when it did he stopped for a moment. It was bigger than he'd expected. As he began walking again he realized the nearer he got that the two wings of the building, although built in the same stone as the main house, were relatively new additions and not weathered in like the original. It seemed as if there was more building work going on to the left of the farmhouse too, and he could make out a cement mixer churning away and a bunch of workmen standing together.

He stopped again, taken aback. It was ridiculous, he admonished himself now, but he had imagined Gina's childhood home to be the proverbial little thatched English farmhouse nestled in countryside, complete with hens scratching outside the door, a cockerel crowing on a fence somewhere and a tabby cat sitting on the doorstep. This was nothing like that.

The sun had turned his hair into a halo of white as he stood there, and as he watched a person detached itself from the others, walking slowly at first and then beginning to run towards him. In the same instant that he realized the figure in boots, dungarees and with a man's cap on her head was Gina, he dropped his suitcase and began to run too. As they met she leaped into his arms and he swung her off the ground, his lips claiming hers in an endless kiss as she clung to him as though she would never let him go. Her cap had fallen off and her hair tumbled about her shoulders in a riot of silky brown curls, and it was an age, an eternity, before he set her back on her feet, his hands still on her waist. She reached up again and put her mouth to his, standing on tiptoe with her arms round his neck, the pair of them murmuring endearments between kisses.

Eventually she drew back a little, her fingers tracing the line of his scar as she whispered, 'Oh, Josef, you were hurt.'

'It is nothing.' He smiled down at her, the piercing blue eyes that could appear cold on occasion warm with love. 'A parting gift from Warrant Officer Proby. It was fortunate that he was intoxicated at the time because he had been aiming for my throat.' His smile died. 'Does it bother you, my face?'

'It's the best face in the world.'

He smiled again. 'Beauty and the Beast.'

'You are not the Beast, not ever. Don't say that.'

'Ah, but he gets his Beauty in the end, does he not?'

Three men had detached themselves from the other two and were now walking towards them. Softly he said, 'I do not wish to make things difficult for you here, Gina. If you want to say that we are just friends I will understand.'

For answer she kissed him again, slipping her arm round his waist as she turned to face Larry, Edwin and James. She could hardly believe Josef was standing next to her, alive and warm and breathing. When she had seen him approaching her heart had stood still for a moment and she'd told herself she was dreaming, she had to be, because how could he have found her?

James was smiling as he reached them and it was he who said, 'I take it you two know each other?' as he winked at Gina.

'This is Josef.' She decided to say it straight off, there was no good beating about the bush. 'We met in Egypt when he was a POW and fell in love.'

Everything about Josef declared his nationality, the more so when he stood straight and clicked his heels together as he said, 'Josef Vetter, at your service.'

If Gina hadn't loved James before, she would have now as he stretched out his hand, saying, 'I'm James, Gina's brother, and these two peas in a pod are Edwin and Larry. It's nice to meet you, Josef.'

'Thank you.' Josef didn't relax a muscle as he shook James's hand. He could see the other two brothers were not at all happy but they did offer their hands after a moment, and then the five of them began to walk up the track to where the two workmen were staring at them quizzically.

Gina had put her hand through his arm and now he felt her squeeze him as she murmured, 'I can't believe you're here. I tried to find out where you'd gone after Egypt but my friend in the office there, at the camp, couldn't help. I think she was shipped back to England shortly after I had to leave for India.'

He didn't reply; they had reached the other two men now who were staring at him and clearly wondering if what they suspected was true and that a German had arrived at the farm, one who was on very friendly terms with Gina by the look of it.

'Come and meet my mother.' Gina didn't even look at the builder and his son as she led Josef past them and round the back of the building to the kitchen, leaving Edwin, Larry and James with the two men. She was furious with the way the twins had looked at Josef and the reluctant way they had shaken his hand, but she supposed that was the way it was going to be with some people from now on. She knew a couple of farmer's daughters hereabouts had got involved with Italian POWs working on their farms during the war – one had even married her Latin lover and already had a bouncing baby boy – and the lads hadn't turned a hair about that, but apparently it was different with Josef, at least for Edwin and Larry. Such hypocrisy!

'Hey.' Josef turned her in to him, pulling her to a stop before they reached the kitchen door. 'It is all right, my Gina. Your brothers are allowed to be suspicious of me, yes?'

'No.' She shook her head, then said, 'Well, yes, I suppose so, but I don't like it.'

'They fought in the war, did they not, and lost comrades, I am sure. It is not going to be easy for this generation to forgive and forget. The war is over but –' he shrugged – 'some people will still see our relationship as collaborating with the enemy. You could be ostracized by friends and family and you must understand this. I will not blame you if it is too high a price to pay and you need to think carefully about it.'

'I don't need to.'

'Yes, you do. Under this fiery exterior there beats a soft heart and I do not want to see it broken because of me. Your happiness is the most important thing. I mean this.'

'I know you do.' She took his hand as she opened the kitchen door. 'Come and meet my mother.'

Elsie turned round from stirring something at the range as they entered and whatever she had been about to say froze on her lips as she saw Gina standing with the tall, fair-haired man. As Gina said, 'This is—', Elsie interrupted her. 'I know who it is,' she said softly, coming forward and smiling. 'Only your Josef could light up your face the way it is now.'

Reaching out, she took one of Josef's hands. 'You are very welcome here for as long as you want to stay, Josef.'

For once Josef's stiff correctness deserted him. There was no formality as his face worked and he looked as though he was going to cry before he pulled himself enough together to say, 'Thank you, I am most grateful.'

'Come and sit down and I'll make a pot of tea. You must be hungry. Gina, fetch out those cheese scones we made this morning and there's some blackberry tarts too. There's cream or butter, Josef. There's always cream and butter on a farm.' She'd turned back to the range as she'd spoken in order to give 'that poor lad' as she'd termed Josef in her mind time to recover his composure.

Josef sat down at the kitchen table, the unexpected kindness and especially the way Gina's mother had said 'your Josef' touching him deeply. He was horrified at how close to tears he was – he hadn't cried in years and the fact that he'd almost broken down in front of Gina and her mother appalled him – but at the same time the feeling was still in the foreground and he didn't trust himself to speak.

Gina sensed how he was feeling and she purposely bustled about fetching the scones and tarts and setting the table for three. Once the tea was mashed the two women joined Josef, who was still sitting quietly and looking slightly dazed. Now the initial surprise and excitement were over Gina was noticing more and more how frail and ill he looked, but she didn't mention it, letting him eat and drink while she and Elsie talked of inconsequential things and nibbled at a scone each although they hadn't long eaten lunch.

It was some time later when Josef had eaten his fill that Elsie suggested he and Gina go for a walk. 'It's a beautiful day,' she said briskly, 'and it might rain tomorrow. Show Josef the farm in the sunshine when it's looking its best, lass.'

Once outside, Gina went in the opposite direction to where the men were working on building the new dairy and milking parlour. The twins were anxious to get it finished before their joint wedding day at the end of July. They and James had been working sixteen or seventeen hours a day, seven days a week, for the last twelve months, helping the builders on the two extensions as well as dealing with the difficulties in getting electricity and a piped water supply to the farm and all the paraphernalia involved with this, which included dealing with the council and endless red tape.

Hand in hand, Gina led him to the orchard. It was one of her favourite places if she ever had a few minutes to herself. The old gnarled trees still produced a good crop of apples, pears, cherries and plums each year with which Elsie made her jams and preserves and pickles, and the grass beneath their feet was full of clover, forget-me-nots, buttercups, daisies and other wild flowers. Bees and butterflies lazily went about their business, and although the sounds of the farm drifted on the warm June breeze, they didn't disturb the tranquillity of the orchard. Once they were seated on an ancient wooden bench under a cherry tree, Josef took her in his arms again, and it was only after a time of kisses and murmured endearments that she drew back and whispered, 'Tell me all that's happened since Egypt. Did your parents survive the camp and are Kirsten and her family safe?'

Josef shook his head and as she said, 'Oh, Josef, I'm so sorry,' he wondered where to start.

A silence ensued between them for a moment; then Josef, not looking directly at her now but with her hand clasped in his, said, 'It is a long story, my Gina, and not a pleasant one. Do you wish to hear it another day perhaps?'

'I'd like to hear it now if it's not going to upset you.' She wanted to know, to understand, what it was that had changed him so much. It wasn't just the fact that he had clearly been ill, it was deeper than that. Even as a POW in Egypt he'd had such a vital life force, such a quiet magnetism, that it had radiated out of him. It was probably one of the things that Proby had hated so much, on reflection. As she thought of the warrant officer, she said, 'You said Proby attacked you?'

'Ah, yes, Warrant Officer Proby.' It was wry but without real resentment. 'On the evening before myself and my comrades were due to leave, he paid us a visit. Germany had surrendered and the war in Europe was over, and we had been told we were being shipped back to our country to join work parties helping to clear rubble, bury bodies, that sort of thing, yes? And so we were pleased. We were going home. Clearly this had occurred to my friend too and he did not like it. So –' he gestured at his face – 'this was the result.'

'Was he disciplined?'

'This I do not know. I imagine so. I was asked to give a statement as to what had occurred before I left with my comrades the following morning. I owe them my life – but for them restraining him he would have come at me again.'

'He was a madman.'

He shrugged but did not comment.

'And so you were taken to Germany?'

'This is so.' He watched a butterfly land on a bunch of forget-me-nots, its wings opening and closing slowly. 'Such beauty in the natural world,' he murmured. 'So unlike the devastation wrought by man. We were taken to Aachen initially. It had been a fine city before the war but the shelling and bombing by the Americans as they fought to break through the Westwall fortifications was severe. It was the first German city within the Third Reich to face an attack by the Americans so therefore from many perspectives became a target of immense importance. One thing I do not and will never understand is that the Nazis had ordered children as young as eight or nine, boys and girls, to participate in the defence of Aachen, and we learned this had been the case all over Germany. I spoke to one American while we were there and he spoke of his shock when he realized children were shooting at him but he was faced with no choice but to return fire and kill them, because they had taken out a number of his comrades. He wept when he told me about a little girl he had killed, about nine years of age, the same as his child back home. A big-bore hunting rifle had lain close to her small body along with several expended cartridge cases. He felt like he had committed murder even though she had killed two soldiers moments before he had shot her.'

Gina stared at him aghast. 'The poor man, and poor bairns too.'

'He told me they captured one young girl who had been injured whilst firing at them, and she told them of a meeting that had taken place with their maidens' league just days before the Americans attacked. Their group head, an older woman, had extolled the virtues of being either a Volkssturm or Werewolf member and instructed them to cause as many enemy casualties as they could whilst remaining elusive. She had likened them to slender, strong wolves of the nation, she-wolves who were natural predators, providers and protectors and who would provide, protect and kill according to their needs. As wolves, they were told, they should fight in the shadows and leave no Americans safe – the enemy should drown in their own blood and in the blood of the she-wolves if that became necessary. It was their duty, she said, as well as their privilege, to die for the Führer and they must never forget this. Girls who had not been taught to shoot could still use grenades or rocket launchers, everyone could play their part.'

He looked at her. 'This American asked me how we

Germans could have so lost our humanity as to make little children into weapons, deadly weapons at that, and I had no answer for him because there is not one. Perhaps the saddest thing is that he remembered the little girl whom they'd captured, who was injured, became quiet and childlike when she realized they were not going to hurt her as she had been told they would. She asked for sweets and chocolate, and when one of the female officers sat with her she cried for her mother. She was just a little girl, she should not have been used to fighting and trying to kill other human beings.'

He sighed. 'The American was so angry and I can understand why. Another man, an interpreter who had been brought in to talk to the children, discovered some had been trained as saboteurs and others to use anti-tank weapons. One of the little ones he talked to said she'd spent weeks learning to handle and use a Panzerfaust, and had been disappointed the Americans had not brought more tanks forward into the battle so that she could shoot at them. She explained that the girls of the Jungvolk had been promised Iron Crosses from the Führer for every tank they killed and destroyed.'

He raked his hair back from his forehead with his free hand before getting up and standing with his back to her. 'Something died in me as I listened to these and other stories, and it was the same with other cities we were sent to. This was not war, this mass sacrifice of little ones. I am ashamed, Gina. Ashamed to be a German and a man.'

'You can't say that.' She jumped to her feet, her voice soft and sad as she put her arms round his waist, her face buried in his back. 'You can't, Josef. You wouldn't have done those things and neither would lots of other of your countrymen. It was the fanatics who committed those crimes and you get such people in every race and in every country of the world.'

He didn't move as he murmured, 'I have always known that war is an incredibly evil thing, but even at its worst it should still be honourable.'

She thought that was a somewhat idealistic way of looking at it, but it wouldn't help to say so. Instead she said, 'You think that because *you* are honourable.'

'You are determined to see the best in me.' He sighed as he spoke but turned and took her in his arms again, settling her against his chest with his chin on her head as they stood together in the scented heat of the orchard. He remained silent for a full minute before continuing with his story. 'It was two years before I was allowed to go back to Berlin to find out what had happened to my family. This was perhaps the hardest thing of all. The American forces in Aachen and other cities we worked in had conducted themselves in a highly professional manner. The inhabitants had been treated with respect on the whole, and there had been no reported cases of rape or sexual violation of young girls or women under the American occupation. This was not the case in Berlin when the Russians took the city. Berlin was the biggest prize of all as far as they were concerned, and they were determined to be the first to occupy the Reich capital. When they did so they began an orgy of rape, torture and killing.'

His voice faltered. 'I found little left of the city I had known and the tension between Russia and the Western zones was palpable. It was well known that Stalin considered Berlin was rightfully his and his alone, and all manner of political and social problems were apparent. Nevertheless, I was determined to try and find out for sure what had happened to my parents and I needed to see if Kirsten was still alive to do this. It was weeks, many weeks, before I traced a neighbour of Kirsten's. Elli was a broken woman. She looked frail and old and could only walk with the help of a crutch. She had suffered terrible indignities at the hands of a group of drunken Russian soldiers and had been told by a doctor she would be a permanent invalid. Elli said my sister had told her my parents were dead. They had died shortly after being interned in the camp, apparently. Kirsten took no responsibility for their demise, saying they had brought their fate on themselves for their disloyalty to the Third Reich.'

Gina looked up into his face, wishing she could take the pain away. 'And Kirsten and her family?'

'Her husband, the SS officer, was held in a prison situated in the Pankow district of north-eastern Russia, accused of committing war crimes. If he wasn't executed he would have been sent to die in the Gulag, the Soviet forced-labour camp system. Elli told me Kirsten and her children were killed after the battle for Seelow when the

Russians were able to fire their guns directly onto Berlin. Many women and young children and babies had retreated to air-raid shelters but when Elli tried to persuade Kirsten to do the same, my sister said she would not be driven from her home by filthy Bolsheviks. Elli offered to take the little ones with her to the shelter, but Kirsten would not allow it. A shell fell directly on the house later that night.'

He pulled her back down onto the wooden bench, putting his arm round her as he said quietly, 'Maybe it was for the best, what Kirsten did in refusing to go to a shelter. My sister was a beautiful woman and Robert and Bärbl were blonde-haired and blue-eyed, the epitome of Aryanism. Elli told me what the Russians did to such children.'

She didn't know what to say. Perhaps there *was* nothing to say.

'After speaking to Elli, I knew it was time to try and find you,' he continued after a few moments. 'I had no money but there was a branch of my father's family living in Wuppertal before the war and I decided to make for there to see if any were still alive, and perhaps to stay with them for a day or two before crossing the border into Belgium and then the English Channel. I was feeling ill but I put this down to exhaustion. I thumbed the lifts, yes? But it was not an easy journey to my aunt's house. I had had to sleep in the open for a few nights and it had rained for days. When I reached my aunt's, I collapsed with pneumonia and problems with my kidneys. I remember little of the next weeks. When I was out of danger there was a long recovery.'

From the tone of his voice Gina could guess the frustration and helplessness he had felt. And all this coming on top of his time as a POW both in Egypt and his own country and then the confirmation that his parents and Kirsten and her family were dead. She put her hand on his. 'I love you,' she said softly.

'And I you.' He lifted her chin, kissing her. 'The thought of you is what has kept me going, even though I told myself that you might not feel the same way now the war was over. And I would have accepted this knowing that you were alive and well.'

'How could you have even thought that for a minute?'

'You are young, free, and ours was after all a brief wartime romance.'

'You are young too.'

'No.' He gave an almost imperceptible shake of his head. 'I shall never be young again and you deserve someone who is.' The sights he had seen among some of the hideous ruins he and his comrades had been ordered to clear came back to him every night when he slept, making him afraid to close his eyes, and some of the stories he'd heard from German survivors who had been near to the central area of Berlin, particularly in the vicinity of the Dorotheenstrasse when the Russians had attacked, were etched in all their hellishness on the screen of his mind. The mindset of many Red Army soldiers had been to make as many German girls and women pregnant as they could, in revenge for the suffering of the Russian people, as well as to teach them a lesson for supporting Hitler and the Nazis. Some suffered worse by having bayonets, knives, broken bottles or gun barrels inserted into their vaginas, as poor Elli had done when they'd finished raping her. Elli's own mother, a sixty-year-old grandmother, had been raped to death by a drunken group of men.

He told himself to stop thinking. He told himself this at least a dozen times a day.

'Josef.' Gina took his face in her hands. 'I want *you*. We can't change what has happened, we never could. The future is a time for rebuilding, not just your country and mine and other shattered nations but men and women and families, otherwise evil wins. And that can't happen, it mustn't. I know you are a good man and your mother and father were good people too, that's what matters. Talking about what you feel, the good and the bad, is the only way to get rid of the demons. I want to know, Josef. I want to share it with you, everything.'

He kissed her again but he knew there were some things he could not burden her with, things he could never speak of. Certain facts had begun to filter through, but the Soviet Rape of Berlin had to some extent been brushed under the diplomatic carpet, along with other inhuman, terrible events of the war that the powers-that-be considered ordinary civilians need not know. And Gina was right, the future had to be faced looking forwards not backwards. He applauded the talk by the

British and Americans of bringing about the complete denazification of his country, targeting the re-education of boys and girls in particular, but he felt tired and weary. Sometimes all he wanted to do was sleep, to shut out the world. It had been selfish and indulgent to come here, he knew that, because Gina deserved better than a burned-out shell of a man. He had needed to know if she was safe and well, but it would have been better for her if he had not come, he realized that now.

They sat for a while longer in the shade of the cherry tree and he steered the conversation away from himself, asking Gina about her time in India, her reunion with her mother and what was happening on the farm. She told him about the CO's generosity and how she had spent her enormous windfall explaining about Edwin and Larry's new contained homes, the weddings in July and the modernization programme.

'It's been a bit tricky,' she said honestly, 'bringing it all together, not least because Betty still isn't fully on board, not really. Mainly I think because I suggested the changes. We tolerate each other but that's about all.'

'But she now owns a quarter of the farm, is that right? Can she not be grateful for what you have brought about?'

'I think she is, in her way.' Gina shrugged. 'She's a lot like her father, she even looks like him. I mean, *really* looks like him. And like him she's determined to dislike me and be suspicious of everything I do and say. But we put on a front for my mam, which is all that matters.'

'A front?' His brow wrinkled. 'What is this?'

'A pretence. We pretend to get on.'

'Ah, yes.' He nodded. 'But your brothers, they do not feel this way?'

'They're fine.'

'So this Betty, she is the lady formidable?'

Gina grinned. 'Very much so. She's at a neighbouring farm at the moment, discussing buying a bull calf. She wants fresh blood in the herd and our bull is getting on now. You'll meet her soon enough but don't be offended if she's not very welcoming – she's like that with everyone.' She leaned against him and he put his arm round her shoulders, and it was like that she said, 'If I left here she'd put the flags out, no doubt about that.'

'Is that a possibility?'

'One day.' She was hoping he would talk about the future, *their* future together, but he didn't.

After a moment or two, he said, 'Your mother would be upset.'

She made no reply to this and the silence stretched on before she stood, pulling him up with her as she said, 'I'd better get back and help Mam with the evening meal. Come on and I'll show you where you can put your things. You can have my old room and I'll sleep with Mam. Edwin and Larry have moved into their new quarters so there'll only be Mam, James and Betty in the house.'

'I do not wish to impose on your family or make things awkward for you with them.'

She stared at him. Was he regretting seeking her out

or was he feeling uncomfortable because of how Edwin and Larry had been? Inwardly cursing the twins, she said quietly, 'I want you to stay for a while, Josef.' For ever actually, but he didn't seem to be in the right frame of mind to hear that. She had thought he had come here to tell her that he wanted to be with her always, that he saw their future together, and certainly initially it had seemed that way, but in the last half-hour or so something had changed. Had she said something wrong? Been too pushy?

As they retraced their footsteps to the farmhouse, hand in hand, she racked her brains to see where she had gone wrong but just got herself in a dither. In the end she decided she would let things be for the moment. She had told him she loved him and he had said he loved her. And she believed that he did. He was here with her now; amazingly, wonderfully, he was here. That would have to be enough for the present and the future could take care of itself.

Chapter Twenty-Seven

Over the next weeks Gina was to remind herself over and over again of the conclusion that she had come to on that first day. It wasn't that she and Josef didn't get on – they did – and she knew she was more deeply in love with him than ever, but never at any point did he mention the future to her and if it came up in conversation he changed the subject. It didn't help that Edwin and Larry clearly disapproved of her relationship with Josef, even though they were civil enough towards him and almost painfully polite. James, on the other hand, treated him as a friend from the first day, joking and laughing with him on occasion and completely at ease. Elsie was the same, and had made it her mission to feed up 'that poor lad', as she privately referred to him. She insisted he stay in bed late in the mornings – 'Sleep is the best medicine in the world, lad, and you can't play silly devils with pneumonia, I of all people know that with our Robin' – mollycoddling him to the point where Gina had to gently remind her mother that Josef was a grown man of twenty-seven, not a toddler in nappies. But it was Betty who was the biggest surprise to Gina, and in a good way. At least initially.

Gina had been on tenterhooks that first afternoon waiting for Betty to return to the farm. She had no idea what the other girl would do or say when she introduced Josef to her, but she had been prepared for harsh words or worse. And Betty had most certainly been shocked at first – it had been written all over her square mannish face – but she had simply shaken Josef's hand and mumbled something about being pleased to meet him. Over the next days Gina had noticed the two of them chatting now and again; Josef had even made Betty laugh once, which had startled everyone because it wasn't a sound one heard very often, and within a couple of weeks it was clear the two of them had become friends. She even allowed Josef to help her with her 'ladies', teaching him how to milk them and telling everyone he had the hands of a dairymaid, which was a great compliment as far as Betty was concerned. And such is the contrariness of human nature, that from being pleased and relieved that Betty liked him and wasn't going to be a problem, Gina found herself becoming jealous of the other girl.

It was ridiculous and she knew it, and she also knew that Josef wasn't interested in Betty in 'that' way, but she envied the easy familiarity that had sprung up between the pair. He was more guarded with her, Gina told herself wretchedly, and she wasn't imagining it. Something was wrong and she couldn't put her finger on it, but neither did she want to put any pressure on him and maybe frighten him away. And then other times, when the two of them took a walk together away from everyone or sat in the orchard, she told herself she was being silly and that everything was fine between them. Josef wouldn't have made the journey to England with all that entailed if he hadn't seen their future as being together. But in spite of herself, all her old insecurities were coming to the surface and she alternated between being wildly happy and desperately miserable.

It was on the day before Larry and Edwin's long-awaited joint weddings at the end of July, six weeks after Josef had arrived at Cowslip Farm, that something happened to bring the situation to a head. The service was being held at the parish church in Hexham, followed by a reception for friends and family at the farm in one of the barns that had been cleared out and decorated for the occasion. Ava, the young widow that Edwin was marrying, had lost her parents some time before the war and had a much older brother and sister who were attending the wedding with their respective families, but it was the parents of Lucy – Larry's bride-to-be – who had been a thorn in Elsie's side concerning the wedding arrangements, particularly Muriel Travis, Lucy's mother.

Once it had been made clear that there was to be a double wedding, Muriel had baulked at holding the reception at their farm, saying there would be too many guests and their farmhouse was too small and there wasn't a barn they could easily use for the purpose. Elsie hadn't objected to this although she had been fully aware that Muriel, who had a well-earned reputation for being parsimonious and penny-pinching, hadn't liked the idea that she might have to contribute towards Larry's brother's nuptials, either financially or in time and effort. And so it had proved. Muriel had seen to it that the amount of food she was providing for the reception was only enough for just one wedding, and the Travises hadn't offered to assist in the clearing out and decorating of the barn, or even bringing over extra trestle tables and chairs. What Muriel had contributed, however, was her tongue, and she used it generously to criticize and find fault wherever she could. So when Lucy and her parents arrived at the farm on the afternoon before the big day, bringing the cooked ham and side of beef and cakes and other bits and pieces they had promised, Elsie had warned everyone to smile and say little and not to rise to any bait Muriel might throw into the equation. 'For Larry and Lucy's sake,' she'd emphasized. 'Let's just keep everything friendly and happy.'

When Silas Travis brought the big farm cart to a halt, the lads, along with Elsie and Gina and Josef and even Betty, dutifully trooped out to welcome them. Muriel sat stiff and straight on the wide plank seat with a face on her like a sow's backside, as Gina said later to Elsie. Muriel was a large woman with jet-black hair that she wore skewered tightly into a bun, and her somewhat flat features and muddy brown eyes added to the overall impression of dourness that enveloped her like a second skin. She hadn't visited the farm since Josef had arrived, and now her small almond-shaped eyes fixed on him standing beside Gina.

There he was, she told herself with the satisfying self-righteous indignation she'd felt ever since Lucy had let slip about Gina's 'friend'. Friend be damned, she'd said to Silas, and he had agreed with her. And as for that girl standing bold as brass with him at her side – a German, a filthy rotten German – she ought to be ashamed of herself. It was a slap in the face for any decent man, woman or child, that's what it was, but then there'd been some rum goings-on at Cowslip Farm from what she could make out. The girl disappearing all those years ago and then turning up out of the blue and as right as rain after the war, what was all that about? She'd asked Lucy umpteen times but she could get nowt out of her, the girl was a closed book, but she could put two and two together as well as the next person.

Why hadn't Elsie sent this German packing with her foot up his backside the minute he'd turned up? That's what she'd have done. What any respectable body would have done. Ee, it fair turned her stomach thinking about what her Lucy was marrying into, but it was too late to call things off now with the scandal that would ensue. And Lucy wouldn't have agreed anyhow, fair barmy about Larry Redfern she was, but she'd live to regret it. She'd told Lucy that last night.

'You'll live to regret marrying him as sure as eggs are eggs,' she'd said, and Lucy had fair gone for her, calling her all the names under the sun. She wouldn't forget that, by, she wouldn't, and when Lucy came crawling back home when it all went wrong, she'd find the door slammed in her face.

The July afternoon was scorching hot and when Silas had helped his wife and daughter down from the cart, Elsie invited them into the house for a glass of lemonade while the menfolk took the food through to the kitchen. Muriel was wearing her Sunday best, the starched pleats in her severe black dress barely moving as she followed Elsie into the large sitting room through the rarely opened front door. It had been a thorn in her side for years that the Redferns' farm was bigger and better than theirs, and now with the two wings added to the house and the new dairy and milking parlour nearly finished, it was even grander in her eyes.

She seated herself on the edge of a chair, gazing about her without speaking and silently accepting the glass of lemonade and slice of seed cake Elsie passed to her. Gina, Betty and Lucy sat in a row on the sofa and Elsie took the other chair opposite their visitor as she said brightly, 'Well, this is nice, isn't it. All set for tomorrow, are you, Muriel?'

Muriel didn't reply to this. She had planned exactly what she would say when she called at the farm. Fixing Elsie with a gimlet stare, she went on the attack. 'I trust *he's* not invited to the church, Elsie? It being a Christian wedding and all?'

Elsie's mouth fell open in a slight gape of shock, but

before she could reply, and as Lucy said, '*Mam!*', Gina said sharply, 'Do I take it you are referring to Mr Vetter?'

Muriel's cold gaze moved to her. 'The German, aye. Your fancy man.'

As Elsie found her voice, saying, 'Now look here—', Gina interrupted her. Her body was taut, her face white, but her voice had a control about it as she said, 'Mr Vetter is a guest here and he is most certainly invited to both the church service and the celebrations to follow, Mrs Travis.'

'And you're happy with that?' Muriel glared at Elsie.

'Of course. Josef is most welcome.'

'Most welcome? Him, a barbarian like all them Nazis are?'

'He is not a Nazi, Muriel.' Elsie was still trying to save the wedding day. 'He's a lovely lad when you get to know him.'

'I'd rather cut me throat.'

'That can be arranged.' Betty's voice was quiet but deadly.

'What did you say?' Muriel's voice had gone up a few octaves. 'Do you know who you're talking to?'

Betty's answer nonplussed her for a moment when it came quick and hard: 'Yes, I do know who I'm talking to and but for the fact it would upset Lucy even more I'd tell you exactly what I think of you an' all.'

Muriel spluttered for a moment, her gaze sweeping over the four women before she said, 'So you're all in this, are you? You'd rather see a swine like him at the wedding than me an' Silas an' our lot? 'Cause I tell you straight, if he's attending, we're not. We might not be much but we're better than murdering scum like him. You're traitors to your country, all of you.'

'Don't be ridiculous.' Gina had risen to her feet and now Betty and Lucy did the same. 'The war's over, or hadn't you heard?'

Whether it was the biting sarcasm in Gina's voice or the fact that all three women, including her own daughter, were looking at Muriel with such contempt, or yet again that Gina had remained perfectly in command of herself, but suddenly Muriel was shrieking at the top of her voice, incoherent in her rage as she jumped to her feet and launched herself at Gina. It was only Betty swiftly stepping between them and grabbing Muriel's flailing arms that prevented Gina being hurt. Muriel was a big woman but Betty was even bigger and her bulk was made of muscle, not fat; she subdued the angry woman without too much trouble. The hullabaloo had brought the men running from the kitchen, and as they crowded into the doorway and surveyed the scene in front of them, in which Betty was holding Larry's future mother-in-law in a kind of headlock that had Muriel's Sunday hat askew and over one eye, it was Silas who bellowed, 'What the hell are you doing? Let go of my wife.'

'Gladly.' Betty pushed Muriel into her husband's arms, saying, 'But if she tries it on again she'll get what's coming to her.'

'What's the matter? What's happened?' Larry went to

Lucy, who was now weeping, and Edwin and James to their mother, who looked ready to collapse.

'It – it was my mam. She – she said—' But Lucy couldn't go on.

The arrival of her husband seemed to have restored Muriel to her right mind and now her head jerked up and her words came rushing out in a vitriolic flow as she hung on to him. 'I told 'em we're not going to the wedding if that filthy Nazi goes. Scum like him in a church, it's not right, anyone would say the same. I said they're traitors and I stand by it – they're a disgrace to what our brave lads fought and died for and I'm not having it. I tell you, Silas, I'm not.'

'All right, all right, calm down.'

It was clear Silas was out of his depth, but Gina wasn't concerned with him or his wife or anyone else but Josef. He was standing in the doorway, as white as a sheet, clearly having heard everything. He stared at her for one long eternal moment and then said very clearly, with his eyes still on her, 'You have been misinformed. I am not attending the wedding tomorrow. I leave here today, in fact.' He turned and was gone.

'No.' As Gina made a move to follow him, Edwin stretched out his hand and took her arm.

His voice low, he muttered, 'I'm sorry, lass, that it's happened like this but perhaps it's for the best, him going, I mean? He'd never fit in here, you must see that? It's too soon after the war to forget and forgive.'

'For you, you mean?' Gina shook his hand from her

arm, her lip curling upwards. 'And him, no doubt?' She jerked her head at Larry.

Her tone catching him on the raw, his voice was louder when he said, 'If you'd seen your mates blown to bits and gone through what we did, you'd feel the same.'

'Don't tell me what I would feel,' she shot back angrily. 'Don't you dare. Don't you think they suffered on the other side, Edwin? That they're still suffering, same as we are? The Nazi regime was a crushing, monstrous thing and lots of good German people stood up to it at the cost of their own lives, Josef's parents included. You act as though it was all angels on one side and demons on the other, but that's not true. Have you ever wondered how Josef got that scar on his face? Well, I'll tell you. One of our soldiers, a warrant officer, took it into his head to slit his throat when Josef was an unarmed POW. Crept up on him at night and tried to murder him in cold blood. So don't make out this war was black and white because war never is, and it's them at the top, like Hitler and his cronies, who are to blame. Not the thousands and thousands of ordinary German people who just wanted to live with their families and get on with their lives before the Nazis took over.'

Muriel pulled herself away from Silas, the fact that Edwin seemed to be supporting her giving fresh venom to her tirade as she spat out, 'See? See, girl? Your own family don't want him here and you ought to be ashamed of yourself, consorting with muck like him. Tainted, you are, you know that? No decent man would look the side you're on after this.'

'Shut up, you old crone.' It was Betty who spoke and as she made a move towards Muriel, the woman shrank back, alarmed at what she could see in Betty's face. 'How you gave birth to a nice lass like Lucy I'll never know, 'cause you're bad through and through. And for your information, I want Josef here, same as my mam, all right?'

'And me.' James had been standing just inside the doorway and now he put his arm round Gina. 'And while we're on the subject of decency, it's common knowledge that your own father-in-law had a woman in Hexham he visited on market days, and you might like to ask your husband what he does on a Thursday night when he's supposed to be playing darts in the pub in the village. Like father, like son, I'd say.'

'James!' Elsie gasped.

'It's true, Mam. If you don't believe me, ask them.' He nodded at Edwin and Larry.

'Is it? Is it true, Silas?' Muriel rounded on her husband and as he began to stutter and stammer, Gina said to James, 'I'm going to find Josef.'

She thought he might have gone to his room and as she ran up the stairs onto the landing she found him packing his few belongings. 'You're not really going?'

He straightened, facing her, and his face spoke for him.

'Because of a vicious old woman like Muriel Travis?'

'No, not altogether.'

'Then why?'

'Listen, Gina.' The noise from the sitting room had increased in volume and added to it was the sound of smashing crockery. 'Listen to that. My being here is tearing your family apart.'

'That's ridiculous. Everything was all right before Muriel Travis came today.' Even as she said it, she knew it wasn't true. But she carried on. 'You can't let a horrible woman like her spoil everything.'

'But it is not just this Muriel, is it, my Gina? Let us be honest with each other. Your brothers were shocked when I came here – they did not know anything about me, did they? I do not blame you for this, being ashamed of associating with a German, not at all—'

'No, no, it wasn't like that.' Is that what he had been thinking, that she had been ashamed of him? 'I told my mam as soon as I came home and I was going to tell the others when I left here to find you. Larry and Edwin don't talk about the war but they're bitter about it, about the friends they lost. It just seemed better to say nothing until I was ready to leave, that was all. There was no question, ever, of my being ashamed of us.' He stared at her without speaking and she said again, 'I've never been ashamed of us, not for a minute.'

'Even if that is so, you must know that Edwin and Larry will never fully accept me, Gina. There is –' he paused – 'what is the English expression? Ah, yes, there is too much water under the bridge. My being here makes them uncomfortable, as does my love for you and yours for me. I will not hurt you in this way.' As she went to speak, he held up his hand. 'And there will be many Edwins and Larrys, make no mistake about that. People are still too raw, too hurt. Maybe if we had met twenty, thirty years from now it might have been different. I knew I should have gone away, left here from the first day I arrived, but I have been weak. I wanted to stay with you. I hoped that somehow things would work out.'

'They will, they will.'

'No, they will not, and part of that is because of me, myself. You deserve someone like *your*self, my Gina. Someone who still has a zest for this life, who is eager, who has hope. I am not like that, not any more. I do not know where I belong or even who I am. Most nights I am afraid to close my eyes in sleep because of the horrors that come, and even in the day the pictures are there. You have found your family and you must be with them. This is good and right.'

'No, what are you saying? I love you and you love me. That is all that matters.'

His voice soft, he said, 'I will write to you and if you wish you can write to me.'

She couldn't take in what she was hearing. She stared at him for some moments and then said dully, 'You can't love me like I love you or else you wouldn't be saying this about leaving.'

He had to do this. He had heard her defending him to either Edwin or Larry after he had come upstairs – the doors had been open and voices carried when they were a certain pitch – and he'd heard what the woman, Muriel Travis, had said about Gina being tainted by association with him. He should never have come here, never put her through this. Quietly, and forcing any emotion from his voice, he said, 'I do love you, Gina.'

'But not enough.'

He knew that when he left here he wouldn't live very long because life without her in it wouldn't be an option, but perhaps it was better she was thinking this way. Here she had her family and friends, people who loved her and would care for her, and what could he offer her? He had no money, no worldly possessions, not even his health. He would be a burden to her here and there would be other people like the Travis woman. However strong she felt now, it would wear her down after a time, sap that vitality and passion and fire that was such a part of her.

When he allowed the silence that had fallen to stretch on, Gina had to bring all her will to bear not to beg him to stay, to throw herself at him and plead and cry. Dignity. The word mocked her with its coldness but she made herself say, 'I hope you will wait until you can say goodbye properly to my mother before you go?'

'Of course.' He seemed shocked she would think anything else.

She nodded, and then turned and retraced her footsteps down the stairs just in time to see Muriel stalking out of the house, her face livid, and Silas trailing after her. The front door banged behind them and she walked into the sitting room where she found Larry sitting with his arm round Lucy who was still quietly weeping, Edwin and

James comforting Elsie, and Betty standing by the window watching the Travises depart.

It was she who said, 'I trust you've talked some sense into him upstairs about this daft idea of leaving?'

She couldn't, she just couldn't cope with Betty even though she was grateful for her championing of Josef. Shrugging, she left them and walked through to the kitchen, exiting the house by the back door. She had intended to walk to the orchard but had only gone a few steps before Betty caught up with her.

'Well?' she said, in her gruff manner. 'What did he say?'

Keeping her voice even with some effort, Gina continued walking. 'He's going, Betty.'

'And you're going to let him?'

'It's not a question of "letting" him.'

'That's exactly what it is. I thought more of you, Gina, or aren't you serious about Josef after all?'

'Don't you dare say that.' They had reached the orchard that was drowsy in the sticky afternoon heat, and Gina swung round to face her adversary, her skin flushing with angry colour. 'I love him, I'd do anything for him, but he obviously doesn't feel the same way.'

'Oh, my giddy aunt, I can't believe you're being so thick. He worships you – everyone can see that.'

'He doesn't think we're suited for each other.' Gina was hanging on to her temper by a thread. She quoted Josef's words: 'He thinks too much water has gone under the bridge for it to work between us.'

'What he *thinks* is that he's protecting you, although why he imagines you need protection I don't know. If anyone can look after themselves, you can.' It wasn't said as a compliment. 'I've told him you're as tough as old boots and not some Victorian maiden who needs to be wrapped up in cotton wool, but he persists in his idea that you're a fragile flower.'

Gina ignored the sarcasm and focused on what really hurt. 'He's discussed me with you?'

'Oh, cut the self-pity, it doesn't suit you. Yes, he's discussed all sorts of things with me but mainly as to how they would affect you. When they shipped him back to Germany as part of one of the work gangs he saw things no human being should see, I mean unimaginable things. Not only that but because our side found out he could speak English as well as German, they used him as a kind of go-between to talk to some of the German civilians about what had happened with the Russians and what they'd gone through. Has he ever told you about the way the Russians liked to set their dogs on women and children, like a sport? If the women and bairns ran from them the Russians would let the dogs off their leads and the animals would run and attack them. He told me he spoke to one family whose little girl had half her face missing as a result of the soldiers' fun. And if they found any German soldiers in uniform the men were made to kneel down, the dogs were set on them, and when the dogs had finished the Germans were shot in the head. No, of course he hasn't told you any of this but it's what he lives with every day of his life, that and worse. Some things he can't come to terms with even now. Ten- and eleven-year-old girls having been raped and sodomized by gangs of drunk soldiers, and yes, in all probability these were German children who had probably been brought up to idolize Hitler, but they were just brainwashed bairns and no one has the right to do that to little ones.'

Gina stared at Betty, shocked to the core. 'Why can't he discuss these things with me if he could with you?'

'Because he's stupid and I've told him that,' said Betty grimly. 'He's beside himself inside, all mixed up and given to some noble idea that he's got to let you go for your sake. It's rubbish and I've told him that. He won't survive without you, Gina. I do believe that.'

'I thought – I thought he didn't love me like I love him.'

'Then you're a damn fool,' said Betty, with characteristic bluntness. 'I dare bet your love for him isn't a patch on what his is for you.'

They stared at each other in the dappled shadows under the trees, birds twittering and bees buzzing, the beauty and serenity of nature all at odds with the horror they were discussing. After a moment, Gina said dazedly, 'He won't stay here, not after what happened today.'

Betty said nothing, continuing to watch her.

'I have to go with him, right now, don't I.'

It wasn't a question, but Betty answered it as though it had been. 'Aye, you do.'

Gina nodded. 'Mam . . .'

'I'll look after Mam, and there'll be Lucy and Ava here from tomorrow, don't forget that.'

'Lucy's still going through with the wedding?'

'Oh, aye. Larry's going to take her back to get her dress and things in a bit and she'll go to the church from here. It'll be up to her mam and da if they want to turn up but no one'll miss 'em if they don't, Lucy least of all. She's had a bellyful of her mam by all accounts, even before this.'

Gina nodded again, somewhat vacantly. 'I have to get my things together.' She hesitated before saying, 'Thanks, Betty.'

'Don't thank me. It's Josef I'm bothered about if you want the truth.'

With a touch of her old spirit, Gina said, 'Don't worry, I didn't think it was me.'

'Don't get me wrong, I'm grateful for what you did for me and James with the farm an' all, 'cause I know full well that Larry and Edwin would never have gone down that route unless you'd pressed them, but –' Betty shrugged her hefty shoulders – 'we'll never see eye to eye, me an' you.'

'No, we never will.' Thanks to Kenneth Redfern. Gina held out her hand. 'Can we part as –' she paused – 'not friends, 'cause I know we're not, but not enemies either?'

'How about as sisters who can't stand the sight of each other, 'cause it's like that in some families?' said Betty, grinning, as she shook Gina's hand.

It was a magnificent concession on Betty's part and Gina recognized it as such. If Betty had been a different individual she would have hugged her, but as it was she smiled, the lump in her throat making it impossible to speak, and then they turned as one and began to walk back to the farmhouse.

Chapter Twenty-Eight

It was late afternoon. The blistering heat of midday had given way to a sultry warmth that was sticky and uncomfortable, but the last thing on Gina's mind was the weather. When she and Betty had got back to the house, Josef was already downstairs talking to Elsie and the others in the sitting room. Gina didn't wait to hear what was being said, and as Betty joined her mother and brothers, she went straight upstairs and began packing. She had asked Betty to send Elsie and James up to her when it was possible, and she had nearly finished drawing her bits and pieces together when they walked into the room. She didn't want to talk to Edwin and Larry; what she saw as their betrayal in front of Muriel Travis was still smarting.

When Elsie bustled into the room she suddenly stopped dead as she saw the suitcase and holdall on the bed, but it was James who said, 'What's going on?'

'Shut the door.' As James obliged she waited until it was closed before she said quietly, 'I'm going with Josef,

Mam. I have to. He won't stay, not after what happened this afternoon, and my place is with him, even though he doesn't think so.'

James's brow wrinkled. 'What?'

'Betty told me he's confided in her and he's got this noble idea that I'll be better off without him. I won't. I'll wither and die, that's how I feel.'

James began to protest but Elsie laid her hand on her son's arm.

'I understand, lass,' she said softly. 'I don't want you to go, you know that, and I was hoping Josef would see his way clear to staying here and settling down on the farm, but after today I can see that's not going to happen. I'm sorry about Edwin and Larry, hinny, and after all you've done for them.'

Gina shook her head. 'I did it for you, Mam, and for James and Betty too, to some extent, but especially for you. Lucy and Ava will be here from tomorrow to help you in the house and dairy and so on.'

'Aye, lass, don't you worry about me. I'll be all right.' Her heart felt like it was being torn out by its roots, but she knew this was hard for her bairn and it wouldn't help Gina if she broke down. Time enough for that when her baby was gone.

'You're not even going to stay for the weddings?' James looked bereft.

'I can't, you must see that? It's Edwin and Larry's big day and they don't want Josef present.'

'Lass—' Elsie began, but Gina stopped her by giving

her mother a hug. 'It's all right, Mam, really it is. They are who they are and like Josef said, us being together is too soon for them to stomach.'

'What will you do, hinny? Where will you go?'

'I wondered if James would drive us into Gateshead and we'll stop overnight somewhere.' She still had a little money left in her bank account. Elsie had insisted that she kept a small nest egg back when Gina had made it clear she wouldn't be one of the partners in the farm. Recently they'd bought a van to make the deliveries to various shops and hotels and businesses easier, and once James had passed his driving test he and Gina had been sharing this job. 'From there, I don't know.' She didn't think it was the right time to say she didn't intend to remain in England, not with Elsie struggling to keep her composure, but she could see now they needed to leave England's shores.

'You'll keep in touch?' In spite of her good intentions, Elsie's voice wobbled.

'Oh, Mam, of course I will. Anyway, I don't know if Josef will agree to me being with him yet. This afternoon he was adamant he was leaving on his own.'

'What will you do if he refuses?'

'Follow him until he changes his mind,' Gina said in all seriousness. The two women stared at each other for a moment and then giggled, breaking the almost unbearable tension.

'Oh, me bairn.' Elsie threw her arms round Gina, hugging her as though she would never let her go and by the time they drew apart their faces were wet with tears, James's too.

Once Gina had gained control of herself, she said softly, 'I don't want Josef to know I'm leaving with him, all right? James, you can put my things in the back of the van while Mam keeps him talking in the house, and I'll make out I'm coming with you to take him into Gateshead to say my goodbyes there. Betty knows what's what, and you can explain to Edwin and Larry when we're gone.'

It was strange, she thought to herself, that all the time she had been thinking it was Betty who was the most like Kenneth Redfern when in fact the twins were even more so. But perhaps she was being unfair. The twins had fought in the war, unlike James and Betty, and although they hadn't been injured physically their mental scars were still real.

'Lass, they'll be heartbroken when they know you've gone.'

Perhaps, but she didn't think so. They hadn't been the same since they'd found out about Josef but in all honesty that was a small price to pay to be with him. Heartbroken was the way she felt about leaving Elsie. Looking at James's dear face, she said, 'You'll look after Mam?'

'Always.' He took her in his arms. 'But this isn't goodbye, I won't let it be.' He kissed her on the cheek, hugging her close for a long moment before whispering, 'You'll always be my precious sister, the other half of me, you know that, don't you? Blood is nothing, it's heart that counts. You were the one who fought Ray Cook in the playground when we started school and he tried to bully me, do you remember? And his pals told us his da thrashed him again when he got home 'cause he'd let a girl give him a black eye.'

She laughed through her tears. 'I remember.'

'You bossed me about and looked after me and tied my boot laces, and I thought my world had ended when you disappeared. I won't let that happen again, I mean it, Gina. I want you to promise me you'll write wherever you settle.'

'I promise.'

They hugged again, and then she and Elsie kissed and cried some more before they all dried their eyes and blew their noses.

'Right.' Gina squared her shoulders and then checked she'd packed everything she needed before shutting the suitcase and holdall. 'Let's do it.'

To Gina's surprise, Josef didn't object when she said she wanted to say goodbye to him in Gateshead rather than at the farm. Perhaps he thought she was less likely to lose control or make a scene in a public place. James made the excuse that he was driving them because he didn't want Gina coming back on her own, probably upset and not thinking clearly. Josef's jaw had tightened at this but he had made no comment.

Edwin and Larry had shaken Josef's hand and stiffly wished him well before disappearing, ostensibly to drive Lucy back home in the farm cart to collect her things, although as James muttered it didn't take two of them to do that. Gina didn't mind; she was glad they'd gone. Josef thanked Elsie for her hospitality and kissed her on both cheeks, but Betty he hugged for a moment, much to the amazement of the others and probably Betty herself.

'You have been the good friend,' he said huskily when he let her go. 'I shall miss you, Betty.'

'I'll miss you too, lad.'

No one commented on the fact that Betty's eyes had watered and her voice was shaky.

'You take care of your ladies, yes? Especially the naughty Buttercup who tries to tread on my toes.'

'I'll do that.' Betty's bottom lip trembled and with a muttered excuse she left the room, James following in her footsteps as he said he would bring the van round to the front of the house.

Elsie was holding herself together with a huge effort, but mindful of the part she was playing she walked with Josef and Gina into the hall. What she really wanted to do was to hug Gina and never let her go, to beg her to stay, to tell her she would do anything if only Gina wouldn't leave. Instead she said quietly as she opened the front door, 'Now I'm not looking on this as goodbye, Josef lad. Do you hear me? Those two numbskulls of mine need a bit of time to adjust, that's all, and you come back and see us again, all right?'

'That is very kind of you.' Josef smiled. 'My good wishes for tomorrow to Edwin and Larry and their brides.'

'Thank you, lad. It's more than they deserve, but thank you.'

James drew up in the van, and Gina said flatly, 'You go and sit in. I want a word with Mam a minute.' Once Josef had left them, she turned to Elsie, the tears she had been holding in for the last minute or two rolling down her cheeks. 'I'm sorry, Mam. I'm so sorry.' She hadn't imagined the actual parting would be so hard but now the moment had come she didn't know if she could leave Elsie. 'I love you so much, you know that, don't you?'

She watched the face she loved crumple into a mass of little lines as Elsie lost control. As they held each other tightly, it was a full minute before Elsie could say, 'There's nowt to be sorry about, me bairn, all right? You're doing the right thing. Your Josef needs you, lass. He's lost, but give him time and he'll recover. And like I said to him, I'm not looking on this as goodbye. We'll write to each other all the time and it's not like before. We've found each other again and that's all that matters.'

'I wish I didn't have to go.'

'Me an' all, lass. Me an' all, but you do and that's that. And listen to me.' She cupped Gina's wet face in her rough hands, her voice soft. 'You an' Josef need to make your own life together now, and you're both young enough to make a success of it. And you will. I know you will. I love you, me bairn, more than life itself, and I want you to be happy, and much as I wish it wasn't so, I can see your place is not here.' She kissed Gina and pulled her close one last time before she said, 'Now wipe your eyes and dry your face else he'll know something's afoot. Once you're in Gateshead, James is going to take your things out of the back of the van and drive off smartish, so Josef can't object, but he'll park somewhere and then double back and see you're all right. Just in case.'

'I'll be all right.'

'Aye, I know you will or I wouldn't let you go.' It was the hardest thing Elsie had ever had to do as she smiled, pushing Gina towards the van and saying, 'Go on, lass, and I'm not going to wish you good luck cause I know you won't need it. You an' him will have a good life together, I feel it in me water.'

'Oh, Mam.' It was an old saying of Elsie's and covered everything from the weather to more important happenings; it brought a wan smile to Gina's face.

Taking a deep breath, she opened the van door and climbed in beside Josef. James bent forward and nodded at her.

'All set?'

'Yes, I was just talking to Mam about some last-minute arrangements for tomorrow she needs to start before I get back.'

'It is not a good time for you to come into Gateshead. You should have stayed and helped your mother.' Josef didn't look at her as he spoke, staring ahead through the windscreen.

Gina made no reply to this and James started the engine, and the next moment they were drawing away from the farmhouse. Gina didn't dare to wind down the window and wave to Elsie, or look back at her, because she knew if she did she would tell James to stop the van. She sat huddled against the door without speaking, her fingers digging into the palms of her hands as she fought back the tears and an overwhelming sense of desolation. She had always known she wouldn't stay at the farm for ever but the way this had happened, so suddenly, had completely thrown her. And it was all Muriel Travis's fault, and Edwin and Larry's too. How could they have sided with that dreadful woman, and after the things she had said about Josef too? They knew he wasn't a Nazi, she'd told them about his parents and what had happened to them and why. She'd never forgive them for this, never.

The evening was mellow and once they were clear of the farm Gina wound down her window to let the summer air in. The countryside was echoing to the cries of swallows as they wheeled in the sky, skilfully hawking airborne insects and skimming the air with graceful movements. She watched them for a few moments, her spirits gradually quietening as the sweet scent of trees and flowers and warm vegetation filled the van. Josef was sitting stiff and immobile at the side of her and she didn't look at him, concentrating on the changing view outside the window and not letting herself dwell on Elsie back at the farmhouse because that was weakening.

'There's a small hotel I know of close to the train station in Gateshead,' James said after a while. 'I'm taking you there, is that all right?'

'Of course. Thank you.' Josef wondered how much it would cost. He had a little money but it wouldn't stretch far. Not that it mattered. Nothing mattered except that he was losing Gina. But it was the right thing he was doing. He had to remember that.

It was a silent journey as the van rattled and bumped along and when they finally drew up at their destination, Gina felt a little better. At some time during the drive she had let go of her resentment towards the twins and felt the stronger for it. They were products of the war, she told herself, and damaged because of it; she hadn't been through what they had and perhaps in time they would regret what they'd said, but even if they didn't it wouldn't impinge on her and Josef. She wouldn't let it. And Betty had come up trumps. She would never have believed that she could think about Kenneth Redfern's daughter with something akin to affection, but she did. Which just showed you never knew what a day would bring forth.

James stopped the vehicle outside a small, distinctly run-down looking hotel with a battered sign declaring itself to be 'The Royal Crown Hotel'. Anything less like a royal crown was hard to imagine. He jumped out of the van and brought Josef's battered little suitcase to where he and Gina were standing, having left Gina's things on the other side of the vehicle where they wouldn't be seen until he had driven away. Holding out his hand, he said warmly, 'Well, goodbye for now, Josef, but I trust we'll meet again in the future.'

'Yes, of course.'

'Good luck.' James smiled and then, because there was no way in the world he was going to drive off without giving Gina a hug, he did just that, kissing her cheek as he whispered, 'Love you, sis.'

She hugged him back. 'Love you too.'

'Be happy,' James said to Josef and with that he walked round to the driver's seat, started the engine and drove off with a screech of the tyres and scattering of gravel.

Josef began to say, 'Where is he—' when he noticed the suitcase and holdall on the pavement.

As he swung to look at Gina, she said, 'I'm leaving with you. It's all sorted.'

'No.' He stared at her. 'No, you are not. You must not do this, Gina.'

'Too late, it's done.'

'No, you must go home. Your mother—'

'She's fully in agreement with me. So are James and Betty.'

'This cannot be.'

'It can be and it is.' She didn't know if that was good grammar and she didn't care.

He shook his head, his voice shaking slightly as he said, 'I will not let you do this. It would be throwing your life away.'

They were facing each other and now she turned and fetched her things, setting them down where he was still standing.

'I'm not going anywhere without you, Josef. You can talk till you're blue in the face, but it won't make any difference. Wherever you go I'll follow you.' And then, her voice softer, she murmured, 'I love you, don't you

453

see? Without you I would have no life – I'd shrivel up and die.'

He swallowed deeply. 'Your family—'

'Will do fine without me, even my mam. She has the lads and Betty, and Lucy and Ava will be there for her from tomorrow.'

He tried again. 'You went through so much before you found them again. I cannot take you away—'

'You're not taking me away, not in that sense. It's my decision, my choice. I can manage without them, even my mam as long as I know she's happy, but I can't manage without you. There, you've made me say it and really it should be you saying these things, as the man.' She moved a step closer, reaching up her hand and touching his marred cheek. 'I love you and I will never love anyone else the way I love you. If you care for me even half as much, I'll be content.'

'Half as much?' His arms went about her and she found herself enveloped, his mouth on hers as he kissed her in a way he had never done before. The narrow, somewhat dingy street was empty but even if it had been full of people it would have made no difference as they stood wrapped in each other's embrace. When he finally raised his head she felt dizzy.

'I love you as a man has never loved a woman, never, in the history of the world, in eternity. I adore you, I worship you.' A shaft of sunlight touched his hair, turning it into a halo of rich vibrant gold that was all at odds with his scarred face. He was only twenty-seven but he could have been thirty-seven, forty, she thought tenderly, and he looked so tired, so worn out and weary, but she would change that.

They would go away, away from England and people like Muriel Travis, somewhere where the things that haunted him would gradually fade and lose their destructive grip on his mind. She would make him well.

'Are you sure you know what you are doing, my Gina?' His blue eyes held hers. 'This – me – is not what I would have wished for you, do you understand? Life with me will be hard and people will judge you.'

'Let them.'

'You say that now, my love, but when you are hurt—'

She stopped him by putting a finger to his lips. 'You are the only person who has the power to hurt me and I know that you will not. Other people don't matter, they really don't. Only if we let them and we won't.'

'I do not want you to regret this in the years to come.'

'Never.' She smiled softly. 'My fate was sealed in a little Egyptian garden years ago.'

'And mine.' He kissed her again but gently this time. 'Will you marry me, my love? I have nothing to offer but myself.'

'That's enough. It will always be enough, and yes, I'd marry you tomorrow if I could.' Still within the circle of his arms, she reached up and placed her lips on his, her fingers tangling in his hair. He kissed her face, her eyes, her throat, muttering words of love in his native tongue before his mouth took hers again, and as they stood there in the summer twilight she thought, Thank you, Betty, thank you. Betty wasn't Kenneth Redfern – she was a far better human being than her father could ever have been – and somehow the knowledge melted the hard bitter lump in her heart with his name on it and she was free of him. For the first time in her life she was truly free of him and it was intoxicating.

Chapter Twenty-Nine

'So, Mrs Vetter, we are on our way to a new life.'

Gina and Josef were standing hand in hand, looking down on the white-crested waves from the deck of the ship taking them across the ocean to New Zealand.

She turned to him, her eyes alight as she murmured, 'And it will be wonderful, I know it will.'

The last years had been nomadic ones, but they had started well and got better as time had gone on. They'd left Gateshead after one night and travelled down country, getting married in a register office in the south where their honeymoon had been spent working in a farmer's fields gathering in the hops because they had needed the money, and Gina's little nest egg would only stretch so far.

Josef had felt wretched about this at first, but Gina had thoroughly enjoyed herself and her enthusiasm had infected him. The fact that she and Josef were husband and wife had made everything else pale into insignificance, besides which the majority of the pickers had been women and once their fellow workers had heard the story of their falling in love and how they'd found each other again, any initial hostility about Josef being a German had melted away. For the rest of her life Gina would look back on this interlude as a magical step out of reality.

At the end of the day's picking they would all return to the hoppers' huts, their temporary homes during the harvest, and the other workers had insisted the good-natured farmer give Gina and Josef a hut of their own. They'd all light their faggot fires on which they cooked their meals, sitting in the deepening twilight talking and gossiping until it was dark, and then Gina and Josef would retire to their mean little dwelling and lie in each other's arms making love until the early hours.

When his nightmares had come she had held him close, speaking words of love to dispel the demons. Gradually over the six weeks they were there a more healthy colour had returned to his skin through working in the warm Kent fields, while the company of folk who were content to 'live and let live' had acted as a soothing balm on his troubled mind. Being surrounded by the countryside and its wildlife in the first gentle days of autumn had been a tonic like no other, and the fact that the huts became hot and stuffy if the day was sunny, and freezing cold in the early mornings, didn't bother them an iota.

Of course, this idyll couldn't last. Once the harvest was gathered in, they had used Gina's small nest egg and their earnings to leave England and travel across the sea to France, working their way through Europe, getting temporary jobs here and there and staying in one place for no longer than six months at a time and sometimes a lot less. Gina wrote to Elsie every month, telling her where they were and what they were doing, sending her postcards and even little gifts she thought her mother would like. They had met lots of other folk like themselves – escapees from real life, Josef liked to call them in his wry manner – and had even been encouraged to join a hippy commune in Spain, which they had politely refused.

They were in Italy when Mao Tse-tung proclaimed China a Communist Republic and in Hungary when North Korea marched into the independent southern half of the divided nation, troops and tanks storming over the frontier. As the months progressed Gina read in the English newspapers, whenever they could get hold of any, of Britain and the United States getting involved in the conflict, and then the United Nations forces being taken by surprise under the impact of a massive assault launched by the Chinese. It seemed as though the nations of the world had forgotten the misery of the last World War and were heading towards a third.

It made them both even more determined to consider carefully where they would settle when their travelling days were done. When they started a family they wanted it to be somewhere where the horrors of the last decade, which seemed to be happening in the present one too, would not touch their children. As Josef had said, many folk were not in the position to choose as they were, having roots and responsibilities that tied them to a particular country and area. Perhaps for the only time in their lives they were free and unhampered but once they had a family that would change. With continuing unrest in East Berlin, Rhodesia, Egypt, Vietnam and other places in the world, it seemed most political leaders were united in one thing only – that war was the answer to any differences.

In his privileged youth, Josef had visited New Zealand with his parents and sister one summer when he was eight years old to stay with relations who had emigrated there. His memories were of lush countryside, wide open spaces, blue skies and a people who had been warm and welcoming, in stark contrast to the Nazi regime which had been gathering steam in the country of his birth. When he had mentioned New Zealand Gina had been a little apprehensive at first – it really was the other side of the world – but after a while the idea had settled on her. What had followed was mountains of red tape, but with Josef's superior education and ability to speak several languages everything had eventually fallen into place.

Gina looked at him now as they stood together holding on to the rails of the ship each with one hand, the other joined. He was her old Josef again, strong in mind and body, his nightmares of their first couple of years of marriage a thing of the past. The travelling had been good for both of them; it had sated the urge that had been with her for a long time and got it out of her system, and it had been a means of healing for Josef. But now they were both ready for the second phase of their marriage, that of starting a family and building a permanent home together. They had visited England and the farm for one last time before setting sail for New Zealand. It had been a good visit. Elsie had been overjoyed to see them and things had gone well, even with Edwin and Larry, who were both fathers now. Edwin and Ava had two little boys and Larry and Lucy a girl and a baby son, and it seemed Betty relished the role of auntie and the children adored her which had, quite honestly, amazed everyone as Elsie had confided to Gina. James was now courting a local lass whom he planned to marry within the year. In the week they'd spent at Cowslip Farm, Elsie and Gina had been all but inseparable, making the most of every precious moment. Josef had resumed his old easy relationship with Betty the minute he'd walked through the door, and both Betty and Elsie had wept unashamedly when the week was up and Gina and Josef had left.

'You don't regret not staying on at the farm?' she asked him softly. Everyone, even Larry and Edwin, had asked them to stay indefinitely, the lads even suggesting that with the farm doing so well they could see their way clear to building a small house for them at the back of the farmhouse. Gina had appreciated the offer, especially because it had been clear her brothers had meant it, and whatever issues they'd had with Josef in the past had disappeared with the march of time, but she had known it wasn't the right thing for them. Josef was no farmer and neither was she; their destiny lay in a different direction.

'It ought to be me asking you that.' Josef put his arm round her, pulling her in to him.

'No regrets for me.' She smiled up into the blue eyes that reflected the clear sky above them. 'I want our future to be ours, just ours, if you know what I mean. Sink or swim, we'll make it together.'

'I thought you might want to stay with your family.'

'Josef, *you* are my family. The rest of it, having found Mam again and the lads, and even Betty,' she added ruefully, because the two of them had still rubbed each other up the wrong way in the short time they'd spent at the farm, 'is just icing on the cake. 'You're what matters to me. You will always be what matters.'

He kissed her. 'You are as necessary to me as breathing,' he murmured huskily. 'My love, my life.' And then he kissed her nose. 'But we *will* swim, my darling, make no mistake about that. A new land, another new beginning, but as long as it is the two of us, it will be wonderful.'

'Actually, regarding the two of us?' She had been going to tell him that night over dinner, but somehow the moment seemed right. 'I think it might be three.'

'Three?' For a moment her Josef, her highly intelligent, well-learned Josef, looked at her blankly, and then as realization dawned, his face lit up. 'You are with child?'

Such a beautifully old-fashioned way of putting it. She grinned. '*Your* child.'

As he lifted her right off her feet, his mouth meeting hers in a kiss that was endless, she experienced one of those moments in life that consisted of pure unadulterated joy. Their baby had been conceived in the week they'd spent at Cowslip Farm and that made the little life growing inside her even more precious. She had no bump as yet, nothing to show for the miracle that was taking place inside her body, but already their baby was the most important thing in the world, a tiny person she would gladly give her life to protect and nurture. And she felt her natural mother had been of like mind about her; battling through a terrible winter storm to give birth in a safe place rather than just giving up and lying down in the snow and taking the easy way out. She had thought a lot about her mother since she had known she was going to have a child, wishing she could have known her and thanking her for being brave enough to give her life.

As Josef set her back on her feet, he hugged her again and again, laughing and almost crying as he murmured, 'A child, our child, oh, my love. And he will be born in a new land, a land where he will be free to be himself.'

'Or herself.'

'Yes, yes, or herself.' He gathered her to him. 'Freedom and liberty, such priceless gifts. I think my father and my mother would be glad to know their grandchild will have such a heritage. Maybe it will make sense of their sacrifice, for speaking truth in the midst of deep darkness as so many others did.'

He rarely mentioned his parents and never Kirsten, and now she reached up and placed her hand on his scarred cheek.

'We'll teach our children what's important, Josef. We'll

show them there's something even more important than freedom, and if they fully embrace it, it will never let them down.'

'Which is?'

'Love, my darling one. Love.'

'Ah, yes.' He settled his chin on her head, his voice deep and throaty as he murmured, 'I remember our old Sunday-school teacher making us learn this passage from the Bible off by heart when I couldn't have been more than six or seven years old. "Love suffers long and is kind; love does not envy; love does not parade itself, is not puffed up; does not behave rudely, does not seek its own, is not provoked, thinks no evil, does not rejoice in iniquity but rejoices in truth; bears all things, believes all things, hopes all things, endures all things. Love never fails."' He nuzzled her hair. 'I think many people forgot this for a while.'

'I think so too.' She slipped her arms round his waist. 'What happened to her, your Sunday-school teacher?'

'Mrs Scholl? When I was in Germany after the war a friend of my father's told me she and her husband sheltered several Jewish families from the Gestapo and helped them escape to Switzerland. Eventually they were betrayed, but before the Gestapo could come for them the underground got them and their three children to safety. They had to leave everything behind, but I think Mrs Scholl would have considered that a small price to pay.'

'I'm glad they got away.'

'Yes, it is good.'

They stood wrapped in each other's arms, the salty sea breeze blowing their hair and the sun bright on their faces, joined in heart and overwhelmingly thankful that in the midst of such a time they'd found each other, and having found each other, hadn't let go. The past was behind them with all its dark twists and turns and the future was full of promise, a future they would embrace together.

Epilogue

1973

Elsie sat in her old rocking chair in front of the glowing range, her slippered feet on the brass fender. It was the week before Christmas, and although she was now eighty-six years old she still insisted on making the whole family's Christmas cakes and puddings, declaring her three daughters-in-laws' weren't a patch on hers. Ava and Lucy and Phyllis, James's wife, never argued with this for the simple reason they knew she was right, besides which they loved her.

Elsie looked down at the package in her hands which the postman had delivered half an hour before in his little red van. He'd been grumbling about the icy conditions and the forecast of heavy snow, but she'd sent him off happy after inviting him in for a mug of her creamy cocoa and two hot mince pies.

She knew who the package was from. Gina had printed her name and address on the back of it for one thing, for another only her bairn sent her parcels in the post. She touched the handwriting on the front of the package, her rheumy eyes misting. She knew in her head it had been the right thing for Gina and Josef to make their life in New Zealand – look at how well they'd done, starting their own haulage business from scratch which now employed umpteen people and had different branches all over the country. Josef certainly had a business head, there was no doubt about that, and their home was beautiful, just beautiful. She nodded to herself. Aye, she knew in her head it had been best for them to spread their wings – it was her heart that was the problem and always would be, she supposed. There wasn't a day that passed that she didn't ache to see her bairn. Just to sit and chat for a few minutes over a cup of tea would be enough.

Pulling herself together, she wiped her eyes on her handkerchief and blew her nose. 'Don't be such a daft old biddy,' she said to herself. 'Count your blessings, woman.' And there were plenty of them. She had her three lads and their families around her, and Betty of course, and the farm was doing well, better than it ever had.

The thought of Betty brought her eyes to the parcel once more. It wouldn't have worked out if Gina had stayed with her, she knew that in her heart of hearts because Betty had always sensed the truth, that she loved Gina more than the rest of them. And God forgive her, she did. Her bairn had always touched something at the core of her that the others couldn't, deep to deep, she supposed.

Realizing that she was verging on maudlin, she shook her head and decided to open the package even though Gina had written on the back of it, 'Do not open till Christmas.' She didn't doubt her bairn had known she wouldn't be able to resist seeing what was inside the moment it arrived; they'd laughed together about this weakness of hers the last time Gina had come over from New Zealand three years ago.

That had been a grand time, she reflected as she worked at the parcel with fingers nobbled by arthritis. All her grandchildren together for once. Gina's four had got on so well with their cousins, bless 'em. The three lads had been out from sunrise to sunset every day, only coming in for meals and as proud as punch at the jobs they'd done with their uncles and cousins, but it had been Sophia, Gina's surprise baby born years after the lads at a time when Gina had thought her childbearing days were over, who'd captured her heart. She was the very image of Gina, bright and bonny and as happy as the day was long. She'd asked Gina why the name Sophia since it didn't sound English or German, and Gina had shaken her head, saying quietly, 'I don't rightly know, Mam. Perhaps it was the time Josef and I spent in Italy when we heard the name a few times, but somehow, as soon as I looked at her when she was born, something said Sophia. Sophia Elsie.'

Elsie smiled to herself. She'd liked that, the bairn having her name too.

She finally managed to undo the outer packaging and

then unwrapped layers of extra padding surrounding what she realized was a framed portrait. It was of Gina and Josef and the bairns and even included their little white dog, Lily. The three lads, young men now, looked very smart in white shirts and ties, but Elsie's eyes were immediately drawn to Sophia. She was sitting at her mother's feet with the dog in her lap, and it was just like seeing a picture of Gina as she'd been in the days before Ken had taken her away, except that Sophia was laughing into the camera without a care in the world, her mother's hand resting on top of her brown curls.

The tears began in earnest then, and it was a little while before Elsie could read the letter which had come with the photograph. Gina had written:

Dear Mam,
I'm sending this before the other Christmas presents which will be delivered in a day or two, but I wanted you to have this separately. I know you'll open it as soon as you get it [Elsie smiled to herself] *and it isn't really a Christmas present anyway. It was taken on our twenty-fifth wedding anniversary and it's specially for you. Sophia is wearing the little silver bangle you sent for her last birthday, she rarely takes it off, and she says she can't wait to see you again. And here's the good news, Mam. We're coming over again in the spring to spend some time with you and the others. We're all very excited and Josef has*

*already arranged everything, you know what he's
like for organization. Everything is fine here
except that you might see Lily looks fat in the
photo. This is because she was expecting a litter
by the spaniel next door at the time who jumped
over the wall attracted by her charms. She had
three puppies, none of which Sophia could bear to
say goodbye to when they were old enough to be
given away, so we now have four dogs instead of
one!*

There followed other bits of news – Gina always wrote
long newsy letters that Elsie loved – before she finished:

*Have a lovely Christmas, Mam. I'll be thinking
of you on Christmas morning and sending you
lots of hugs and kisses. I love you so so much
and I miss you every day.*
Your Gina xxx

'Not as much as I miss you, me bairn,' Elsie whispered.
It had started to snow again, and as she glanced at the
window she thought of that day so many years ago now
when a young frightened girl had taken refuge in the hay
barn and the result had been her Gina.

She hadn't guessed then that there would be so much
pain connected to the gift God had given her, but it had
been worth it. In spite of the years of sorrow, she could
say now it had been worth it. She still grieved for her

Robin, of course, and always would, but that was different somehow. It had been the not knowing with Gina that had sent her half-mad with grief.

She raised the portrait to her lips and kissed the radiantly smiling woman in the picture, sending up a little prayer of thanks that her bairn had come into a safe harbour where she was well and happy and surrounded by those she loved. And then, as she heard Betty calling to someone in the yard outside, she stuffed the letter into her pinny pocket to read again and again when she was alone in her bedroom. Standing up, she walked creakily out of the kitchen and through to the sitting room, her arthritic knees protesting, and placed the portrait with the rest of the family photographs on the long sideboard.

She heard the back door open as she left the sitting room and then Betty's voice calling her, a faint note of anxiety in her tone. It had been after she'd had a fall some years ago that Betty had started worrying about her, and her daughter's concern took the irritating form of trying to wrap her up in cotton wool. Or at least she'd found it irritating until Josef had taken her aside on their last visit three years ago.

'You mean a great deal to Betty,' he'd said quietly in his precise German way. 'Your sons have their wives and families, but all Betty really has is you, her mother. She may not express this in words, but she is aware of it just the same.' He'd patted her shoulder gently. 'It would be good to let her in, I think?'

She'd been offended initially, thinking he was criticizing

her – which he probably had been – but the more she'd thought about it, the more she'd realized he had a point. Kenneth had monopolized Betty from the moment she was born and in a strange way she'd been relieved about this. It had meant she could grieve for Gina without feeling guilty that Betty was being neglected, and then, by the time Gina had come back into her life, a pattern had been set and one which she had had no desire to change if she was being truthful. Betty was too like Ken for one thing, and she'd told herself her daughter neither needed her nor even particularly liked her, let alone loved her.

She had been wrong on both counts.

Now, as she walked into the kitchen, she smiled at Betty, saying, 'Fancy a brew, lass? Just the two of us?' Her daughters-in-law were busy in the dairy and the menfolk were somewhere or other on the farm. 'I made you a sly cake earlier an' it'll still be warm if you want a slice?'

Betty smiled back, her dour face softening. 'Aye, lovely. Thanks, Mam.'

Something had changed in the last three years since she'd heeded what Josef had been trying to tell her. Never in her wildest dreams would she have imagined that Betty would be a comfort to her but she was, and the more she had shown this, the closer they had become.

It would never be like the bond she had with Gina – nothing could come close to that – but nevertheless, she knew in her heart that Betty needed her in a way that

Gina never had. Gina would always have left the nest at some point and flown to pastures new, she understood that now. Her bairn had been born with the desire to see new things, new sights, to embrace the world fully and to take it by the throat if she had to. It was the way Gina was, the way she'd always been even as a small bairn. She had been born to fly, her storm child. Her tempestuous, mercurial, wonderful storm child. It had been her destiny.

Dancing in the Moonlight

By Rita Bradshaw

As her mother lies dying, twelve-year-old Lucy Fallow promises to look after her younger siblings and keep house for her father and two older brothers.

Over the following years the Depression tightens its grip. Times are hard and Lucy's situation is made more difficult by the ominous presence of Tom Crawford, the eldest son of her mother's lifelong friend, who lives next door.

Lucy's growing friendship with Tom's younger brother, Jacob, only fuels Tom's obsession with her. He persuades Lucy's father and brothers to work for him on the wrong side of the law as part of his plan to force Lucy to marry him.

Tom sees Lucy and Jacob dancing together one night and a chain of heartbreaking events is set in motion. Torn apart from the boy she loves, Lucy wonders if she and Jacob will ever dance in the moonlight again . . .

Beyond the Veil of Tears

By Rita Bradshaw

Fifteen-year-old Angeline Stewart is heartbroken when her beloved parents are killed in a coaching accident, leaving her an only child in the care of her uncle.

Naive and innocent, Angeline is easy prey for the handsome and ruthless Oswald Golding. He is looking for a rich heiress to solve the money troubles his gambling and womanizing have caused.

On her wedding night, Angeline enters a nightmare from which there is no awakening. Oswald proves to be more sadistic and violent than she could ever have imagined. When she finds out she is expecting a child, Angeline makes plans to run away and decides to take her chances fending for herself and her baby. But then tragedy strikes again . . .

The Colours of Love

By Rita Bradshaw

England is at war, but nothing can dim land girl Esther Wynford's happiness at marrying the love of her life – fighter pilot Monty Grant. But months later, on the birth of her daughter Joy, Esther's world falls apart.

Esther's dying mother confesses to a dark secret that she has kept to herself for twenty years: Esther is not her natural daughter. Esther's real mother was forced to give up her baby to an orphanage – and now Joy's birth makes the reason for this clear, as Esther's true parentage is revealed.

Harshly rejected by Monty, and with the man Esther believed was her father breathing fire and damnation, she takes her precious baby and leaves everything and everyone she's ever known, determined to fend for herself and her child. But her fight is just beginning . . .

Snowflakes in the Wind

By Rita Bradshaw

It's Christmas Eve 1920 when nine-year-old Abby Kirby's family is ripped apart by a terrible tragedy. Leaving everything she's ever known, Abby takes her younger brother and runs away to the tough existence of the Border farming community.

Years pass. Abby becomes a beautiful young woman and falls in love, but her past haunts her, casting dark shadows. Furthermore, in the very place she's taken refuge is someone who wishes her harm.

With her heart broken, Abby decides to make a new life as a nurse. When the Second World War breaks out, she volunteers as a QA nurse and is sent overseas. However, life takes another unexpected and dangerous turn when she becomes a prisoner of the Japanese. It is then that Abby realizes that whatever has gone before is nothing compared to what lies ahead . . .

A Winter Love Song

By Rita Bradshaw

Bonnie Lindsay is born into a travelling fair community in the north-east of England in 1918, and when her mother dies just months later Bonnie's beloved father becomes everything to her. Then, at the tender age of ten years old, disaster strikes. Heartbroken, Bonnie's left at the mercy of her embittered grandmother and her lecherous step-grandfather.

Five years later, the events of one terrible night cause Bonnie to flee to London, where she starts to earn her living as a singer. She changes her name and cuts all links with the past.

Time passes. Bonnie falls in love, but just when she dares to hope for a rosy future, the Second World War is declared. She does her bit for the war effort, singing for the troops and travelling to Burma to boost morale, but heartache and pain are just around the corner, and she begins to ask herself if she will ever find happiness again.

Beneath a Frosty Moon

By Rita Bradshaw

It's 1940 and Britain is at war with Germany. For Cora Stubbs and her younger siblings this means being evacuated to the safety of the English countryside. But little does Cora know that Hitler's bombs are nothing compared to the danger she will face in her new home, and she is forced to grow up fast.

However, Cora is a fighter and she strives to carve out a new life for herself and her siblings. Time passes, and in the midst of grief and loss she falls in love, but what other tragedies lie around the corner?

As womanhood beckons, can Cora ever escape her troubled past and the lost love who continues to haunt her dreams and cast shadows over her days?

One Snowy Night

By Rita Bradshaw

It's 1922 and the Depression is just beginning to rear its head in Britain, but Ruby Morgan is about to marry her childhood sweetheart and nothing can mar her happiness. Or so she thinks. An unimaginable betrayal by those she loves causes her to flee her home and family one snowy night.

Crushed and heartbroken, Ruby vows that, despite the odds stacked against her, she will not only survive but one day will show the ones she left behind that she's succeeded in making something of herself. Brave words, but the reality is far from easy.

Dangers Ruby could never have foreseen and more tragedy threaten her new life, and love always seems just out of reach. Can a happy ending ever be hers?

'Catherine Cookson would have been proud to put her name to this heartfelt and moving saga'
                    Peterborough Evening Telegraph